Janey's War

It is not easy to lead a normal life in the midst of war.
This book is dedicated to those who struggled to hold the
family together between 1939 and 1945.
They should be treated with respect, and remembered with pride.

Janey's War

Barbara Murphy

PIATKUS

✿✿ Visit the Piatkus website!

Piatkus publishes a wide range of bestselling fiction and non-fiction, including books on health, mind, body & spirit, sex, self-help, cookery, biography and the paranormal.

If you want to:

- read descriptions of our popular titles
- buy our books over the internet
- take advantage of our special offers
- enter our monthly competition
- learn more about your favourite Piatkus authors

VISIT OUR WEBSITE AT: www.piatkus.co.uk

Acknowledgements

Research is a painstaking part of writing, but certain people have been particularly helpful with this task, and my thanks go to the staff of Hythe Library; the Museum of Army Flying at Middle Wallop; and the Medical Officer Recruitment, RAMC Training Group.

Good constructive critisism is needed before a first novel is ready for publication, and I shall always be grateful to my agent, Judith Murdoch, for pointing me in the right direction – and to Judy Piatkus for opening the door.

Set in 11/12pt times by
Action Typesetting Ltd, Northgate Street, Gloucester

Printed and bound in Great Britain by
Mackays 0f Chatham plc, Chatham, Kent

Chapter One

The two girls stood side by side, close, but not touching. One held the woman's gaze. The other looked away. She knew what to expect.

'I don't want that'n.' The woman half nodded in Jane's direction. 'But this'n ...' Rose, her vivid blue eyes still fixed on the woman, smiled. 'I'll take her.'

The billeting officer consulted her notebook. 'I'm sorry, Mrs Walton,' she said. 'Their mother particularly requested that they are billeted together.'

Mrs Walton's head swivelled towards Jane, noting her tall, skinny frame and straight hair. The gaze then went back to Rose, with her rounded features and halo of tumbling ringlets. Not even the dreadful po-shaped hat could disguise the fact that here was the child whose photograph had once been chosen to bear the famous soap caption, 'Preparing to be a Beautiful Lady'.

'You're never telling me they be sisters.'

'Actually, they're twins.' Pencil poised, the billeting officer waited.

Mrs Walton looked even more surprised, then her eyes narrowed. 'They'd be twice as much trouble, egging each other into mischief, no doubt. I'd want extra.'

'The allowance is eight shillings and sixpence for each child, Mrs Walton.'

'Well, there'll be no pudding or cakes. We'm not made of money.' Mrs Walton clucked her tongue and looked around the village hall. At the door, a policeman shuffled his feet and examined the ceiling. In the corner by an ancient upright

1

piano, the only other child stood alone, clasping and unclasping her hands. The girl was tiny and not wearing school uniform, just the hat. If she was a brand-new first-year pupil like the twins, she had to be eleven at least, although she looked much younger. Her mop of jet-black hair was stuffed under her hat, and thick lashes shielded her eyes, which widened with anxiety as Mrs Walton lifted the large label pinned to her coat. 'What be wrong with Theresa O'Connor?' she asked.

Jane thought she knew why the girl had not yet been selected. She had heard her softly praying, 'Please, Holy Mother of God, don't let me be the last.'

The billeting officer sounded weary as she said, 'There is nothing wrong with her. But she comes from an Irish Catholic background. Does that present a problem to you?'

Mrs Walton circled the twins, then walked back to the corner. Finally, she said, 'Not such a problem as having two mouths to feed. And this'n looks as though she won't eat too much. Has she had all her jabs?'

'Theresa has been vaccinated and inoculated against diphtheria, and her mother says she's a healthy child.'

'Good. I can't abide sickly children.' Mrs Walton turned to Theresa. 'Can 'ee make bread?' she asked. 'No? Then it's time 'ee learned. Come along.'

Theresa fumbled with the buttons on her coat. At the door, Mrs Walton called out, 'Don't dawdle, child. We've wasted enough time already.' The handle of the girl's carrier bag had broken, so she bundled it under her arm and hurried after her new 'mother', almost colliding with the heavily built man coming in.

He stared thoughtfully after the two figures, then nodded to the policeman and the billeting officer. 'Couldn't get here sooner. Cow be a rum'n today. Animals know when something's amiss.' Slowly, he shook his head. 'Never thought I'd live to see it again.'

The billeting officer finished writing. 'They didn't send the children away last time,' she said.

'True enough. How's it been, then?'

For the first time, the policeman spoke. 'More like market day in Norwich.' He sounded angry. 'Old Sam Grimshaw had the nerve to feel the boys' muscles. And Clara Walton only be after a skivvy.'

Glancing warningly in the direction of the twins, the billeting officer put a finger to her lips. Then she asked the man who'd just arrived, 'Is Mrs Edwards with you?'

'No. Young George be poorly. But she told 'ee yesterday we've room for one, didn't she?'

'Oh, yes. But I don't know what to do about these two girls. Their headmistress has my bedroom, and I'm sharing with Mother. I suppose I could take one at a pinch, but they're twins.' The woman looked at him without hope. 'Still, you have a houseful with your own family.'

The silence was almost painful. Jane was afraid to look at the man's face, so she studied his boots. They laced up to his ankles and had the thickest soles she had ever seen. And they were caked with mud. Mum would have gone mad if she had seen so much dirt.

For the second time that day, Jane felt a longing to see her mother. The first time had been when the coach stopped outside a paper shop, and she had seen the placard. Just one word, with three huge letters: WAR! The word everyone had been repeating in hushed tones for days. A girl had begun to cry and, for a moment, Jane had wished Mum were sitting beside her. She wasn't scared, but she felt confused. She didn't even know where they were. Just somewhere in Norfolk.

It wasn't as if Mum would cuddle her or anything. Mum wasn't like that. But it would be nice to hear her say, 'Don't be silly, Janey. There's nothing to worry about.'

Now, as she waited in the village hall, she again felt the need for those words, half scolding, that would tell her everything was going to be all right. Even yesterday morning, while they queued in the damp darkness at the jetty, Mum had calmly reminded them to say 'please' and 'thank you', do as they were told, and make sure they had a clean hankie. It was as though they were going on a Sunday-school outing down the Thames. And when their turn came to walk up the gangway of the *Golden Eagle*, Mum just gave them a quick hug and walked away, past the sobbing mothers clinging to their children. The fact that she had hugged Rose a little closer than Jane didn't matter. That was normal. And what Jane wanted more than anything was to be normal. Not having a lot of strangers stare at her. Not wondering where she would sleep, or when she would see Mum and Dad again.

Bits of dried mud fell off the boots as they moved. He's bound to choose Rose, thought Jane. What will I do without her?

Mr Edwards leaned forward and grasped the string handle of Rose's carrier bag. He smelled of the cattle pens in Romford Market. Then he turned to the billeting officer.

'You be doing enough, Miss Robertson,' he said, 'with the school to run, and your mother.'

He picked up Jane's bag. Startled, she looked up at him. He was smiling. 'You'll have to share a bed, but 'ee won't be separated,' he said. 'Don't forget they gas masks, my darlings.'

As Jane followed Rose through the door, she wondered what their new home would be like.

'Are you awake, Rose?'

'Yes.'

Submerged in the feather bed, Jane snuggled closer to her sister. 'How long do you think the war will last?' she asked.

'Grandad reckons it'll be over by Christmas.'

'But I heard Dad telling Mum it might go on longer than the first one. That's more than four years.'

'Could be, I suppose.'

'Will we have to live here for four years?'

'Hope not. Couldn't put up with your fidgeting for four weeks, let alone four years. Go to sleep, Janey.'

Jane stopped trying to pull her nightdress straight and poked her nose out above the eiderdown. A nightlight sent shadows onto the ceiling. The room was bigger than their bedroom at home, but the furniture was bigger, too, and old-fashioned, like Gran's. The wardrobe had huge double doors that creaked, and there was a washstand with a marble top. Jane and Rose had been given the bottom drawer of the tallboy, but they could hardly drag it open, it was so heavy. On top, a looking glass swung in a wooden frame.

The bumps in the other two beds belonged to Kitty and Doris Edwards.

'It's not too bad here, is it?' Jane ventured.

Rose lifted her head from the pillow and looked around. 'There's no gas laid on, and no bathroom. I haven't used a po since I was a baby.'

'They've got an outside privvy, like Gran's.'

'At least Gran's is right by the back door. I don't fancy having to walk miles down the garden every time I want to go. And they use bits of newspaper.'

After a while, Jane said, 'Mr and Mrs Edwards seem kind, don't they? They made us a lovely tea.'

Kitty's voice sounded irritable as she mumbled, 'Will you 'vacuees shut up? I've got to be up at six for work.'

A few minutes later, Jane thought of something. It had to be asked. She whispered, 'Rose. Will the siren go again tonight?'

'How should I know? And if it does, you're not to play the piano.'

'But –'

A loud 'Ssh' came from the direction of Kitty's bed. Rose turned over.

Hurt, Jane watched the flickering shadow on the ceiling. It wasn't her fault. If the teacher had left them alone last night, most of the evacuees would have slept through it. They'd been up since four, picked up by lorries, dumped at the dock and told to find the right queue for their schools. Not easy in the dark, drizzling rain, with every school in the area to choose from and officials scurrying around, trying to separate hundreds of mothers and toddlers from the schoolchildren. Then they'd been on the paddle steamer for hours. After that, they'd had to wait around at Great Yarmouth until the buses came to take them to a dance hall on the seafront. First, they'd queued up for bangers and mash and slabs of fruitcake. It wasn't as good as Mum made, but their sandwiches were long gone and they were starving.

Afterwards, one of the teachers had suggested a talent show and asked if any of them could do anything. One boy played 'Good King Wenceslas' on his comb, another did a card trick which went wrong, and an older girl sang 'Ave Maria'. She had a nice voice, even though it wobbled a bit. The next minute, Rose had jumped up and dragged Jane onto the stage. 'I can dance and my sister can play the piano,' she'd announced. But Jane couldn't remember 'Bye Bye Blues' without the music, so

5

the teacher vamped it. When she'd finished, the teacher asked Jane if there was anything she could play for them. She made a mistake at the beginning of 'Umbrella Man' and was glad to get back to her seat. They were all given a toffee, but Rose won a bar of chocolate for being the best turn.

By that time hundreds of sacks filled with straw had been laid out all around the dance floor. There wasn't a single light along the promenade. Suddenly, the curtain was yanked from her hand and firmly straightened. A woman said, 'Leave the blackout alone, dear. Don't want the Jerries to see us, do we?'

The straw didn't smell very nice, but Rose and Jane huddled together under the stiff grey blanket and were soon asleep. It seemed like only the next minute when Jane's shoulder was shaken and a torch flashed in her face. Then she heard the wailing noise. A voice whispered loudly in her ear, 'Will you play the piano for us, dear, in case some of the children are nervous?' It was the teacher who had organised the concert. Halfway through the second chorus of 'Umbrella Man', Jane heard an aeroplane, but it sounded different to the ones she'd heard before. Her fingers faltered, but the teacher had gripped her shoulder. 'Keep going, dear,' she ordered. The noise grew louder and louder until it was overhead. Then it began to fade. Jane finished the third chorus and looked at the teacher, who held up her hand. It was quiet again. Then another sound, wailing up until it reached a pitch and stayed there. The teacher clapped her hands and cried, 'All clear. Well done, dear.'

Just then, one of the outer doors had clattered and a man in a tin hat came in. His voice boomed, 'Just a reconnaissance sortie. Nothing to worry about.' Nearby a baby began to cry and a woman called out, 'Now we've all been bloody well woken up for nothing, is there any chance of a cup of tea?'

Looking around the dimly lit hall, Jane felt uncomfortable. People raised their heads, and she asked the teacher if she could go back to bed, hoping to escape before anyone recognised her.

'Of course, dear, and I'm sure we all give Jane a round of applause for rising to the occasion, don't we?'

Picking her way through the bodies strewn around the floor, Jane heard, above the thin clapping, a voice saying, 'I used to like "Umbrella Man".'

6

When Jane crawled back under the blanket, Rose muttered, 'I've never been so humiliated.'

Close to tears, Jane had protested, 'What else could I do?'

'Pretend to be asleep, or deaf or something.'

Now, watching Mrs Edwards's nightlight, Jane thought about Mum and Dad and hoped Jack would remember to feed her rabbit. Then she wondered what to do if the siren went again. Wake Rose up and ask her, I suppose, she thought, just before she drifted into sleep.

It was barely daylight when Mrs Edwards brought in a jug of hot water and tipped some into a china bowl on the washstand.

In the kitchen, steam rose from three bowls of porridge, but only Doris sat at the table, yawning. Mrs Edwards explained, 'Kitty's already had her breakfast. Every other week she goes early to sort they newspapers. Father and Jim have their breakfast after they've seen to the animals.' She put three eggs into a saucepan of boiling water on the range, smiling as she noticed the twins gawping. 'Never seen duck eggs before?' she asked. 'They be better than chicken eggs just now.'

The eggs tasted stronger than the ones Mum bought from the milkman and were much bigger. Jane was spreading blackberry jam on a second slice of bread when Mr Edwards and his eldest son came in through the scullery.

'I don't suppose 'ee brought Wellingtons?' Mr Edwards asked as he tugged off his boots at the door.

Her eyes on the tall, gangly youth, Rose said, 'We were only allowed to bring one change of clothes and toilet things with us.'

Thick slices of bacon sizzled as Mrs Edwards turned them over. 'Never mind, we'll keep to the road. Can't cross fields in they thin shoes,' she said, cracking eggs into the frying pan. 'They'll be as much good as a dog with side pockets.'

Rose giggled as she said, 'The weather's been lovely lately. Surely it can't be that muddy?'

'We had quite a downpour Saturday night. And it's not only mud to watch out for, is it Father?'

Chuckling, Mr Edwards said, 'They cows aren't fussy where they leave their dollops. But you'll soon learn country ways.' After he'd washed his hands at the stone sink, Mr Edwards held out an enamel jug to his son. 'Fetch more water for

7

Mother, Jim.' Through the open door, Jane saw the boy glance sideways at Rose as he pumped water into the jug.

Doris cut several slices of bread and spread them lavishly with creamy butter. 'George doesn't want any breakfast,' she announced. 'And he's not going to school. Can I stay home, too?'

'No.' Mr Edwards put three slices onto his plate and looked enquiringly at his wife.

'His ear still hurts bad,' she said. 'I'll take him to the doctor's after I've found out what they be doing up at the school.'

Today should have been the day that Jane and Rose started at the County High School. The bus from the corner of their road would have stopped right outside the lovely new building, with its hockey pitches and tennis courts. Instead, they had to walk for half an hour before crowding into the village hall. Four teachers sat on the platform, deep in discussion.

Jane had been so proud when she'd first tried on her uniform. Now her navy velour coat felt damp and heavy from Saturday morning's rain, and her ankle socks were grubby. Mrs Edwards left George with the twins while she took Doris across to the school. His eyes were red and puffy, so Jane held his hand while she searched in vain for familiar faces from the elementary school.

Rose couldn't find any of her friends, either. 'I thought Edna Browning had passed,' she said, looking fed up.

'She might have gone to the technical college. Oh, look! There's Theresa O'Connor.' The girl, standing alone, smiled back at Jane, but didn't move nearer.

It seemed ages before Mrs Edwards came back, without Doris. 'Your headmistress is coming over to talk to 'ee,' she said. 'So I'll get along now. I had hoped you might be in the same class as Doris, but never mind. Wait outside at twelve and she'll bring 'ee home.'

Miss Bellinger, the headmistress, stood on the platform with two teachers on either side. She was a tall, well-built woman with dark, cropped hair and an expression that made it plain she would tolerate no nonsense. All she did was raise her hand and the hubbub quietened.

'As you can see, there is insufficient room for two schools to

8

conduct classes at the same time,' she said. 'So Miss Robertson has kindly agreed that we shall have the use of the school building for mornings, or afternoons, on alternate weeks. But you will be expected to do homework for the other half of the day.' Groans from some boys near Jane brought a reproving frown from Miss Bellinger, before she continued, 'Even so, we are a greater number than the children who live in the village, so we will use this hall for assembly and as an additional classroom.' She looked around the room. 'For the present, we only have a skeleton staff, as three teachers have joined the armed forces and the others remain in Essex.'

Miss Bellinger paused for a moment, as if trying to find the right words, then went on, 'These are troubled times, and I appreciate that you will miss your families. However, we must not forget that the good people of this village have taken us into their homes at some inconvenience to themselves. Therefore, we must behave with courtesy and dignity while we are guests, and always remember the honour of the school. I wish you to remain here this morning, so that we may talk to you individually. Then you may go back to your billets, but please return to the school at one thirty. Now, let us pray for our families in Essex, for our new families here in Norfolk, and for an early peace.'

Jane peeped through her fingers at the rows of boys and girls who stood with bowed heads. One or two first-year pupils, like Theresa, wore their own, rather shabby clothes, with just the school hat or tie. She was glad that Mum and Dad had bought the whole uniform, even though it had cost a lot of money. It made her feel as though she belonged.

This was going to be different from the elementary school in a lot of ways, not just lessons. These bigger boys, in their long trousers and blazers with the school badge on the pocket, they wouldn't punch each other in the playground. And the girls, with their blue and yellow striped ties and smart gymslips, they wouldn't do handstands against the wall. Jane felt a surge of excitement as she realised that she stood at the threshold of an entirely new way of life.

Later that evening Jane wrote the date, Monday 4th September 1939, and the words 'Dear Mum and Dad', on Mrs Edwards's lined writing pad. She described the journey, the 'air raid' and the village.

It's two villages really and we live in the lower one. There's nothing here except a few houses, a little shop and the chapel. Mrs Edwards's grandmother runs the shop. She's very old and her name is Mrs Oliver.

Yesterday Mrs Edwards took us to chapel. Mrs Oliver played a funny little organ and her voice squeaks when she sings, but she doesn't wear glasses, not even when she reads from her Bible. Mr and Mrs Edwards are very kind and try to make us feel at home. George is the youngest, then there's Doris, who is 10, and Jim has just left school. They are all very shy, but Kitty bosses the others. She told us she's nearly eighteen but Mr Edwards called her 'Sweet Sixteen'. She works in Mrs Oliver's shop.

School is in the upper village, which is a bit bigger. There's a bus to Cromer, but only twice a week. We started classes this afternoon. The books haven't arrived yet but Miss Fredericks said my spelling is quite good and she also praised the way Rose read a piece of poetry by William Wordsworth. It was all about daffodils and she read it ever so well.

Jane dipped her pen in the ink bottle again.

Three of the boys from the fourth year walked home with us. They are billeted next door and I think one of them has a crush on Rose because he carried her gas mask for her.

There's a piano in the parlour but the music is mainly hymns and classical pieces which are a bit hard. I brought some work home from school to do in the morning but Rose forgot hers so she's going into Cromer with Mrs Edwards. I offered to stay with George because he's got an infection in his ear. Mrs Edwards said she'll take me next time.

There's lots of chickens and things here. It's like a farm really although Mr Edwards calls it a holding. He offered to let me milk the cow but its horns look sharp so I said I'd rather help make the butter and cheese. The ducks and geese cackle a lot and look ever so funny as they waddle up to the pond. I like the pigs, except they pong a bit.

10

One of them has got ten babies and they squeal like mad when they're feeding. Fancy having ten babies hanging on to you like that all the time!

I said my prayers last night and cleaned my teeth like you told us but it's not so good without a tap. You have to tip the slops into a bucket under the washstand and carry it downstairs.

Good night, Mum and Dad, and God bless. I'll pray tonight that this rotten old war will be over soon and me and Rose will be back with you again. Give my love to Jack and ask him to make sure Snowy has some clean straw. Do you think Rover and Tibs are missing us as much as we miss them? From your loving daughter, Jane x x

P.S. Will you send our Wellington boots please so we can walk to school across the fields and save half a mile?

Jane wiped the nib clean with a piece of blotting paper. Across the table, Rose folded her single sheet of paper.

'I don't know how you find so much to write about, Janey,' she said, 'Mum and Dad will never have time to read all that.' She reached across the table and tried to turn the knob on the oil lamp.

'Careful!' Jane rescued the ink bottle.

'Stop fussing. Nothing would get through all this newspaper.'

'Well, it is their parlour, and it's very kind of Mrs Edwards to let us use it for our homework.'

'I'm not doing any. This light's bad for my eyes.'

'But you must.'

'Why? It's not proper homework. They're just finding things for us to do. We could learn more by exploring the village.'

'It'll be better when the books come.' Jane began to fold the newspapers. They were filled with news about the war and pictures of Mr Chamberlain and Adolf Hitler, and Polish people walking along a road.

Rose wandered around the room, picking up ornaments. 'Why do they hang on to all this old stuff?' she asked, pulling a face at the painted cows with enormous horns which stared back at her from a pair of huge vases on the mantelpiece.

'Mum says if you keep things long enough, they'll be fashionable again one day, and valuable.'

'Well, this lot will be worth a fortune.'

11

Jane thought it must take hours to dust the vast collection of china and bits and pieces.

'Just look at that!' Rose pointed to a glass dome covering some faded flowers in the centre of an enormous sideboard. She ran her fingers down the twisted pillars, like sticks of black barley sugar, that supported the ornate canopy. 'Mum would have a fit is she saw this.' Rose's fingers were streaked with grime.

Both girls jumped as the grandfather clock in the corner began to chime the hour. At that moment, the door opened and Kitty said, 'You'd better be finishing now. It's bedtime. Don't forget to take the newspaper back. We needs 'im to light the fire in the morning.'

'What about the lamp?' Jane asked.

'I'll see to 'im. Don't want the house on fire. You go and get your cocoa.'

As Jane carried the pile of newspapers back to the kitchen, she heard Kitty and Rose laughing in the parlour. It made her feel strangely shut out.

The suitcase was waiting for them when they arrived home from school on Friday afternoon. It was the big one Mum and Dad used when they went to Margate.

Even George came into the kitchen to watch as everyone fumbled with knots and buckles. Eventually, the clasps clicked open and six pairs of hands raised the lid.

On top lay two new dolls, dressed in matching dresses and hats, one pink, one blue. Rose picked up the pink doll. 'This one's got hair like mine,' she said.

Eyes round, Doris touched the golden curls. 'It feels real,' she gasped. 'And the eyes open and shut. You ought to call her Shirley. She's my favourite film star.'

Mrs Edwards handed the blue doll to Jane. 'What be 'ee going to call this one, my darling?' she asked.

'I don't know.' Actually, Jane would have preferred her shabby Old Tedbear rather than the dark-haired beauty blinking back at her. But it would be nice to have something of her own to talk to.

'What about Elizabeth?' Doris suggested, 'After our princess.'

Jane smiled. 'That's a good idea. And you can play with it whenever you want.'

Mr Edwards lifted out the two new Bibles. 'Glad to see 'ee comes from a God-fearing family,' he said. 'You can read a verse to us after supper.'

Jane didn't dare look at Rose, in case they giggled. She delved into the layers of clothing until her fingers touched something wrapped in brown paper. Two pairs of shiny black Wellington boots. Good old Mum! Right at the bottom, she found what she was searching for: some familiar pieces of piano music, 'In a Monastery Garden', 'Wish me luck as you wave me goodbye' and a book of Souza marches.

George pointed to some more papers. 'Are they comics?'

Eagerly, Rose grabbed the *Film Fun* and Jane scanned the *Girl's Crystal* to see if the serial had ended yet. There was also a *Beano*, and Mum had written across the top, 'For the little boy with the bad ear.' It was the first time Jane had seen George's gappy smile.

Mr Edwards nodded approvingly again. 'That's very kind of your folks,' he said.

In the folds of the school raincoats Mum had packed a book of knitting patterns for doll's clothes, knitting needles and several balls of different-coloured wool. The last thing that brought 'oohs' and 'aahs' were two books, *Little Women* and *Heidi*, and two letters.

Doris sat back on her heels, face flushed, and sighed, 'That were real exciting. Wish I could be a 'vacuee.'

Mr Edwards patted her head. 'I thank the Lord you've not had to go away, my darling.'

Mrs Edwards cut thick doorsteps of bread and dripping and slabs of seedcake, as parts of the letters were shared. Mrs Harrison had written to Rose, her husband to Jane.

'Dad says there was an air raid, but nothing happened.'

'Gran crocheted the dolls' clothes, Janey, because Mum's knitting me a complicated jumper in Fair Isle.'

'His prize chrysanths are full of earwigs.'

'Guess what! Jack's had another row with Betty. Mum reckons the engagement's off.'

'They're bound to make it up again. They always do. Oh,

13

poor Dad! He's got to dig up his potato patch and put in an Anderson shelter, whatever that is.'

George looked up from his comic and asked, 'Does he say anything about your rabbit?'

Jane shook her head, her attention on the letter. 'Listen, Rose! You know that man with the Austin Seven? Well, he took his children to Cornwall to be safe, but he wasn't allowed to have any lights on, and on the way back he crashed into another car and was killed.'

Mrs Edwards shook her head sorrowfully. 'Like that poor postman at Cromer. Rode his bike straight into a tree. They say hundreds of folks have been killed already, all because of the blackout.'

Rose finished reading her letter. 'I suppose they'll tell us to eat more carrots now, so we can see in the dark. What else does Dad say, Janey?'

'He sends his love, and regards to everyone else.'

'Mum's writing to you separately, Mrs Edwards.'

'That be very kind of her, my dear, but she don't need to bother. I expect they're busy getting ready in case they bombers come ...'

For a moment, the room was silent.

Later, as they unpacked the suitcase, Rose said, 'I nearly died when Mr Edwards said we were a God-fearing family.'

'Well, we do go to Sunday school.'

'But Mum and Dad only go to church at Christmas.'

'You read that bit from St John ever so nice, Rose. Do you still want to be an actress when you grow up?'

Rose mused for a moment. 'Not just an actress. One like Jessie Matthews, so I can sing and dance as well. Have you made up your mind yet what you want to do?'

'I'd like to be a proper pianist, like Myra Hess. But I know I'm not good enough.'

'All I hope is that they don't want us to go to university just because we've passed the scholarship. I couldn't stand being at school for another ten years.'

As Jane lay staring at the light dancing on the ceiling, she wondered what they would all be doing in ten years' time. Mr Edwards would still be milking a cow called Daisy. Whenever they had a new cow, he called it Daisy. Made life simpler, he

14

said. Mrs Edwards would still be baking bread, always smiling. Kitty would be married with lots of children, and Doris would have taken her place at the shop. How old would Mrs Oliver be, if she was still alive? She'd be nearly a hundred, and little George would be seventeen, working on the holding with Jim.

What about Mum and Dad? Jane couldn't imagine them being any different, Dad pottering about his garden and Mum polishing everything in sight.

There were no doubts about Rose. With her looks she was bound to be famous. A star. She would sweep into a room, wearing a slinky satin dress and a fur wrap, just like Ginger Rogers. People would beg for her autograph. Men would gasp at her beauty.

And Jane? Try as she might, Jane couldn't picture herself at twenty-one. She might work in a post office or a library. Her hair would still be straight and dark, her eyes brownish, her legs and arms bony.

She knew she wouldn't have a boyfriend. Because when people talked about her, they always said, 'Jane's one of the Harrison twins. Pity she's so plain.' Sometimes they didn't even bother to lower their voices, and it made her angry that she wasn't supposed to mind, just because she was a child.

Chapter Two

It was better having school in the morning and the rest of the day free, Jane decided, especially now a crate of books had arrived. They had to share because the rest were needed back in Essex, but at least she was given proper homework.

George's crying could be heard before they opened the back door. It wasn't so much a cry, more a wail. Mrs Edwards looked worried. 'Had to take him to the doctor's again,' she said. 'If they new drops don't work, George will have to go into hospital.'

Jane noticed a tear drop onto the back of Mrs Edwards's hand. 'Would you like me to read him a story?' she asked. 'Might take his mind off the pain.'

'Would 'ee, Janey? I'm only just starting on the potatoes, and Father will be in any minute. I haven't even collected the eggs yet.'

'Shall I do that first?' Jane liked rummaging around the straw for warm brown eggs.

'No thank 'ee, dear. They hens be rum'ns today. Don't like waiting for their feed.'

Rose tied an apron around her waist and picked up the knife, just as Mr Edwards and Jim walked in from the scullery. 'I'll do the potatoes,' she said. 'Janey, do you think you could pacify poor little George?'

Mr Edwards beamed as he unlaced his boots. 'Proper little mother, aren't we, Rose? I can see you've done it afore.'

Jane wondered why Rose offered to peel the potatoes. Usually she preferred to lay the table.

George lay muffled by his eiderdown, eyes tightly closed.

16

The wailing had stopped, but from time to time a little whimper raised the bedclothes, like a hiccup. The room was almost identical to the girls' bedroom, except that there were only two beds. Lying on a chair, the comic her mother had sent looked rather dog-eared, as though it had been read several times.

He didn't hear her whisper his name at first. Then his eyes opened. 'Have 'ee got something to make the pain go away?' he asked.

'Your mum said you can have another half Aspro soon. George, who's your favourite in *Beano*?'

'Dennis the Menace.'

'Would you like me to read it to you?'

'Would 'ee ...?'

Jane tried out funny voices for the different characters. She knew she didn't read aloud as good as Rose but, at one point, George almost smiled. Eventually, he dozed off. Jane smoothed the damp hair back from his forehead, remembering.

She had been about George's age when Lennie had diphtheria. As soon as her mother had heard about the epidemic, she'd rushed the twins to the doctor for an inoculation. The boys were older, said it was sissy to be scared. Secretly, Jane thought they were afraid of the needle, but it hadn't hurt much.

Lennie was first with a sore throat, then Jack and Dad. While they waited for the ambulance, Jane had sat on Lennie's bed. His face was red and hot, and he kept asking for lemonade.

At the hospital, he'd been put into an iron lung, and her father and Jack into the isolation ward. The first day they were allowed out into the grounds, Mum had taken the girls to visit. They'd bought a basket of strawberries, and Jane remembered hearing the iron lung pumping life into Lennie. Just as Mum was handing Dad the biggest, juiciest strawberry, it stopped. Mum's hand shook and she dropped the strawberry. Then she'd whispered, 'Oh, no,' and held Dad's hand tight as they all watched the nurse walking across the grass towards them. Lennie was just fourteen.

Jane sat with George and her memories until Mrs Edwards put her head around the door and whispered that dinner was ready. 'A sleep will do him good,' she said.

The sleep didn't last long enough to do much good. George was still crying when Kitty came home from work, closely followed by Mrs Oliver. The old lady peered into the inflamed ear. Then she straightened up. 'I've a better cure than all they drops and operations. Come into the kitchen, Lizzie.'

Curious, Jane followed and watched as Mrs Oliver sprinkled a slice of bread thickly with pepper, while Mrs Edwards held a piece of flannel in front of the range. Then the grandmother put the bread in the flannel and hurried back to George. Ignoring his protests, she wrapped a woollen scarf around his head to hold the poultice in place.

'That'll do it,' she said. 'Tonight.'

George's scream woke Jane from a deep sleep and she collided with Doris as they ran onto the landing. Holding a candle, Mr Edwards led the way into the boys' room, where Mrs Edwards sat, rocking George to and fro. Tears streaming down her face, she looked up at her husband.

'It burst,' she cried. Then she began to laugh. 'Now 'ee won't have to go away, will 'ee, my darling.'

Mr Edwards closed his eyes for a moment before he turned to the group huddled in the doorway. 'Back to bed with 'ee,' he said, 'or we'll never wake in the morning. I'll help Mother clean up in here.'

Jane shivered. 'Shall I get your dressing gowns?' she asked.

Mr Edwards glanced down at his pyjamas. 'We don't bother much with things like that,' he said. 'But it were a kind thought.'

Within a few days, George was back at school. At home, he constantly begged, 'Read me a story, Janey, please.'

Every Monday, a letter plopped onto the mat for the girls. Dad was working a lot of overtime. Gran's legs were bad again. Sheila Green next door had been evacuated with her firm. Mr Green had fallen down the kerb in the blackout and hurt his ankle. Jack and Betty were engaged again. The twins couldn't understand why Jack had fallen for Betty. She was pretty enough in an insipid sort of way, but never seemed to care what Jack wanted. There must be other girls who would be nicer to him.

Jane wondered how her mother would take it if Jack was called up. She had been bad for a long time after Lennie died,

18

and young Jack was all she had left from her first marriage. Grandad had told Jane that 'Big' Jack Taylor had been in the cavalry. When he got shot in the foot, TB set into the wound and Nell Taylor was a widow at twenty, with little Jack to look after, and Lennie on the way.

It was seven years before she remarried. Fred Harrison liked reading books by Arthur Conan Doyle or playing classical gramophone records. Not a bit like Big Jack Taylor, who'd been good at sport and a bit of a lad. Grandad said young Jack was a right chip off the old block, and Jane was sure he'd go looking for adventure in the forces, even though his work in the drawing office was classified as a reserved occupation.

True to her word, Mrs Edwards took Jane to Cromer, and bought her a skein of rainbow wool. She also bought a remnant of pink material and showed Rose how to cut out a Shirley Temple dress for her doll. Jane couldn't sew for toffee, but Rose took to it like a duck to water.

It usually took Jane a while to make close friends, but gradually she began to break through the barrier of Theresa O'Connor's shyness. She was quite a bright girl, but tended to be overlooked, probably because she was so tiny.

The boy next door, Bill Thompson, still hung around Rose. One Saturday afternoon, a crowd of fourth- and fifth-formers decided to get together, and invited the twins. Jane wasn't sure what it was all about, but was flattered to be included, especially when Bill suggested that Jane be the one to ask permission from Mrs Edwards, since she was good at that sort of thing. But Rose wouldn't let her invite Theresa as well. Apparently, they were the only new ones allowed inside the select circle of older students. When Jane asked why Kitty was going, she was told sharply it was none of her business.

It was a hot afternoon and they all met by the stile in the upper village. Kitty looked nice in her best dress, fair hair tightly waved and curled. She claimed it was naturally curly, but Jane knew she used rags and kirby grips every night. Soon she was the centre of a group of boys. As they stood around, waiting for someone called Isabel, Jane nudged Rose. 'What are we supposed to do?' she asked.

Rose looked at Bill Thompson, who winked slowly. Then

19

she murmured, 'You'll find out soon enough.' Jane didn't think Rose knew what was going to happen, either.

When Isabel finally arrived, she was greeted with raucous comments and whistles. Here was a girl who had looks and figure and knew it. With dark hair sleekly cut into a bob, the fringe almost resting on carefully plucked eyebrows, and an incredibly white skin, she reminded Jane of the vamp image from the twenties. But her eyes were really dramatic. Brilliantly green, they seemed to change colour as her head turned away from the sun. Slowly, Isabel began to climb the stile and stood for a moment, surveying the small group. As her gaze reached Kitty, those strange eyes narrowed.

'I thought we weren't inviting the yokels,' she said.

A fair-haired boy spoke up. Jane recognised him as Arnold, one of the boys billeted next door. 'I invited Kitty. What's wrong with that?'

Isabel's gaze travelled from Kitty's head to her shoes, and back again. Then she thrust her breasts out against her tight-fitting jumper, so that everyone could see she was wearing a brassiere. 'Nothing,' she drawled, half smiling. 'If you like fat country bumpkins.'

Her rosy cheeks colouring even deeper, Kitty tried unsuccessfully to force her belt through the buckle. She must have been two sizes smaller when Mrs Edwards made the dress.

Turning away, Isabel frowned. 'Who invited Shirley Temple?' she asked, nodding in Rose's direction.

Bill Thompson moved closer to Rose. 'I'll ask who I like,' he said. 'And nobody else has objected to the twins being here.'

Isabel stared at him. 'Wouldn't have thought you went in for cradle-snatching,' she said. 'But there's no accounting for taste.' Her glance barely flickered at Jane. 'And I suppose she brought the ugly sister along to carry the sandwiches.'

Rose stepped forward. 'Don't you talk about my sister like that, you bitch,' she cried.

Isabel examined her nails. 'Ah, yes. I did hear that there were some new scholarship kids from the council estate.'

Undaunted, Rose battled on. 'That doesn't make you anything special.' She treated her adversary to the same scornful appraisal Isabel had given Kitty. 'At least when I'm your age, I won't have to wear a brassiere before boys will notice my tits.'

Giggles were bitten back as the two girls glared at each other. Then Isabel turned back to the fifth-formers. 'Will someone help me over this damned stile?' she demanded.

Two boys detached themselves from the group around Kitty and held out their hands to Isabel, who lingered just a shade too long, showing a brief glimpse of knicker before she led the way across the field.

Near Jane, a girl's voice muttered, 'Looks like Lady Isabel has met her match at last,' as they headed towards a haystack.

A rickety ladder lay on the ground and the dozen or so youngsters soon clambered to the top of the stack. Isabel sat in the centre of the largest group of seniors. She pretended to ignore Kitty, but Jane was sure she was watching out of the corner of her eye, probably noting who was attending Kitty's court instead of her own.

Rose sat on the far side, with Bill and the other boy from next door. Unable to get near her, Jane squatted on the edge, studying the view across the patchwork fields.

A roar of laughter from the boys around Kitty disturbed her reverie. Isabel murmured something to a girl sitting at her feet, who turned to her companion. Soon, a chain of giggles drowned the guffaws from Kitty's corner. Then Kitty leaned over and whispered in Arnold's ear. And so it went on. Murmurs. Giggles. Asides. Laughter. Jane wished she could hear what they were saying. She tried to catch Rose's eye, but she was deep in conversation with Bill. He was by far the best-looking of the boys, his dark, wavy hair obviously treated to more than a smoothing of Brylcreem. His voice was deeper, too, unlike one or two of his classmates, who still croaked a little as they laughed or shouted.

With no one to talk to, Jane wondered if she could slip down the ladder without being seen.

'Hullo.'

Startled, she looked around. The boy's pale face was sprinkled with freckles and his mop of straw-coloured hair made him look as though he'd been thatched. But he had a nice smile.

'My name is Clive Randall, better known as Sandy,' he said. 'I'm billeted with the Morrises.'

Jane nodded. 'I've seen you with Bill and Arnold.'

'You're Rose's twin, aren't you?'

'Yes. The plain one.'

'Why do you say that?'

She shrugged. 'Everybody else does. And it's true.'

Facing the sun, Sandy squinted at her. 'You remind me of that new singer, Judy Garland,' he said. 'And she's not plain.'

For a long moment Jane watched an ant crawling along a blade of straw. Then she said, 'What's your billet like?'

'Not quite home from home, but they're decent enough. How about you?'

'Oh, Mr and Mrs Edwards are ever so nice.' The ant fell off the blade and began climbing again. 'Do you know why we've come here?' she asked. 'Is it a meeting?'

'Just a get-together, really. Sometimes in the holidays we meet in the park.'

'But what do you do?'

Sandy smiled. 'Sit around and talk, and eat.'

'Eat?'

'Haven't you brought anything?'

Jane felt in her skirt pocket. Two mint humbugs were the best she could do. 'If I'd known, I'd have asked Mrs Edwards for some sandwiches. But she'll have tea ready in a minute, anyway. And I've got homework to finish.'

'Do it tomorrow.'

She shook her head. 'There's chapel in the morning, Sunday school in the afternoon, and chapel again in the evening. Anyway, they don't like you doing any work on a Sunday. Not even knitting or sewing.'

'Gosh! That sounds awful. Aren't you allowed to do anything at all?'

'We can read the Bible, and I can play hymns. Or go for a walk.'

'Don't you get bored?'

'I did at first, but you get used to it. Look, I'd better go now.'

He put a hand on her arm. 'Not yet. I've got a couple of apples and a Mars bar. Be back in a mo'.'

Before she could protest, he crawled away. That was when

she heard, above the hubbub, Isabel's high-pitched voice saying, 'Now I know what they mean by muck spreading. Everybody who sits near it stinks.'

Arnold jumped to his feet. 'You shut your big mouth, Isabel Wallis,' he ordered.

'And what if I don't? Will you and who else shut it for me?'

'If you keep on insulting Kitty, I might at that.'

Another boy stood up. 'Take an order point, Godwin,' he said. 'And apologise to Isabel.'

'We're not in school now, so you can't tell me what to do.'

Fists clenched, the two boys faced each other. Then Isabel, her sharp features challenging, said, 'Why don't you biff him one, Leslie, for threatening me?'

Jane wasn't quite sure who struck the first blow but, as soon as the two boys locked in combat, their friends joined in. Some of the girls screamed, others urged them on. Trying to distance herself from the flailing arms and legs, Jane edged backwards. She never knew whether it was Isabel's or Kitty's champion who hurtled towards her.

As she hit the ground, Jane felt an explosion inside her chest. Conscious, but unable to speak, she gasped for breath. The most agonising pain she had ever known seemed to tear her body apart.

'Nobody told me that dying would hurt so much,' she thought.

'What shall I say to Father? I'm not supposed to go near they ricks.'

'Will you shut up whining, Kitty! My sister's dying and all you can think about is saving your own skin.'

Each attempt to breathe was more painful than the last. No matter how Jane struggled, no air reached her lungs, only searing, terrifying pain. If she couldn't breathe, she would die. Why didn't they shut up yapping and help her?

Fragments of voices: '... ambulance?' 'Grandad sounded like that, before he ...' '... broken neck?'

Jane tried to scream at them to get help, but no words came, only a hoarse moan. Don't let me die, Rose. Oh, Mum! Take the pain away. But Mum isn't here. Where is she? I want Mum.

23

Confused, Jane thrashed wildly as she made another agonising attempt to draw breath. Someone tried to lift her shoulders, making it worse.

Rose was there, kneeling at her side. She was holding her hand and appealing to the others, 'Haven't any of you done first aid?'

Sandy stepped forward. Gently, he touched her wrist, eyelids, the sides of her neck. 'She'll be all right. Just badly winded.'

Winded? Nobody could suffer as much as this just by being winded, Jane thought.

'How do you know?' Rose wasn't convinced, either.

'Fell out of the apple tree once. Thought I was a goner. But Mum knew what to do. She's a nurse.'

'What did she do?'

'Checked the pupils of my eyes, and my pulse. Then waited till I got my breath back.'

'What's the neck bit for?'

'Er … swelling, I think. Anyway, I don't think Jane's badly injured. But she won't want to find you lot crowding around.'

Again, Jane tried to take a deep breath, but only managed a gasp and wheeze.

'Don't try so hard. It will ease off in a minute,' Sandy said.

He was right. The air finally filtered through to her lungs. She tried to sit up, but Sandy shook his head. 'Lie there for a bit,' he ordered. 'And don't try to talk, either. When you're feeling better, I'll take you home.'

Kitty stepped forward, twisting her handkerchief. 'You won't tell Father what happened, will you, Janey?' she asked.

Rose looked at her. 'Why not?'

'He'll be mad if he knows the 'vacuees have been up on Mr Porter's haystack.'

'We weren't doing any harm.'

'It's because of they pitchforks and things lying around. And if someone lit a cigarette …'

Sandy said, 'It's against school rules to smoke.'

Arnold looked around. 'Isabel does, when she thinks nobody's looking. Someone ought to warn her.'

A voice from the crowd said, 'She's gone off with Leslie.'

Sandy looked up at the haystack. 'Still, your dad's right, Kitty,' he said. 'We were daft not to see the danger.'

Although it still hurt to breathe, Jane could just about whisper, 'I won't tell anyone.'

'But we can't pretend nothing happened,' Rose protested. 'You're as white as a sheet.'

'If Father finds out ...' Kitty wailed.

Jane had no great affection for the girl, but she didn't want anyone to get into trouble. She made another effort. 'I'll say I fell off the stile,' she croaked.

'OK.' Rose squeezed Jane's hand. 'Do you think I ought to take you to the doctor?'

Sandy helped Jane to her feet. 'Did you bang your head?' he asked.

'No. Mrs Edwards will know what to do.'

Rose did most of the talking, while Mrs Edwards dabbed white spirit on Jane's back, 'to bring out they bruises,' and made her a cup of strong, sweet tea, 'for the shock'. Mr Edwards looked thoughtful.

After supper, Jane was glad that Mrs Edwards insisted she go straight to bed.

The click of the door awakened her. Kitty stood by her bedside, holding the green tin candlestick. 'I knew Father would be mad,' she snivelled. 'And now he's forbidden me to go out with the 'vacuees.'

'But I told them it wasn't your fault.'

'He reckons it'll lead to trouble.'

'Perhaps he'll change his mind later on.'

Kitty shook her head. 'You don't know Father. Other girls my age go out with boys, but when I said it wasn't fair, he made me come to bed. Before Doris and Rose.'

Nothing more was said about the incident until the following Friday, when Jane went to the shop for another writing pad. Mrs Oliver was bagging up sugar in the back room. Kitty glanced over her shoulder, then leaned across the counter and whispered, 'Janey. Arnold has asked me to go and see that Alfred Hitchcock picture with him next Tuesday. It's my afternoon off.'

'I thought your dad said ...'

'He did. But I can manage it, if you'll help me.'

'How?'

'If I tell Father I'm taking you to the pictures, he'll let me go.'

'No, he won't. I'm an evacuee, too.'

'He didn't mean you and Rose, daft, he meant the ... the older ones. Go on. Be a sport.'

'I'm sorry, Kitty. I don't want to tell fibs to your dad. And there's no point in asking Rose. She's got a rehearsal for the school concert.'

'I know. But you could walk round the shops or something. It would only be a little white lie.'

Jane studied the shilling in her hand. Secretly, she thought Mr Edwards was a bit hard on Kitty, but she didn't want to risk upsetting him. If he found out, Kitty would be in worse trouble than ever. Not looking up, she mumbled, 'I'm no good at telling lies, even little ones. I always go red.'

'Rose said you wouldn't help me out.' Kitty shouted. 'If you hadn't been daft enough to fall off the haystack, none of this would have happened. Just don't ever ask me a favour, that's –'

Mrs Oliver's squeaky voice interrupted. 'What's going on out there, Kitty?' she called 'Has the delivery man brought the wrong order again?'

For a moment, Kitty continued to glare at Jane. Then she called back. 'It's all right, Great-Gran. Just one of they stupid 'vacuees.'

Forgetting her writing pad, Jane ran out of the shop. Best keep out of Kitty's way for a bit, she decided.

What with Kitty barely speaking to her, Doris on a different school timetable, and Rose making new friends in the upper village, Jane was left to her own interests. It didn't bother her. The twins had always had separate friends and activities. Usually Rose was the centre of a crowd, and Jane just had one best friend. This time it was Theresa. Most days they walked home from school together, exchanging confidences, talking about their previous schools, future plans, families. Theresa dreamed of university, but knew her father would never be able to afford it. Her eyes glowed whenever she mentioned her parents and the large brood of brothers and sisters.

Jane was glad she hadn't been billeted with the Waltons. Their house was even more isolated, with lamps never lit until you had to grope around for matches.

'What's Mr Walton like?' Jane asked.

'He never opens his mouth except to say "Yes, dear," or "No, dear,", so I wouldn't be knowing. I think the poor man's just as afraid of her as I am.'

'Why don't you write to your mum?' Jane suggested. 'Tell her you want to go home.'

'I'd like to. But she's enough to put up with, what with her expecting again. Then there's Grannie O'Connor.'

'What about her?'

'She wants to go back to Ireland. Keeps on all the time about the air raids. But Mam won't leave me da.'

'They've not had any air raids worth talking about. Dad calls it the Phoney War.'

'What about you, Janey? Do you want to go home?'

'Once or twice I've cried myself to sleep, thinking about it. But Mr and Mrs Edwards are really nice, and I do like living in the country.'

The days settled into a comfortable routine of schoolwork, piano practice, reading and walks around the country lanes. Once, Mr Morris next door let Jane sit on his big carthorse when he led it back to the stable. It was the first time she had ridden a horse. She was a bit scared at first, being up so high. But once she got used to it, it was quite exciting.

There were many things Jane was getting used to. Oil lamps seemed cosier than electric light, more like the gas lamps they used to have, with their soft hissing sound. She enjoyed chatting to Mrs Edwards in the kitchen as she helped knead the dough, and Saturday nights were quite a laugh. Mr Edwards dragged the tin bath into the kitchen and they waited their turn in the parlour, singing around the piano, then went in two at a time, like animals into the ark. Underclothes were given to Mrs Edwards for the big wash on Monday. Rose complained about having to share Jane's bathwater, but Jane quite enjoyed bathing in front of the range, with the big kettles and saucepans steaming on top. The only thing she didn't like was washing her hair. Mrs Edwards melted bits of soap down, but it didn't rinse out properly. Mum had always been very fussy with their hair, using Amami shampoo and adding lemon juice to Rose's rinse water, and vinegar for a shine on Jane's darker hair.

27

Even Sundays were not too bad if the weather was dry enough for a walk with the family, George usually clutching her hand. His parents talked about the old days, before the regular bus service into Cromer.

Mrs Edwards reflected, 'My mother didn't even have a bicycle.'

The day Mr Edwards found Jane examining his wife's 'sit up and beg' bike, he offered to teach her to ride. At first, he held the bike and walked alongside until Jane felt confident enough to try it alone. 'It's easy,' she said, before the front wheel wobbled and she fell into the ditch. After a few more tumbles, she reached the corner, but couldn't manage the curve. When she crawled out of the ditch for the umpteenth time, Mr Edwards suggested they try again the next day.

'Oh, no,' Jane protested. 'I don't want to give up. Please.'

'All right. But instead of thinking about falling off, think about riding round that corner, and the nice straight road in front of you.'

She pictured herself cycling around the bend, like Mrs Edwards. Just steady pedalling. Not a wobble. And there was the straight stretch. It worked.

When she stopped and looked back, Mr Edwards was smiling. 'Come you here,' he said.

Again she imagined turning the corner safely, then pedalled past his burly figure.

'Good girl,' he panted as he caught up with her. 'Once you learn, you never forget it.'

She felt so exhilarated, all she could say was, 'Thank you. Can we come again tomorrow?'

'As long as your bruises aren't too bad. See what Mother thinks.'

'Oh, I've had worse falls than that.'

'True. The haystack was a fair height.'

'About twelve feet –' Hand to her mouth, Jane stopped. 'How did you know?' she faltered.

'Bert Porter mentioned he'd seen a crowd of 'vacuees up on the rick. I put two and two together.'

She whispered, 'I'm sorry.'

'What for?'

'For not owning up.'

'Did you know they haystacks are out of bounds?'

'No. None of us did.'

'Kitty knew.'

'I think the others were up there before she realised. Or perhaps she forgot.'

Slowly, he pushed the bike towards the house. Then he said, 'You're loyal as well as brave. That's good.' He wagged his finger at her. 'But no more lies, not even half-truths. This time I'll let it go but, remember, I can't abide dishonesty. Never could and never will.'

Although he'd reprimanded her, Jane was pleased he thought she was loyal. And brave. It was nice to have someone on her side.

Chapter Three

'Never in the field of human conflict has so much been owed by so many to so few.'

Settling herself more comfortably against the stone wall, warmed by the August sun, Jane completed her diary entry.

> Stirring words from Mr Churchill. I don't want to forget them. Dad wrote that they can see the planes fighting high up in the sky. If we keep on shooting the Jerries down, they won't have enough planes left to bomb London, please God. Doesn't seem possible we've been away nearly a year. Looking forward to seeing Mum next week.

Jane flicked back through the pages. Her mother had visited them twice. The first time had been in December, and was ghastly. Mrs Harrison thought it safe to take them home for Christmas, and Jane had been keen, but Rose wanted to stay in Norfolk. Of course, she couldn't tell her mother she was planning to go to the school dance with Bill, so she tried to persuade Jane to join sides with her. They'd had the most awful row. But when Jane told her mother she was excited at the prospect of seeing her pets again, there was a long silence, and Mrs Harrison didn't look at them as she confessed that Rover had been put to sleep in the first week of the war. Mr Green was an air-raid protection warden and he'd told everyone all the animals would run wild with rabies as soon as the bombs dropped. To make matters worse, Jack had left the latch loose on the rabbit hutch and Snowy had escaped.

Unable to bear the thought of not being greeted by her tail-wagging, face-licking mongrel, Jane backed Rose's pleas to stay, and their mother went home alone.

The last visit, for their twelfth birthday in April, had been much happier. Among the cards and presents had been money from Gran and stylish pyjamas in different colours from Aunt Grace. They had a Selfridges label, so they must have been expensive, but Aunt Grace always put a lot of thought into her gifts. Not like her sister, Auntie Vi, who rummaged around the back of the storeroom for something she couldn't sell in Uncle Arthur's shop. This time it had been a battered box of stale chocolates, a joint present for the twins.

Best of all, Mrs Harrison brought the wedding pictures. Jack looked smart in his army uniform. It had been a quiet do, not a white wedding, apart from the snow. The twins were heartbroken they couldn't be bridesmaids, but the weather was atrocious at the beginning of 1940, and Jack only managed a forty-eight-hour pass, so he and Betty went straight off to Torquay after the service, to stay at Uncle Joe and Aunt Peggy's boarding house. Jane missed her brother, he was always good for a laugh. Which was more than could be said for his wife. Jane wondered whether Betty would cheer up a bit now she was pregnant.

Nothing much had changed in Norfolk. A trickle of homesick evacuees had returned to London. The Edwardses were as kind as ever, although they still treated their eldest daughter like a child. Rose had let her hair grow. She said ringlets were too childish. And she had enrolled with a dancing school in Cromer. Jane suspected her sister sometimes met Bill Thompson afterwards, away from inquisitive eyes. Sandy was nice. He often talked to Jane when the crowd ignored her, said he could hear her when she played the piano, and enjoyed it.

She had tried a music teacher in the next village, but it was a waste of money going back to Grade I. Better to keep practising. School was OK. Both sisters had good marks in the end-of-term exam, for different reasons. Jane had to work hard to keep up with the class. Rose had a photographic memory, so she was able to swot at the last minute and come out with flying colours.

Jane looked ahead in the diary. Back to school Monday week. Mum's birthday the Saturday after, 7th September. She had saved nearly enough pocket money to buy her the new Gracie Fields record.

As she closed her diary, Jane noticed a tiny figure, and waved. Theresa raced along the footpath and dropped down beside her friend.

'Can't stop long, Janey,' she panted. 'Mrs Walton has run out of flour and threatened all sorts of things if I don't hurry.'

Horrified, Jane stared at the little Irish girl. 'What's happened to your hair?' she asked.

'She said it took too long to look after, and chopped it all off. The scissors weren't very sharp.' Tears welled in Theresa's eyes, so Jane quickly changed the subject.

'Did you tell her that Mrs Edwards had invited you to tea next week, to meet my mother?'

'I did, too. And the answer was same as last time. We're too busy for me to go gallivanting around.' Another tear escaped.

'Oh, Theresa! You've got to tell your mother.'

Miserably, Theresa shook her head. 'The new baby is very fractious, and Grannie O'Connor is sure the Germans will bomb London because it's a heathen place and God will have his vengeance.'

'That's ridiculous.'

'I know it, Janey. And you know it. But once Grannie O'Connor gets going on something, she doesn't stop. She's making me mam's life a misery. I can't make it worse.'

For a moment the two girls sat quietly, watching a sparrow hawk hovering. Then Theresa jumped to her feet. 'I'd better be on my way,' she said. 'Enjoy your mam's visit. I'll be wanting to hear all about it.'

Jane smiled. 'I can't wait,' she said.

Next morning, after chapel, Jane was sitting on the bed, reading a letter, when Kitty came into the room and closed the door.

'Rose asked me to speak to you,' she said.

'What about?'

'You know you said you would come with us to see *The Wizard of Oz* on Tuesday?' Jane nodded. 'Well, we'd be glad if you'd back out.'

'Why?'

'Because we're friends and we like being on our own.'

'Rose is nearly five years younger than you.'

'That doesn't matter. She acts older, and we like the same things.' Kitty's voice rose. 'So we'd rather you didn't come.'

'I was going into Cromer anyway, to get Mum's birthday present,' Jane said. 'And I want to see *The Wizard of Oz.*'

'Even though you know you're not welcome?'

Jane's voice was slightly shaky, but she stood her ground. 'If my sister doesn't want me along, she can tell me herself. And I've as much right to go to the pictures with her as you have.'

'Why, you little –' Kitty raised her arm, but was interrupted by Rose opening the door.

She looked from one to the other, then said to Kitty, 'You'd better not lay a finger on my sister. And for goodness' sake keep your voice down, or none of us will be going anywhere next week. Your mum sent me to remind you that it's the Lord's day. And dinner's ready.'

The Tuesday bus was nearly full when it arrived, and by the time they reached Cromer it was packed. Some of the women turned towards the market, but the younger passengers headed for the cinema.

'So you made it all right, Kitty.'

Jane turned round at the sound of Arnold's voice. 'I didn't see you on the bus,' she said.

'That's because we got on at the first stop and went upstairs.'

Suddenly, Bill was walking alongside Rose, and Arnold with Kitty. Jane began to feel apprehensive, but she wasn't prepared for the scene when they stopped outside the cinema. 'Shall I get the tickets, or will you?' she asked Rose.

Glancing at Bill, Rose mumbled, 'Actually, Bill's paying for me.'

Then the penny dropped. Angrily, Jane said, 'No wonder you tried to persuade me to back out. You and Kitty had this planned all along, didn't you?'

With a smirk, Kitty butted in, 'Now perhaps you'll clear off.'

'Why should I?'

'Because you'll be a ruddy gooseberry, that's why. You tell her, Rose.'

33

Not meeting Jane's eyes, Rose said, 'Look, Janey, I know it's a rotten trick, but would you mind not coming with us?'

'But I was looking forward to the picture.'

'I know. And I'll make it up to you, I promise.' Rose bit her lip. 'Why don't you look round the market when you've bought your record? We'll see you at the bus stop.' The boys had bought the tickets and were waiting. 'Please don't tell anyone, Janey,' Rose pleaded, 'or we'll all get into trouble.'

After they disappeared through the swing doors, Jane turned away, fighting back the tears. Why hadn't Rose been honest about it? Not let her come for nothing. How could she be so mean?

A cool wind began to penetrate Jane's dress, so she took refuge in a café. After a while, she moved on to her favourite bookshop. But today she had no enthusiasm for browsing. Dark clouds threatened rain as Jane walked slowly, head down, towards the bus stop. 'Sorry,' she muttered, as she bumped into someone coming out of a shop. It was Sandy.

'What's up?' he asked. 'Lost a tanner and found a penny?'

'Just a bit cold, that's all. Wish I'd worn my blazer.' She buttoned her cardigan. 'Did you come on the bus?'

'No. Mr Morris gave me a lift in his van, but I'm catching the bus back.' He eyed the flat package under her arm. 'Is that your mum's record?'

'Yes.' She noticed his carrier bag. 'What did you buy?' she asked.

'Only plimsolls. Come on. If we walk a bit quicker, it'll warm you up.' He bustled her along the pavement until she was quite breathless.

As the they reached the café, a crowd of youngsters, noisily singing, 'We're off to see the Wizard', danced out onto the pavement. Sandy propelled Jane towards his friends. 'Did you enjoy the picture?' he asked Bill.

Jane didn't want to look at her sister, or any of them, but she couldn't help noticing Arnold slip his arm loosely around Kitty's shoulders. He laughed loudly as Bill recounted the Cowardly Lion scene. Jane turned away, wishing they would get a move on. Already cold, she suddenly felt chilled to her bones.

Further along the road, a stout figure watched them, stony-faced. It was Mr Edwards. They fell silent as he came up to them.

His eyes flickered from Kitty to Rose, then to Jane, showing feelings so aggrieved that Jane wanted to cry out that she hadn't been involved. But she couldn't, not without blaming his daughter and her sister. Finally, he spoke.

'We're all going home in Mr Morris's van,' he said 'There's a storm brewing.'

She expected a different kind of storm when they arrived home, but he didn't shout, nor even ask them to account for themselves. When Kitty ran up to her bedroom and burst into tears, Mrs Edwards came out of the kitchen and asked what on earth was the matter. Jane looked appealingly at Rose. Surely she would clear her sister.

'Just a silly misunderstanding,' Rose said. 'The boys next door had gone to see the picture as well, and we bumped into them.' Rose waited for the crack of thunder to stop, then went on, 'Unfortunately, Mr Edwards saw us all coming out, put two and two together, and made five. That's all there is to it.'

All coming out? I hadn't even gone in, Jane thought, but that was Rose's story, and she was sticking to it. Sadly, Jane watched the unbelieving expressions. It was apparent that Mr and Mrs Edwards thought she had been as much a part of the conspiracy as the others.

As another rumble of thunder added to the oppressive atmosphere, Jane realised her mother would be told. Oh, goodness! She'd been looking forward to Mum's visit on Friday. Now she was dreading it. It just wasn't fair.

Chapter Four

It was awful. Worse than the first visit. After Mrs Harrison
had been in the parlour for some minutes with Mr and Mrs
Edwards, she came into the kitchen.

'Mum, I can explain –' Rose began.

'Not a word! From either of you. You'd better start packing
your things. We're going home tomorrow.'

'But, Mum –'

'You heard what I said, Rose.' When Mrs Harrison used that
tone of voice, you didn't argue.

After supper, Mrs Harrison said she would like an early
night, thanked her hosts politely for the meal, and retired to
the parlour, where a camp bed had been made up.

Saturday was just as uncomfortable, with Rose trying to
avoid Jane, and only the two mothers making any attempt at
polite conversation. If she could have got away with it, Jane
would have avoided meals as well, just so she didn't have to
tolerate Kitty looking daggers in her direction and snivelling,
as though she were the injured party and it were all Jane's
fault. Eventually, she overplayed her martyred hand and was
sent out of the room by her father.

When it was time to leave, Jane asked her mother if she
could leave her doll with Doris, and received a curt nod. She
didn't have anything suitable for George, so she gave him the
remains of her pocket money. The poor little fellow didn't
understand what was going on. Howling, he clung to Jane
when she said goodbye. Then she turned to Mrs Edwards.

'I'm sorry we didn't get a chance to say goodbye to Mr
Edwards and Jim,' she said.

'They're helping out over at Bert Porter's place.'

'Will you tell him goodbye, please? And thanks for everything you've done for us. And ...' Jane was close to tears. 'I'm sorry about ...' She couldn't say any more.

There were tears in Mrs Edwards's eyes as she leaned over to kiss the girls. Then she handed a packet of sandwiches to Mrs Harrison, shook hands, and closed the front door.

The coach journey was long, tedious and ominous. Jane knew they hadn't heard the last of the incident. She hoped her father would be at home. He usually managed to calm down Mum when she lost her temper.

No such luck. The house was dark and empty.

Mrs Harrison carried the suitcase upstairs. 'I'll do the blackout in your room first,' she said. 'When you've put your things away, come straight down.'

Their bedroom looked smaller than Jane remembered. A wooden frame covered with thick black paper made sure no light escaped from the window. The brown lino and oak furniture gleamed with wax polish. Crumpled newspapers were stuffed into the black-leaded fireplace, and starched doilies protected the dressing table. Cotton bedspreads covered the eiderdowns until the end of October, when summer bedding and curtains would be packed away in the loft and replaced with heavy folkweave, smelling of mothballs.

Old Tedbear stared sightlessly from his one eye, waiting to be cuddled and tucked inside the sheet. Rose zipped up the pink crinoline nightdress case, a Christmas present from Gran, sat her doll on the dressing table, and went downstairs, still not saying a word. For a moment Jane lingered, reluctant to enter the lion's den.

Sprawled on the fender seat, Tibs waited hopefully for someone to light the first fire as the evenings cooled. Wisely he'd disappeared for a few days when most of his furry neighbours were taken for their final trip to the vet. As Jane put out her hand to stroke his plush coat, he jumped down and walked out of the door. Either he's forgotten me, she thought, or he's hurt because I went away.

After vigorously plumping up the cushions and tucking a stray newspaper out of sight, Mrs Harrison faced her daughters. 'I hope you two are thoroughly ashamed of yourselves,' she began, 'because I certainly am. To be asked to bring you home, in disgrace –'

Jane was shocked. 'They didn't, did they?'

'Not in so many words. But I had no choice. You knew Mr Edwards's views on lying, yet you went ahead with your cock-and-bull story. He wouldn't ever be able to trust you again. And neither can I. As for –'

Rose broke in, 'It was Kitty's idea, Mum. We only went along to help her out. There didn't seem any harm in it.'

'No harm in it! When the whole of Cromer saw you giggling and cavorting with boys –'

'I wouldn't call half a dozen people the whole of Cromer.'

'Don't be cheeky, Rose. You know what I mean. At your age you have no right to be out alone with boys, especially boys of fourteen and fifteen.'

'We weren't on our own. There was a crowd of us. We didn't even sit on the bus with the boys.'

'Only because you didn't want anyone to find out about your furtive little plan. And how could you be so deceitful to those kind people, Janey?'

Jane thought it best to remain silent. Nothing would stop her mother now, unless Rose owned up that Jane hadn't known about the deception until it was too late.

'I only hope the teachers don't get to hear about it,' Mrs Harrison went on.

Quietly, Jane asked, 'What did you say to Miss Bellinger?'

'What could I say? I told her I didn't think there was any danger now, so I would be taking you home.'

'Will we be able to start at the high school on Monday?'

'Miss Bellinger said it might be difficult. The County High is the only one still open, and it's full up with all the kids from the other grammar schools who didn't want to be evacuated.'

Rose brightened visibly. 'So we might not have to go to school?'

'It's up to the deputy headmaster. He'll give you homework if there's no room. I've got to see him on Monday – as if I haven't enough to do.' Mrs Harrison's voice became even more irritable. 'What on earth your father will say about all this, I really don't know.'

Rose said, 'He won't say much. He never does.'

Mrs Harrison's face was livid. 'I've warned you once about answering back, my girl. And don't think you're too old for a hiding, because you're not, and never will be, either of you.' Wagging her finger, she swung angrily round towards Jane, just as Mr Harrison pushed open the door.

He looked at the twins, then at his wife, and sighed, 'Oh, dear.'

Mrs Harrison blinked and took a deep breath. 'I didn't hear you come in, Fred,' she said.

'There did seem to be a lively discussion going on.' He hung his cap and raincoat on the hallstand with his gas mask. 'What's up?'

'Your daughters have been branded as deceitful liars, that's what's up.'

For the next five minutes, Mrs Harrison repeated the whole sorry story, finishing, 'I don't know what to do with them. You'd better give them a good talking-to while I get on with supper.'

Mr Harrison slumped into an armchair and reached for his slippers. He looked tired as he said, 'I'm listening.'

Rose was quick off the mark. 'It wasn't as bad as all that, Dad,' she said. 'Mum only heard Mr Edwards's side of the story, and we couldn't very well land Kitty in it.'

'How do you mean?'

'She only wanted to go to the pictures with Arnold, and her dad was ever so strict. So she said she was taking Janey and me. When we got there, we found she'd arranged to meet the boys. It was too late to do anything about it, so we didn't have much choice, did we?'

Mr Harrison rolled a cigarette and fumbled in his pocket. As he blew out the match, his eyes searched Jane's face, as though searching for the truth. 'Is that what you think, Jane?' he asked.

Quickly, Rose said, 'She was in the same boat as me. Couldn't snitch on the others without causing a rumpus.'

Mr Harrison held up his hand. 'You've had your say, Rose,' he said. 'It's Jane's turn now.'

To tell the truth would be to accuse Rose of lying. She would probably deny it, anyway. Jane averted her eyes as she mumbled, 'I'm sorry Mr Edwards was so upset, especially as he was kind enough to come and take us home.'

39

Rose scoffed, 'To spy on Kitty, more likely. He was really hard on her.'

Mr Harrison's face was stern as he said, 'Mr Edwards has the right to make rules in his own home. The fact that you don't agree with them is neither here nor there. If I thought that you'd plotted together behind his back ...' He relit his cigarette, then lifted the cushion and found his newspaper. 'Let's just say there may have been some extenuating circumstances. Now go and help Mum with supper.'

Rose said, 'Can't we stay in here with you, Dad? You know what Mum's like when she's wild.'

'You'd better go and tell her you're sorry, then. That's the best way to get back into her good books.'

Supper was another uncomfortable meal. Jane asked about Jack. He'd volunteered for the new Airborne Division. Wanted to be a glider pilot, of all things. Betty had bad morning sickness, so she had given up her job at the bakery.

Jane took the dishes to the scullery and slipped into the bathroom. The tiny room was filled with buckets of sand, huge rolls of sticky tape and cardboard boxes labelled *First Aid* and *Emergency Supplies*. Feeling uneasy, she hoped they wouldn't need to use them, and wondered what the Anderson shelter looked like. Opening the back door a fraction, she peered into the darkness. Watery moonlight showed a mound where potatoes had once sprouted, but little else, except for the mangle. And the kennel, chain hanging. She was about to close the door when a voice roared, 'Put that light out!' It was Mr Green.

'How many other dogs were put down for nothing?' Jane shouted back, as she slammed the door and ran up the stairs.

A tap on the door interrupted her sobs. Mr Harrison put a cup of tea on the dressing table, then sat on the bed. 'I'm sorry about the animals,' he said.

'Why did you listen to him, Dad? You know he spouts rubbish.'

'At the time it seemed the best thing to do.'

'If only you'd told us! I kept asking about him. And Snowy.'

'Yes, that was rotten luck.' Mr Harrison sighed. 'We wanted to let you know, but couldn't find the right words. It seemed

40

better to tell you in person. And don't forget, I was fond of that little dog, too.'

Jane sniffled and nodded. After a moment, her father went on, 'It's a pity I couldn't have got down myself to see you, and meet Mr and Mrs Edwards.'

'You'd have liked them, Dad,' Jane said. 'But we did understand that you were busy at the Arsenal.'

'Working flat out. Didn't even get my week's holiday this summer.'

Suddenly, Jane felt guilty. 'I'm sorry we've made things worse, Dad,' she whispered. 'Mum's really upset.'

'Well, she's had a lot to put up with. She's worried sick about Jack. Then there's the baby coming. And your gran's legs.' Jane smiled faintly. 'Food rationing doesn't help. Try and see things from her point of view.'

'I do try. Honest. But I can't talk to Mum like I do with you. Sometimes I feel as if she doesn't like me very much, only Rose.'

'That's nonsense. Mum thinks the world of you two, even though she doesn't show it.' Mr Harrison's voice was unusually sharp. 'I found her crying her eyes out last Christmas Eve, because she missed her girls. That's what she said. Not Rose. Both of you.'

'I wish I'd known,' Jane whispered miserably. 'Do you think she'll ever forgive us?'

''Course she will. Mum might have a bit of a paddy, but she doesn't bear a grudge. Come on, give your old dad a cuddle, then drink your tea.'

As she snuggled into his shoulder, the faint smell of Erinmore tobacco reminded her just how much she'd missed him.

After he'd gone, Jane thought about her father's words. Fancy Mum fretting like that. She'd always been one to get in a tizz about silly things, like wiping your feet on the doormat, or what the neighbours might say, but seemed to take everything else in her stride, even war.

Next morning, Jane went out to get the Sunday paper. Shop windows were crisscrossed with sticky tape, and pavement edges were painted with white stripes. Sandbags everywhere, even around the telephone box, and a square concrete shelter replaced the patch of shrubs on the corner.

41

Back home she explored the garden. An ugly corrugated-iron arch was sunk into the ground and covered with about a foot of earth. Jane peeped inside at a puddle under the wooden bench.

Rose peered over her shoulder. 'You won't get me down there,' she said.

'Not very big, is it?'

'We'd catch our deaths. Look at the water running down the walls.'

Mr Harrison joined them. 'It's only condensation. Mum wants me to get a little oil heater. That'll help.'

Rose protested, 'You're surely not expecting us to sit down there? We'd get more protection in the house.'

'I know this isn't any good against a direct hit. But we won't get injured by blast or flying glass, or trapped under wreckage.'

Quietly, Jane asked, 'Do you think the Germans will bomb us, Dad?'

Mr Harrison straightened up and looked at the shiny silver balloons dotted thickly around the sky, like drifting whales. 'Let's hope not, love,' he said. 'But just as well to be ready if they do come.'

Despite the warmth of the day, Jane felt a chill shiver of fear. Suddenly the war seemed much closer.

Chapter Five

Gradually, the shelter filled. Shoppers, assistants, bus drivers and passengers, all sought refuge in the tunnel under the pavement. There was no panic. People glanced upwards when a bomb landed near enough to vibrate the damp walls, then smiled nervously at each other. A tiny baby began to cry, pitifully at first, then more demanding, until the young mother unbuttoned her frock and huddled into the corner, bending low over the greedily sucking infant. One or two women smiled with compassion, and children stared curiously, but the men looked uncomfortably at their shoes, or concentrated on the torn poster, as though *Careless Talk Costs Lives* had to be memorised. Even Nell Harrison searched her handbag until she found a letter from Jack to reread.

Poor Mum! Not much of a birthday treat for her. Dad had planned it all carefully: tea in Lyons, then the pictures. A surprise. The biggest surprise was hearing the siren, hurrying out of the teashop and seeing hundreds of planes droning steadily through puffs of smoke.

Now the gunfire was louder and more intense. Jane's knees began to tremble. She could be killed or badly injured. Suppose her hands were maimed? Oh, God! They'd been safe in Norfolk. Suddenly she was not only frightened, but angry. It was one thing being under suspicion, thanks to Rose and Kitty. But now her life was at risk, and for what? A stupid liaison with a couple of boys. There were times, Jane thought, and this was one of them, when she really hated her sister.

If only she had a book or some knitting, anything to take her mind off the noise. A particularly loud explosion brought a young seaman scurrying through the entrance, brushing the remains of a burst sandbag from his shoulders as he looked intently along the benches.

The warden offered him a cigarette. 'Expect you're used to all this racket?' he said.

The sailor nodded. 'First leave I've had this year and I've got no bleedin' ceiling in me bedroom.'

'Where do you live, mate?'

'Canning Town. It's bad round the docks.'

'What about your family?'

'The neighbours said Mum had come here to do some shopping, so she don't know what's happened yet.' Again he searched the faces, then shook his head.

'Have you tried the big shelter near the station?'

'That's next on my list. Thanks for the fag.'

Jane watched her mother's face. She knew what was going through her mind before Mrs Harrison spoke. 'I do hope Gran is all right, Fred. She won't go down the shelter if she can help it.'

'Grace will make sure they do. She can be quite firm when need be.' Fred Harrison patted his wife's hand. 'It's quiet now. Let's go home.'

They surfaced to a pall of dust and a pavement littered with broken glass. Bell ringing shrilly, a fire engine raced past.

Rose looked at her father. 'There's still time to catch the last show,' she said.

Mrs Harrison shook her head. 'Sorry, dear, but I couldn't settle for worrying about Gran and Grandad. Can we go there now, Fred? To put my mind at rest.'

'The buses will be right up the creek for a bit. I'll go myself first thing in the morning.'

'But the raid's over now.' Rose pouted. 'And I was looking forward to it.'

'So was your mother. If the shop's open we'll take in some fish and chips, and a bottle of cherryade.'

They were sprinkling salt and vinegar on their supper when the gunfire started again. Mr Harrison reached for the torch. 'Good job we came home when we did,' he commented.

Mrs Harrison looked uncertain. 'Shall I put the food in the oven?' she asked her husband.

'No. We'll take it down with us, just in case.'

A distant rumble warned them not to waste time. Probably

because their Anderson was not so deep or thick-walled as the street shelter, the hysterical sounds of gunfire going up and bombs coming down seemed louder.

Just before midnight a brief lull enabled them to dash into the house. On the way back to the shelter, Jane slowed for a moment. Even when the Crystal Palace burned down, the sky had not been as red as this.

Her mother's sharp voice interrupted her thoughts, 'Don't drag that blanket in the dirt, Janey.'

Mr Harrison had grabbed some nightlights and pillows, Rose had a pile of magazines, and Jane her knitting. Mrs Harrison made a flask of tea and brought a packet of custard creams. When her husband had secured the wooden door, he tucked a blanket around her knees and said, 'Not quite the celebration I had in mind, but happy birthday, Nell. And if you don't mind my saying so, you don't look forty-two, even with a smudge on your nose.' Gently he wiped the mark away with his handkerchief, then kissed her cheek.

'As long as you don't wish me many happy returns of the day.' Mrs Harrison smiled wryly, then jumped as a shower of dirt fell from the juddering doorway. 'That was close. Was it our house?'

Mr Harrison opened the door and peered over the pile of sandbags. 'No. It looks like the two on the corner.' He quickly closed the door as another bomb whistled earthwards. 'Any idea where Tibs has got to?' he asked Jane. 'Couldn't see him in the kennel.'

'He was hiding under the bath, so I put his blanket in there. They say cats usually manage to find the safest place.'

Her mother screwed the lid back on the Thermos. 'Do you reckon we're in for a few nights of this, Fred, like they had in Liverpool last month?' she asked.

'There's no way of telling what Hitler's got in mind. A lot depends on the weather, of course.'

'Only I've been thinking. We ought to get the shelter a bit better organised. Deck chairs are all right for a little while, but not for as long as this. My bedclothes will be ruined, draped around the floor. We need better lighting, as well. And a bucket.'

Slowly nodding, Fred Harrison looked around. 'The only thing I can think of is to put the mattress from Jack's bed on the floor, and the old camp bed that's up in the loft.'

'All this damp will ruin the mattress.'

45

'I suppose I could knock up some sort of floor and cover it with a groundsheet. And I'll hunt around for some hurricane lamps and a heater. The man at the oil shop said they're like gold dust.'

'Try Arthur. He manages to get hold of things that are in short supply.'

'And charges the earth for them. But I'll ask him. Meantime, we'll have to make do the best we can. It can't go on for ever.'

A fresh crump-crump warned it might go on for a long time. Nerves on edge, they flinched as shrapnel pinged against an exposed corner of the Anderson, covered their ears against tortuous sounds, like nails rattling in a tin bucket, when the anit-aircraft batteries cracked into action, and held hands as bombs whooshed or screamed downwards. Jane prayed as she had never prayed before, mainly for courage and the strength to hold back her cries.

Dawn was breaking as the last batch of raiders turned homewards. The Harrisons crawled out of their hole in the ground and blinked at Mrs Green, who was examining a tile blown from her roof. Mr Harrison picked up two more tiles and commented, 'If that's the only damage, we haven't got much to moan about. Not like those poor devils.'

Silently they watched the thin spiral of dust and listened to the sounds of shovelling from behind the broken wall at the far end of the road.

'Is Mr Green down there with the rescue workers?' Mrs Harrison asked.

'No. He's still in the Anderson, trying to catch up on some sleep.'

'Wasn't he on duty last night?'

Mrs Green shook her head, not meeting her neighbour's eyes. 'He didn't think it was right to leave me on my own.'

'You could have come in with us, couldn't she, Fred?'

'I told Wilf I'd be all right, but he said his bad ankle hurt.' Cissie Green thrust the tile into her overall pocket and looked towards the wrecked houses. 'Old Mrs Johnson lived there. She refused to go down the shelter. Said she'd rather die in her own armchair. Reckon she got her wish.'

Nell Harrison looked anxiously at her husband, who nodded. 'Just let me have a quick wash and brush-up, then I'll be on my way,' he said.

46

'Have some breakfast first. There's something I want to talk about before you go.'

Once they were settled at the table, Mrs Harrison looked at her husband. 'Go on, Fred,' she said.

Finishing his mouthful of fried bread, her husband quietly said, 'Last night wasn't very pleasant. And your Mum and I are bothered that it might go on for a bit.' He cut the rind from his bacon. 'We'd rather you were somewhere safe until this little lot's over.'

'What do you mean by somewhere safe?' Rose asked. 'Norfolk?'

Mrs Harrison shook her head. 'Torquay. Aunt Peggy put a letter in with my birthday card. Said she was worried London might be bombed, and you were welcome to stay there as long as you like.'

As Jane and Rose exchanged glances, silent messages passed between them. Although they were chalk and cheese in looks and personality, they shared a special bond from having shared the same womb. Often, each sensed what the other was thinking. In this instance, both girls were remembering past holidays in Devon with great affection. Aunt Peggy and Uncle Joe adored children, though they hadn't any of their own. It would be wonderful to see them again. And safe. But ...

Rose voiced their fear. 'Do you think Hitler plans to invade us, Dad?' she asked.

Mr Harrison wiped his plate with a piece of bread before he answered, 'Yes, I do think Hitler plans to invade us.' Placing his knife and fork neatly on the empty plate, he said, 'Whether he succeeds or not is a different matter. He should have come earlier in the year, when we were unprepared.'

Rose giggled, 'Apart from the Home Guard with their broomsticks.'

Seriously, Jane persisted, 'But all this bombing could be a preamble to an invasion, couldn't it, Dad?'

'Yes. I'm afraid it's a possibility.'

SHaring thoughts, the girls stared at each other. Then Jane motioned for Rose to be their spokeswoman. 'We want to stay here.'

Mrs Harrison began to argue. 'And we want you to go to Aunt Peggy today. She'll look after you well.'

47

'I know, Mum. But we won't be safer down there if the Germans do invade. We need Dad to protect us, not Uncle Joe with his wooden leg.' Rose ploughed on, 'God knows what the soldiers might do to us.'

'Don't, Rose!' Mrs Harrison shuddered. 'I don't want to think about such things. And I don't want to be worrying about you every time the siren goes.'

'Mum, if we go away, we'll all be worrying about each other all the time. You here and us down there.'

'Oh, Fred,' Mrs Harrison appealed for help. 'I really don't know what to do for the best.'

After a moment, Mr Harrison asked, 'What do you think, Jane?'

'I agree with Rose,' Jane answered without hesitation. 'Whatever happens, I think I can face it better if we're all together.'

Five minutes later, Jane opened the front door for her father and handed him his gas mask. Then they both gasped. Waddling along the pavement, Gran and Grandad carried bulging carrier bags. Behind them, Aunt Grace had stopped for a moment to rest from the weight of two suitcases.

Horrified, Jane watched her grandmother's face crumple as the old lady burst into tears.

Six weeks later, Jane sat on her bed, chin hunched over her knees, and wondered. What made it possible for her, night after night, to go through the routine of collecting her knitting and books five minutes before the alert was due, put the kettle on for the flask of cocoa, and help Gran along the garden path as calmly as if they were going to pick some brussels sprouts?

She still shook inside every time the siren started, but when she looked around at Gran's dropped crochet hook, Grandad's fingers fumbling with his newspaper, and Rose's bright smile as she buttoned his coat, she had to control her own feelings. Most of all, it was the expression on Mum's face, especially when Dad was on nights.

Please don't let them know I'm so frightened, she prayed, Mum's got enough to put up with.

The nights in the shelter were particularly difficult. With two extra chairs, it was a tight squeeze. Mum had bought navy serge slacks to pull over their pyjamas, so Gran could have the hot-water bottles. She also had the eiderdown, two pillows, the leanest meat, most of the best butter, and Dad's chair by the fire. Still she complained.

Although it was better since her father had made the wooden floor, Jane was squashed in the corner on a low stool, unable to sit away from the corrugated-iron walls. She could feel the damp coldness through her thickest jumper and dressing gown

It would have been even more cramped if Aunt Grace had stayed as well. But someone had to look after the house and feed Grandad's birds. Jane felt sorry for her mother's older sister. She was quite a jolly soul, really. Not a bit like an old maid.

Jane collected her notes. Better finish the essay in the shelter. Dad was on his way upstairs to check the blackout. As he pushed the frame more securely against the window, he said, 'Can you try to keep Gran on the path, Jane? She flattened a row of my young savoys last night.'

'I do try, Dad, but she won't listen, and she won't follow Mum. She just stands and watches the flares, then complains her eyes have gone funny and she can't see where she's going. When are they going home?'

'Not till Jerry stops bombing the docks. Gran is convinced she's safer here, even though we've had our share. That first raid really shook her up.'

'I know, and I try to be patient, honest. But ...'

'But what?'

'It's the way she has us all waiting on her hand and foot, and running backwards and forwards to West Ham. Did you know Mum strained her back yesterday, carrying two cases full of their winter clothes?'

'No, she never mentioned it. I'd have gone after work if I'd known.'

'I wish they'd go home. It's not as though the house was badly damaged. You boarded up the windows and helped get the place straight again. Poor Aunt Grace! She's there all by herself. How can Gran do that to her?'

'I didn't know it bothered you as much as that, Jane.'

'It's just that she's so ungrateful. Grandad's all right, except for those awful sucking noises when he eats, and he will keep taking his teeth out. But Gran is always moaning. I don't think it's fair on Mum.'

49

'I agree, love. But nothing is fair in this ruddy war. And I can't throw the old people out. The best thing we can do is to try and ease Mum's burden a bit.'

At supper, Gran said, 'You forgot to pack my brown cardigan, Nell. Will you get it in the morning?'

Mr Harrison smiled as he said, 'I'll go over on Sunday, Gran. Grace might want some jobs done. We can come back together for dinner.'

'But it's my warmest one. Nell won't mind.'

'Nell ought to rest her back. Another couple of days won't hurt.'

Open-mouthed, Gran stared at her son-in-law. Mrs Harrison frowned. 'How did you know about my back?'

'Never mind. But a strained back needs warmth and rest. Put a bottle on it when you go down the shelter.' He looked pointedly at Gran, who glared, but said nothing.

'Are you fire-watching tonight?' Mrs Harrison asked.

'Only till midnight. I'll bring a fresh jug of cocoa down with me.' He put a restraining hand on her arm as she pushed back her chair. 'We'll wash up, won't we, girls?' he said. 'You sit by the fire for a bit, dear. Have a little snooze while you've got the chance.'

Nobody snoozed in the shelter that night. For eight hours the bombers attacked, as though determined to deafen those they couldn't kill.

Gran was as determined as the bombers. As they surfaced in the morning, she said, 'I'm frozen stiff. Can't Janey get my cardigan, Fred? Give her something to do while she's got no school.'

'Jane and Rose have got homework to do before they start school again on Monday. Borrow one of mine.' He kissed his wife. 'Bye, dear. Don't forget to rest that back.'

On Monday Jane scowled at her reflection as she tried to pull down the sleeves of her blouse. She'd grown inches since she'd last worn the winter uniform. And the hat looked ridiculous, perched on top of her head. She yanked it down hard. Now it pushed her ears right out. Rose managed to look pretty whatever she wore. She'd had a good moan about having to go to school again, but Jane was looking forward to it. The quicker they could catch up, the better. Set homework wasn't the same as being at school.

The assembly hall was packed. Jane looked around for famil-iar faces. Two girls from her class in Norfolk were sitting in the row behind, and Sandy was right at the back, with Bill and Arnold. Looking as disdainful as ever, Isabel sat next to Leslie Saunders.

She had hoped Theresa might have plucked up courage to tell her mother about Mrs Walton, but there was no sign of her. In her last letter, Theresa had said Mrs Walton intercepted her letters and insisted on reading everything she wrote before she would allow it to be posted. Jane decided to write again that night.

The chattering stopped abruptly, and Jane was surprised to see Miss Bellinger climb the stairs to the platform, followed by a line of teachers.

'I expect you are wondering why I have returned to Essex,' she began. 'The reason is that it was felt our evacuated pupils would be safer in the West Country. However, despite the air attacks upon London, some decided not to transfer to the new destina-tion and, with the influx from other schools in this area, it has been necessary to increase staffing here.'

Nodding towards the man at her side, the headmistress contin-ued, 'I know the school has maintained its high standards while I have been in Norfolk, and I would like to thank Mr McEwen for his sterling work.'

Miss Bellinger's expression changed. Feeling uneasy, Jane waited for the headmistress to continue.

'After prayers, Mr McEwen will explain the revised schedules. First, though, we must remember a second-year pupil, whose name will be on the Roll of Honour. The child who was killed by one stray bomb, jettisoned from a German plane returning home. Let us stand silently for one minute and pray for Theresa O'Connor.'

Jane stuffed her hands into her mouth to stifle the cry of anguish as she visualised her friend running along a country lane, worrying that she might receive a tongue-lashing from Mrs Walton. One single bomb, whistling down towards a vast, empty space. And finding Theresa O'Connor who'd never hurt anyone in her short life. She'd been sent there to be safe. But nowhere was safe. Not any more.

Chapter Six

The twins were packing their satchels when they heard the knocker. On the doorstep waited Auntie Vi, Peter and a small suitcase.

Jane had never had much time for her mother's younger sister, with her prying eyes and penny-pinching ways. Uncle Arthur was just as bad, furtively counting his takings from their poky little shop. But she and cousin Peter had always been good mates, even though he was a year older, and she didn't mind his coming to stay with them at all.

Mrs Harrison poured her sister another cup of tea. 'How bad was it?' she asked.

'They'll have to shore up the wall of the shop. It's only Peter's room that's unsafe.'

'We were lucky to get away with it. Last night was the worst I've known.'

'Becton Gas Works copped it.' Auntie Vi looked at the door, then lowered her voice. 'How are you getting on with Mum and Dad under your feet all the time?'

'It's not easy for any of us, but we manage.'

'Why didn't they go up to Herbert's? There's nothing worth bombing in Warwickshire.'

'They're not keen on the country, and –'

'And they're not keen on Dolly, either. Who is? But at least they'd be out of the raids. And he's the eldest. He ought to help out a bit more.' Auntie Vi put her cup back on the table. 'Does Len know they're with you?'

'I've written, but goodness knows how long it'll take to reach the ship. We've not heard anything for ages.'

'See if you can tap him for a bit of help.'

'What can Len do from the middle of the Atlantic?'

'He could give you an allowance for them. Must have a bob or two stashed away, all those trips he used to get. Not like us, with families and homes to fork out for.'

'Mum and Dad will go home as soon as the bombing stops. Please God it won't go on for much longer' Mrs Harrison glanced at the clock. 'You girls had better get a move on, or you'll be late.' She turned to her sister. 'Have you sent a note to Peter's school?'

'No point. It was flattened last night.' Auntie Vi picked up her handbag. 'All I hope is that Peter will get a good enough education here.'

'This is the best grammar school in the area,' Mrs Harrison retorted. 'The twins had to get very good marks to be accepted.'

'Oh, they'll be glad to have Peter. His teacher says he's exceptionally bright, and I've got his report.'

'It will all depend on whether there's enough room, Vi. The girls had to wait seven weeks, and it's their own school. I'd better come with you.'

Peter was in luck. A third-year girl had decided to join the evacuated group that day.

After dinner, Jane found him standing at the edge of the playing fields, alone.

'How are you getting on?' she asked.

'OK.' He looked around. 'Where's Rose?'

'With Bill, I expect.' She studied his face as he cleaned his glasses. 'Don't worry, I'm sure you'll be back home before long.'

Peter smiled. 'Oh, I like the idea of being with you and Rose. But I can't help worrying. The shop's right in the thick of it all.' He adjusted the glasses on his nose. 'And Auntie Nell's got Gran and Grandad, and now me dumped on her as well. Mum didn't even ask if she minded.'

'Of course Mum doesn't mind, silly. She thrives on sorting out problems. Says that's what families are for.'

Peter was not the only unexpected guest to arrive that day. Aunt Grace was normally the neatest of ladies, as befitted a supervisor of a typing pool. But not today.

Her hair was smothered in brick dust, grime streaked her face and her eyes were red, as though she'd been crying.

Jane's heart sank as she looked at her grandparents. She'd never seen a grown man in tears before, and it distressed her to see Grandad fumbling for his handkerchief.

'My lovely budgies,' he mumbled. 'They're all dead.'

The huge aviary in the back garden had been Grandad's lifetime hobby. Some of his birds had won prizes at shows.

Gran sobbed, 'We've lost our home. Lived there for nearly fifty years. Now it's gone.'

Swiftly, Rose moved across the room and put her arms around the old lady.

Jane looked at Aunt Grace, who raised her head and attempted to smile. 'I'm sorry,' she said. 'I didn't mean to frighten you. But I haven't had time to take it all in.'

'Where were you when it happened, Aunt Grace?' Jane asked.

'With the Hopkinses. They insisted I share their shelter. Saved my life. Ours had the direct hit.'

'Have you been here all day?'

'No. The ARP men said there wasn't anything I could do, so I decided to call in at the office to let them know I was coming over here. But Wainwright and Pettifer's was badly damaged, and we had to move the documents and typewriters to our office in Lincoln's Inn.'

'Poor Aunt Grace, you must be exhausted. Are your girls OK?'

Wearily, Aunt Grace brushed a strand of hair back from her face. 'All except young Eileen Cavanagh.' Her voice faltered, then she went on, 'She lived in one of the flats near the office. They didn't find her till lunchtime.'

'She's not dead?'

'No. But her legs were too bad to save. She'd just got her silver medal for ballroom dancing, too.'

Rose whispered, 'Oh, no.'

'Such a brave girl! Sadly, her parents were killed.' Aunt Grace dabbed at her eyes. 'I stayed with Eileen at the hospital until they took her into the operating theatre, then came straight here.' Ineffectively she brushed dirt from her skirt. 'I must look a right mess.'

'The copper's lit.' Her sister stood up. 'You can have the first bath while I sort out the bedrooms.'

Mrs Harrison tried to make room for Peter's clothes in the twins' wardrobe. 'With Gran and Grandad in Jack's room, Grace in here on the camp bed, and Peter on the settee, we can manage the sleeping. Not that we sleep in the house these days.' She peered into the suitcase. 'Janey, I keep telling you to keep that cat out of the bedrooms.'

'Sorry, Mum.' Laughing, Jane lifted Tibs from the suitcase and put him on the landing. 'He just wants to know what's going on.'

'So tell him what happens to curious cats. And do the best you can with the rest of Peter's things.' Mrs Harrison winced as she bent over the suitcase.

Jane said, 'Why don't you lie down for a while, Mum?'

'How can I, with supper to get before the siren goes? Talk sense, Janey. Oh, Tibs! Do get out of the way.' Her voice was sharp with pain as she stepped over the cat.

'You shouldn't have carried those suitcases. Dad was quite concerned about you.'

'Was it you that told him? You know I don't like worrying him.'

Watching her mother's face, Rose said, 'Mum, I've been thinking. Why don't I stay home from school tomorrow? I can give you a hand, so you can rest your back.'

'That's very kind of you, dear, but you need your lessons. You'll have exams in a few weeks.'

'I can always swot at the last minute, and get by.'

'Just getting by isn't good enough, Rose.'

'You don't need top marks in algebra to get into films. Dad was telling me about a concert at the Arsenal the other day, by a new branch of the army called ENSA.'

'What's that when it's at home?'

'Entertainment something or other. Anyway, I'm going to join that as soon as I'm old enough.'

'A good education is never wasted. I only wish I'd had the opportunities you two have got.'

'It's different for Janey. She likes school. I hate it. Go on, Mum. Write a note for Peter to take.'

Mrs Harrison hesitated. Then she shook her head. 'It would

be nice to have you home, Rose,' she said, 'but your father wouldn't like it. And I must go along to the Housing Office. Put in for a bigger place.'

There was no good news for Mrs Harrison. 'Everybody's in the same boat,' she explained later. 'The only thing they could offer was one of the new semidetached houses up near the school.'

Rose became excited. 'Oh, Mum! They've got a separate dining room with a hatch into a kitchenette. And the bathroom is upstairs. It's even got a washbasin, so we wouldn't have to queue up for the scullery sink.'

'And no pumping up baths on a Friday night. Just switch on the hot water.' Mrs Harrison sighed. 'But it's ten shillings a week dearer, and we just can't afford it.'

'Can't the others give you a bit more towards the housekeeping? They're living rent-free.'

'Grace is giving as much as she can, but she has extra fares to pay, and lost most of her things.'

'Gran and Grandad have enough clothes to last the rest of their lives, judging by the way they've overflowed into your wardrobe.'

'But they don't get much pension, and they need money for their personal expenses.'

'Grandad will have to cut down on his beer, then. And Uncle Arthur isn't hard up for a bob or two.'

'Shush, Rose. Peter might hear you.'

'He's filling the coal scuttle. Anyway, he knows his dad has more lolly than the rest of us put together.'

'According to your auntie Vi, they're feeling the pinch because of rationing and shortages. She's giving me a few groceries each week instead of money towards Peter's keep.'

'You can bet your boots you'll get broken biscuits and sweepings from the tea chest. It makes me sick when I think how hard Dad has to work for a pittance, while Uncle Arthur is feathering his nest from the black market.'

'Rose!'

'Gran said he's got masses of stuff hidden away in the back room. Buys it cheap off one of the dockers and sells it for a fat profit.'

'You haven't told anyone else about this, have you, Rose? Outside the family, I mean.'

'Of course not. Anyway, what about the house, Mum? I'd love to live there.'

'I know you would, dear, but everything is going up. Dad said it's due to the Battle of the Atlantic.' Mrs Harrison laughed. 'I have a Battle in the Co-op every day. And there's other things as well. Christmas club, your dancing lessons, Janey's music. That reminds me.' Mrs Harrison hesitated. 'You'll have to miss your piano lesson tonight, Janey. I had to sort out the ration books, then queue over an hour for the sheep's hearts, and I haven't started to stuff them yet.'

'You don't need to come with me, Mum.'

'There's been a man hanging around, talking dirty to little girls.'

'I'll go with her, Auntie Nell.'

Mrs Harrison dropped a spoon as she swung around towards the door. 'Oh, Peter. You gave me quite a turn. How long have you been there?'

'Only just. Sorry I made you jump. But let me go with Janey. I like listening to her playing.'

'Well, if you're sure you don't mind.' Mrs Harrison turned to Jane. 'There's one and sixpence on the mantelpiece for your lesson. Off you go, and straight back, mind. I want to get supper over before the siren goes.'

After the lesson, Miss Palmer asked Jane if she'd seriously considered music as a career. 'Do think about it, my dear. Your exam marks were excellent.'

Jane had often daydreamed about performing at the Royal Albert Hall, wearing a velvet evening gown. She would play Grieg's Piano Concerto. As the last notes died away, the audience would rise to their feet, crying, 'Bravo! Bravo!', the orchestra would tap their appreciation of her excellence on the music rests, and she would leave the platform in joyful tears, carrying an armful of flowers.

As they walked home, Peter asked, 'Have you ever been to a proper concert?'

'No. But I saw a film about a pianist once. The music was so beautiful, I cried all the way home.' Jane reflected on the film for a while, then said, 'I know I couldn't ever be a real concert pianist, however much I wanted to.'

'Why not?'

'Because it takes years of training and Dad couldn't afford it. And I'm not good enough.'

''Course you are. I don't know anyone who plays as good as you.'

'Thanks, Peter. But you have to be more than good. I've got a bit of talent, but I'm not a genius.'

'Then what did you music teacher mean when she talked about you having a musical career?'

'I'm not sure. Perhaps she was thinking I could play with a dance band or theatre orchestra.'

'And spend the rest of your life buried in a pit?'

The cousins laughed. Jane said, 'I wouldn't mind being an accompanist. I think I could be good enough for that, if I studied properly. Not as good as Ivor Newton or Gerald Moore, of course. But there must be lots of opportunities.'

They walked through the quiet streets in silence for a while. Then Peter said, 'Seriously, though, Janey. You don't really want to take up music, do you?'

'Why shouldn't I? Have you changed you mind about my being good enough?'

'No. But it's a waste of time for a girl.'

Surprised, Jane stopped. 'Why?'

'Because girls get married and have babies.'

'Aunt Grace didn't.'

'Only because her fiancé was killed.'

'So what you're saying is that a girl can't have a career if she wants to get married?'

'I'd want my wife to give up work when we got married.'

'To do what?'

'Look after the house, of course, like my mum.'

'I suppose you think girls shouldn't be at grammar school, either?'

Peter shrugged. 'I wouldn't want to marry a girl who wasn't intelligent.'

Resisting the urge to kick him, Jane walked on. 'And what is your intelligent wife supposed to do, apart from housework?'

The scorn in her voice was not lost on Peter. 'This is silly,' he mumbled, digging his hands deep into his pockets. 'Girls always find things to do. Knitting, and sewing, and things. And they visit friends for chats over cups of tea.'

'What about her ambitions? Things she's studied? Like my music?'

'Well, I suppose you could play at a local concert sometimes. But you wouldn't have time to do more than that. Not if you're bringing up a family.'

'Women are doing war work now, then going home and looking after the children.'

'That's different. When the war ends, everything will be just as it was before.'

'With men having careers, and women looking after the home?'

'Yes. Isn't that what you want?'

Jane shook her head. 'I don't know what I'll want when the war's over. But I know one thing – I won't want any man telling me I've got to give up something I like doing.'

'Then you'll probably end up an old maid, Janey. Because no man in his right senses is going to put up with coming home to an empty house and his dinner in the oven, just so his wife can go gallivanting night after night, playing the piano.'

Bright colour flushed Jane's cheeks as she flounced through the gate with a parting shot. 'Don't ever ask me to marry you, then! I'd rather be an old maid.'

As she took off her hat and looked in the hallstand mirror, an unpleasant thought occurred to Jane. With her looks, she might not be able to choose whether to be an old maid.

Chapter Seven

Uncle Len and his shipmate, Nobby Clark, had been stewards together for years, staying at Gran's house between cruises, taking the twins to the zoo, then pantomime or tea at the Corner House. When war broke out, they'd transferred from luxury liners to armed merchantmen, crossing and recrossing the Atlantic together. Always together.

But on a cold November day in 1940, there was only one peaked Merchant Navy cap on the hallstand. Jane threw her school satchel over the top and rushed into the living room. Yes, there he was, grey eyes twinkling as ever, dark hair now flecked with silver, sleeves rolled up, revealing a small tattooed heart framing the word MOTHER. Known as Lucky Len, he had missed only one sailing in his life, the ship that disappeared without trace in 1914.

'Nobby's in hospital,' Len explained, a niece on each knee. 'Now, don't panic. He's not dying. Just got a couple of bullets in his leg. He'll be down to see you as soon as he can walk.'

Horrified, Jane asked, 'How did it happen?'

'He won't talk about it, and we were picked up by different boats. First thing I knew was when I went looking for him in Liverpool.'

'Was it awful?' Rose asked.

'It's not very nice seeing your mates machine-gunned.' He threw his cigarette end into the fire. 'We lost a few good blokes.'

Flashing her brother a warning look, Nell said, 'Thank God you're safe, anyway. And you've brought something back from Canada, haven't you?'

'I have indeed, though I'm not sure I've bought the right thing. Your girls have grown a bit since I last saw them.' Two small teddy bears each had a maple leaf taped to a paw. 'Sorry they're a bit bedraggled. I stuffed them up my shirt before I got in the lifeboat.'

Jane was thrilled. 'He's lovely! I'll call him Lucky, after you.'

As she hugged her uncle, Rose asked, 'Can you get real French scent from Canada?'

'Don't know. But if I can find a pretty girl to help me, I'll buy something more suitable for a beautiful young lady next time.' He winked and ruffled Rose's curls, then turned to Jane. 'Give us a tune, Janey. Whenever I get homesick, I think of you playing 'Alice Blue Gown'. Your mum used to sing it when we were kids. She should have gone on the stage.'

With the family sitting around the fire and singing, it was just like Christmas. Even Gran and Grandad were enjoying themselves. While Jane put the music back in the stool, Uncle Len told Peter he'd gone over to the shop after he found his own home flattened.

'Your bedroom's a right mess. Reckon you'll be here for the duration.'

'I don't mind.' Peter grinned.

'Bit crowded, though. I'll book into the Merchant Navy Hostel, Nell.'

'There's always room for you, Len, and Fred's on nights, so there's a seat in the shelter.'

Although they managed to persuade Uncle Len to stay, he refused to go into the shelter. It was a particularly noisy night and bombs dropped close. In the morning, Mrs Harrison surveyed the broken glass on her bed. 'I'll have to see to this first,' she said. 'Fred must have somewhere to sleep.'

'Is it always as bad as last night?' Uncle Len asked.

Wearily, his sister nodded. 'It's been more than two months nonstop. We could do with a break.'

'Well, at least you won't need a chimney sweep for a while.' A pile of soot lay in the hearth, and the bedroom suite was covered with a black layer.

Mrs Harrison turned to Jane. 'Help me carry the bedspread out into the graden. Careful, now.'

When the three cousins came home from school that afternoon, Uncle Len had gone. So had Gran and Grandad.

'Your uncle was concerned about them, and the overcrowding here,' Mrs Harrison explained. 'So he insisted on taking them up to Uncle Herbert's.'

Rose laughed. 'I'd love to see Aunt Dolly's face when they turn up.'

'We phoned them first, to make sure it was all right.'

Jane said, 'I'm sorry we couldn't say goodbye.'

'There wasn't time. Poor Gran was so exhausted after last night, she didn't even argue when I packed their bags. Thank goodness they'll get a good night's sleep tonight.'

Jane noticed the shadows under her mother's eyes. 'Pity you couldn't have gone with them, Mum,' she said.

'And who'd have looked after the rest of you?' Mrs Harrison spread the cloth across the table. 'I only hope Dolly doesn't argue with Gran all the time.'

No siren sounded that night. Aunt Grace moved her things into Jack's room and, for the first time in weeks, the twins slept in their own beds. It was wonderful to be indoors on such a night.

For once, Mrs Harrison was grateful the fog stayed with them. It kept the bombers away and gave her a chance to turn her attention to the Christmas pudding. 'Couldn't get any lemons, so I'll have to improvise with grated carrot. They're talking about rationing marge and lard now, as well.' She frowned at the recipe. 'Switch on the wireless, Janey. There might be something about it on the news.'

She was right about cooking fats. But the main news was that Coventry had been repeatedly bombed for ten hours, and the old city centre and cathedral destroyed. Nell Harrison groped for a chair.

'They'll be all right.' Jane tried to reassure her mother. 'Uncle Herbert lives miles away.'

'But he works in Coventry, and he might have been on nights.'

Peter jumped up. 'If you've got some change, I'll nip up the road and phone them.'

He was smiling when he came back. 'They're fine. Uncle Herbert was on day shift. They heard it, but it was in the distance.'

'Thanks, Peter. You're a good boy. Did he say how Gran and Grandad are getting on?'

'All right, I think. He said not to worry about them.'

As soon as the fog lifted, the Luftwaffe returned. Jane hated seeing the aftermath of damaged homes, rooms exposed like doll's houses, furniture tottering precariously on the edge as rescue workers sifted through debris. She turned away from the meshed window of the bus. As if reading her thoughts, Rose squeezed her arm.

'Don't worry, Janey. They might not come over tonight.'

'You must think I'm a right idiot, being so scared.'

'Why should I? Every night my heart beats so fast I'm sure you must hear it, and I bet Mum's just as bad.'

'Mum? She's ever so brave. Remember the time when that drunk on the tram was after a fight? It was Mum who pushed us behind her and batted him one with her umbrella. Nothing scares Mum.'

'Except a harmless cow. Or a spider.'

'That's different. I mean, really bad things don't frighten her.'

''Course they do. Everybody gets frightened inside.'

'What do you do to stop the fear showing?'

'I try to make a joke. It's the only way I can handle it. But it doesn't really matter what you do, unless it's something daft, like wetting your knickers.'

A week before Christmas, Nell Harrison returned from the hairdresser tight-lipped. 'The Eugene perms have gone up to twenty-five shillings,' she complained to Jane. 'So I had to have the cheaper one. Only hope it won't go frizzy.'

'Why don't you have a shampoo and set on Christmas Eve, to soften it up?'

'And fork out another three shillings? I'm not made of money, Janey. Had to pay elevenpence for a toilet roll today, and –' She was interrupted by a knock at the front door. 'That'll be the window cleaner. Take a shilling out of my purse.'

It wasn't the window cleaner who stood on the doorstep, grinning. Astonished, Jane stared. Not at the man, nor at his crutches. But at the woman standing by his side.

63

Her dark hair was swept into a sleek pageboy bob under a tiny felt hat, its short veil barely concealing her eyes. When she smiled, her teeth were perfectly shaped. She was the most beautiful woman Jane had ever seen.

'Hey, Janey. Haven't you a kiss for your uncle Nobby?'

Dragging her gaze away from his companion, Jane hugged him, calling out, 'Mum! Guess who's here.'

'For goodness' sake, Janey, I'm not in the mood for guessing games. Who is it?' Mrs Harrison appeared at the top of the stairs. When she saw the two visitors, her expression changed from irritation to amazement. 'Why, Nobby! What a lovely surprise! I didn't expect you to be out of hospital till the New Year.'

'Twisted Sister's arm. Told her Santa wouldn't know where to leave my toys. She finally relented when Laura said she was coming back to London and offered to give me a hand.' He smiled at his companion. 'So, here we are. Oh, sorry. I haven't introduced you. Laura Marshall. Nell Harrison.'

'Please forgive me for intruding like this.' The woman held out her hand. 'I'm afraid there's a slight problem with the trains.'

Nobby explained. 'It was "everybody out" at Barking. I knew you wouldn't mind Laura waiting here for a couple of hours.'

'No. No, of course not.' Mrs Harrison sounded flustered. She always panicked when people called unexpectedly. 'Come into the living room,' she said. 'You'll have to excuse the place.'

Nobby kissed her cheek. 'Stop fussing, Nell, and put the kettle on.'

A delicate aura of perfume wafted past Jane. She touched the fur coat, quite unlike the shabby musquash her mother wore.

While she set out the best cups on a tray, Jane studied their visitor. The plain black suit was relieved only by a sparkling brooch in the shape of a rose. Jane wondered if they were real rubies and diamonds. Her nails glowed ruby red, too, the exact colour of her lipstick. It was difficult to tell how old she was. Must be at least thirty. Wherever had Uncle Nobby met such a gorgeous creature?

Her mother had been wondering, too. 'Have you known

64

Nobby for long, Mrs Marshall?' she asked, using her 'polite' voice.

'Only a few weeks. My brother was on the same ship. When it went down, Nobby saved his life.'

Excited, Jane asked, 'What happened?'

'Robert was drifting towards a pool of burning oil, half conscious. Nobby saw what was happening, and rescued him.'

'Gosh!' Jane turned to Uncle Nobby. 'Weren't you afraid of getting burned?'

'I only dived down and pulled him under the oil patch.' He looked uncomfortable. 'Anyone would have done the same.'

Hand to her throat, Nell murmured, 'Len didn't mention it.'

'He doesn't know,' Nobby said. 'He was picked up straight away. Lived up to his name, thank God.'

'When did your legs get hurt?'

Quietly, he said, 'Jerry came back and strafed the survivors in the water.'

'People don't realise ...' Nell Harrison turned to her guest. 'Is your brother fully recovered, Mrs Marshall?'

'From his injuries, yes. He now has to go to East Grinstead.'

Jane said, 'Isn't that where they operate on burned airmen?'

'Yes. It's the finest hospital for skin grafts.'

'Oh, the poor man!' Mrs Harrison shuddered, then prodded the fire. 'Can't get any heat out of these dust briquettes,' she apologised. 'But it's all we have. I only hope the coalman comes before Christmas. Let me pour you another cup of tea, Mrs Marshall. It'll warm you up.'

'Thank you.' Mrs Marshall's eyes went to the piano. 'Who is the pianist?' she asked.

'Janey. And her sister sings and dances ever so well. Rose will be in any minute now. She's out looking for remnants. You should see the marvellous presents she makes from scraps of material. Don't know where she gets all her cleverness from.'

Mrs Marshall's eyes flickered from mother to daughter, and back again. 'You must be very proud of them both,' she said. 'They're twins, I believe.'

'Yes, but not a bit alike. Rose has blue eyes and naturally curly blonde hair.'

The dark eyes studied Jane. 'I used to envy girls with curly hair until the short bob became fashionable,' she said.

Jane said, 'It looks lovely in a pageboy.'

'It was my husband's favourite style.'

Why the past tense? Jane wondered. The awkward silence was broken by Nobby Clark. 'Laura's husband was killed at Dunkirk,' he said.

'Oh, I am sorry,' Mrs Harrison sympathised. 'I saw some of the soldiers on a train. They looked worn out.'

'My husband was on one of the little rescue boats. It was my father's, actually.' Mrs Marshall's voice was low. 'They had made two successful runs before they received a direct hit.' She noticed the questioning expressions and nodded. 'Both of them, I'm afraid.'

There were tears in Mrs Harrison's eyes as she softly said, 'I know how you feel. My first husband died in 1919. I was six months gone with my second son. Do you have any children?'

'Two boys. Lawrence is ten, Desmond nearly nine. It's not easy bringing up sons alone, is it?'

The two women shared a sad little smile. 'They need a father,' Nell Harrison agreed. 'I was lucky. Some women don't get one good husband. I've had two.'

Rose and Peter arrived home together. They were obviously fascinated by their visitor. Peter asked her if she thought Apple Blossom talcum powder was a suitable gift for his mother, and Rose proudly showed the red velvet which would become part of her costume in the Christmas concert. 'Do come and see me dance,' she pleaded.

'My sons are singing in the church choir on Christmas Eve. Otherwise I would have brought them to your concert.'

Nell Harrison glanced at Nobby. 'How long will you be staying here?' she asked.

'I'm to report back to Liverpool on the first of January. But I'll be sleeping at the hostel.'

'No, you won't. You need someone to look after you.' She frowned in concentration. 'You and Peter could share Jack's room. I'm sure Grace won't mind moving back in with the girls for a few days. Now she's joined the Red Cross, she's out most evenings, anyway.'

'It's good of you, Nell, but I couldn't impose.'

'Nonsense. You look tired out.'

'It was a long journey,' Mrs Marshall agreed. 'You should stay here and rest.'

'That's settled then.' Mrs Harrison hesitated for a moment. 'Mrs Marshall, I've been wondering. Would you like to bring the boys to tea the Sunday after Christmas? It would only be simple, but you'd be very welcome.'

'I shall look forward to it.' Laura Marshall smiled.

It was a happy Christmas. Mrs Harrison was in her element bustling around the kitchen, putting the Dundee cake and tin of ham on one side, already thinking ahead to the 29th.

There was even a lull in the air raids. And Peter was pleased to have his parents there for the day. On the way home from church, Mrs Harrison decided to telephone her brother in Warwickshire. The trouble was, Gran thought nobody could hear her unless she raised her voice.

'Dolly keeps making me go out,' she bellowed. 'Mother's Union. Walks after dinner. They call it lunch.' She snorted. 'When did the likes of us have napkins on the table? It's all bloody show.'

Rose talked about the concert, and Jane thanked her grandmother for the two-shilling postal order, then told her about Mrs Marshall's anticipated visit. For a moment there was silence, then Gran said, 'Let me talk to Nell again.'

Squeezed in the doorway of the telephone box, Jane saw her mother's expression change as she tried to get a word in. 'No, Gran, I don't think more of strangers ... They're only coming to tea ... Of course I care how you feel.'

As Mrs Harrison replaced the receiver, she sighed, 'I wish you hadn't mentioned it, Janey. Now Gran's all upset.'

'Sorry, Mum. When you told her about Uncle Nobby and Mrs Marshall, I thought it would be all right.'

The highlight of Christmas Day was Jack and Betty's arrival. Not that Betty contributed much to the festivities, but that was not unusual. She'd only visited the Harrisons once since the twins came home, and barely said a word. But Jack, as lively as ever, insisted that his wife join in the ritual singing of 'Twelve Days of Christmas'.

'Oh, no! I can't sing,' Betty protested.

'Neither can I. You be "eleven pipers piping".' He counted heads. 'I'll be "four calling birds", as well as bringing up the rear.'

The song ended with more than the usual hysterical laughter, due partly to Jack's raucous bird imitations, and partly to Aunt Grace's partiality to port and lemon. When they'd regained their composure, Uncle Nobby asked Jack about the new Airborne Division.

'It's so new, nobody knows what we're about. Should be moving to Haddenham any day, then perhaps I'll learn to fly at last.'

'So what are you doing at the moment?'

'Fitness training, stuff like that. But I hate all this hanging around. Can't wait to see some real action. After all, that's what I joined for.' Jack grinned, then noticed the expression on Betty's face. Quickly turning to his sisters, he changed the subject. 'How are you getting on at that new school of yours?'

Rose pulled a face. 'It's all rules and regulations. If you talk, or run along the corridor, they dish out house points. Then you get it in the neck again from the other kids because they say you've let the side down.'

'Just like the Army. Don't worry, you'll get used to it. What about you, Janey? Do you find it tough?'

'I'm struggling a bit with algebra and French. But the other subjects aren't too bad.'

'Wish I was old enough to join up.' Rose sighed.

Jack ruffled her hair. 'You leave the fighting to the menfolk, little doll, and enjoy your schooldays while you can. Have any of your friends from Norfolk come back?'

'The boys billeted next door have, and a few from the Upper Village. And I've made lots of new friends.'

Jane carried the tray to the scullery. Jack followed and watched as she rinsed the glasses under the tap. Eventually, he said, 'I was sorry to hear about your friend. That was rotten luck.'

It was still difficult for Jane to talk about Theresa, but she knew Jack would understand. 'I feel so guilty about her,' she murmured.

'Why on earth should you feel guilty?'

'I knew she was being badly treated. If I'd reported it to the

68

school, or tried to find out where her parents live, they'd have brought her home. And ...' Jane dissolved into tears, burying her face in her brother's shoulder. After she'd recovered, he lifted her chin and smiled gently.

'Life is full of "ifs",' he said. 'If Hitler hadn't marched into Poland. If the German pilot had flown another minute before pulling the plug. If the little girl had run a bit faster, or a bit slower.' He wiped her tears with his handkerchief, and advised, 'Forget the guilt, Janey. Just remember the friendship.'

He was right, of course, and Jane was glad she'd talked to him. Nothing could take away her memories of Theresa.

'Thanks, Jack.' She hugged him. 'I do miss you. But Dad's very understanding.'

'Dad's a wise old owl. You're like him, Janey. I never quite know what you're thinking, but always feel there's a lot of common sense behind that funny little face of yours.'

Playfully, Jane punched her brother on the chin. 'Seems strange to think that the next time you're on leave you'll be a dad yourself.'

Chapter Eight

The Sunday after Christmas, Mrs Harrison was humming and hawing over tablecloths. 'Perhaps the damask is too ostentatious,' she mused. 'What do you think, Fred?'

'I don't suppose it'll matter one way or the other. We're not entertaining royalty.'

'Mrs Marshall lives in Westcliff. I don't want her to think I don't know how to do things properly.'

Nobby Clark grinned. 'You always do things properly, Nell. But you are an old worryguts.'

'Someone's got to plan things.' Mrs Harrison sighed. 'At least I won't have to worry about Gran and Grandad showing us up. And what are you grinning at, Nobby?' There's nothing wrong with good manners.'

'I was just wondering how Dolly is getting on with the old folks. Now *she* really is a snob.'

'I know, but I can't have them back here. This house just isn't big enough.'

The house might not be big enough, but it was polished from top to bottom. Bread was thinly cut, home-made jam spooned into the Devon Pottery dish, and scones piled on a tiered cake dish with jam tarts and fairy cakes. The Dundee cake took pride of place in the centre of the embroidered tablecloth. Jane and Rose had made jelly in the fancy mould, and a jug of sherbet-powder lemonade for the boys. As she placed the sliced ham on the last clear space, Mrs Harrison cast a worried eye over the table.

'I do hope there's enough to go round,' she said.

Jane smiled. 'You could feed an army on this, Mum. Why don't you get changed while I lay the tea tray?'

When Mrs Harrison came downstairs, Jane felt a swell of pride. The woollen frock exactly matched the cornflower blue of her mother's eyes, and she was wearing the pearls Fred Harrison had given her on their wedding day.

'Oh, Mum! You do look lovely,' she said. 'Rose, come and see.'

For the umpteenth time, Rose ran back from the front door. 'Gosh,' she said. 'You look just like Carole Lombard.' She studied her mother's make-up. 'Except for the lipstick. You need a bit more colour.'

'No, she doesn't.' Mr Harrison stood in the doorway, buttoning his cardigan. 'Your mother looks perfect just as she is.'

'Go on with you, Fred. Wait till you see Mrs Marshall.'

'I don't care if the Queen of Sheba comes through that door. She won't hold a candle to you, love.'

Rose tidied her hair in the mirror. 'It's ever so windy,' she said. 'Next door's dustbin lid has blown down the road. There's rubbish all over the path.'

As Mr Harrison was putting the broom away, their visitors knocked at the front door. The next few minutes were a flurry of introductions and nervous laughter. When Jane took the coats upstairs, she couldn't resist stroking the fur and peeking at the label: Swears & Wells. Must have cost hundreds. 'Oh no, you don't!' A tabby tail swished defiantly as Tibs was shushed from the bed.

At first, the boys were shy, but their eyes gleamed when they saw the table, and soon there was a hubbub of conversation in the room. Lawrence chatted to Jane and Peter, but his younger brother's attention was fixed on Nobby Clark, sitting next to his mother. Jane wondered if he was afraid another man would take his father's place. But that was silly. Uncle Nobby was a confirmed bachelor, like Uncle Len. Then she glanced at her father and wondered how she would feel if she were told he wouldn't be coming home any more.

Jane thought again how pretty her mother looked, with a flush of excitement on her cheeks and eyes sparkling. Dad was right. She could hold her own against any beauty, even the lovely guest of honour. Today, the rose brooch glowed at the neck of Laura Marshall's black crepe dress and she had swept her hair up into a mass of tiny curls.

71

Suddenly, Jane realised that Aunt Grace was also staring, and Mrs Marshall had noticed.

'I'm sorry,' Aunt Grace apologised, 'I didn't mean to be rude. But I feel sure we've met before.'

'I'm afraid I don't recall ...'

'Have you ever been a client of Wainwright and Pettifer?'

'The solicitors? Why, yes. I did call there once, many years ago.'

'Now I remember.' Aunt Grace sounded excited. 'You were going to Paris to model the Coco Chanel collection. I typed the contract.'

Open-mouthed, Rose got her breath back. 'Were you really a mannequin in Paris?' she asked Mrs Marshall.

'Yes, and in London.'

'How exciting!'

'Sometimes. But it's also very hard work.'

Rose sighed. 'If I couldn't be an actress, I'd want to be a model. How did you become one?'

Mrs Marshall laughed. 'There wasn't much else I could do. Drifting around the world is pleasant, and you learn languages, but little else. So, when a family friend offered me a job in their fashion house, I took it.'

'Why did you drift around the world?'

'Rose!' her mother admonished. 'You really shouldn't ask so many questions.'

'I don't mind.' Mrs Marshall spread jam on her scone. 'After my mother died, Daddy sold the house and bought a boat. The boys loved it.' She smiled at Mrs Harrison. 'I can make exotic dishes, but have never managed scones as good as these. May I have another one, please?'

Rose didn't stop asking their visitor questions until the table was cleared and music put on the stand. After Rose had sung her party piece, Jane played a Chopin nocturne, then out came the song album. They were singing 'Happy Days Are Here Again' at the top of their voices, Nobby beating time with his crutch, when Aunt Grace realised someone was knocking at the front door. Very loudly.

Jane's heart sank when she heard Gran's voice in the hall. 'About bloody time. It's blowing a gale out there.'

'But Gran, why have you come back?' Mrs Harrison's voice sounded dismayed. 'I told you –'

'I know what you told me. But I wasn't staying with that snooty cow another minute.'

'What happened?'

'She made a fuss because Dad was picking his nose in front of 'er precious kids. So I told Madam Dolly exactly what I thought of 'er, packed our bags, and 'ere we are.' Gran stood in the doorway. 'Fred. There's a taxi outside needs paying.' Her eyes scanned the room, resting briefly on Laura Marshall. 'You must be their new mate,' she said.

'I'm Laura Marshall, and I'm very pleased to meet you.'

Gran ignored the outstretched hand and turned to Nobby. 'Well, young man, where's that scallywag Len? I 'aven't even 'ad a bleedin' Christmas card from him.'

Nobby struggled to his feet and kissed the old lady. 'The post isn't too regular when you're at sea, Ma,' he said. 'Come and sit down. You must be tired.'

'Fair worn out, and not a bite since breakfast. I 'ope you've got some shrimps and winkles left.'

Aunt Grace said, 'I'll get you something in a minute. Where's Dad?'

'In the lav. Put the kettle on, girl. I'm parched.'

Mrs Marshall smiled at the twins. 'Would you be kind enough to fetch our coats, please?'

Disappointment showed in Rose's face. 'You're not going already?'

'The boys have had too many late nights recently. I really ought to take them home.'

Nodding miserably, they went up to their mother's bedroom. 'She did it on purpose,' Rose burst out.

'Why couldn't she have said Grandad was in the bathroom? "Lav" sounds so common.'

'For the same reason she's swearing and dropping her aitches more than usual. She's letting Mrs Marshall know they're East Enders and prahd of it,' Rose mimicked. 'I hope Mum sends them packing.'

'Ssh! Grandad's coming upstairs.'

'I don't care. She only came back because she thought we might be having a bit of fun and she wanted to spoil it. Why did you have to tell her about the tea party?'

Tears pricked Jane's eyes. 'I wouldn't have done if I'd

known,' she murmured. 'Where are they going to sleep?'

'In Jack's room, I suppose.'

'But we've put Uncle Nobby and Peter in there.'

'Gran won't care who sleeps out in the dog kennel as long as she's comfortable.'

Jane had to agree. Feeling thoroughly fed up, she draped the mink coat over her arm. At that moment, a crump of gunfire sent them scurrying downstairs.

Their father took charge. 'You can't leave yet, Mrs Marshall,' he said. 'I'll check the shelter and light the heater, just in case.'

Grandad moaned, 'I said we shouldn't come back, Rosie. At least we were safe at Herbert's.'

'How was I to know the Blitz would start up again?' Gran began to cry.

Mrs Marshall tried to comfort the old lady. 'We haven't had so many bad raids recently,' she said.

A whistling bomb belied her words. Torch in hand, Fred Harrison came back. 'If you and I stay up here, Nobby, there's room enough for the others down the shelter.'

Mrs Harrison began to argue, 'But Fred –'

'No time for buts, Nell. Come on, Gran. You first.'

Some explosions were too close for comfort, but mainly the noise was distant.

'Seems like they're going for the City,' commented Aunt Grace, during a brief lull.

Desmond whispered in his mother's ear. She nodded and stood up. 'May we use your bathroom, while it's quiet?'

Jane said. 'I'll come with you. Tibs usually hides under the bath and I like to make sure he's all right.'

Crawling out from under the canopy of sandbags, she stopped, filled with horror. Reflecting the flames that must be devouring everything in their path, billowing crimson clouds crept slowly towards them from the west, tainting the night with evil. She heard Mrs Marshall murmur, 'Oh, dear God,' under her breath. It was as though the end of the world had come.

In the scullery, Mr Harrison was making a jug of cocoa, while Nobby Clark put sandwiches in a paper bag. When Jane told them about the sky, they switched off the light and opened the back door.

'Christ almighty,' Nobby muttered. 'They've done for London this time. With this wind, they haven't a chance.'

Desmond looked at his mother. He didn't cry or say anything, just began to shiver.

Jane was upstairs, looking for blankets, when she heard the knock at the door, and a woman crying. In the hall, Betty leaned against the wall, tears streaming down her grime-streaked face. Mr Harrison helped her into the living room and insisted she drink some cocoa.

'Now, love,' he said gently. 'What made you come round on a night like this? Has your place been hit?'

Betty shook her head. 'It was Auntie Vera's flat,' she sobbed. 'In Peabody Buildings. We'd gone to tea. But Dad forgot the sandwich box. So I took it round to the station. Then the siren went.' Her tears seemed to choke her.

'Take your time,' Mr Harrison soothed. 'Just tell us what happened.'

'Dad made me wait in the Underground. When it got quiet, I went up to the street. The buildings were on fire.' Her body shook as she gasped, 'They're all gone. Auntie Vera. Uncle Bert. Grandma. And Mum.'

'You poor child!' Mrs Marshall put her arm around Betty's shoulders. 'Where's your father now?'

'He went to the hospital. But they were all burned up. We couldn't even recognise them properly. Then he collapsed, so they kept him in.'

'Didn't they want to keep you in, too, because of your condition?'

'They moved all the maternity cases out. I was supposed to come to Oldchurch, but the ambulance couldn't get through. Two of the women were in labour. They were making a dreadful noise.' Betty groped for her sodden handkerchief. 'I couldn't stand it any longer. So I started to walk.'

'Where were you?' Mr Harrison asked.

'Manor Park, I think. I just kept walking away from the fires. I didn't know where else to go.'

'We'll look after you. Drink your cocoa.' As Mr Harrison handed the cup to the distraught girl, Betty gasped and clutched her stomach. 'I think something's happened to the baby. This awful pain!'

'How long have you had it?'

'Twice in the last half-hour. But it's not due for another month. Oh, God!' Betty's eyes suddenly filled with fear. Mrs Marshall felt the girl's clothing, then turned to Mr Harrison.

'You'd better get your wife,' she said quietly. 'Her waters have broken.'

They all looked upwards as another wave of bombers droned overhead.

The screams went on and on. From the shelter, Jane heard them above the whoosh of bombs and clanging bells of fire engines and ambulances. Above the howling wind. Above the eventual wailing of the all clear.

Gran walked straight into the living room. Anxious, Jane looked at her father. 'Your Aunt Grace has gone to telephone the doctor again,' he said. 'The district nurse got blown off her bike and broke her arm. All the others are out seeing to casualties, and there's no ambulance available.'

'What are we going to do?'

He shrugged. 'Your mum and Mrs Marshall are doing their best.'

'Shall I make some tea?'

'Good idea. Rose, take the boys upstairs and find somewhere for them to sleep. I don't think Mrs Marshall will leave just yet. You too, Peter.'

Jane was pouring the tea when Gran came back into the scullery. 'It's the wrong way round,' she announced. 'And the cord's round it's neck, just like I had with my stillborn. I don't hold out much hope for either of them.'

Mr Harrison rubbed a hand wearily across the stubble on his chin. 'You'd best get some sleep while you can,' he said. 'They'll manage in there till the doctor comes.'

The old lady grunted. 'That's what Nell said. You forget I've had more babies than all of them put together. And lost more, too. But you're never wanted when you're old. Where's the old man?'

'He's gone up to our bed. I'll bring your tea.'

Jane carried two cups into the living room. At first she couldn't see Betty, then realised a mattress was wedged behind the piano. Laura Marshall was on her knees, bathing the girl's

76

flushed face. Mrs Harrison sat by the fire, eyes drooping. Jane had never seen her mother look so exhausted.

'Lawrence and Desmond are quite all right, Mrs Marshall,' she whispered. 'They're upstairs with Rose.'

'Thank you, dear. Were they very frightened?'

'They were ever so good. Didn't make a fuss at all.'

An ear-splitting shriek filled the room as Betty clutched at Mrs Marshall's hands. She seemed to be straining and pushing, then the cries faded into moaning. Knowing she couldn't help, Jane quietly closed the door behind her and went back into the scullery.

'Are they going to die?' she asked her father.

Mr Harrison spooned sugar into his cup and shook his head. He didn't know.

'Betty's been in agony all night. How much longer can she go...?'

Betty's scream cut across Jane's words just as Aunt Grace put her key in the front door. Her expression was not hopeful. Jane poured another cup of tea and handed it to her aunt, as Laura Marshall came into the scullery. 'No doctors. No nurses. No ambulances.' Aunt Grace sipped her tea. 'For another hour, at least.'

Through the open doorway they heard Betty whimper, 'Let me die. Please ... Jack ...' Her voice rose to a shriek.

Swiftly, Mrs Marshall closed the door. 'Do you know where he is?' she asked Mr Harrison.

'Most of the training section is in transit between Manchester and some place in Oxfordshire. It's a chaotic state of affairs. I don't know whether to phone the War Office or the Air Ministry.'

Jane was becoming frightened by their serious expressions and the sounds of torment. 'Isn't there some way we can get her to hospital ourselves?' she asked. Her father and aunt looked despairingly at each other, but Mrs Marshall suddenly said, 'Do you know anyone who has a car?'

'Mr Green has an old flivver. It's the only one in the road, now,' Jane said.

Her aunt sighed. 'He's on early shift. I saw him go off just now, on his bike.'

'That's it, then,' said Mr Harrison. 'Cissie Green would

never dare let anyone use his precious car, let alone the petrol. Especially us.'

'It's our only chance, Dad. We don't know anyone else.'

'Even if she agreed, Jane, there's no one to drive it.'

'I can drive.'

They all stared at Laura Marshall. Aunt Grace stood up. 'Will you come with me, Mrs Marshall?' she asked.

Five minutes later, Jane was sitting in the back of the little Ford Eight with her almost unconscious sister-in-law.

'How did you manage to persuade Mrs Green?' she asked.

Laura Marshall concentrated on avoiding a crater in the road. 'Mrs Green had heard Betty,' she said. 'But she doesn't want her husband to find out about the car.'

'She'll be lucky, with our nosy neighbours.'

'Why is she afraid of him?'

'I don't know, really. He shouts a lot, but I don't think he hits her. She ought to stand up to him. Turn right at the crossroads.'

'I'd never have found the way without you, Jane. It was very good of you to offer to come.'

'Well, Aunt Grace had to go to work, and Mum was really needed at home to see to everything.'

'I can understand that she wanted to come with Betty. After all, it is her first grandchild. But it might be a long wait, and – oh, dear. Another road blocked.'

Eventually, they stopped outside a drab Victorian building. Still looking elegant, despite her sleepless night, Mrs Marshall ran up the steps of the hospital.

An ambulance clanged into the courtyard and porters dashed out to help the driver unload the casualties. Jane had to turn away. She knew she could never be a nurse.

Betty's head rolled from side to side. It was as though she were too exhausted to make a sound. A nurse opened the car door and moved the blanket covering Betty, then signalled to a porter with a stretcher. 'How long has she been bleeding like this?' she asked.

Jane stared at the stained blanket. 'Only just now, I think.'

The nurse nodded and helped lift Betty from the car. 'Come with me. I'll need her details,' she said.

How could they all remain so calm? Jane wondered, as she

78

waited in the corridor, watching nurses and doctors move among the patients. Most of the injured quietly awaited treatment or X-rays, but some were visibly distressed. In a curtained cubicle, a child cried. The woman sitting next to Jane rocked backwards and forwards, holding a bloodstained towel to her shoulder. Suddenly she grasped Jane's arm and muttered, 'I'm going to be sick.'

There were no nurses in sight so Jane ran along the corridor and knocked on a door marked SISTER'S OFFICE. In the tiny room two white-coated doctors were holding X-rays up to the light.

'Excuse me,' Jane faltered. 'There's a lady who feels sick ...' At first, she didn't recognise the Sister when she turned around. She had never seen Sandy's mother in uniform.

Mrs Randall murmured something to the doctors, picked up a steel bowl, and followed Jane along the corridor. They were too late. After a brief word with the woman, Mrs Randall turned to Jane. 'You won't be able to sit here until it's cleaned up. Are you waiting for treatment, Jane?'

'No, I'm here with Betty.'

'Your sister-in-law? Was she injured?'

Jane shook her head. 'The baby started too early, and it's the wrong way round, and ...' At first the tears came slowly, then gathered momentum. 'Gran said they might both die.' Choking sobs stuck in her throat.

Lowering her voice, Mrs Randall said, 'Wait outside my office. When I've attended to this patient, I'll pop up to Maternity.'

Jane knew people were watching her. She felt ashamed, but couldn't help herself. Leaning against the wall, she stuffed a handkerchief in her mouth in an attempt to stem the flow of tears. An arm went round her shoulder and she smelled the distinctive scent as Laura Marshall knelt by her side.

'I'm sorry.' Jane's voice was muffled by the fur coat, but she felt comforted.

'There's nothing to apologise for, my dear. You're worried about the baby, and you've had a very bad night.'

'But so have all these people. I don't know what you must think of me.'

Mrs Marshall took the handkerchief and gently wiped Jane's

79

face. 'I think you're very brave,' she said. 'You insisted on accompanying me, even though you knew it wouldn't be very pleasant. Now, have a good blow.'

Within a few minutes Jane felt better. 'Did you manage to get rid of the bloodstains?' she sniffed.

'I hope so. We won't know for sure until it dries.'

'Mrs Green goes mad if there's as much as a crumb –' Jane stopped as Sandy's mother returned. Ushering them into her office, Mrs Randall stood behind the desk, frowning slightly. Jane feared the worst.

'It was touch and go, Jane, and your sister-in-law isn't quite out of the woods yet. She's lost a lot of blood.' Mrs Randall's glance moved to Jane's companion. 'Thankfully, you were able to get her here in time, but she is very weak.'

Jane hardly dared ask, 'What about the baby?'

'The little boy is in an incubator. If his respiratory problems don't worsen, he's got a chance.'

Softly, Mrs Marshall asked, 'Are there any other complications?'

'He's tiny, of course. Not quite five pounds. And there is some damage to one of his legs.'

'Serious damage?'

'It's too early to assess yet. But he was in the breech position for some time, and it was twisted. At the moment, however, we are more concerned with the possibility of brain damage.'

After a long silence, Mrs Marshall said, 'Is there anything we can do?'

'She needs her husband, but I understand he's in the services.'

'Jane's father is trying to contact him, but his whereabouts are rather vague.'

'Ah.' Mrs Randall sighed. 'Then there's nothing else one can do, but wait and hope.'

'We can pray.'

'Yes.' Mrs Randall half smiled at Laura Marshall as she said, 'We will pray.' She wrote something on a piece of paper and handed it to Jane. 'That's the telephone number for the Maternity Ward. Someone can phone later today.'

'Can we visit her?'

'Only her husband and parents are allowed while she's on the critical list, I'm afraid.'

'Her mother was killed last night, and her father's in hospital.'

Momentarily Mrs Randall closed her eyes. 'Oh, the poor child! No wonder she's –' A nurse peered round the door.

'Excuse me, Sister. We have a little girl with serious burns.'

'I'll come at once.' Mrs Randall patted Jane's shoulder. 'Go home and get some sleep, dear,' she advised.

As she stared out of the car window at the devastation, Jane wondered how she was going to tell her mother that her grandson might be crippled, or worse. And would Dad be able to trace Jack before he had to leave for work? Betty needed her husband. Where on earth was Haddenham?

Wherever it was, Jane knew she had to find her brother, even if it meant going up to Whitehall and knocking on the doors of all the War Minsitries and Air Ministries. Even Number 10 if need be. After all, the Airborne Division had been Mr Churchill's idea. He should know where the trainee glider pilots were.

Chapter Nine

The train whistled as it wove in and out of the tunnels. On one side brick-red cliffs towered above the train; on the other, waves almost lapped the track. Wiping a smut from her eye, Jane tugged at the strap to ease the window open again, breathing deeply. She had always loved this first sight and smell of the English Channel as the *Devon Belle* puffed around the curve of coastline.

But there were many changes. On a mild day in May like this, there would normally be children paddling, their parents snoozing in deck chairs. Now barbed wire coiled along the deserted beaches, anit-tank traps and concrete gun posts guarded against the threatened invasion. How long would it be before her world was peaceful again, she wondered.

Her mind flitted back to the dreadful night last December. Thanks to Jane's persistent telephone calls, a sympathetic secretary in the War Office had finally tracked down Jack, who'd spent most of his short compassionate leave willing his son to live, talking to him, gently massaging the tiny, crippled leg, urging him to fight.

Five months later, the doctors were unable to say how badly he might be affected. Still in mourning, her sister-in-law hadn't recovered from her ordeal, and didn't seem concerned about little Johnny. So it was Mrs Harrison who nursed Betty, and walked the floor when the baby was fretful, which was most nights. Jane wondered where her mother found the strength to cope with it all.

Even last Sunday morning, when they'd climbed out of the shelter after another savage attack had fired London from

Hammersmith to Romford, Mum hadn't gone to pieces. She'd just gripped Dad's arm for a moment, and told the family to stay in the shelter until they were taken to a centre. Then she calmly moved among the drenched remains of her home, picking up a saucepan here, an ornament there.

The incendiary had actually fallen on the Greens' house, spreading the fire each side until powerful hoses halted its progress. Jane managed to hide her own distress at the charred remains of her beloved piano. But when she couldn't find Tibs, the tears couldn't be held back. Later she realised just how lucky they'd been.

She would never forget the sight of all those families in the infants' school, staring blankly into space, as though too stunned to cry. Even the children were quiet, huddling close to their mothers, some in nightclothes. The warden eyed Mr Harrison's suitcase. 'Good job you've got a bit more than the clothes you stand up in,' he observed. 'The WVS are running out of everything. If Adolf keeps this up much longer, we'll be wearing fig leaves.'

Most of Sunday had been spent salvaging what they could and taking it back to the centre. When they returned from the final trip, Rose glanced at Peter and burst out laughing. 'You look like Al Jolson,' she said.

Dropping to one knee and spreading his arms, Peter sang a few bars of 'Mammy'. Then he retaliated, 'Wait till you look in a mirror, Rose.' They were still laughing as he pushed open the swing doors.

'Ssh!' Her mother put a finger to her lips.

Rose surveyed the sad faces. Slowly, she said, 'They need cheering up. And we're the ones to do it.'

Peter said, 'How?'

'A concert. You can tell some of your soppy jokes.' Her voice warmed. 'Come on, Janey, let's see what that piano's like.'

Jane had looked uncertainly at her father, who shrugged his shoulders and said, 'It's up to you.'

There wasn't much response when Rose called for 'turns', but she was undaunted. Her dancing shoes had escaped the fire, and she brightly tapped her way through 'In the Mood' before introducing Peter as 'the corniest stand-up comic I know, even when he's lying down'. He did quite well, even raised a few titters. Then, to Jane's horror, Rose asked for suggestions for a sing-song. 'A Nightingale Sang in Berkeley Square' was the only one Jane could remember without her music. Red-faced, she shook her head again and again. It looked as though the impromptu concert would fizz out, until a little man in a cloth cap came over to the piano.

'I can vamp a bit,' he said, nipping out his cigarette and putting it behind his ear. Whatever was called out, he played it, and everyone joined in. It hadn't mattered that he thumped out the same bass. By the time he closed the piano lid, they were chatting to each other, smiling again.

Rose told her father, 'You'll have to get another piano, Dad, Janey's Grade IV is in November. And I need her to help me practise for my Silver.'

Angrily, Jane had protested, 'For goodness' sake, Rose! Mum and Dad have more important things to think about than a piano. We've got to find somewhere to live first.'

Now, as she sat in the railway carriage, she was sorry she'd snapped. Rose had only been trying to take everyone's mind off things. As if reading her thoughts, Rose looked up from her *Picturegoer* and smiled. Rose never harboured a grudge.

Absentmindedly, her mother murmured, 'I hope Gran and Grandad settle down all right with the Randalls.'

'Sandy's mum and dad are really nice. They get on ever so well with Aunt Grace. And there's not been any more raids all week.'

'I know. But I'd feel more comfortable if they were with me. I don't know why Gran wouldn't come.'

Rose pulled a face. 'The only seaside place she likes is Margate, or Southend.' She sighed. 'I wish you'd taken up Mrs Marshall's offer to have the upstairs of her house, Mum. It's smashing.'

'I couldn't. You've seen what lovely things she has. I'd never know a minute's peace in case we broke something. Still, it was good of her to store all our things.' Mrs Harrison wiped a dribble from Johnny's mouth with her handkerchief. 'Let's hope it won't be too long before the council give us another house.'

Jane jumped to her feet. 'Here we are, Mum – Torquay.

Once we get to Aunt Peggy's, you can have a nice rest.'

'How can I rest, with no home, your grandparents in one house, your dad in another, and God knows what Jack's getting up to?' Mrs Harrison pulled the shawl closer around the baby. 'You do talk nonsense sometimes, Janey. Now make yourself useful and help Peter with the bags.'

Joe Taylor was at the barrier. 'Peg's cooking supper,' he explained. 'She can't wait to see this little fellow.' He chucked Johnny under the chin, then took the big suitcase from Peter. Outside, they piled into a taxi and drove along the seafront, past the harbour and up the long hill, stopping outside the three-storey house Jane loved.

Aunt Peggy, plump and jovial as ever, wiped floury hands on her overall as she greeted them at the door.

'Come along, my pretties. You must be starving.'

Mrs Harrison kissed her sister-in-law. 'I'm gasping for a cup of tea.'

'You'll get more than a cup of tea, Nell dear. Joe's been fattening a chicken for Whitsun, and her be roasting in the oven alongside my Devonshire dumplings.' Jane had forgotten the pleasure of Aunt Peggy's soft West Country burr.

When she awoke next morning, Jane heard seagulls. And something else: men singing. Both girls dashed over to the window.

'Look!' Rose cried.

About thirty young men in singlets and shorts, towels slung around their necks, ran up the hill, their feet marking time as they chanted, 'I've got sixpence,' and waved cheerily to the sisters. Rose leaned out of the window and joined in the singing. As she was belting out, 'and tuppence to send home to my wife,' the bedroom door burst open.

Mrs Harrison was not amused. 'Janey! Rose! Come away from that window. Whatever will the neighbours think?'

With a final wave, Rose ducked back under the sash. 'There's no harm in it, Mum.' She was laughing. 'We've got to cheer the boys on, haven't we?'

'Not in your nightie, you haven't. As soon as you're both washed and dressed, go down and help with breakfast.' Little Johnny wailed, and Mrs Harrison sighed. 'That racket has woken the baby. He's hardly slept all night. I'd better see to him. Betty will need to lie-in after her long journey yesterday.'

When the bedroom door had closed, Rose commented 'Anyone would think Betty was the only one on the train.'

'I suppose Mum fusses because she's been so ill.'

'It's time she started getting better. She'll never be able to look after Johnny if Mum does it all the time.'

Breakfast was another splendid meal. Creamy porridge, followed by two new-laid eggs each and, warm from the oven, a huge cottage loaf, its topknot golden and shiny.

Aunt Peggy beamed as they tucked in. 'Start the day with a hearty breakfast, and you'll not go far wrong.' She pushed a dish of marmalade towards Betty. 'Try some of this, my pretty,' she said.

Betty crumbled the bread on her plate, her eggs untouched. 'I've not been able to face breakfast since I was expecting,' she murmured. Quietly, she left the room.

'Us'll soon put the roses in her cheeks,' Aunt Peggy said. 'Now then, I'm sure a growing lad like Peter can manage another egg.'

After breakfast, the twins took Peter for a walk along Babbacombe Downs. Halfway along the clifftop, Jane stopped. This was her favourite view, with twin crescent beaches far below and red cliffs stretching towards the horizon. Today the sea was sapphire blue and frisky, its white-capped waves lightly whipped by the same breeze that sent cotton wool puffs of cloud scudding across the sky.

Shading his eyes, Peter said, 'I see what you mean, Janey. It does take your breath away.'

Rose peered over the railings. 'That's where we used to cut through to Oddicombe Beach,' she said. 'It's overgrown now, but I reckon I could still find the way.'

'You mustn't,' Jane said sharply. 'It's mined.'

'Can't be. Aunt Peggy told me the RAF go down there for PT every day. I'm going to get up early tomorrow and watch.'

'Mum won't let you.'

'Mum won't know. I'll be back before breakfast.'

Peter said, 'No good, Rose. It's a restricted area, so it would be dangerous to stray from the main path.'

'How come you know so much?'

'Your uncle told me.'

Sensing a quarrel, Jane hastily said, 'We could walk down to Torquay this afternoon, if you like. It's nice around the harbour.'

Rose brightened. 'At least there's some decent shops down there. All you've got up here is empty hotels and seagulls.'

'It's much prettier than London.'

'But it's so boring. There's nothing to do. Not even a decent picture on, only a thriller. I hate thrillers.'

'Never mind. There'll be something else on in Torquay.'

The local paper advertised a new James Stewart comedy. Rose had everything planned. There was time to window-shop before the film.

Mrs Harrison looked dubious as she said, 'There's a lot of troops around.'

'Don't worry,' Peter said, 'I'll look after them.'

'You're a good boy, Peter, but I'd still be worried. Some of the forces are foreign.'

'Why don't you go with them?' suggested Aunt Peggy. 'You like the pictures. I remember Big Jack saying you ought to have been an actress.'

Mrs Harrison hesitated, then shook her head. 'I'd like to, but now you've borrowed a pram, I want Johnny to get some fresh air, then perhaps he'll sleep better tonight.'

'I'll take him out,' Aunt Peggy announced. 'My friend at the pottery wants to see Betty and the baby.'

'Oh, no,' Betty said. 'I don't really feel up to it.'

'It'll do you good, my pretty,' Aunt Peggy said briskly. 'And we'll have a lovely cream tea.'

It was just like before the war, strolling along streets with unboarded shop windows displaying sparkling jewels without fear of bombing or looting. Their favourite little café still made mouth-watering chocolates. Despite her laughing protestations of extravagance, Mrs Harrison was persuaded to buy some.

'We deserve a treat,' Rose said, 'after all we've been through. They don't know there's a war on down here. No Blitz, nothing.'

'Aunt Peggy said they've had a few raids,' Jane said.

'Only the odd hit-and-run,' Rose scoffed. She leaned

87

forward to admire a window. 'Look at that gold evening dress with the sequins, Mum,' she said. 'I'll have one just like it when I'm famous.'

Her mother wasn't listening. Dreamily, she stared into another window. The twins followed her gaze and gasped.

Rose said, 'What a gorgeous coat! It's just like Mrs Marshall's.'

Jane wished she had five hundred pounds to buy it for her mother. She also wished she could buy some music, but her pocket money was spoken for.

Later, Peter handed her a copy of 'I'll Be Seeing You'. Pleased, she hugged him. 'Thanks, Peter. But you shouldn't have.'

'That's all right.' He shrugged. 'It was only a bob. You can try it out after supper.'

Uncle Joe told Jane to help herself to his music. 'I'd give you the piano as well, love,' he said, 'but it'd cost too much to ship it up to London.'

While Jane was sorting through the music, Aunt Peggy said, 'Jess has asked us over to dinner tomorrow. The young folks can help feed the animals. They'll like that.'

'That's very kind of your sister, Peg.' Looking at the clock, Mrs Harrison said, 'I think I'll go up now. I want to write to Fred before Johnny wakes up again.'

'That's right, dear. And don't you worry about the baby. Us'll have him in our room.'

'But that's not fair on you and Joe. And there's his feed –'

'No arguments, now. I may not have little ones of my own, but I'm quite capable of making up a bottle. You'll feel better for a good night's sleep.'

Certainly Mrs Harrison didn't look so worn next morning, Jane thought, as the bus rattled along narrow lanes towards the farm.

Jane thought it wonderful, as ever. Uncle Amos let them hold the newborn lambs and, after great helpings of bacon roly-poly and treacle tart with custard, they helped him drive the cows into the yard, and watched the thick creamy liquid spurt noisily into the pail.

'Want to have a go?' he asked, a mischievous twinkle in his eye as Rose wrinkled her nose and backed away. Peter was not very successful. Uncle Amos looked at Jane. 'I'll wager you'm better at it, girlie,' he said. 'She gives a good yield for our land girls. Must be them warm fingers.'

The cow looked around thoughtfully at Jane, then resumed munching oats and obligingly cooperated with the girl's gentle tugging. It was the most satisfying sense of achievement. Jane felt as though she never wanted to see London again, and said so to Rose, when they were feeding the geese.

'You must be joking, Janey. What would you do in the country, apart from feeding smelly animals?' Rose squelched her rubber boot out of the mud. 'Give me London any time. At least it's got dance halls and picture palaces, even if they do have to close early.'

'I thought you wanted to come to Devon.'

'Only to dodge school. And I'd heard there were airmen stationed here. Thought they'd liven the place up a bit. But fat chance I've got of talking to any of them, with Mum breathing down my neck.'

During the next few days, Rose took every opportunity to slip away from the others. One evening she seemed quite excited. Jane knew she was concealing a secret, but had to wait until bedtime.

'I've found the café they use,' Rose said. 'It's in a side street off the Downs. And you'll never guess ...'

Jane bounced up and down on the bed. 'What won't I guess? Come on, Rose, tell me.'

Breathlessly, Rose bubbled, 'I've got a job. Start on Monday.'

'I made hundreds of cups of tea, forty-two ham sandwiches, two bob in tips –' Rose kicked her high wedge shoes across the kitchen – 'and my feet are killing me. Really, there's nothing else to tell.' But the glint in her eyes told a different story, which she confided in Jane when they were alone.

'It was smashing. For the first time in my life I wasn't treated like a kid.'

'How do you mean?'

'Well, when they came in for their break, they chatted to me. Asked if I had a boyfriend. Things like that.'

Eyes popping, Jane said, 'Gosh! Weren't you scared?'

"Course not, silly. Can't wait for tomorrow.'

Nobody had been more surprised than Jane when her mother had given in about the part-time job, mainly because Aunt Peggy reassured her that it was quite a respectable little place.

Within a few days Rose knew the names of most of the airmen who frequented the café, and had made friends with a waitress named Joyce. Her first pay packet contained a pound note and a shilling.

'You'll have to open a Post Office savings account,' Mrs Harrison said.

'Oh, Mum,' Rose wailed. 'Can't I keep this? It's the first money I've ever earned.'

'A guinea is a lot of money, Rose. And you've already had almost ten shillings in tips.'

'That's gone, Mum. I bought presents for everyone, didn't I?' Rose looked appealingly at Aunt Peggy.

'It's true, Nell. Those lovely chocolates, and baccy for Joe.'

'Well, all right then. Just this once.' Mrs Harrison smiled. 'What are you going to do with all that money?'

'I've seen a gorgeous dress. It's only fifteen and eleven-pence, and no coupons if I get it this week.'

'All right, dear. I'll come with you in the morning before you start work.'

'No need,' Rose said, hastily. 'I've tried it on, and they're keeping it by for me.'

'But Rose -'

'By the way, Mum.' As Rose interrupted, Jane thought her voice sounded too casual. 'Joyce is going to a dance tomorrow night with some of her friends. She asked me. To celebrate my first week's work.' Rose licked her lips and went on, 'And Janey and Peter, of course. I'll treat them.'

'A dance? What would your father say?'

'He wouldn't mind. You've got to let us go to our first dance some time. And Peter will take care of us.'

'Where is this dance?'

'Torquay, I think. I'll find out for you tomorrow.'

Mrs Harrison still looked dubious as she asked her sister-in-law, 'What do you think, Peg?'

Aunt Peggy pursed her lips for a moment, then smiled.

'They're only young once, bless 'em,' she said. 'Although they'd have to leave early to catch the last bus.'

'Joyce's uncle is bringing us home in his taxi. And we won't be late, I promise.'

In the bedroom, Jane turned on Rose. 'I hope you're not thinking of pulling the same rotten trick you did in Norfolk, because I won't play ball this time.'

'Of course not. What do you take me for?'

Jane didn't want to go to the dance, and she suspected Peter felt the same. He wasn't keen on dancing, and they didn't know Joyce. To make matters worse, Jane had an ugly spot on her chin the day of the dance.

'Janey! You can't wear ankle socks to a dance.' Rose glared at her sister.

'I didn't bring any stockings with me.'

'I'll have to ask Joyce to lend you a pair. Don't want you showing me up.' Rose hesitated, then went on, 'Joyce thinks I'm fourteen, but you look much younger than me. So I haven't told her we're twins.'

'Hadn't you better put on your new dress?' Jane's voice was terse. 'It's getting late.'

'It's at Joyce's. We're going straight from there.'

'Aren't you going to show it to Mum?'

'She can see it tomorrow.'

Joyce's mother told Peter and Jane to wait in the front room. 'She'll be ages putting her powder and paint on,' she said, before she disappeared.

It wasn't only Joyce who had powder and paint on. Jane wouldn't have recognised her sister in the street. Layers of sticky black mascara hid the blue eyes, and she wore scarlet lipstick and huge gold earrings. Joyce had obviously helped with the upswept hairstyle. As for the dress, it was black satin and skin-tight, with a slit skirt.

Horrified, Jane said, 'Rose, you can't go out like that. Mum would have a fit.'

'Don't be a spoilsport, Janey, or I won't take you.'

Quietly, Peter said, 'You go with us, or not at all.' Rose opened her mouth as if to argue, then lowered her eyes beneath his steady gaze.

'OK.' Rose tottered forward a couple of steps.

'You'll cripple yourself in those heels,' Peter said.

'They're Joyce's. I've only borrowed them for tonight. Listen, you two. I've looked forward to this all week. Don't ruin it by nagging.'

Joyce also wore black and was heavily made up. Jane thought they looked like a couple of tarts, but she hadn't the heart to argue any more. She just hoped that the other teenagers would be more suitably dressed, so that Rose would feel too uncomfortable to do it again.

When they were on the steps of the biggest hotel in Torquay, Joyce's uncle leaned out of the taxi. 'Enjoy yourself,' he said. 'I'll see you here at midnight.'

Peter stopped. 'We promised Auntie Nell we'd be back by eleven,' he said.

'Mum won't know,' Rose argued. 'She goes to bed as soon as she's given Johnny his ten-o'clock feed.'

'She'll wait up tonight.'

'For goodness' sake, Peter! Anyone would think I was a child. Joyce is allowed to stay out as late as she likes, and she's not much older than me.'

Peter turned back towards the taxi. 'Will you please come back at a quarter to eleven?' he said.

Jane asked Rose, 'Did you tell Mum it was here?'

'I forgot. Doesn't matter.' Voice still angry, Rose rummaged in her handbag. 'Joyce found you a pair of stockings. There's a ladder in one of them but it won't show if you're careful. Here's your ticket, and yours, Peter, in case we get separated.'

When Jane came out of the ladies' room, Peter was waiting for her. Rose had gone ahead, with Joyce, to look for her friends.

The ballroom was enormous, with a huge faceted globe flashing splinters of light from the ceiling. Hundreds of people tried to move around the dance floor. It could hardly be called dancing. Most of the men and some women were in uniform.

'Gosh!' Jane surveyed the scene. 'How are we going to find Rose?'

'Let's make our way towards the refreshments. You look on your left, I'll watch the other side.' Peter took Jane's elbow and guided her through the crowd.

At the bar, a group of airmen clustered around a blonde in a black satin dress, clutching a glass of orange drink. The bright smile left Rose's face when she saw Peter and Jane.

'Where's Joyce?' asked Jane.

'Dancing with Frank. Why don't you two dance? It's a waltz. Peter can just about manage that.'

He looked at the shuffling crowd and commented, 'Doesn't seem to make much difference in here. Anyway, I want a glass of orange squash. Janey?'

The airman standing next to Rose put his hand in his pocket and pulled out a handful of change. 'I'll get them,' he said. 'You'll never be heard through that lot, but the barmaid knows me.' He leaned conspiratorially close to Peter and winked. 'Straight orange, son, or a dash of something to liven it up?'

'Just two orange squashes, thanks.'

Jane whispered to Rose, 'Are they Joyce's friends?'

'And mine. They come into the café.'

'But they're old. He must be at least twenty-five.'

'So what? At least Reggie knows how to have fun.'

Peter muttered under his breath, 'I bet he does.'

'Here we are, kiddoes.' Reggie was back. 'One straight orange for ...?'

'Peter. Thanks.'

'And you must be the kid sister. Nice of Blondie to bring you.' Jane glimpsed a flash of gold in his front teeth. 'Here.' Reggie took Rose's glass and handed it to Peter. 'Hold that while I dance with this beautiful doll.'

Peter sniffed Rose's glass. 'Thought so,' he murmured.

'What's up?'

'There's gin in it. We'd better keep an eye on friend Reggie.'

Miserably, Jane said, 'I think we ought to go home.'

'Rose would make a scene. We'll hang on for a bit, make sure he doesn't slip her any more Mickey Finns.'

The crush at the bar became thicker, helping Jane to knock the glass from Rose's hand. Peter insisted on buying a replacement, allowing others to be served before him. Just as Reggie bought another round, Peter whisked Rose onto the dance floor in an atrocious attempt at a quickstep.

'I'm crippled,' she complained afterwards.

'I told you those shoes were deadly.'

'It's not the shoes, idiot, but your clumsy feet. Where's my drink?'

Innocently, Jane looked around. 'It was here just now. Someone must have taken it. What a shame.'

Reggie said, 'I'll get another one.'

'No time, I'm afraid.' Peter looked at the clock. 'It's gone half past ten. We'd better be making a move.'

Reggie slipped an arm around Rose's waist. 'You two kids take the taxi. Frank and I will bring the girls home in the truck, later.'

'That's right, Janey.' Rose smiled sweetly. 'You know how Mum worries about you.'

Reggie squeezed Rose closer as he said, 'And I'll get you another orange special, darling.'

Peter put his hand on Rose's arm and said, 'Come on.'

She looked appealingly at Reggie, who stepped forward, staggering slightly.

'Listen, sonny,' he said. 'You take the little girl home and leave the grown-ups alone.'

'You do realise they're under age?' Peter said quietly.

As though anticipating a fight, a small crowd gathered.

Reggie shrugged. 'There's plenty of sixteen-year-olds drinking.'

'Joyce may be just about sixteen, but Rose isn't.'

'Almost. She told me.'

'She was thirteen last month.'

Reggie leaned forward until his face was level with Peter's. 'You don't know what you're talking about.' His voice was slurred. He jerked a thumb in Jane's direction. 'It's the pain in the arse who's under age, not Blondie.'

'They're twins. And please don't insult my cousin.'

For a moment there was silence, until one of the airmen sniggered, 'What will your wife say, Reggie, when she hears you've been cradle-snatching?'

Reggie's face darkened as he swung around. A sea of grinning faces confronted him. As the laughter spread, he pushed through the crowd, which began a slow handclap.

Peter turned to Joyce. 'The taxi's outside,' he said.

'You take it. I'll go back later.' Joyce drained her glass and handed it to her companion. 'Get me another, Frank, there's a love.' She didn't look at Rose.

Outside the hotel, Rose swung round and slapped her cousin

94

across the face. 'I'll never forgive you, Peter,' she shouted.

'Stop it, Rose,' Jane cried. 'You're only making things worse.'

'How could you humiliate me so? In front of my friends.' Rose dabbed at her eyes. 'You could have pretended I was older, Janey. I only wanted a bit of fun, for once.'

'What you wanted was for me to lie, and make Peter out to be a liar. Just so you could go off with a married man.'

'How was I to know he was married?'

'Here's the taxi.' Peter bundled the girls into the cab, and explained about Joyce to her uncle. When they reached the house, Rose said, 'I think I'm going to be sick. Tell Mum I've a headache.'

Evading the questions wasn't easy. 'It was a bit hot in there and the band was noisy.'

'But did Rose enjoy herself? What about dancing partners?'

'She danced a lot, Mum. I'm sure she'll tell you about it tomorrow. Good night, everyone.'

While she undressed, Jane heard Rose weeping into her pillow. The black dress and shoes were thrown into the wardrobe. Jane decided to leave well alone, for tonight.

Some hours later, she was awakened by an explosion. She switched on the light. Rubbing red-rimmed eyes, Rose sat up. 'What was that?' she mumbled.

'Don't know. Didn't hear a siren.'

Johnny began to cry. On the landing, Aunt Peggy looked bewildered. 'Was that a bomb?' she asked.

'I don't think so.' Mrs Harrison had to talk loudly above the baby's yells. 'It didn't sound big enough.'

Tying the cord of his dressing gown, Uncle Joe said, 'I'm going out to have a look.'

'Do be careful, Joe dear,' Aunt Peggy fussed.

They huddled in the hall, watching him cross the road. Jane heard a voice call out, 'Perhaps it's the invasion.'

Uncle Joe came back. 'Mr Prince reckons it's a mine. Probably a fox.'

'Oh, dear. Poor little critter.' Auntie Peggy shook her mass of metal curlers and led the way back upstairs.

Rose slept late, skipping breakfast. The disturbed night seemed to have taken Aunt Peggy's mind off the dance, and Mrs Harrison had her hands full with a restless grandson.

When Jane went up to the bedroom to put on her shoes, Rose was fully dressed.

'Are you coming to church?' Jane asked.

'No. I'm going round to give Joyce her shoes back and pick up my skirt and blouse. Where are her stockings?'

'On the line. I've just washed them. Tell her you'll take them in to work tomorrow.'

'You must be joking if you think I'm going into that café again. I'd be a laughing stock, thanks to you two.'

Jane ran down the stairs to join her aunt and uncle. All through the service, she recalled the hateful look on her sister's face.

As soon as they were home, Jane knew something was wrong. It was the crying. Not normal crying, but hysteria. In the kitchen, Rose sat at the table, head buried on her arms. Mrs Harrison turned round, a bottle of smelling salts in her hand.

'Oh, Peg! Am I glad to see you,' she cried. 'She's been like this ever since she came in. I can't make head or tail of her babbling.'

Aunt Peggy wrapped her jacket around the girl's shaking shoulders. 'Shock,' she said. 'Get the brandy, Joe, there's a dear. Now then, my pretty. What's upset you so?'

Rose raised her head and looked at Jane. 'That noise last night ...' A convulsive shudder ran through her body. 'It wasn't a fox. It was Joyce and Frank,' Rose gasped. 'They went down to the beach, and trod on a mine.'

The brandy and hot, sweet tea calmed Rose a little, but she would only allow Jane to help her back to their room. Feeling sick, Jane sat by Rose's bed, listening to the sobbing. After a few minutes, Rose whimpered, 'I'm so sorry, Janey.'

'It wasn't your fault.'

'But you were right. And I should have stopped them.'

'Ssh.' Jane tried to comfort her sister. 'You weren't to know they would go down the cliff.'

'But we'd arranged to go together. They said it would be all right.' Shivering, she clutched at the bedcover. 'A few hours ago they were dancing. Enjoying themselves. Now they're dead. Blown to bits.'

Realisation struck Jane deep in her stomach. It could have been Rose who trod on the mine.

Chapter Ten

'Here we are, old girl, five mattresses, all the way from
Torquay to Paddington in the guard's van and not a mark ...'
Fred Harrison's smile faded when he saw the expression on his
wife's face.'

'What happened to the removal van, Fred?'

'Ran out of petrol along the Barking Road. The driver
borrowed this.'

'But it's a rag-and-bone barrow. The name's on the side.
And this is such a nice neighbourhood. What will people
think?'

In a patient voice, Mr Harrison said, 'Would you prefer us
to sleep on the floor? Right, then we'd better get this lot
unloaded. It's coming on to rain.'

Upstairs, a loud baritone voice burst into song, 'Any old
iron, any old iron ...'

Not daring to look at her mother, Jane saw her father and
cousin pause on the stairs, their shoulders shaking. In the
dining-room doorway, Aunt Grace held a hand over her mouth.

'Len!' Mrs Harrison sounded furious.

A dark head peered over the banister, eyes innocently wide.
'Did you call me, sister dear?'

Waiting for the explosion, Jane ventured a glance. At first,
her mother's face was a picture of angry confusion. Then her
lips began to twitch, and the whole family burst into laughter.

Still chuckling, Mr Harrison unwrapped a sacking bundle. 'I
went back to the old house,' he said. 'Unscrewed the curtain
wires. You'll need them later on.'

Mrs Harrison fingered a blackened stair rod. 'These will

clean up with a bit of Brasso,' she said. 'Was there anything still in the shed?'

'No. But there were a few things in the shelter. Surprised they hadn't been pinched.'

'Those two cushions can go on the bed-chair in the front room, for Peter. Anything else?'

'The bucket. Your knitting. And these.'

As Jane gleefully pounced on her two bears, Uncle Len called out, 'There's a fish lorry stopping outside.'

'For goodness' sake, Len,' Mrs Harrison called back, 'do stop teasing.'

'He's right, Mum,' Jane said. 'It is a fish lorry.'

Everyone rushed to peer out of the window at the lorry parking behind the barrow. Clearly marked on the side was the name JOSHUA SMITH, SUPPLIER OF COCKLES AND WHELKS.

'Oh, dear, I'd forgotten,' Mrs Harrison murmured. A curtain across the road moved slightly.

'Who is it, Mum?'

'It's the man from Southend. Give him a hand, Len.'

Suddenly, Jane understood why her uncle didn't answer. His attention was fixed on the second figure climbing down from the cab. Slowly, he whistled. 'I've travelled the world a few times, but I've never seen a finer-looking woman,' he said.

Laura Marshall wore a navy stockinette siren suit, her hair in a scarlet snood. She pulled up the hood, then turned with a dazzling smile as the twins hurled out of the front door to greet her, both gabbling at once.

'Do you like the house?'

'Daphne Jarvis lives at number 61.'

'The garden goes right down to the railway.'

Laughing, Mrs Marshall extricated herself from two pairs of arms. 'It's a lovely house. Hullo, Mr Harrison. I hope the bedsteads aren't too damp.'

'They're well wrapped up. Get inside out of the rain, Mrs Marshall. I'll help Josh.'

Within minutes, the lorry was empty, apart from two pieces of furniture, shrouded in sacking. At the front door, Mrs Marshall whispered something to Mr Harrison. He looked startled, then grinned. With much puffing and panting, the larger item was pushed and pulled into the living room. Finally, the ropes were untied, the covering removed.

Unable to speak, Jane could only stare. Her mother turned to Mrs Marshall. 'I'm afraid we can't afford –' she began.

'You don't have to. It's a gift.'

'But we couldn't possibly –'

'It was my husband's, and I know he would want it to be used.' As if anticipating the next question, Mrs Marshall said, 'The boys aren't really interested.'

Jane lifted the polished mahogany lid and gasped, 'It's a Broadwood.' Lightly she touched a note, then another. The tone was exquisite.

Sharply her mother reminded Jane of her manners.

'Thank you,' Jane cried, impetuously throwing her arms around Mrs Marshall. 'Oh, thank you, thank you ...'

'Does that mean you're pleased?' Mrs Marshall laughed, then looked at Uncle Len. 'There's a stool on the lorry. Could you bring it in, please, Mr Davies? You are Mr Davies, aren't you?'

Mrs Harrison became flustered. 'I'd forgotten you hadn't met my brother. Len, this is Mrs Marshall, who's been so kind to us.'

'I'm very pleased to meet you at last, Mrs Marshall.'

Her smile was warm. 'How do you do, Mr Davies.'

'Call me Len, please.'

Rose nudged Jane as Uncle Len took Laura Marshall's hand and held it for a long moment, until it was gently withdrawn.

Jane could have sworn her uncle coloured a little as he murmured, 'I'll get the piano stool.' Certainly, he couldn't take his eyes off Laura Marshall, not even when they gathered around the table for dinner.

'It's not much, I'm afraid,' Mrs Harrison apologised as she sliced corned beef. 'Janey, did you find the tin opener?'

'Yes, Mum, and I've put two tins of peas in the saucepan. Is that enough?'

'Not for all of us, silly. Open another tin, while I dish up the potatoes. Len, will you pass the bread to Mrs Marshall and Josh?'

'Do call me Laura, please. I'd like to feel we are friends.'

'Oh ...' Mrs Harrison looked embarrassed but pleased. 'Well, if you're sure. Thank you.'

After dinner, Laura Marshall picked up her handbag. 'Do you mind if I smoke?' she asked. Mrs Harrison shook her head, and her husband produced his little rolling machine.

'Fred,' Mrs Harrison said, 'Mrs Mar – Laura might not like the smell of roll-ups.'

Josh Smith reached into his pockets for a packet of cigarette papers. 'Laura's used to it,' he said. 'We all rolled our own, except the skipper. He smoked a pipe. Now that really did stink, didn't it, Laura?'

'I hated the smell of Daddy's pipe, yet now I miss it. I suppose that's one of the penalties of not having a man around.'

Uncle Len held a match to her cigarette, and Jane noticed his hand shake slightly as Laura Marshall steadied it with her fingers. The match burned low before he recovered and blew it out. Jane had never seen her uncle like this before. Come to that, she had never seen anyone like this before, with such an expression of adoration. Not even on the films.

Mrs Marshall pushed back her chair. 'I forgot the strawberries,' she said. 'They're in the cab.'

Quick as a flash, Uncle Len was on his feet. 'Let me get them for you,' he said. 'It's still raining.'

The strawberries were impressive. 'Wish I could get them to that size,' Mr Harrison commented. 'You're obviously a keen gardener.'

'Only because I don't like to waste all the years Douglas put into it. Like many sailors, he was quite happy working with the land, but it is quite a size.' She smiled. 'Fortunately, it won't be long before the boys are big enough to help with the heavier tasks.'

Len pushed an ashtray towards her. 'I'd be glad to lend a hand when I'm on leave,' he said. 'Like you say, sailors enjoy pottering around a garden.'

From the expression on their faces, Jane knew what her parents were thinking. Uncle Len had never shown the slightest interest in their garden.

Quietly, Laura Marshall said, 'That's a very kind offer, but I know your shore leave is precious.'

'I'd like to help, honest. You just say the word.'

'I will, thank you.' Mrs Marshall turned to Mrs Harrison. 'Shall we make up the beds?'

Still thinking about Uncle Len, Jane sorted through the blankets and pillows Aunt Peggy had sent, half listening to the conversation between Mrs Marshall and her mother.

'Has Betty's health improved at all?'

'A little, but she wasn't too happy about going to her Dad's for a couple of days. Doesn't feel confident about looking after the baby on her own. Anyway, I'll bring her back tomorrow.'

'I expect her father enjoys their company.'

'You'd think so, but he never visits his grandson. Quite honestly, I don't reckon he'll ever get over losing his ...' Mrs Harrison's voice trailed as sounds of an argument reached them from the next room.

'But Dad, I particularly wanted my bed near the fireplace. Why can't you move it?'

'Because they're not easy to make if they're flush against the wall. Think of your mother's back.'

'Janey usually makes her own bed. She hasn't got a bad back.'

'What about your bed? Do you make it yourself?'

'If I'm up early enough.'

'Then you'd better get up early enough, from now on. Your mother is going to have her hands full with this big house, and nine people to cook and wash for, not to mention the baby. I'll do what I can, but you'll have to help out a bit more.'

'And Janey.'

'Janey's like Aunt Grace. You don't have to ask.'

At that moment the front door banged, and Mrs Harrison, rather red-faced, called out, 'Is that you, Peter? Have you taken the barrow back?'

'Yes, Aunt Nell. And guess what?' His voice was full of excitement. 'On the way back I met the warden from the rest centre. He told me someone had seen a stray tabby in the next street to your old house. So I went round ...'

Jane pushed past her mother and Mrs Marshall. Wrapped in a piece of sacking, a damp, emaciated cat clutched Peter's coat. 'Tibs! Oh, Tibs.' Tears rolled down her cheeks as she gently lifted her pet from Peter's arms. Wide-eyed, the cat looked around at the sea of smiling faces, then stared at Jane. As she stroked his matted fur, he began to purr and nuzzled into her neck.

'He's been living wild for weeks,' Peter said. 'Wouldn't let anyone near him.'

'Bring him into the kitchenette,' Aunt Grace said. 'You can give him a saucer of milk while I open the sardines. Oh, dear! We ought to butter his paws, but there's barely enough for Fred's sandwiches.'

Peter roared with laughter. 'Butter his paws? Pull the other one, Aunt Grace, it's got bells on.'

'I'm not joking, dear. It's so they don't get lost if they move to a new house.'

'How? That's not logical.'

'I don't know how. But it works.'

Laura Marshall said, 'Daddy had a theory that because they keep stopping to lick the butter off, it helps them to become familiar with their surroundings.' She looked thoughtfully at Tibs. 'We used fish oil once, on the boat.'

Half an hour later, Tibs was sniffing each corner of the kitchen, stopping every few yards to lick at the sardine oil on his paws.

When Sandy knocked on the front door, Jane dragged him into the kitchenette. 'Look,' she cried, 'Tibs is alive. Isn't it marvellous?'

Sandy held out a hand towards the cat, then pulled a face. 'Crikey, he smells like a day trip to Southend.'

Mrs Harrison said, 'Does your mother know you're here, Sandy?'

'Mmm. She wants to know if you'd like her to bring Mr and Mrs Davies tomorrow.' He grinned cheerfully. 'And I'm here to offer my services.'

'That really is most kind of both of you.'

Rose said, 'Is Bill with you, Sandy?'

'No. He stayed on to play tennis.'

'I haven't played tennis for ages. Think I'll go over, now it's stopped raining. Coming?'

'Not now, Rose. I came to help. There must be a lot to do.'

'Well, I've been on the go all day, and I deserve a break. Can I borrow your racquet? Thanks. I'll just get my plimsolls.' With a cheery wave, Rose ran upstairs.

Laura Marshall rinsed the teapot and dried her hands. 'We'd better be on our way, too, Josh,' she said.

Jane carried the empty shopping basket to the lorry. She was curious why Uncle Len had been hovering, shifting from one foot to the other. As Mrs Marshall stepped up into the cab, he ran down the path.

'Laura.'

'Yes, Len?'

'Laura ...' He hesitated, glancing at Jane. Racquet in hand, Rose had followed him, obviously also curious.

'Yes?'

'My ship doesn't sail till Sunday. Could I come down on Friday? Take a look at your garden?'

'Of course. Until Friday, then.'

'And ...' He fidgeted with the door of the cab. 'As Saturday is my last night, I was wondering ...' Jane strained her ears as he lowered his voice, and Rose winked broadly behind her uncle's back. 'Perhaps we could go to the pictures, or something?'

Laura Marshall tucked a strand of hair into her snood. 'I'm afraid I'm not free on Saturday. But thank you for asking.'

'Oh. I should have known, being Saturday night and all. You probably go dancing.'

'Actually, I'm going to a concert. At the Albert Hall.'

'I've never been to the Albert Hall.'

Josh grinned as he hauled himself up into the driver's seat. 'Neither had your shipmate, until he met Laura,' he said.

'My shipmate?' Uncle Len looked perplexed.

A slight frown crossed Laura Marshall's face as she sighed. Then she said, 'I'm going to the concert with Nobby.'

As the lorry drove away, Jane's heart ached for her favourite uncle.

Someone had made an effort with tarnished tinsel and paper chains, and a crudely painted banner pronounced the CHRIST-MAS 1941 AMATEUR TALENT CONTEST, but the Working Men's Club remained defiantly cheerless and shabby. A pall of cigarette smoke hung from the grimy ceiling and men held their pints high as they jostled to find a seat. Women in headscarves sipped port and lemon, leaning forward in an attempt to hear what their companion was saying. To add to the cacophony, children outshrieked each other as they ran amok.

103

'What am I doing here?' Jane wondered. It was all Rose's fault.

Last week, she'd come home from rehearsal in a tearfully pleading mood. Madame Delia's pianist had joined ENSA and wouldn't be available to play for the big concert at the Town Hall. They would have to cancel, unless they could find someone else. After all the work they'd put in, they couldn't let that happen, could they? All the tickets had been sold, and yes, she realised there would be only two weeks' rehearsal. That was why they needed someone who could sight-read very well. Someone like her sister. She'd told Madame Delia that Janey wouldn't let them down, so please, please, please!

Despite all her arguments, Jane found herself peering through a hole in a dingy curtain a week later, wondering why she'd allowed Rose to talk her into using tonight's event as an audition, and feeling sick at the thought.

'You'll be fine, Janey.' Once again Rose had read her mind.

'How can you do it, Rose? In this atmosphere?'

'They're not all as bad as this.'

'Why couldn't Madame Delia have auditioned me at her studio? You know I hate amateur talent contests.'

'Because we're providing a short cabaret and this way she can see both of you.'

'Where's the other pianist?'

'I don't know.' Rose looked closely at her sister. 'You could do with a bit of make-up. These lights drain all your colour. And your plaits are much too tight. Come on, I'll do them again.'

In the cold little room backstage, Rose dabbed her sister's face with powder, touched her lips lightly with lipstick and smoothed a little rouge on her cheeks.

'There, that's much better.'

Jane looked into the dusty mirror. Although the make-up helped, she still felt plain. It was a pity she'd inherited her father's sallow complexion.

A woman elbowed her out of the way and placed a girl in front of the mirror. The girl smiled apologetically at Jane as the woman began to tie a huge pink satin bow.

'Give me the bobby pins, Christabel,' the woman said.

'Sorry, Mummy. I forgot them.'

104

'Well, I can't fix this on your hair without them.' She turned to Jane. 'Have you got any?'

'Here.' Rose held out two hairgrips. 'Let me have them back, won't you?'

The girl's mother eyed Rose's white satin dress suit. 'Are you one of the contestants?' she asked.

'I'm part of the cabaret. My sister's a contestant.'

The woman's mouth dropped open. 'Are you sisters? I'd never have guessed it.'

'We're twins.'

'Really!' The woman stared rudely at Jane, then continued teasing even more curls into her daughter's hair. 'Christabel has a lovely voice. She's bound to win.'

'Mummy, please ...'

Jane felt sorry for Christabel. She looked about fifteen and wore a vivid pink taffeta dress covered with huge polka dots, the short flounced skirt and tight sash accentuating the girl's puppy fat.

The chairman told Jane she was on fifth, and not to mind too much about the piano. It had seen better days, but the judges would take that into consideration. 'All we want now is the piano player. Will someone drag Sam away from the bar?'

Tripping on the steps at the side of the stage, Sam swore as he staggered towards the piano, tankard in hand. 'Right,' he wheezed, slopping his beer, 'put all your music on top of the joanna. Who's first? Some bloody comic, I suppose. He'll be lucky to get a laugh out of that lot.'

A man in a check suit did a reasonable impersonation of Max Miller, followed by a singer who, although flat, managed to reach all but the lowest notes of 'Old Man River', despite Sam's time changes and vamping. It was Christabel's turn next. She paused by the piano, whispered, 'Apple Blossom Time', and smiled at her mother, sitting at the same table as Mrs Harrison. Sam ferreted through the pile, and nodded.

Christabel's warbled C sharp didn't match the one-note introduction. In the confusion of the restart, still in unharmonised keys, neither singer nor pianist seemed aware that they were performing totally different songs. When Christabel spread wide her arms, waltzed sideways, and valiantly began, 'I'll be with you in apple-blossom time' for the third time,

Same shifted a stub of cigarette to the opposite corner of his mouth, squinted through the smoke and continued to play, 'Ma, I miss your apple pie' in a lively four-four. Titters from the audience built up into guffaws, until poor Christabel flapped her arms helplessly, burst into tears and fled. Jane watched in horror as pennies were thrown onto the stage and a voice shouted, 'If eggs weren't rationed, you'd get them as well.' Sam shuffled off into the wings, raising two fingers in the air as he went.

Red-faced, the chairman hurried onto the stage, shouting, 'Order, ladies and gentlemen! Order, please.' As the noise abated, he mopped his brow. 'Thank you. Now, I'm sure you'll want to welcome our next act. Jane's going to play a medley of popular music on the piano.'

A voice yelled, 'If she's no better than the last one, she knows what to expect.'

The chairman held up his hands. 'There's no need for that. They're doing their best.'

'If that's their best, Gawd save us from their worst.'

The chairman beckoned Jane, but she shook her head. As he came to talk to her, the slow handclaps began.

'Come on, they're waiting,' he hissed.

'It's the juggler's turn, not mine.'

'I know, but Sam won't play while the audience are in this mood, so you'll have to go on next.'

Dismayed, Jane listened to the sounds of discontent. 'I don't think I can –' she began.

Suddenly, Rose pushed through the crowd in the wings. 'Go out there and show them how a piano should really be played,' she said. 'Good luck, Janey.'

Clutching her music, Jane walked across the stage. The handclapping stopped, but the silence was even more nerve-racking, and her hands shook as she placed the music on the rest. The next moment, music rest and music were scattered around the floor.

Jane froze, listening to the roars of laughter from the audience. The heckler yelled, 'We've got ourselves another comic', and she wished the floor would open up and swallow her. But it didn't. If she obeyed her instincts and walked off, they would win – the audience, the heckler, Sam, smirking in the wings. He would be Madame Delia's new accompanist, because there wasn't anyone else. She couldn't do that to Rose. But she couldn't crawl around the stage collecting her music, not while they were laughing at her. Thank goodness she'd practised.

She went straight into 'The White Cliffs of Dover'. The piano was badly out of tune and she soon found out which keys were soundless. The audience helped by singing with her. After the final bar of 'Wish Me Luck as You Wave Me Goodbye', she sat for a moment, eyes closed. She knew it had sounded awful, but at least she had tried. And, in a funny sort of way, she had enjoyed it.

Suddenly she was conscious of the clapping. Not slow hand-clapping, but enthusiastic applause, accompanied by whistles and shouts of 'More'. Hardly daring to look, she faced the audience. The table where her mother had sat was empty.

In the wings, Rose hugged her. 'You were terrific, Janey. Go back and take another bow.'

'No, Rose. I couldn't.'

The chairman smiled sheepishly at Jane. 'Forgot to warn you about the dodgy music rest. Would you like me to pick up your music, duckie?'

Several people patted Jane on the shoulder and said, 'Well done, dear.' Sam belched as he pushed past, but didn't look in her direction. Jane decided to stay in the wings with Rose. Her mother slipped back into her seat, but the other chair remained empty.

After the juggler had dropped his batons twice, the audience became restless again. The tenor was better, but struggled with the top notes of 'Your tiny hand is frozen'. Sam's accompaniment was appalling. Jane admired the accordionist's bravery in tackling 'The Comedian's Gallop', but felt he really should have chosen something less ambitious.

Finally, the chairman announced, 'While the judges deliberate over the contestants, we will be entertained by Madame Delia's Dancettes, led by Rose, the pretty sister of the young piano player.'

In the wings, Madame Delia put on a record, Rose put on a bright smile, and the girls were on. There was no doubt they were good, and the audience was still cheering when the contestants were ushered back onto the stage. The chairman stepped forward.

'And now, ladies and gentlemen, the moment we have all been waiting for. It was a hard decision, but the judges have at last chosen the best three entries. You won't be surprised to learn that the winner is our own cheeky chappie, Benny Brown.' The man in the check suit took the first envelope from the chairman, then came the accordionist, the tenor third.

Jane hid her disappointment as she clapped the smiling trio. She hadn't expected to win, but had thought she might be one of the runners-up.

As soon as Mrs Harrison joined them backstage, Jane eagerly asked, 'Did you hear any of my medley, Mum?'

'No. When they started throwing things I went out to the ladies'. I knew you wouldn't be any good on that piano.'

'I'm sorry, Mum, but I did try, honest.'

'Well, no use crying over spilt milk. And as you weren't even in the first three, I don't suppose Madame Delia will be interested.'

Wiping cream from her face, Rose said, 'That wasn't a fair decision. Janey was the best one. And the audience think so, too. Listen to them.'

Above the boos, they heard the heckler's voice. 'What about the kid on the piano?'

'You see?' Rose grinned. 'There's a fiddle going on.'

'Nobody would cheat for two pounds,' her mother said. 'But you were very good, Rose.'

The room was a hubbub of activity and chatter as mothers helped the dancers change back into warmer clothes. Madame Delia beckoned. At first sight, the dancing teacher appeared rather hard, but Rose said she was all right as long as you did your job properly. She wasn't as elegant as Mrs Marshall, Jane thought, but had a certain style, with her auburn hair in a thick roll and false eyelashes. She continued to repack the make-up while she talked.

'I appreciate that the piano is badly in need of attention, if not total demolition,' she said, 'so it was rather difficult for me to judge the standard –'

Rose interrupted, 'Janey got a first class in her exam.'

'An accompanist also needs other talents. The ability to pick up and repeat passages endlessly during rehearsal, and to assess what is happening on stage during a performance. It comes with experience.'

That's it, thought Jane, as she watched the woman slot the last tube of greasepaint into the box. I'm not good enough.

Before Madam Delia could say any more, they were interrupted by the chairman. 'I believe you wanted me,' he simpered.

She eyed him coldly as she said, 'The next time you recommend a drunken oaf, make sure everyone has earplugs.'

He began to bluster, 'The piano was a bit dicky –'

'Jane managed to overcome the problem. And she should have been among the prize winners. Why wasn't she?'

'I'm sorry, Madam Delia, but rules is rules.'

'What are you talking about?'

'They voted her the winner, but Christabel's mother found out ...' He glanced at Mrs Harrison. 'Jane's under fourteen and there were money prizes. So we had to disqualify her.'

Madame Delia glared at him, then turned back to Jane. 'I'll be honest,' she said. 'You are a little young, but Rose tells me you sight-read well, and you can obviously memorise.' She shrugged into her leopard-skin coat. 'Because of your inexperience, I can only offer you five shillings for the rehearsals and a pound for the show. Do you think you can learn the music in time?'

'I'll do my best, Madame Delia.'

'You'll need to.' The dancing teacher stared hard at Jane. 'I'm risking my reputation, but I really haven't any choice.'

On the bus going home, Jane couldn't stop smiling to herself. She was going to play the piano at the Town Hall on Christmas Eve. Accompany Rose. They would do a show together, in front of the Mayor and Mayoress. Even if Madame Delia didn't keep her on as the troupe pianist, she would have that one moment of glory.

Chapter Eleven

The Harrisons had booked almost the whole of the fourth row. 'No peeking through the curtains, please, Jane,' Madam Delia reproved. 'It's not professional.'

'Sorry, Madame Delia.'

'I'll give you the signal to go out after the Mayor and Mayoress have arrived. When the house lights dim, you can start the opening number.'

As she waited, Jane studied her pencilled notes on 'Let the People Sing'; '4-bar intro, 2 chorus, coda, repeat last 8 bars for play-off.' She'd practised every possible moment for the past week, but there was so much to remember, so much that could go wrong. Would the light be good enough? Suppose she turned over two pages together? Silently, she prayed that she wouldn't let anyone down.

As always, Rose led the troupe onstage with a brilliant smile. Her timing was so good, it made Jane's task almost easy, whereas the Babes were quite a challenge. None was older than five years, and they faltered several times during 'The Wedding of the Painted Doll', but Jane held back, then picked up the melody again. The audience loved them.

The interval was a chaotic flurry of costume changes and make-up renewals. Jane kept out of the way. All too soon it was time for the second half. It wasn't until a young acrobat gracefully somersaulted offstage to the final bars of 'Rustle of Spring' that Jane began to relax. Now there was only the finale, and she had never heard 'There'll Always Be an England' sung with more fervour. The applause was deafening. Jane felt exhausted, but exhilarated at the same time. Even if Madame Delia wasn't satisfied, it had been the most wonderful experience.

As she gathered her music together, she looked towards row D. Her father and Peter beamed and Uncle Len gave her the thumbs-up sign. Laura Marshall came across to the piano.

'Well done, Jane!' she said with a big smile. 'You were splendid.'

'Thank you.' Jane looked at an empty seat. 'Where's Mum?'

'She's helping Rose change.' Mrs Marshall handed Jane a small package. 'Happy Christmas, my dear.'

'Aren't you coming on Boxing Day?'

'I'm afraid it's not possible.'

'But your presents –'

'I'll try to see you again after Christmas.'

'When?'

Mrs Marshall hesitated, then said, 'I may not be able to visit for a while.'

'Why not?'

'The WVS need drivers for their mobile canteens, and it is something I can do.'

'But why does that stop you visiting us?'

'It's not only that.' Mrs Marshall looked uncomfortable. 'Robert is living with me between his hospital visits, and my mother-in-law is far from well.'

Jane didn't answer. She couldn't understand the real reason behind the excuses.

Mrs Marshall went on. 'You're going to be busier than ever, anyway, with your music and studies.'

Tears began to hurt Jane's eyes. 'I'll miss you,' she mumbled.

'I shall miss you, too. Wll you write to me?'

Jane nodded, and the familiar waft of perfume accompanied the kiss.

Slowly, Jane made her way backstage. One shoe on, one off, Rose hopped across the dressing room and flung her arms around her sister. 'You were wonderful, Janey. Wasn't she, Mum?'

Folding Rose's costume, her mother said, 'Not bad, considering it was your first time. But you made a mistake in the second chorus of "Yours". Has Madame Delia said whether she wants to keep you on or not?'

Rose laughed. 'Of course she'll keep her on. We've been asked to appear in a pantomime in January.'

Madame Delia told Jane she had done very well, and suggested a trial period. 'I've had more pianists come and go than hot dinners,' she said. 'Some only like the shows, get bored with rehearsals. Others find it interferes with their social life.' Ruefully, she looked at Jane. 'I suppose exams will be the problem in your case.'

On the crowded bus, Jane looked at her pound note. Thirty shillings earned in one week. If she saved half, that would leave fifteen shillings to buy something nice for her mother in the January sales. But it wasn't only the money that filled her with pleasure. It was the memory of the atmosphere, the buzz of anticipation just before the lights went down, the sound of the audience laughing at the comedy routines, and clapping for ages after the finale. Desperately she hoped that Madame Delia would keep her on as the regular pianist.

Suddenly she heard the name 'Laura' mentioned. Her mother and Aunt Grace sat nearby, talking in hushed tones.

'Len will be disappointed,' her aunt was saying. 'I've never seen him so smitten.'

'It's a pity, but there was no future in it.'

'How do you know? Did Laura say anything?'

'Of course not. Len told me he didn't have anything to offer her, always being away, so he was leaving the field clear for Nobby.'

'That's funny, Nobby told me he thought she was too far above him. He thought she only went out with him because of her brother. You know, gratitude.'

'Well, it looks as though she's not really interested in either of them. I just hope they – ssh, they're coming downstairs. Tell the others it's our stop.'

As they walked along the cold, dark streets, Jane wondered. Did Uncle Nobby hopelessly love Laura Marshall? With his slight stoop and thinning hair, he wasn't exactly a darkly brooding Heathcliffe, yet Jane couldn't help comparing his plight with that of the tragic lover in *Wuthering Heights*.

And what about Uncle Len? There was no doubt that he was

attracted to the beautiful widow. Had his luck finally run out? Falling in love certainly seemed to be a precarious business.

For the next few months, Jane had other things on her mind than wondering about love. Things like learning the music for tap-dancing and ballet exams, rehearsals and concerts. And choosing the right matriculation subjects. Her mother said it didn't matter. She was determined that Jane should become a music teacher, but the thought of spending her life watching reluctant youngsters being dragged into the front room by their mothers was unbearable to Jane. The only alternative she could think of was to take a secretarial course, but that would mean transferring to the technical college. She would have liked to discuss it with her father, but he had volunteered for extra overtime. Miss Bellinger had her own views upon the matter: both sisters should go on to university. A transfer was not possible.

Rose wasn't much help, but she was single-minded. You didn't need a degree to go on the films.

Jane explained the eventual solution to Laura Marshall's mother-in-law as they washed up the dishes after Desmond's tenth birthday party in August. 'It was Aunt Grace who suggested I enrol for evening classes in shorthand and typing, Mrs Marshall.'

'A sensible idea, Jane. And why don't you call me Auntie Bea? Less confusing than having two Mrs Marshall's'.

Jane smiled. 'I noticed the boys call you Granbea. That's a lovely pet name.'

'Much more friendly than Grandmother.'

As they chatted, Jane couldn't help making comparisons with her own grandmother. At sixty-six, probably about the same age as Auntie Bea, Gran would never carry a cup into the kitchenette, let alone wash up. And it wasn't long since this old lady had been at death's door.

'Sandy's father is working on a cure for pneumonia,' she commented.

'Sandy? Is that the young man who wants to be a doctor?' Jane nodded. 'Laura was quite impressed with him. Said he had nice manners.' Auntie Bea handed Jane a tea towel. 'But won't military service hinder his plans?'

'He's applied for a place at medical school. If he passes the board interview, he'll be exempt from call-up for the time being.'

'What about the other young man? Your sister's beau.'

'Bill?' Jane giggled at the quaint expression. 'He's talking about volunteering.'

'I suppose most of the sixth-form students go straight into the forces.'

'Quite a few. Isabel Wallis joined the WAAFs, and Arnold Godwin has just been accepted into the Marines.' Jane paused for a moment. 'The one I feel sad about is Leslie Saunders. He could have gone to Oxford, but he chose the army. Got his commission just before the Dieppe raid.' Her voice faltered. 'They say he may get a posthumous medal.'

Momentarily, Auntie Bea's eyes closed, before she said, 'I was thinking only this morning how sad it is that the Duke of Kent's children will be fatherless.' She shook her head. 'And the poor mothers. It's hard to lose a child, whether you're Queen Mary or Mrs Saunders.'

Jane stammered, 'I'm sorry. I shouldn't have mentioned it.'

'Don't apologise, dear.' Auntie Bea touched Jane's arm. 'Douglas is never far from my thoughts. And the boys are a constant reminder –' She was interrupted by a burst of childish laughter from upstairs.

Amazed, Jane stared at the ceiling. 'It isn't often you hear Johnny laughing like that.'

'Such a handsome child. Is he having treatment?'

'Betty only takes him to the hospital because Jack insists. She doesn't keep up his exercises at home, or work on his speech.'

'What a pity.'

Jane nodded. 'The only one he really responds to is Jack. He adores Johnny. Spends every moment with him when he's on leave.'

As they smiled at another peal of laughter, Auntie Bea commented, 'Desmond is very good with small children. But he clings too much to his mother, I'm afraid. Douglas was the same.' Auntie Bea stared out of the window, but Jane knew she was looking beyond the rain dripping from the trees, far into the past. 'I took Douglas to Southampton so that he would remember the maiden voyage of the world's finest liner. They said she was unsinkable.' Jane's sharp intake of breath must have disturbed her reverie, for she turned and said, 'I'm sorry, Jane. I thought you knew. My husband went down with the *Titanic*.'

'No, I didn't. How ghastly!'

'It was a tragedy that shouldn't have happened.'

'Uncle Len told me about it. He tried to get taken on as a cabin boy.'

'Ah, the aptly named Lucky Len. Such a nice young man.' Jane smiled at the thought of her uncle being called a 'young' man, as Auntie Bea went on, 'Desmond is so like Douglas, it troubles me.'

'Because he still grieves for his father? That's natural, isn't it?'

'But Desmond seems to resent anyone getting close to Laura. And Laura is too nice a person to live alone. The boys won't be at home for ever.'

Jane was thoughtful for a moment. Then she said, 'I hope I don't sound rude, but ... why don't you live here?'

'Goodness me, no.' Auntie Bea shook her head. 'We both value our independence too much. And our friendship.'

'I wish my grandparents felt the same.'

A spate of shouting and cheering interrupted the conversation. Auntie Bea chuckled. 'Have you ever played Monopoly?' Jane shook her head. 'Then it's time we added to your education. Let's challenge those young scoundrels upstairs.'

It took a while for Jane to learn the rules, but she enjoyed the game. Rose became bored and wandered into Desmond's room, but Peter soon grasped the finer points and turned Rose's mediocre little wooden houses into hotels in Park Lane and a pile of 'funny money'.

'Beginner's luck,' Lawrence scoffed cheerfully. The noise built to an excited pitch as they squatted on the floor, throwing dice, buying and selling property.

Jane wailed, 'Oh, no! That's the third time!' as she read her card, 'Go to gaol. Pay £200.'

Just as she reached for her dwindling bank balance, the telephone rang in the hall. They all turned towards the open door as Laura Marshall called into the sitting room, 'Nell, it's your sister – Vi.'

Peter's face was anxious as he stood up. They followed him onto the landing. Only Desmond stayed in his room, patiently amusing Johnny with a clockwork clown on a trapeze. For some minutes, the only sound was the whirring toy and Johnny's squeals. Then Mrs Harrison said, 'Find out where they're taking him, and phone Grace. You'll need a solicitor. And, Vi, try to calm down. We'll get the next train back.' She replaced the receiver and looked up at Peter.

He walked slowly down the stairs. 'Has Dad had an accident?' he asked.

'No, Peter. Nothing like that.' Mrs Harrison bit her lip. 'Oh, well, it will be in the papers, I suppose,' she sighed. 'The police have just arrested your father.'

'I won't go. And you can't make me.'

Rose's defiant voice rang through the house. Jane glanced at Aunt Grace, who raised her eyebrows, then examined the stocking she was darning. Slowly, Jane ironed her school blouse. Neither of them looked at Peter, head bent over a cash-book.

Only Rose's voice penetrated two closed doors. 'Fat chance I've got of being prefect now.' Muffled responses from her parents, then, 'Of course they'll know. It's in the paper.' More murmurings, followed by, 'It's different for Jane. She hasn't got many friends at school.' Her father's voice, a little sharper, and Rose's final outburst, 'What am I supposed to say when they ask whether my uncle is in Wormwood Scrubs or Brixton? I'll die of shame.'

Peter's head jerked towards the door, his face so drained of colour Jane thought he was going to faint. Then he quietly closed the book, pushed back his chair and walked out of the back door, into the gathering dusk.

Aunt Grace sat motionless, a look of great pain on her face. As the dining-room door slammed and footsteps were heard running upstairs, she pushed her needle into the pincushion. 'I think a pot of tea is called for.'

Uncertain whether to comfort cousin or sister, Jane stared at the bottles of red and black ink, pens and ruler, neatly arranged on the blotting paper. She couldn't quite believe that Peter wouldn't be living with them any longer.

Her mother pushed open the kitchenette door. 'Haven't you finished your ironing yet, Janey?' she asked. 'You know I've still got some to do, and I don't want to be up all night.'

'I did Dad's shirts while I was about it.' Jane stood on a chair to unplug the iron from the light fitting.

'Oh. Well, I hope you've done the collars properly.'

Mr Harrison followed his wife. 'Where's Peter?' he asked Aunt Grace.

'In the garden.'

'Do you think he heard?'

She nodded. Mr Harrison's face was troubled as he said, 'I'll have a word with him.'

Jane watched her mother flop onto a chair. 'Are you all right, Mum?' she asked.

'Of course I'm not all right,' Mrs Harrison snapped. 'You girls know it upsets me when you answer back.'

Changing the subject, Jane said, 'It's a shame you've got to start doing fire duty, on top of everything else. If you'd been a year older, you'd have missed it.'

'Well, no use crying over spilt milk.'

'No. And at least things are quieter now.'

'That's no consolation. The way we're bombing Germany, Hitler is bound to retaliate.'

As Jane turned away, she felt a comforting squeeze on her arm from Aunt Grace. 'There's your tea, dear.'

'Thanks. Shall I take one up to –?'

'No.' her mother interrupted. 'You keep out of it, Janey. I haven't finished with that young lady yet.'

Gently, Aunt Grace said, 'Why don't you leave it till the morning, Nell? Far better to sleep on it.'

Mrs Harrison sipped her tea in silence. Then she said, 'Perhaps you're right, Grace. Anyway, Jack and Betty will be back from the pictures soon. I don't want anything to upset him on his last night.'

Suddenly, there was a screech, thump and yowl from the living room. The door opened and Tibs shot out, closely followed by a slipper. He ran straight through Aunt Grace's legs and out of the back door. Gran's voice shouted after him, 'And stay away from those birds, or you'll finish up in the glue factory.' Then she called out, 'Isn't anyone going to bring us a cup of tea?'

117

Gran complained bitterly to Jane about the cat, Rose's shouting, Uncle Arthur, her legs, having to wait so long for her tea, and only having one biscuit. By the time she'd finished, there was another complaint. The tea was cold.

Grandad's mumblings were incoherent, because his teeth were wrapped in a handkerchief on the mantelpiece. Jane sorted out the pages of his *News of the World*, scattered all over the floor, threw the night cover over the birdcage, and retrieved Gran's slipper from the hall. It was a relief to close the door and go back to the kitchenette.

Her father was sitting at the table, gazing out into the garden. He looked round at Jane and smiled.

'Why don't you take Peter's tea out to him?' he suggested. 'And remind him that he promised to be home by nine o'clock.'

The scent of roses over the arch was almost overpowering. Jane thought how well her father had developed the garden in little more than a year, considering the hours he worked. Rows of onions, carrots and beetroot stood to attention, while carefully nurtured marrows were growing to mammoth proportions.

When Jane's eyes became accustomed to the half-light, she saw Peter. Partly hidden by the air-raid shelter, he leaned over the fence, watching a train hurtling along the track. There was no point in talking till it had thundered past, the cab alive with sparks and flames as the fireman shovelled coal.

When all was quiet again, Jane ventured, 'Rose didn't mean to hurt your feelings.' Peter didn't answer. 'She's been trying to get out of school for ages. This was just another excuse.'

'I know. That's the tough part about it.'

'What do you mean?'

'The fact that Rose will do anything to leave school, and I'd give anything to stay on.'

'Oh, Peter! Isn't there anything we can do?'

'Mum needs me in the shop,' he said. 'She's got no one to help with the heavy lugging, and she was never much good with accounts.'

'But when Uncle Arthur is home again, you'll be able to carry on with your education, won't you?'

He shook his head. 'Dad will probably keep out of the way

118

till the fuss has died down. The people who were willing enough to pay a bit more for a tin of salmon are scared stiff they're going to be hauled before the beak, and the others are very holier-than-thou. Some have transferred their ration books to other grocers.' He leaned back against the fence. 'He's such a fool!'

'Three months seems a bit hard for a first offence. I'd have thought they would have fined him, it was such a petty thing.'

'I think the magistrate was trying to make an example of him. Everyone thinks Dad made a pile out of the black market, but if he did, I can't find it. I've gone through the books and the bank balance is just about enough to pay this month's bills. I'll have to sort out the paperwork for them. It's a right mess.'

'Will you give up your plans to be an accountant?'

'Good heavens, no! I told Mum I would only leave school on condition that I can take evening classes. University is out of the question now, but I can still qualify on my own. It'll take a bit longer, but –'

Mr Harrison called from the back door, 'Pe-ter!'

'Coming, Uncle Fred.' Peter gulped the last of his tea and looked at Jane. 'Will you be all right tomorrow?'

''Course I will. It'll be a nine days' wonder till they find something else to whisper about.'

Peter leaned forward and kissed her cheek. 'You're a brick, Janey,' he said. 'I shall miss you.'

'It won't be the same without you,' she said. 'And Rose is really upset that you're going.'

He put his head on one side. 'You two are so different,' he observed. 'Like somebody said at school, Rose is the one you'd want as a girlfriend, but Janey's the one you'd want to marry.'

Jane felt the colour glow in her cheeks as she asked, 'Who said that?'

At first Peter didn't answer, just grinned. Then he said, 'Me,' turned on his heel and raced back to the house.

Mrs Harrison took a shilling from her purse. 'Your mum asked me to give you your bus fare. We weren't sure how much it was going to cost her to get to ... to see your dad.' She paused, then went on, 'Don't forget, you're both coming to dinner again next Sunday.'

'We won't forget, Aunt Nell. And –' Peter fumbled with his suitcase – 'thanks for putting up with me for the last two years ...' His voice faltered. 'And everything.' The room was quiet for a moment, until he said, 'I'll get my coat.'

Jane followed him into the dinning room. As Peter picked up his blazer, he nodded towards the bed-chair. 'That's a lot more comfortable than the camp bed at the shop.'

'Perhaps Mum would let you have it.'

He shook his head. 'That poky little room isn't big enough,' he said. 'I have to put the two wooden chairs out in the scullery each night to make room for the camp bed.'

'What do you sit on, when you're all home?'

'The rickety old stool under the table. The table covered with oil cloth. It's funny,' he reflected, 'I don't think of it as home any more, just the shop.' Peter looked around the polished dining suite, vase of roses standing on a crochet runner, studio portrait of Jack and Betty in pride of place on the sideboard alongside brass Buddhas and pagodas, once blackened by fire and now gleaming. 'This is home,' he said.

As they were all saying goodbye in the hall, Rose hurtled down the stairs and flung herself at her cousin.

'I'm sorry,' she cried. 'It's not your fault. I don't want you to go ...'

Over the top of her blonde curls, Peter and Jane exchanged understanding smiles. He patted Rose's back. 'Just think,' he said, 'you'll have longer in the bathroom in the morning, without me yelling at you to hurry up.'

'It's not fair,' she sobbed.

'No. But no use crying over spilt milk. That's what you always say, Auntie Nell, isn't it?' As Jack opened the front gate, Rose ran back upstairs.

Betty went straight up to bed without a word, but Jack talked to Peter for a moment, then shook his hand and came into the kitchenette. 'Rotten thing to happen,' he observed. 'Wish I had his brains.'

'You did very well at the technical college,' Mrs Harrison protested.

'Peter has a brilliant mind, Mum. He'll go far, given half a chance. And he's a worker, like Janey. I get by, but most of the time I'm just looking for a bit of fun. Rose is the same.'

'Hmm.' Mrs Harrison snorted. 'Don't mention that young lady to me.'

'Jane shook her head as her brother was about to open his mouth. 'How's Mr Churchill's famous Airborne Division coming along?' she asked.

'Well, like Topsy, it's certainly growing.' He grinned. 'And at last I've crossed the Channel.'

Mrs Harrison looked more worried than ever. 'You haven't been flying over enemy lines, have you?'

'Only dropping a few leaflets. I'm probably in more danger crossing the road in the blackout, Mum.' Jack hugged her. 'How about a cup of cocoa? I don't suppose Betty will want one. She's usually asleep by the time I go up.'

Jane carried her ironing upstairs, expecting to find Rose sobbing her heart out on the bed. Instead, she was staring into the dressing-table mirror. Jane knew that look.

'Now what are you up to?' she asked, as she stepped over Aunt Grace's camp bed.

'I've had an idea,' Rose said, grinning.

'So I see. Is it about school?'

'Yes. It'll solve all our problems.'

'You mean it'll solve your problem.' Jane sat on the edge of the bed. 'Listen, Rose. Mum and Dad have got enough on their plates just now. Don't make things worse.'

'I'm not. I'm making things better.'

Jane doubted that, but she went on. 'If you lose your temper the way you did tonight, they won't even listen to you. You know what Mum's like.'

'I can always get round Mum, you know I can.'

'Not over leaving school, you won't. They can't afford the five pounds to buy you out.' Jane tried pleading. 'Why not give it a try? I'll be with you.'

'No.' Rose's voice was adamant. 'I hate school and I'm not going back there. Ever.'

Jane sighed. 'Then I suggest that you talk to them very calmly and reasonably. What is this idea, anyway?'

Excitedly, Rose turned towards her sister. 'It's –' She stopped. 'No. Aunt Grace will be up in a minute.'

'But Rose ...'

'I need to work it out properly.' A secretive little smile

121

on her lips, Rose turned back to the mirror. 'Tell you tomorrow.'

In the classroom marked FORM 4A, Jane gave her mother's hastily written note to Mr McEwen, who nodded and pointed towards one of the desks at the back of the room, away from prying eyes boring into the back of her neck. Peter had said Mac was OK.

While the register was being called, she thought about her class mates. Rose was right, she didn't have many friends. Until now, her life had revolved around her sparkling sister, watching admirers gather as she recounted the latest happening. Rose had 'a talent to amuse'; Jane was always reminded of Noël Coward's phrase.

It wouldn't have been so bad if Sandy and Bill were still in the sixth form. Never before had Jane felt so alone.

During the morning break she went straight to the library, but it wasn't so easy to hide at dinnertime. Her form-mates sat in companionable groups, not looking up as she stood with her tray, uncertain where to sit. She wondered if they were avoiding her, embarrassed by Uncle Arthur's misdemeanour.

'Hullo, Jane.'

The girl behind her was Daphne Jarvis, Rose's friend who lived across the road. She went on, 'They asked me to take Rose's place as form prefect for today.' Daphne smiled hesitantly. 'I suggested you should be the replacement, but I was next on the list. Sorry ...'

'That's all right.' Jane hadn't expected to be nominated.

Then Daphne said, 'Could you do me a favour?'

Surprised, Jane answered, 'If I can.'

'The kids in 1A haven't a prefect at their table. Would you mind keeping an eye on them?'

The first-formers were the quietest group in the room. They smiled nervously at each other and at Jane. One tiny lad in short trousers actually called her 'Miss'. They all had that mixed expression of apprehension and eagerness. She had almost forgotten what it was like to be so new.

At the far end of the table, a girl sat with head bowed, savoury rissoles barely touched. A slight movement of her shoulders suggested she might be weeping. Jane picked up her

122

own plate and sat next to the girl, who glanced round like a startled rabbit, tear-filled eyes wide, then again concentrated on her lap.

Quietly, Jane said, 'I don't blame you for not liking the rissoles, but if you don't eat you'll be starving before the afternoon is over.'

A muffled voice replied, 'The dinner is very nice, to be sure, but I'm really not at all hungry.'

There was something familiar about the brilliance of the girl's violet eyes, with the double row of lashes, her blue-black hair tied back with a ribbon, the soft Irish accent.

'What's your name?' Jane asked.

Again the girl looked up, fear replacing misery. 'You're not going to give me another order point, are you? Oh, please don't! I'll eat my dinner. All of it.' She grabbed her knife and fork and frantically cut the rissole.

'Of course not.' Jane placed her hand on the girl's arm. 'I just want to know your name, that's all. You remind me of someone.'

The girl looked relieved but continued to put the food onto her fork. 'Me name's Kathleen O'Connor. Did you know my sister Theresa?'

'We were evacuated together. I'm Jane Harrison.'

For the first time, a tiny smile touched the younger girl's face. 'She wrote to me mam about you, all the time. Said you were her best friend.'

Jane watched Kathleen, seeing again the vulnerability of Theresa, remembering their long walks together in Norfolk. She wondered why Kathleen had received an order point so soon.

Kathleen whispered, 'I wasn't sure that I would be allowed in assembly, so I hid in the cloakroom.'

'Why shouldn't you be allowed?'

'Because I'm Catholic. Me gran said the Protestants are heretics and don't use the proper language, and I wasn't to take part.'

'Wouldn't your parents have preferred you to go to the convent school?'

'Da wanted us to, but me mam was dead against it. Oh, there were some terrible rows at home, I can tell you. It was just the same with Theresa.'

123

'Do you think you'll go back to Galway when the war's over?'

Kathleen shook her head. 'There's no work. I wouldn't want to be that hungry again.'

'Are your parents happy here?'

'Da's got regular work and me mam's thankful to have a house with no pigs and chickens in and out. But Grannie O'Connor ...' Her voice trailed off.

'My gran and grandad live with us. He's no bother, but Gran is always complaining.'

'Grannie O'Connor has never forgiven Da for marrying out of the faith. She says this is a heathen country and if we worship with the Protestants we'll be damned for eternity.' Kathleen ate the last soggy chip. 'That's what I was trying to say this morning. But the prefect said I was insolent.' The tears were close again.

Jane stood up. 'If you point her out to me, I'll try to explain. Now, how about some chocolate pudding and custard?'

In the afternoon break Daphne thanked her for helping out, and confirmed that the fifth-form prefect had cancelled the order point for Kathleen. Then she asked if Rose was ill. Jane mumbled something about a painful period, and tried not to think about tomorrow, or the day after.

She hurried home across the park, for once not pausing to talk to the ducks, ran around the back of the house, and stopped. Normally on a Monday there would be a line of washing. The kitchenette was empty. So were the other rooms. Calling her mother, she took the stairs two at a time.

Rose's bed was littered with clothes, as though she had tried on and discarded everything in her wardrobe. Her mother's bedroom was empty, and there was no sign of Betty and Johnny. Jane tapped on the door of her grandparent's room and peeped in. Grandad snored softly, but Gran's eyes opened and glared at Jane.

'You're late,' she accused.

There was no point in arguing. 'Where's Mum and Rose?' Jane asked.

'How should I know? They've all buggered off.'

'But where? Mum must have said something.'

'Nobody tells me anything. There's a note somewhere.' As Jane turned, Gran called out, 'Hurry up and put the kettle on. I'm gasping.'

The note was brief. Mrs Harrison and Rose had gone to London, Betty and Johnny were visiting Mr Kennedy. Following instructions, Jane dug up potatoes and picked runner beans, calling Tibs at the same time. She hadn't seen him since Gran had thrown her slipper at him.

Johnny's cries were heard long before Betty appeared at the back door.

'Whatever is wrong with him?' Jane asked.

'I don't know. He's been like it all afternoon. Are the others back yet?'

'No. Why have they gone to London?'

'Blowed if I know. They went out as soon as I got back from seeing Jack off.'

'Didn't Mum say anything?'

Betty frowned. 'I was so upset, I wasn't really listening. Anyway, I didn't fancy staying in by myself. Your gran always has a go at me when Mum's out. So I decided to take Johnny round to Dad's, and your mum said she would leave you a note.'

As Johnny's cries became more insistent, Betty put a hand to her head. 'I've got to lie down,' she said. 'Call me when supper's ready, will you.'

'What about Johnny? Doesn't he need feeding, or changing, or something?'

'Probably. I forgot to take any nappies with me. You see to him, Janey.'

'But I've got homework to do before my typing class.'

'Then he'll have to stay out there till Mum comes back. I've got a headache.'

It was impossible to ignore Johnny. Annoyed with Betty, Jane closed her French grammar book and went out into the garden. As she picked up her nephew, she smelled the reason for his distress. And Tibs was sitting by the back door, waiting for his supper.

Half an hour later, the satisfied cat licked his whiskers, and a bathed and pyjama-clad infant sat in his highchair. Just as Jane began to spoon mashed vegetables into his mouth, her mother and sister arrived home.

125

Chapter Twelve

'I'm going to be a model!'

Potatoes remained poised on forks. Even Betty looked interested.

Mrs Harrison murmured, 'Well, we're not quite sure, Rose.' But she smiled proudly.

'That's what the man said, Mum. You were there.'

Gran asked, 'What sort of model? You're not going to pose in the altogether, are you?'

''Course not, Gran. Much better than that.'

Aunt Grace guessed, 'You're training to be a fashion mannequin. Like Laura Marshall?'

'Something like that.'

Betty gasped. 'I can just imagine you at the Ritz.'

'Not straight away.' Rose smiled dreamily. 'Actually, I'm more likely to be on the pictures. The stage schools were quite impressed.' She paused, observing the dramatic effect of her words.

Impatient, Jane cried, 'What stage schools? Oh, come on, Rose, do tell us the whole story.'

'Well ...' Rose was obviously enjoying the spotlight. 'Mum and Dad agreed I could go to stage school, and we went to Lavinia Lamont first. She runs the biggest school in London. It was ever so fancy, wasn't it, Mum?'

Her mouth full, Mrs Harrison nodded.

'They wouldn't let us in to see her, though. The secretary said there was a two-year waiting list. She was a snooty old bird.'

'But she did say to try the Dance and Drama Academy in Tottenham Court Road, Rose, so she must have liked the look of you.'

Betty asked, 'Were they full up as well?'

'Only for this term. They suggested I get some decent photographs taken and try again next year.'

Mrs Harrison took up the story. 'So we went into the Corner House for a cup of tea and the waitress told Rose about the Starstruck School for Girls. It was a funny little place, but at least the man gave Rose an audition.'

'Told me I had good potential,' Rose said.

'When do you start?' Jane asked.

'I'm not sure. He's going to let us know as soon as there's a vacancy.'

Aunt Grace reached for the breadboard. 'Wouldn't you feel happier with a woman?'

'That's what I thought at first,' Mrs Harrison said, 'but Mr McGlusky seemed to know what he was talking about. He used to be with the G. H. Eliott show.'

Gran looked up. 'I saw the "Chocolate-Coloured Coon" once at the Stratford Empire,' she said. 'Lovely turn, he was.' She began to hum a few bars from 'Lily of Laguna'.

'Where does the modelling come in?' Jane asked.

'Well, who should we bump into but Edna Browning, my friend from the elementary school? She's a machinist with a posh fashion firm in Soho, and said they were desperate for someone to help out in the salon, so we went back with her, saw the boss, and I start next Monday.'

'But Rose,' Jane said, 'what will you do if Mr McGlusky has a vacancy?'

'Take it, of course. Meantime, I'll be getting experience, and twenty-two shillings a week.'

Aunt Grace frowned. 'That doesn't sound much,' she said. 'What will you be doing exactly?'

'Oh, this and that. Helping to look after customers, modelling for them. Mr Cohen said some of the customers tip the girls, and he'll give me a rise after three months if I help sell a lot of dresses.'

Gran said, 'Sounds like a shop assistant to me.'

Jane looked at the clock. 'I must hurry,' she said, 'or I'll miss the bus. Don't want to be late for my first typing class.'

There were no typewriters in room 16. Jane thought she was in the wrong room until Mrs Rhodes introduced herself. She was a jolly soul who seemed to enjoy their reaction when she demonstrated the first step, finding the typewriter. After the giggles had died away they all managed to up-end the desktops so that the typewriters swivelled up until they sat firmly in the centre of the desk, like Mrs Edwards's sewing machine. The next twenty minutes were spent learning the intricacies of the QWERTY keyboard. Then, and only then, were they allowed to place their hands on the keys and attempt to type one line from Lesson One of the manual.

Jane hadn't expected the keys to be so stiff, but she was pleasantly surprised when complimented upon her even touch.

'Your "a" and semicolon are just as distinct as the other letters,' Mrs Rhodes said. 'Something you don't often find with a beginner. Are you by any chance a musician?'

'I play the piano. Does that help?'

'Oh, indubitably. You have equal strength in the little finger.' Mrs Rhodes addressed the class. 'Before you go home, I want all of you to look at Jane's work. It is an excellent example of how to type neatly and evenly.'

It was the first time Jane had been singled out for praise in a school class. She dashed home to tell her mother, but Mrs Harrison was busy preparing her husband's supper.

Aunt Grace congratulated Jane on her neat page of typing, then said, 'I didn't have a chance to ask you earlier, dear, but how was your first day as a fourth-former?'

'Missed Rose, of course. But met Theresa's younger sister Kathleen. Nice girl. Is Rose upstairs?'

Gran looked up from her crochet. 'She's still round at her friend's house. Never did care much for that girl.'

'Edna Browning?'

'That's the one. Too giggly for my liking. I hope she doesn't lead our Rose astray.'

It was gone ten o'clock before Rose came home. 'I bet they all wondered where I was today,' she said to Jane. 'What did you say?'

'I told Daphne you had a bad period.'

'Oh.' Rose looked slightly put out. 'Well, Mum is going to

see old Bellringer tomorrow. Make arrangements to buy me out.' She brightened. 'Wait till they find out I'm a model. Pity Isabel isn't still there. She'd be green with envy.'

Carrying the tray, Mrs Harrison came into the dining room. 'Time you cleared up here and went to bed, Janey,' she said. 'Your father will be home soon and we've things to talk over with Rose.' She lifted two cups of cocoa from the tray. 'Give one of these to Betty when you go upstairs.'

Rose took a cup. 'Dad won't half be surprised when he hears about my job,' she said.

'Don't forget you have to ask his permission, Rose,' her mother reminded. 'Your father only agreed to a transfer to stage school, not leaving school altogether.'

'Dad won't refuse, not when he knows how much it means to me.'

Later, Jane listened to the murmur of voices downstairs. It was impossible to tell which way things were going between Rose and her parents.

When the voices had died down, there was a light tap on the door and a soft, 'Jane, are you awake?' It was her father.

He sat on the bed and asked how her day had been, smiling when she told him about the typing class. Then he said, 'What's your opinion about this job Rose wants to take?'

Jane hadn't had much opportunity to form an opinion, but she knew she had to answer carefully. 'I don't really know, Dad. But Mum has met Mr Cohen, and she doesn't seem too worried.'

Mr Harrison sighed. 'Trouble is, your mother and Rose both dream about the same castle in the air, with Rose's name in huge lights over the door. You're the one with feet firmly on the ground.'

Slowly, Jane said, 'I'm not sure whether the job will amount to much more than a glorified shop assistant. But I am sure of one thing.' Her father listened attentively as she went on, 'Rose is unhappy at school. Has been for the last couple of terms. And this business with Uncle Arthur has made things worse. Even if she's forced to go back, I don't think she'll ever settle down.' Jane thought for a moment, then met his gaze. 'Perhaps Rose needs to find out for herself what it's like in the real world outside school.'

Quietly, Mr Harrison digested her words. Then he nodded, and stood up. At the door he turned. 'Will you miss Rose a great deal if she leaves school?' he asked.

Jane's eyes filled with tears. 'Yes,' she whispered.

'I thought so.' He smiled at her. 'Good night, love. God bless.'

She was drifting into sleep when Rose came to bed. As she listened to her sister cheerfully humming, 'I Don't Want to Set the World on Fire', Jane was prepared for the whispered announcement, 'Dad said OK. I knew I could get him round to my way of thinking. Isn't it marvellous?'

'Marvellous,' Jane echoed. Her tears had to wait until Rose was asleep before they could dampen the pillow.

Chapter Thirteen

Nell Harrison was called up to do war work in 1943. She hadn't worked in a factory before, and wasn't happy about it, but Jane tried to console her with the thought that she could leave once she was forty-five.

Strangely, as her birthday approached, Mrs Harrison complained less. Finally, she told them she would carry on, for the time being at least.

Gran put up quite an argument, well matched by her daughter. 'I've made friends now, and I need the money.' Jane had never seen her mother so spirited with Gran. 'Anyway, it's nothing to do with you.'

'Nice thing, I must say, talking to your mother like that. You're getting as common as those women you work with.'

Nell Harrison stopped clearing the table. 'Listen,' she said. 'For years I've done nothing but look after the home and children. That might have been enough for your generation, but things are different now. Besides, I feel as if drilling holes in army lorries is doing something useful for the war effort.'

'What use are you going to be if you neglect your family, I'd like to know?'

'Don't talk daft. I'm only out a few hours each morning, and Betty's here.'

'Hmmph.' Gran sucked her teeth. 'If I ask her to make a cup of tea she tells me to wait till you come home.'

Betty protested, 'That's not fair. I made you a cup of tea only yesterday.'

'More like cat's wee.'

'Then you'd better get it yourself. I've got Johnny to look after.'

'You leave him in bed till Nell gets home.'

'Mum knows I can't cope with Johnny when I'm worried sick about Jack.'

'He's only in Bournemouth. Said the most dangerous thing he had to do was jump in the deep end at the baths with all his clothes on.'

'But what about when he had to take those gliders all the way to Africa?'

'He came back, didn't he? More than could be said for those other poor sods who went down in the sea.'

'And Jack was supposed to be with them.'

'Then thank Gawd he had the runs, and stop snivelling.'

'You're wicked, Gran. You don't care how I feel.'

'Shut up, you two!' Mrs Harrison snapped. 'I don't want to be reminded that Jack could have been killed at Sicily. All I hope is that they stop flying those stupid things.' She stacked another plate on the pile. 'But whatever happens, I'm going to carry on working.'

Betty's lip quivered. 'I don't see why. Dad's a charge hand now, and he does plenty of overtime, so it can't be the money.'

Nell Harrison looked from one to the other. 'You really don't have a clue, do you?' she said. 'Have you looked at Fred lately? He's wearing himself to a frazzle, and I want him to ease up. But we're still replacing things from the fire, and there's eight mouths to feed.'

Gran grunted, 'We all pay our way, so I don't know what you're going on about.'

'I'm trying to make you understand. It's not only food, you know. Rose has to look nice for her job, and Janey outgrows her uniform as soon as she puts it on. They must think we're made of money at that school. There's always something.'

As Jane washed up, she wondered whether she should leave school and get a job? Now she was fifteen they wouldn't have to pay fees in lieu.

Her mother brought another tray into the kitchenette. 'Are you rehearsing tonight?' she asked.

'Yes. It's the last open-air concert tomorrow. That'll pay for my shorthand class and textbook. Or would you rather have it towards our fare to Torquay?'

'Doesn't matter, really. It's all got to be paid for, one way or another.' Her mother sighed. 'Still, Rose needs a holiday, and Peg is lonely with Uncle Joe in hospital.'

'Have you heard any more about his injuries?'

'Only that he's got a piece of shrapnel lodged in his spine, and will probably be in a wheelchair for the rest of his life.'

'Oh, no!' Jane fought back a tear. 'Was there much damage to the house?'

'She said the blast hit the front windows, but the rooms at the back are safe.'

'Why on earth would they want to bomb a lovely place like Babbacombe?'

'God knows. They just strafed the Downs from one end to the other.' Mrs Harrison briskly wiped up a saucepan as she changed the subject. 'If Rose is going straight from work tonight, you'd better take her a sandwich. She'll be tired and hungry after being on her feet all day.'

The following afternoon, a brisk breeze sent clouds scudding across a blue sky, and Jane was glad she'd taken a couple of clothespegs to anchor her music. The Holidays at Home concerts had been particularly successful, and by the time Rose led the girls onto the bandstand, every deck chair was taken. Their rendition of 'This Is the Army, Mr Jones' was warmly applauded, especially by a small group of American servicemen.

Everything was fine until the finale, a medley of song and dance representing the Allies. As Jane was changing music at the end of Offenbach's 'Can-Can', the peg sprang out of her hand and sheets of music scattered in the wind. Arms akimbo, three of the troupe waited for the introduction to their Cossack dance. She hadn't had a chance to memorise the music for it. Scarlet-faced and aware of the laughter, she improvised, but improvisation wasn't her strong point, and Madame Delia knew this. The dancing teacher began to clap the rhythm and la-la the melody, encouraging the audience and gathering music at the same time. Soon, they all joined in, and it didn't matter what Jane was playing.

Swiftly, Madame Delia slipped 'Star-Spangled Banner' onto the music rest, holding it securely with one hand while she reshuffled the last few pieces with the other. The audience rose as one to sing 'Land of Hope and Glory', with two encores, before the national anthem.

Eventually the applause died away. Fathers in uniform linked arms with their wives and walked in the park, making the most of the rare August sunshine.

Humiliated, Jane tried to apologise. Instead of the fury she'd expected, Madame Delia laughed. 'Brahms is probably turning in his grave, but you didn't panic. Now, I think the only one still astray is page four –'

'Would this be what you're looking for, ma'am?' A tall, well-built American, wearing wings above his breast pocket, held out the missing music.

Smiling, Madame Delia studied him for a moment. 'Why, yes, it is. Thank you, sergeant.'

'My pleasure.' He saluted, then turned and watched Rose running towards them across the grass.

'Hi, Chuck,' she cried. 'You found the place OK?'

'Sure did. And the show was great. You're quite the little star.' Rose grinned. 'Did Denny come with you?'

'He's over there with Al.' Two younger men waved. 'And would this young lady be your sister?' Chuck asked, nodding towards the dancing teacher.

'Sorry. I should have introduced Madame Delia.'

'Well, I'm real pleased to meet you, ma'am. I sort of imagined it would be someone older directing the girls. You must be very proud of them.'

'I am, sergeant. And thank you.'

'Chuck, please.'

Eagerly, Rose asked, 'What do you boys have in mind now the show's over?'

'Whatever you want, Rose.'

'I'd love to go dancing.'

He laughed. 'Sure. Perhaps we could try the Lyceum, maybe call in at the Rainbow Club.'

'Gosh! Could we?'

He turned to Madame Delia. 'She's been dancing all afternoon, now she wants to dance all evening. Gee, I wish I was that young again. What vitality!'

'Rose was born to dance,' Madame Delia smiled.

'I can believe that.' He looked thoughtful. 'And from what I hear, you're a pretty mean hoofer yourself. Medals and things.'

'A long time ago.'

'Once a dancer, always a dancer. Say, why don't you come with us? I'm not in Denny's league, but I'd sure be honoured if you'd be my partner.'

'I don't know,' she murmured. 'It's years ...'

Rose nodded excitedly. 'Oh, please say yes. You love dancing.'

'Well ...'

The sergeant grinned. 'Swell. How long before you're through?'

'About half an hour. I'll have to go home first. Rose?'

'I brought my dress with me.'

'You'd better come back to my house.' She hesitated. 'Perhaps, Chuck, you and your friends would like to come with us, have a cup of tea while you're waiting.'

'Why, thank you, Delia, that would be swell. Now, Rose, where's this sister of yours? Maybe she'd like to make a threesome, with Al.'

Rose's voice was subdued as she introduced Jane. His handshake was warm, but he was obviously uncomfortable. 'Hi, Janey. Didn't realise you were Rose's kid sister. You sure can tickle those ivories.'

Rose looked appealingly at Jane. Madame Delia opened her mouth as if to speak, then changed her mind.

Jane murmured, 'Thank you. But I'm afraid I've got ironing to do, and packing.'

Quickly, Rose said, 'We're off to Torquay tomorrow, on holiday. See you in a minute, Chuck.'

In the makeshift changing room, Rose told her she'd met the Americans one lunchtime when walking down Wardour Street, looking at pictures outside the trade cinemas, where movie people hung out. Denny was from New York and had won Jitterbug contests. He was wonderful. And she was so thrilled about tonight.

'Rose, don't be late. We've got to leave early tomorrow and you haven't packed yet.'

'Just throw a few things in the case for me. And could you rub the iron over my pink blouse? Oh, and Janey ...'

'Yes?'

'Don't tell Mum and Dad I'm going out with Americans.'

'What am I supposed to say?'

'Say I'm with Madame Delia and some friends. That's why I wanted her to come. She's a perfect chaperone.'

135

Chapter Fourteen

'Sally, dear.' Madame Delia knelt to grasp the tiny foot. 'It's shuffle-back-one-two, shuffle-back-one-two.'

Jane played eight bars of 'Toy-Town Soldiers' for the sixth time, and marvelled. With older pupils Madame Delia was demanding, with adults she could be brusque, but she had endless patience and gentleness for her Babes.

'That's right, sweetheart.' She moved the electric fire closer to the piano. 'Once more from the top, please, Jane.'

This time Jane was able to play right through without interruption. 'Good girls!' Madame Delia looked at her watch. 'Let's skip around the room now, warm you up before you go out into the cold.' An almost forgotten siren froze the scene into a tableau. Jane was the first to speak.

'It may be a false alarm. We haven't had anything for nearly a year.'

'I'm sure you're right.' Madame Delia's voice was reassuring, but the rumble of distant gunfire wasn't. Calmly, she asked the children, 'Have you heard of a game called sardines? You follow me into the other room and crawl inside a cage. Make believe you're sardines trying to squash into a tin.'

A voice shrilled, 'Are there any prizes?'

'Of course, dear. Sweeties for everyone.'

As Jane helped pack the little bodies into the Morrison shelter, she understood why the children laughed with delight. They were too young to remember air raids.

'What do we do now?' Sally asked.

'Practise our singing.' Madame Delia paused briefly as the first aircraft droned overhead and glanced at Jane. 'Sorry there's no room for you in there,' she said in a low voice, 'but I'm afraid the sides will burst.'

'I know.' The wire walls of the table shelter were bulging. 'What shall we sing?'

Voice at full pitch, Madame Delia instructed, 'We'll start with "Ten Green Bottles".'

All went well for two choruses, until the sounds of gunfire and bombs threatened to swamp the voices. Madame Delia crouched to talk to the children.

'Let's pretend we're on the stage of the biggest theatre you can imagine.'

A voice piped, 'The London Palladium?'

'That's the one. Imagine that Granny is sitting right up in the gods. In the back row. You want her to hear you, don't you?'

A chorus shouted, 'Yes, Madame Delia.'

'Right then, off we go. "Eight green bottles …"'

As six green bottles struggled for survival, the house shook and the lights went out. For a split second, there was nothing but silence and darkness. Then a child whimpered.

Madame Delia lowered her voice to a dramatic whisper. 'When all the sardines are in the tin, and the lid is on, it's very, very dark.'

'But I don't like the dark.'

'That's because you don't know what fun it can be. You can stick your tongue out in the dark and nobody tells you to stop. Go on. Do it.' For some minutes the children squeaked and giggled. Then the dancing teacher said, 'And you can pull funny faces while you're singing. You can't do that when the light's on, it would look silly.' More giggles. 'Try to sing louder than anyone else and pull the funniest face at the same time. But when I shine the torch on you, you must stop.'

'Like playing statues?'

'Just like that. All together now, "Five green bottles standing on the wall …"'

Jane would never have believed that a dozen small children could make such a noise. But it worked. When Madame Delia flashed her torch, they were all trying to contort their faces into ghastly expressions. Jane wasn't sure that they would hear the all clear above the din.

137

Someone was calling through the letter box. It was Sally's mother. 'I could hear you right down the street, even above the all clear.'

'Good. That was the idea.' Madame Delia flashed her torch. 'Now, let's see if we can find Sally among this little lot.'

While Jane sorted through knitted pixie hoods and mittens, another mother arrived. Jane held the candle closer while two tots were buttoned into coats. 'Did they bomb the substation?' she asked.

'No, ducky. One of our rockets misfired and landed smack on it. Warden told me.' The woman roared with laughter. 'Silly sods!'

'Do you know where the bombs fell?'

'Mostly over Plaistow way, I reckon. Not much for you to worry about, love.' She straightened up. 'Come on, kids. Say goodbye.'

The house was suddenly quiet. 'I'll get my music from the other room,' Jane said. 'I expect the buses will be running again now.'

'Not just yet, Jane. I want to discuss the concert with you. See if you can poke a bit of life into that fire while I put the kettle on. We could use a hot drink.'

It was the first time Jane had been in the living room. In the dim light from the fire and candle, she could see that the three-piece suite was made from real cow hide. And the thick beige carpet stretched almost to the walls, protected by a tiger-skin rug in front of the fireplace. Only the metal table shelter marred the effect.

A glass-fronted showcase, filled with trophies, caught her eye, as did the framed photograph on top, showing Madame Delia wearing a stunning evening dress, the hem trimmed with a deep band of feathers. Her partner, in white tie and tails, was tall and thin, with a pencil-line moustache. Both were smiling and holding the huge silver cup that was prominently displayed in the cabinet. Jane was about to pick up the photograph when Madame Delia came back into the room, carrying a tray.

'People often say Bernard looks a bit like Ronald Colman. And he danced like Fred Astaire.' Madame Delia paused by the photograph. 'That was taken in thirty-eight. Our finest hour, you might say.' She set the tray on the coffee table, opened the

138

showcase and took out two silver candlesticks. 'We won these in Paris the year before.' She lit the candles. 'Oh, we had wonderful plans! We were going to run our own school of ballroom dancing. That's why we had the studio built on at the back. What with the sprung floor and mirror walls, it cost over three hundred pounds, almost as much as the house.'

'When he comes home, you'll be able to –'

Madame Delia shook her head. 'Four winters in a freezing camp have ended his dancing days.' She poured two cups of tea and lit a cigarette. 'I've just heard that they had to amputate two of his toes. Frostbite.'

Jane shuddered as she wondered how she would feel if her fingers had to be amputated. Then her thoughts wandered.

'Jane?'

'Sorry, Madame Delia. I was miles away.'

'Anywhere in particular?'

Jane smiled. 'Devonshire, actually. Uncle Amos has Italian prisoners of war working on the farm, and they're terribly homesick. Hate our winters. I was just thinking it must be rotten to be a prisoner in another country, whatever side you're on.'

After another little silence, Madame Delia said, 'It's four years today.'

Confused, Jane tried to think what might be significant about January 1940. That had been when Jack and Betty were married. When Jack joined up.

Madame Delia went on, 'Four years since I waved goodbye to Bernard. He didn't have to go, you know.'

'Then, why ...?'

'There wasn't any future in ballroom dancing during a war. So he went in as a PT instructor. I suppose it made sense, in a way.' Picking up a candle, she went over to the cocktail cabinet, selected a bottle and poured a generous measure of tawny liquid into her teacup. 'What didn't make sense,' she continued, 'was his volunteering for overseas duty. That could have been left for the younger chaps. But he couldn't resist the chance of a bit of travel and adventure.'

'Jack's like that.'

Madame Delia refilled her cup from the teapot and the bottle. 'How's your brother getting on in India?'

'He's a staff sergeant now.'

'Does he enjoy flying gliders as much as ever?'

'Loves it. Tried desperately to get on the operation dropping supplies to the Chindits in Burma, but they only used Americans. He feels frustrated that he was one of the first volunteers and still hasn't seen any real action.'

'What is he doing, then?'

'He's part of the training unit.'

'It must be a relief to Betty.'

'Not really. She stays in bed most of the time. Leaves Mum to look after Johnny as soon as she gets home from work. And Gran has been in bed since she had the flu at Christmas, so the brunt of the work falls on Mum. It's too much for her, really.'

Madame Delia nodded, then changed the subject. 'Chuck's back on duty.'

'Has he flown again yet?'

'No. They suspended the daylight missions in October. Lost too many B-17s.' She stubbed out her cigarette. 'Such a waste. Denny and Al were barely out of their teens. And if he hadn't had appendicitis, Chuck would have gone with them.'

The proverbial blessing in disguise, Jane thought, like Jack's bout of dysentery last July.

Madame Delia poked angrily at the fire. 'Chuck was a sort of father figure to those boys.'

'It hit Rose hard.'

The dancing teacher lit another cigarette. 'Rose troubles me. I get the impression that she's disappointed in her job.'

'I think the main problem is the boss's wife. Mrs Cohen picks on Rose, probably because she's the prettiest.'

'It's a pity she couldn't get in at one of the reputable stage schools.'

'Mr McGlusky took some more photographs, but he's as bad as Mr Cohen, all promises and excuses.'

'I'm afraid I have little faith in Mr McGlusky. He's a third-rate agent. What Rose needs is the discipline of someone like Lavinia Lamont.' Madame Delia brushed cigarette ash from her trousers. 'Bernard's sister Eunice was one of the Bluebell dancers. Those girls were precision-tuned. I never tired of watching them.'

'Gosh! Did she work in Paris?'

'As far as I know, she's still there.'

'Gosh,' Jane said again. Her thoughts returned to Rose. 'Is it possible for Rose to become a film star? It's all she's ever dreamed of.'

Eventually, Madam Delia answered, 'Your sister has more talent than any other pupil I've taught. She also has the rare quality of stage presence.'

'So you do think she can make it?'

'It's very competitive out there, Jane. Most girls never get beyond the chorus line, although it's possible with a bit of luck, for a talent scout to spot a likely lass. However, she sometimes has to pay for the privilege.'

'That's what Mr McGlusky said.'

'Exactly! And the favours don't always buy success. Now, if Rose had your ability to work she'd be giving Lady Luck a helping hand. Which reminds me –' Madame Delia took a candle over to the walnut bureau – 'I've been asked if the older girls can take part in three Workers' Playtime concerts in factory canteens. I know you're busy with your studies, but can you manage the extra time?'

Jane nodded. 'I need to buy more textbooks.'

'Good. We can use the "Wonderland" opener from the pantomime, followed by Rose's "I Got Rhythm".' She scribbled on a piece of paper, then paused. 'We'll need a sing-song. Any ideas?'

Mentally, Jane ran through songs. 'I already have "Don't Sit Under the Apple Tree" and "Ma, I Miss Your Apple Pie". If we get "Apple Blossom Time" we could do a medley with a theme.'

'Good idea.' Madame Delia suddenly chuckled. 'Remember that poor kid at the Working Men's Club?'

'Christabel? I felt so sorry for her.'

'That was your audition. Over two years ago.' Madame Delia stared at Jane. 'How old are you now?'

'Sixteen in April.'

'You know, I still find it hard to believe that you and Rose are the same age.'

'Most people do.'

'You look nice when Rose makes you up for a show, but have you thought of trying a different hairstyle?'

'Rose is always trying to pin it this way or that, but there isn't an ounce of curl in my hair, and plaiting is the only way I can keep it tidy. Can't afford a perm.'

'It's time I gave you a raise. Or would you rather I paid your fares?'

'The fares would be a great help. Thank you.'

'Now, for the finale we'd better have "London Pride", and Rose can lead "There'll Always Be an England". Nice patriotic finish.' She handed the sheet of paper to Jane. 'What grade are you at now?'

'Coming up to my sixth, but I'm not sure how much longer I can keep it going, with two nights here, two at the tech, and homework. I've been seriously thinking about giving it up and doing book-keeping and calculating machines on Sunday mornings instead.'

'Sounds a bit heavy going. I thought you were keen to get your cap and gown.'

'I was. But if I'm not going to make a career out of music, it might be better to concentrate on commerce. Peter said trained comptometer operators will be in great demand after the war.'

Madame Delia locked the bureau. 'Sensible young man, Peter,' she said. 'It was a shame about his father.'

Surprised, Jane said, 'I suppose you read about it in the paper.'

'Yes. Anyway, it's none of my business. And I think people like you and Peter will get there in the end, whatever happens. You're both workers.' She picked up the tray. 'Just as long as you don't find it all too much and want to give up being my accompanist.'

'Oh, no! I like this best of all.' Jane peered at the slim marble clock on the mantelpiece. 'I must go,' she gasped.

'I was going to make another pot of tea. Can't you stay a little while?'

'Mum will be wondering what –' The shrill ring of the telephone on the bureau made them both jump. Jane took the torch into the studio and found her music and coat.

'That was your mother.' Madame Delia stood in the doorway. 'I explained what had happened.'

'Was she cross that she'd had to go out to phone? It's very cold.'

'I think she was anxious more than cross. She was trying to phone your Aunt Grace's office and Rose's shop as well. They're not home, either.'

'Oh, dear.'

'I expect it's just the trains up the creek after the air raid. Wait a moment and I'll walk to the bus stop with you.'

'Really, I'll be all right. Thank you for the tea.'

'No, please wait. I could do with some air. And I'm nearly out of cigarettes.' She flicked the light switch on and off. 'Still not working. Hold the torch a moment while I put my coat on.'

Madame Delia took back the torch to search for her handbag. As it illuminated the photograph on the display cabinet, she muttered, 'Bloody war!'

It was the first time Jane had heard the dancing teacher swear.

Chapter Fifteen

The new wave of bombing at the beginning of 1944 was persistent and disruptive. As sirens warned, buses disgorged passengers into dark streets to fend for themselves. Jane grew accustomed to walking three miles from the technical college, ducking into street shelters and emerging during a lull, eyes and ears alert, like a nocturnal animal sniffing for the hunter.

Madame Delia considered cancelling the canteen concerts, but the girls wanted to go ahead, and the factories had good shelters.

There was no doubt that the audience enjoyed the star of the first concert. They banged their knives on the tables and stamped their feet. Waiting for her music cue, Jane watched 'Sid the Spiv' move around the canteen, shrugging the enormous padded shoulders of his jacket, small brown trilby perched on the side of his head, eyes darting to see which victim to pounce on next.

'The way you're laughing, love, you might need another pair of these.' Grinning cheekily, he held up a voluminous pair of knickers. 'Talk about passion killers.' The woman screeched. 'And I've just found out that ladies are starching their brassieres to make 'em last longer.' He leaned towards the woman. 'So long as they don't expect us blokes to starch our underpants. It brings tears to me eyes just thinking about it.'

Timing the laughter perfectly, he sidled up to the plant manager. 'I've got just the thing for a man about town.' With an exaggerated glance over each shoulder, Sid reached inside his jacket. 'Interested, guv?' His voice was a hoarse whisper from behind his hand. The manager looked uncomfortable, but played the game.

'I might be,' he said.

'Might be!' Sid bellowed. 'Might be? Gawd, I've got the answer to all your prayers. In fact, I've got three hundred and sixty five of them, one for every night of the year.' The women cackled and Sid rounded on them, wagging a finger. 'Naughty, naughty,' he scolded. Then he draped an arm around the manager's shoulders. 'Now, mate, usually I won't let them out of my sight for less than a fiver. But for you ...' He slapped the man heartily on the back. 'Six quid. Cheap at half the price.' The manager grinned sheepishly. Sid shook his head. 'Bit 'ard up this week are we? Paid out too many bonuses to all these lovely workers?' The audience roared. 'Tell you wot,' Sid went on, 'seeing as how you're on hard times, you can have the lot for a quid.' He nudged the man in the ribs. 'Be prepared, I say, just like the Boy Scouts.' Again he timed the guffaws before he went on, 'When the wife's waiting for you with the rolling pin every night, what do you tell her?'

Rolling his eyes to the heavens, he took a large package from his pocket and held it high so the audience could read the printed words, *365 Tall Stories*.

As the audience began to laugh, he banged on the piano. 'Right, girlie, music time.' Jane began the introduction and Sid paced up and down. 'You all know this, so leave your spotted dick and custard, if you'll pardon the expression, loosen your corsets, and let's go. "You put your right arm in ..." '

By the time they'd finished the hokey-cokey, the audience were hoarse. Fingers poised over the keys, Jane waited for the cheers and whistles to fade, but the workers were reluctant to let him go. He blew kisses, flung his arms wide and shouted, 'You're lovely! God bless you all', before running jauntily from the room, still waving.

The opening bars of 'London Pride' were lost among the cries of 'More! More!' and the Dancettes, dressed as Pearly Kings and Queens, had to work hard to catch the attention of the audience, until Rose's entrance. In her diminutive costume, made from sheer parachute nylon and with the Union Jack draped over one bare shoulder, she drew wolf whistles from the men and envious glances from the women.

Madame Delia was right, Jane thought, her sister had marvellous stage presence and, like Sid, she knew how to play to the crowd. They stood to join her in the second chorus of 'There'll Always Be an England'. The national anthem afterwards was almost an anticlimax.

Repacking her music, Jane heard two men sniggering as they filed back to their assembly lines. 'Wouldn't mind unfurling that little blonde's flag.'

'You wouldn't be the first, not with those "come to bed" eyes.'

Jane tried to hide her disgust. How could they say such things? Was that what men thought whenever they looked at a girl? Or was there something in her sister that provoked such comments?

'Here.' Rose handed Jane a piece of music. She looked angry.

'Thanks.' Jane wondered if Rose had overheard the two men. 'Can you see "The Hokey-Cokey"? It belongs to Sid.'

'If that bloke puts his hand up my skirt once more, he'll get my knee in his crotch.'

'Who? Sid?'

'No. He hasn't got the balls.'

'Rose!'

'It's that slimy toad of a manager. He's worse than Sammy Cohen. Look out, here he comes again.'

Rose shrugged the twitching hand of the plant manager from her shoulder. 'Excuse me, I have to change,' she said.

Undaunted, he pinned her against the piano. 'Not yet, dear. I've laid on some refreshments in my office.'

Kneeling under the piano, Jane saw his hand slide up her sister's thigh. She also saw Rose's foot swivel until the heel of her tap shoe rested on the arch of his foot and heard his grunt as Rose suddenly shifted her weight.

'Was that your foot? Sorry.' Rose sidestepped as Jane stood up. The manager's face was almost purple as he tried to conceal his pain. Rose smiled sweetly at him. 'We'd love to join you in your office, wouldn't we, Jane?'

'But it's for you. You're the star,' he muttered through clenched teeth, barely glancing at Jane.

'How kind! But we couldn't have a show without a pianist,

146

could we?' Rose cooed. 'And I never go anywhere without my sister.'

His head swung towards Jane. 'You're having me on,' he said. 'You can't possibly be sisters.'

'Actually, we're twins, and quite inseparable.' Rose moved closer to Jane. 'Why don't you go with this nice man, while I get changed? Tell him about your secretarial course. He might offer you a job.'

Holding on to the piano as he rubbed his injured foot, the manager glared at Jane. 'I've just remembered,' he blustered. 'There's a meeting ...'

Jane couldn't resist the temptation. Picking up her music case, she slammed the piano lid shut. 'Was that your hand?' she said. 'Sorry.' She didn't smile, and she didn't look back.

In the dressing room, Madame Delia packed costumes into a suitcase. 'If Rose doesn't hurry, you'll miss the last bus,' she said.

'I'm here, Madame Delia.' Stripping off her costume, Rose told the story of the hapless manager with great delight. Still angry, Jane remained silent as she changed.

Madame Delia was not amused. 'You should have told me before it got out of hand, Rose,' she said. 'You know my views on that sort of thing.'

'You were busy. Don't worry, Janey and I handled it beautifully. What a team!'

'That's not the point. It's my responsibility, and I'm quite capable of dealing with anyone who oversteps the mark.'

'But –'

'I won't have my girls running around inflicting injuries on every lecherous stage-door Johnny they come across, unless they're in danger of being raped or injured, which is hardly likely in a place like this.'

'Well, he didn't invite me into his office for a cheese sandwich, that's for sure.'

'Neither did he chloroform you and drag you behind the desk.'

Huffily, Rose turned away.

Madame Delia went on. 'If any man touches you again or makes suspicious invitations, just say no quite firmly, then come straight to me, no matter how busy I am. And that goes for –'

Madame Delia's eyes rested briefly upon Jane, then scanned the other girls – 'all of you. Is that quite clear?'

A subdued chorus of 'Yes, Madame Delia' was interrupted by a familiar wail preceding the drone of engines. The factory siren blasted their eardrums. Calmly, Madame Delia took a large torch from her bag. 'Follow me, girls,' she said. 'We have to use Shelter C.'

A full moon illuminated the frosty yard with its row of shelters. Jane glanced up at the beams of crisscross lights and saw one sweep past a bomber, then return to pinpoint the aircraft. Immediately, the gunners sent a stream of shells up through the beam, straight onto target. As they watched the ball of fire spinning earthwards, Rose murmured, 'Well, they won't come back and –'

An almighty explosion from the rear of the factory lifted them both off their feet and down the steps. Jane collided with Madame Delia, who was waiting by the door. Rose landed on top of the plant manager.

'Don't make a meal of it,' she said, pushing away his arm. 'Let me get to my sister.'

Jane examined her hands, always her first fear. 'I'm OK, thanks. How about you?'

'Fine, apart from being mauled. Madame Delia, will you please ask this gentleman to keep his hands to himself?'

Rose and Jane helped the dancing teacher to her feet. Brushing the dirt from her clothes, she said tersely, 'You heard the young lady, Mr Williams.'

'I was only trying to help her up. And my hand is injured, so I couldn't –'

'It wasn't necessary to fondle her breasts. Even with one hand.'

'Are you suggesting ...?'

'No, I'm telling you. If you don't leave my girls alone, I shall make a formal complaint. You know they're all under age.'

Spluttering something unintelligible, the manager shuffled past the smirking workers.

Jane turned to Madame Delia. 'Did I hurt you?' she asked.

'No. But you didn't come off so lightly.'

Dismayed, Jane stared at the gaping hole in her trousers.

'Oh, dear,' she wailed. 'What will Mum say? She only bought these last month.'

'I think she'll be more concerned with the state of your knee. Let's have a look.'

While Madame Delia tried to stem the bleeding with a handkerchief, Rose went in search of first aid, and returned with the factory nurse, who cleaned the gash and bandaged it tightly. 'Get your mother to take you to the doctor in the morning, dear,' she said. 'You might need a couple of stitches, but this will hold for now.'

Madame Delia lit a cigarette. 'Were there many casualties?' she asked.

'It fell on the dump of empty canisters. Good job they weren't full of chemicals, or we'd all be flying up there with Jerry.' The nurse neatly tied the ends of the bandage. 'The only other casualty I've had is the boss. Got his hand shut in the piano.' She chuckled and lowered her voice. 'Pity it wasn't his dick. It could do with a rest.' She snipped the loose ends and turned back to Jane. 'There you are, dear. It'll be sore for a few days, but at least it wasn't your hands. I enjoyed your playing.'

Rose put her arm around Jane's shoulders and they huddled together for warmth, listening to the bombardment. Eventually, the factory hooter signalled a return to work.

Madame Delia and Rose helped Jane up the steps. A powerful stench almost overwhelmed them and they gazed in wonder at the multicoloured flames flickering across the sky.

'It's like the northern lights,' said one of the dancers. 'Is it dangerous?'

'No, love,' a factory worker reassured. 'Just the vapour from those empty drums. It'll burn itself out by morning. Pretty, isn't it?'

Madame Delia looked thoughtful. 'There won't be any more buses,' she said. 'Wait here, I'm going to find that comedian. He's got a taxi meeting him.'

A few minutes later, she was back. 'I told his wife you can't walk five yards on that leg, Jane, let alone five miles, and she's agreed you can share their taxi. They go past your road.'

'What about the rest of you?'

'We haven't so far to walk. Better hurry, though. Sid's getting fretful about the meter.'

The meter wasn't the only thing Sid was fretful about. As soon as Jane and Rose were in the taxi, he asked for his music. 'Too dear to give away,' he grumbled, snatching it from Jane's hand.

At her side, his wife whispered, 'Don't mind him, love. He's always tired after a performance. Does your leg hurt?'

'A bit. It's not too bad.'

'Your mum must be proud as punch, having two such talented daughters,' she said. 'When Rose sang "There'll Always Be an England", it brought a lump to my throat.'

From the front seat, Sid complained, 'I told you I was to be the last act. Bad enough having to play up to all those stupid cows in the audience, but to be ousted from the finale by a bunch of bloody schoolkids ...'

'Come on, Sid. You know they always have something patriotic at the end.'

'Not when I'm on the bill, they don't. Just you make sure it doesn't happen again.'

There was an uncomfortable silence until Jane asked Sid's wife whether she had been a performer.

'I was in the chorus when I met Sid,' she answered. '*Cinderella*, at East Ham Palace. Gave it up to be his business manager.' Her laugh was bitter.

'Do you miss it?'

'Not really. The glamour wears a bit thin after years of traipsing from one shabby digs to another. I'd have liked to have had kids, but it wasn't to be.'

Sid glanced over his shoulder. 'They don't want the story of your life. Why don't you shut your mouth and think about getting me some decent bookings?'

'Quite the Prince Charming tonight, aren't we?' she snapped back. They didn't speak again until Sid told the driver to stop at the far end of the girls' road.

'You can't drop the girls here,' Mrs Sid protested.

'Why not? I've done them a favour as it is.'

'Favour my arse. Madame Delia gave you five bob towards the fare. Turn down here, Bob.'

Mrs Harrison was waiting. 'I've been so worried.' She noticed Jane's torn trousers. 'Trust you to fall over,' she complained. 'What's that stain? Mud?'

Rose said. 'It's blood, Mum. And Janey didn't fall over. She was blown over. We both were.'

Mr Harrison stood in the living-room doorway. 'How about some cocoa, Nell?' he said. 'The girls look as if they could do with a hot drink.'

Jane limped across to the chair her father pulled out near the fire. 'What are you doing home, Dad?' she asked. 'I thought you were back on nights for a bit.'

'Swopped with Charlie Blake. His eldest girl is getting married tomorrow.' Mr Harrison picked up the coal scuttle and left the room.

For some minutes the girls sat silently, warming their hands. Then Rose said, 'What's up, Janey?'

'My knee hurts, that's all.'

'I know when something's needling you.'

'It's nothing, really. Just that incident with Mr Williams.'

'Forget it. I expect his pride was more hurt than his fingers.'

'No, not that. It was the way he looked at you. Talked to you. And you said Mr Cohen was the same.'

'That's nothing. You should have heard some of the blokes in the canteen.'

'I did. It was horrible.'

'Listen. Men are easy to handle, once you realise that they're only thinking of one thing when they look at you.'

'Not when they look at me, they're not, thank goodness.'

Rose put her head on one side. 'You're still a baby, aren't you, Janey? But you'll know what I mean when you're a bit older. Men will start looking at you. It's all part of growing up.'

'If that's what it's all about, I don't want to –' She broke off as her parents came back into the room.

Mrs Harrison's hand trembled slightly as she examined the swelling around Jane's knee. 'I'll get a couple of aspirin,' she said. 'Good job it wasn't Rose.'

'Nell!' Her husband looked shocked.

'You know what I mean. They've got another factory concert next Friday, and Rose couldn't dance with a leg like that.'

'Well, I'm thankful Jane's hands weren't injured. And I'm not sure I want the girls out at night if these raids continue.'

151

Jane touched her father's arm. 'I have to go out at night for my classes, Dad. And we're just as much at risk here.'

When the twins were in bed, Mrs Harrison put a cushion under Jane's knee. 'Best to keep it raised,' she said. 'If the siren goes again, wait for Dad and me to help you downstairs.'

Trying to get comfortable, Jane hoped the aspirin would soon ease the pain. She heard her sister softly call.

'Yes, Rose. I'm still awake.'

'Do you mind that people notice me more than you?'

'No, I'm used to it.'

'But it was different when we were little. Things hurt more when you get older, don't they?'

'I'm not jealous of you, Rose, if that's what you mean.'

'No. You've too nice a nature to be jealous. Not like me. I do rotten things without realising it. Like setting you up with Mr Williams.'

It had been a rotten thing to do, and Jane had been angry, but she knew her sister hadn't intended to be cruel. 'Try to get some sleep, Rose,' she said. 'You've got to work tomorrow morning.'

Yawning, Rose mumbled, 'And if I'm late, Old Mother Cohen will put me on shoulder pads. She knows I hate stitching fiddly ...' For a brief moment there was silence until Rose muttered, 'Damn.'

Jane didn't want to ask the question. 'How long have you been in the machine room?'

'Since we came back from Aunt Peggy's.'

'Six months! Do Mum and Dad know?'

' 'Course not. They'd only make a fuss.'

'What are you afraid of, Rose?' There was no answer, so Jane asked, 'Why are you working in the machine room?'

'Mrs Cohen moved me. She said I was insolent to a customer.'

'Were you?'

'Not so you'd notice. Mrs la-di-da Vernon couldn't make her mind up so I huffed a bit, but she didn't complain.'

'Couldn't you explain to Mr Cohen? He's supposed to be the boss.'

'Not when his wife's around, he's not. And he's the real reason I was moved.'

'I don't understand.'

'Oh, Janey, you're so ...' Rose sighed. 'I heard them arguing after she caught him putting his arm round me. He said it was just to welcome me back. She said it was the machine room for me or the sack.'

'Oh, Rose! How rotten for you!'

'It's not so bad most of the time. Working with Edna and the girls is better than having to be polite to those snooty old bitches in the salon. But Myra Cohen never takes her eagle eye off me. My stitching is better than the others' so she can't find much fault with it, but God help me if I do slip up.'

'For goodness' sake, why don't you leave?'

Rose's laugh was short. 'I've thought about it often enough. Even applied to a shoe shop, but it's on commission and all the senior staff grab the best customers, so the pay would be worse than I'm getting now.'

'You could try to get in an office.'

'Only as a general dogsbody. I can't type and I've no qualifications. And don't you dare say it.'

Jane had no intention of saying 'I told you so'. But she was concerned about her sister. 'You must tell Mum and Dad. They're the best ones to advise you.'

'I can't, Janey. Not yet.'

'They'll be much more hurt if someone else tells them.'

'Edna Browning has promised, and I know you won't tell, so there's no way they can find out.'

Jane wasn't convinced. 'Do you have any plans?' she asked.

'Mike McGlusky said something might come up at any moment, and I've left my photographs with all the theatrical agents. I know I'll get into films eventually.'

'I hope you're right, Rose. But I still think you should tell Mum and Dad.'

'I got myself into this mess, Janey. I'll get myself out of it. Then I'll tell them.'

Chapter Sixteen

After three hours in Outpatients, Jane hobbled home on crutches, a new dressing on her stitched knee. As Mrs Harrison put the key in the front door, she commented, 'I hope Betty has started dinner. Gran doesn't like to wait too long.'

There were no saucepans on the cooker. Jane glanced at her mother. It was too quiet.

In the living room Gran and Grandad stared into the meagre fire. Betty looked as though she had been crying.

'Oh, my God!' Mrs Harrison gasped. 'Have you heard something about Jack?'

'It's Dad.' Betty sniffed. 'I didn't know what to do, so I made him a cup of tea.'

'But Fred's supposed to be at work.'

'He's in the other room.'

Fred Harrison's face was ashen under the grime, his clothes torn and filthy. When he raised a hand to brush back his hair, Jane noticed his palm was bleeding. He sat hunched in a chair; the cup of tea was untouched.

'Oh, Dad! What's happened?' she asked.

His eyes were glazed, as though not really seeing her. 'They're gone,' he muttered.

Mrs Harrison knelt in front of him. Her voice was gentle as she said, 'Who's gone, Fred? Tell me about it.'

His speech was fragmented. 'All my mates. Dug for hours. Couldn't find them. Only bits.' The nightmare reflected in his eyes. 'Direct hit on the shop.'

Mrs Harrison gathered her husband into her arms as though he were a baby, holding him while he grieved for his friends.

Feeling almost guilty, Jane said a prayer of thanks that her father had changed shifts.

Fred Harrison was made foreman to replace Charlie Blake, and given a new team to train. Crutches discarded, Jane settled down to study for her final exams. She was becoming more and more concerned about her mother's health. Her hair, once her crowning glory, was more pepper and salt than ash-blonde, and her legs were a mass of protruding veins. Standing at a workbench for five hours each day didn't help. After a night punctuated by sirens, Jane suggested that her mother stay home and catch up on some sleep.

'Don't be ridiculous, Janey. I can't take time off every time there's an air raid.'

'But you're worn out, Mum. Look at yourself.' Jane turned her mother towards the mirror.

Faded blue eyes sunk in deep sockets stared back. Then Mrs Harrison shrugged. 'Your father has to go in to work, no matter what. Stop fussing, for goodness' sake.'

Jane bit back the retort that Dad didn't also have to run the home, nor look after a cantankerous parent, neurotic daughter-in-law and handicapped grandchild. There must be a way that some of her load could be eased. All day Jane mulled over a plan of campaign. Aunt Grace would be her best ally, and the others would have to make a little more effort. If they didn't, Mum would crack up.

Her fears were put to the test that afternoon. Instead of being in the kitchenette, preparing tea, her mother was sitting by the living-room fire. Her left arm was in a sling.

Gran was first to speak. 'I knew it,' she said. 'First Janey's leg. Then Fred's mates. Now this. It always comes in threes.' She became angry. 'Why didn't you jack it in when I told you? You could have lost your hand.'

'But I didn't, Gran, so don't go on about it, please.'

The old lady shook her head. 'It's no good expecting me to get supper. I can't move without coughing.'

'Janey will see to things.'

Jane noted the padded bandage around her mother's hand. 'How badly is it hurt?' she asked.

'The doctor said there's no damage to the bones. I only

155

turned round for a second, to see if the next batch of tailplates had come. It must have caught my sleeve. Next thing I knew, my hand was dragged under.' She winced.

'Oh, Mum! I was afraid something like this ... Have you had any dinner?'

'No. I felt a bit sick when they brought me home, so I lay on the bed.'

Gran said, 'Dad and I only had a drop of soup. Can you get us something, Janey? I'm famished.'

'In a minute, Gran. Where's Betty?'

'After she warmed up the soup, she buggered off round to her dad's with the boy. Didn't even wash up, lazy cow.'

Wearily, Mrs Harrison passed a hand across her forehead. 'Don't go on so, Gran. You know she gets upset at the thought of blood, so she's better out of the way.' Again she winced.

Jane asked, 'Did they give you any painkillers?'

'They're in my handbag.' Mrs Harrison began to rise, then flopped back in the chair. 'Oh, dear. My legs are all wobbly. Daft, isn't it?'

'No, Mum. You've had a nasty shock.' Jane found the tablets. 'I'll get you a glass of water before I start supper.'

There was little in the larder. Gran disliked rissoles, but the piece of beef was too tiny for anything else. Just as Jane was slicing potatoes thinly for scallops, Aunt Grace put her key in the door. Ten minutes later, a pot of tea was ready and the table laid. Rose and Betty came through the back door together.

'I met Betty on the corner and she told me.' Rose threw her scarf and gloves onto the table. 'Where's Mum? I must see her.'

'In the living room,' said Aunt Grace. 'Put your things away first, Rose. We're trying to dish up.'

Betty poured herself a cup of tea. 'I'll take this upstairs,' she said. 'Bring the pushchair in for me, Janey. I'm frozen.'

Sharply, Aunt Grace said, 'So is that child. And we're all busy. I'll give you a lift one end. Come on.'

As they heaved the pushchair into the kitchenette, Betty grumbled, 'He's hungry, as usual.'

'Then chop up one of those rissoles and a couple of scallops,' Aunt Grace retorted. 'There's gravy in the saucepan. How was your dad?'

'I really don't know why I bother to visit him. He just sits looking at Mum's photo albums and crying. Keeps saying he wishes he was dead. He's so depressing.'

Jane glanced sideways at Aunt Grace and saw her lips twitch.

As expected, Gran complained about the rissoles. Surprisingly, it was Grandad who told her to shut up and eat. Too shocked to argue, Gran just stared at him.

'Nell's got enough to put up with,' he said. 'And don't forget, she was the only one who had the presence of mind to switch off that drill, while everyone else was trying to drag her hand away.' He pulled a handkerchief from his pocket and blew his nose. 'I reckon our girl's a bloody heroine,' he went on. 'And the least we can do is to make things easier for her, not worse.'

Aunt Grace smiled. 'That's right, Dad. If we all pull our weight a little bit more, Nell will recover quicker. Jane and I have just been talking about it.'

'I'll be all right in a day or two, Grace.' Nell Harrison looked uncomfortable. 'And Janey's quite capable of holding the fort. Or she ought to be, at her age.'

'Of course she is, but it's not fair to leave it all to her.' Aunt Grace looked around the table. 'There's enough of us here to share the chores.'

Gran looked horrified. 'And what am I supposed to do, with my cough and bad legs? Scrub the floor?'

Aunt Grace pushed a plate towards her mother. 'You can cut up Nell's food. That'll be a great help.'

Grandad asked, 'Is there anything I can do, Grace?'

'Yes, Dad. Keep the papers tidy and see to the fires.'

'He can't carry the scuttle when it's full,' her sister protested.

'I can manage it half-full,' Grandad said.

'Good for you.' Aunt Grace turned to Betty. 'You'll have to look after Johnny, and clean your own room.'

'But –'

'One day you'll have a whole house to clean. Might as well start getting used to it.'

Nell Harrison smiled wryly, 'Looks like you've got it all planned out, Grace.'

'It was Jane's idea. She was worried about you. We're going to tackle the washing on Saturdays between us.'

Rose spoke for the first time. 'What can I do?' she asked.

Her mother smiled. 'You're on your feet all day, dear, so we wouldn't expect too much from you. And you work Saturday mornings.'

'So do I,' Aunt Grace said, tartly. 'And Jane has her studies, night classes and rehearsals. If we're prepared to pitch in, I'm sure Rose will. After all, she often goes out dancing, despite having been on her feet all day.'

Rose avoided Jane's eyes as she said, 'Of course I don't mind. Shall I do the other bedrooms?'

Mrs Harrison picked up her fork. 'That's very good of you, Rose.' She looked at the scallops. 'I hope you didn't use up all the lard ration, Janey. I was saving that to make a pie.'

Later that evening, Jane reminded Rose that she should tell her parents about her change of job.

'I know I should, Janey. And I felt awful downstairs when Mum was being so nice to me. But I can't. Not yet.'

'You've got to do it some time, Rose. Get it over and done with, for goodness' sake.'

'Not while Mum is hurt. It would only make her feel worse.'

'How do you think she'll feel if she finds out from soneone else?'

'I'll tell her as soon as she's a bit better. Stop worrying. There's no possible way she can find out.'

Jane hoped her sister was right, but the fear remained with her as their 16th birthday approached and still Rose said nothing. The raids were diminishing and Mrs Harrison's hand slowly healing, so a family tea party was arranged on the actual day. Rose was bringing Edna Browning home, and Jane invited Kathleen O'Connor. The young Irish girl was a frequent visitor and the only one, apart from Jack and Desmond, who seemed able to communicate with Johnny. Gently she talked to him, encouraged him to say 'Please' and 'Ta', instead of grunting. Even Gran admitted that the girl had the patience of a saint, and Grandad said she was the prettiest child he'd seen, apart from Rose, of course.

When they arrived home from school, Auntie Vi and Peter

were in the living room. 'I've just been telling your mother she ought to claim compensation,' Auntie Vi said.

Mrs Harrison frowned. 'Not if that wretched shop steward has anything to do with it. He keeps coming round here, talking about bringing everyone out on strike. All I want to do is forget it. Dr Norman said I can't work on machinery again, anyway.'

'You're a fool, Nell. But then you always were. When are we having tea?'

'Not till Grace and Rose are home, and Rose doesn't leave work till six. Such a long day for her. Janey, when you've hung up the coats, will you make a cup of tea, to keep us going? Don't forget to warm the pot. And make sure the kettle's boiling properly.'

Peter followed Jane into the kitchenette. 'Why does she do it?' he asked.

'Do what?'

'Talk about Rose as though she's God's gift.'

'She is, as far as Mum is concerned.'

'But she either ignores or nags you. I noticed it when I lived here, but it's getting worse. It's straight out of "Cinderella".'

Jane laughed as she set the cups on a tray. 'Except in this case, Cinderella is the ugly sister.'

'It's not funny Janey. Why don't you stick up for yourself? Doesn't it hurt you?'

Frowning, Jane poured boiling water into the pot. 'Yes,' she admitted. 'But I know Mum doesn't mean to hurt. It's just her way.'

'But it's so unfair.'

'Life hasn't exactly been fair to Mum, either,' she reminded him. 'And she doesn't complain, so how can I?' Changing the subject, Jane held out her hand. 'Do you like my present from Aunt Peggy and Uncle Joe?'

'That's terrific.' Peter bent over the gold signet ring set with a small garnet. 'And it's engraved with your initial. Did Rose have one, too?'

'Mmm. And we've vowed not to take them off, ever.'

Laura Marshall bought Jane several pieces of sheet music. 'The Warsaw Concerto!' Jane exclaimed. 'How did you know I wanted that? And Rose loves records.'

'I hope she likes Frank Sinatra.'

'They say he's going to be a big star.' Jane found Glenn Miller's 'American Patrol' and wound up the portable gramophone. Soon, everyone was clapping as Desmond supported Johnny, and Kathleen moved his weak leg backwards and forwards in time to the rhythm.

As the music faded, Peter glanced out of the window, an anxious expression on his face. 'It's a telegraph boy.'

The plain envelope was addressed to Betty. Jane moved closer to her mother as her sister-in-law read the single sheet of paper. She knew what Betty would say before the words came.

'It's Jack,' she whispered. 'He's missing. Believed killed.'

Jane grabbed her mother and motioned to Peter to pull the armchair forward. For once Gran did the right thing and produced a bottle of smelling salts.

Betty sat in the chair, clutching the telegram. Suddenly, as though sensing her distress, Johnny whimpered. Kathleen lifted him into her arms and took him through to the kitchenette as his mother began to scream.

Laura Marshall stood up. 'Help me to get her upstairs,' she asked Peter.

It took all their strength to drag the hysterical girl out into the hall. The screams built in intensity, reminding Jane of the night when Betty had been in labour. Then came the sound of a sharp slap, followed by silence, eventually broken by deep sobs.

In the sideboard, Jane found the bottle of brandy, hoarded to celebrate victory. She poured a little into a glass and gave it to Lawrence to take upstairs. Then she held another glass to her mother's lips. Some of the spirit trickled down Mrs Harrison's chin, but she swallowed enough to make her splutter and push Jane's hand away.

'I want Fred,' she mumbled. 'And Rose.' Her head fell back against the chair and her eyes closed.

Auntie Vi asked Jane, 'Will they let your dad come home if I phone the Arsenal?'

Good idea. The number's on that piece of paper behind the clock.'

After a few minutes, Laura Marshall and Peter came downstairs. 'She's calmer now,' Mrs Marshall said. 'Just crying quietly. The brandy helped.' She reached for the bottle. 'Your grandparents should have a nip.'

They sat quietly in their armchairs, but Gran's eyes were full of tears and Grandad's hands shaking. After Gran had sipped her brandy, she murmured, 'First his father, then his brother, now Jack. All before their time.'

Grandad moaned, 'I wish I could change places with him. I've had my life. Jack's hadn't even started.'

'Don't, Grandad! Please don't.' Kneeling, Jane stroked his hand. 'We don't know for sure that Jack is dead,' she said. 'They automatically send that telegram first, but he may be a prisoner, or hurt somewhere.' She looked at Mrs Marshall. 'How can we find out what happened?'

'As next-of-kin, Betty will have to make the enquiries. I'll find out what I can tomorrow. But you're right, of course. Jack probably is still alive. We must pray.'

Jane realised that this must be bringing back distressing memories to Mrs Marshall. Then she remembered Rose. What a ghastly birthday present for her!

She became aware of the solemn ticking of the clock. Where was Auntie Vi? It shouldn't have taken so long to make one phone call.

But Auntie Vi had made more than one phone call. When she finally reappeared, there was a flush on her cheeks, almost of excitement.

'Fred is on his way home,' she said. 'And I thought Rose ought to know as well. After all, Nell was calling for her, and the telephone number was on the back of that piece of paper.' Jane felt sick as she realised what her aunt was about to divulge. 'And guess what?' Making the most of her moment, Auntie Vi waited until she had everyone's attention. 'Rose doesn't work in the shop any more.'

Nell Harrison sat forward, her eyes upon her sister.

'She's in the machine room. Has been for some time.' Auntie Vi took off her hat and fluffed her hair. 'Didn't you know?'

Chapter Seventeen

Exactly a week after the Allies invaded Normandy, Jane and Rose were awakened by a single plane. But it was not the familiar sound of a British plane they heard, nor the distinctive fluctuating drone of a German bomber. In fact, they had never heard this peculiar engine before. Both girls rushed to peek behind the blackout.

'Oh, my God,' Jane gasped. 'It's on fire!'

In a sky not yet lit by dawn, the flame streaked like a comet towards London.

Rose gripped Jane's shoulder. 'That was no ordinary plane. Not sounding like that.'

Heart pounding, Jane pushed the blackout back into place. 'What on earth was it?' she asked.

A quiet voice said, 'I can tell you.' Aunt Grace stood in the doorway. 'Come downstairs.'

When the family had gathered in the living room, she explained that they had just seen Hitler's long-threatened secret weapon. A pilotless plane, filled with high explosives. When it ran out of fuel, the plane would go into its final dive.

Fred Harrison broke the long silence after she'd finished speaking. 'How do you know all this?' he asked.

'We were warned last month that this type of weapon might be used.'

'You never said a word.'

'I was sworn to secrecy by the ARP warden. He wanted us to be prepared for extra duty.' Aunt Grace tucked a stray curler under her hairnet. 'I kept hoping it was just another rumour.'

'Are they planning to send many of these over, Grace?'

'I don't know. We can only hope that our troops will reach the sites in France soon.'

Grandad looked bewildered. 'Aeroplanes without pilots. It can't be possible. Can it?'

Devoid of teeth, Gran's mouth sank between nose and chin. 'This is what comes of going against nature,' she declared. 'If we'd been meant to fly, we'd be born with wings. I always said it, and always will.'

The whole concept reminded Jane of H. G. Wells's *The War of the Worlds*. Anxiously, she asked, 'How will we be able to shoot them down? They go so fast. And it wasn't very big.'

'About half the size of a fighter plane, I believe.' Aunt Grace smiled at Jane. 'We'll find some way of stopping them, dear, I'm sure.'

They came in their hundreds. Night and day. Nicknames were promptly given to the missile: flying bombs, buzz-bombs, doodlebugs. Jane grew to detest the evil little monsters more deeply than anything else she had experienced.

When little Johnny began wetting himself every time he heard the distinctive sound, Betty fled to the arms of Aunt Peggy. Uncle Herbert offered a safe home to his parents and Gran almost weakened, but decided she would rather face Hitler's wrath than Auntie Dolly's. And Madame Delia was forced to suspend her dancing classes.

Jane tried to convince herself that she would become accustomed to the new onslaught, but the fear wouldn't go away. Like a dark shadow, it was there. She was always listening. At home, she did the Hoovering as quickly as possible, fearing what the noise might mask. Hurrying along the streets, she kept her ears strained to catch the first wail of a siren or distant rattle of a V-1's engine. Even worse was the silence after the engine cut out, when she flung herself to the ground and counted the seconds, heard the whoosh overhead, felt the ground judder as the missile reached its destination. And whenever she saw a plume of smoke, she would pray it was not her home, not her family.

At school, all pupils were moved to the ground floor, the long corridor tightly packed with desks and barricaded with sandbags. Nothing was allowed to interrupt the process of matriculation. After four explosions, too close for comfort,

Jane doubted she would ever finish her maths paper, and Peter's helpful advice vanished from her mind as she listened to the fifth approach. Two desks in front, Daphne Jarvis's shaking hand knocked over a bottle of ink. Watching the weeping girl trying to blot the stains from her exam papers, Jane felt physically sick.

As soon as the bell rang and her uncompleted papers were collected, Jane grabbed her hat and blazer. She knew she should have stayed to comfort Daphne, but she was too distraught to be of any help.

Her father was in the kitchenette, lighting the gas under the kettle.

'Nice timing, dear. I'm just making a cuppa. How was it?'

At first the words wouldn't come. Only the tears. Eventually, Jane was able to control her sobs, sip the tea her father pushed in front of her, and talk. She told him of her fears and the disastrous exam. She told him she couldn't see the point of continuing.

He didn't interrupt. Just rolled a cigarette and listened intently as the frustrations were allowed to flow.

'I'm so fed up. Dad. Here I am working like a slave for my future, and I don't even know if I'm going to have a future.'

She paused to wipe her eyes, wondering what her father was thinking. After a while, he asked, 'What exams are you taking tomorrow?'

'English grammar and French oral. I hate oral tests.'

'But you like English grammar, and it's the most useful one of all if you're going to be a secretary.'

Bitterly she cried, 'It won't be of much use to me if I'm blown to pieces. At least Rose gets to have a bit of fun. I don't even have time to go to the pictures.'

At the mention of her sister, his brow furrowed. Jane knew he had been bitterly hurt by Rose's deception over her job. Just like Mr Edwards in Norfolk, her father expected total honesty from his family.

He was speaking again. 'Have you talked to anyone else about this? Teachers? Aunt Grace? Mum?' Jane shook her head and looked for a dry patch on her handkerchief. 'You might be in for a surprise if you did.'

'What do you mean, Dad?'

'Has it ever occurred to you that they might all be feeling the same?'

Jane was shocked. 'Of course not. They're much stronger than me. And braver. Otherwise they wouldn't be able to carry on as though nothing was happening.'

'But inside, Jane, they're just as scared. The teachers probably wonder whether they'll be around to mark homework. Aunt Grace types letters that might not arrive. Your mother polishes a house that could be demolished.'

'Why do they bother?'

Mr Harrison smiled wryly. 'What choice do they have?'

'I have a choice, Dad. I can get a job in one of the factories and earn more than I ever could as a typist.'

'True. But I don't think you will.'

'Why not?'

'Because one day this war is going to end. Some people won't live to see that day, but suppose you're one of the lucky ones who survive. What then?' He leaned across the table and took her hands. 'You'd be wasted on an assembly line,' he said. 'Your exam results show that you're a very good typist.'

'There'll be lots of good typists coming out of the services,' Jane cried. 'It's going to be too competitive.'

'Exactly. And those who get the good jobs will be those who have the edge. Those with more certificates.'

'Rita Brooks had certificates. She only gets twenty-four shillings a week as a filing clerk.'

'To start with. And she's gaining experience.'

'But her sister has no qualifications at all, and she gets two pounds ten at Fords.'

The steaming kettle reminded Mr Harrison he needed another cup of tea. 'And she'll still be earning two pounds ten next year, and the year after. I wonder what Rita Brooks will be earning when she's a qualified secretary? Wasn't that what you had in mind, once upon a time?'

Jane watched as her father added tea to the pot. 'A time before flying bombs,' she said, quietly. 'I'm scared, Dad. And I don't know what to do.'

He kissed the top of her head. 'You said Sandy's coming home at the weekend. Have a word with him. He's in the same boat, and you've always respected his opinion.'

It was true. But it wouldn't help Jane to get through to the weekend.

'I respect your opinion even more, Dad. What do you think I should do?'

'I think you should go to school tomorrow, and do the best you can. Then see how you feel about the next day.'

Jane stirred her tea. 'Would you be very disappointed if I gave it all up?'

Mr Harrison thought for a long moment before he said, 'I've always had the feeling that one of my girls would amount to something. And to be honest, Jane, I hoped it would be you.'

Uncle Len's laugh was unmistakable. Jane heard it before she saw his cap on the hall stand. It was good to hear Gran and Grandad chuckling. But Uncle Len looked different. The stocky figure was much thinner, his hair completely grey. One thing hadn't changed, though: his bear hug was as strong as ever.

'Christ, Janey,' he exclaimed. 'You're nearly as tall as me.'

'Language, Len. Language,' his sister reproved.

'Sorry, Nell. But I can't get over it. What have you been doing? Putting manure in her shoes?'

'Whatever it is, I wish she wasn't such a beanpole. I can't keep up with her clothes. But wait until you see Rose. She's the image of Carole Landis.'

Later, when he followed her into the kitchenette, Uncle Len asked Jane how her exams were going. 'It can't be easy, trying to concentrate while those bastards keep chucking their latest filth at you. Sorry, Janey.'

'I call them some pretty wicked names myself, sometimes. When Mum's not around.' Jane shrugged.

'How long has Nell had that funny twitch in her eye?'

'Since the telegram about Jack.'

'Let's hope he's a prisoner,' he said, then changed the subject. 'I suppose you'll be going out to work soon, like Rose. Got a job lined up?' Jane shook her head. 'You'll do all right. At least you know what you want to do. Wish I did.'

Amazed, Jane stared at him. 'I thought you only ever wanted to be at sea.'

166

'So did I, love.' He looked thoughtful. 'Thirty years is a long time. And I don't know that I want to go back to being a steward on a cruise liner when this lot's over.'

'Why ever not?'

'I'm nearly forty-eight. Sailed the world a few times, but never had a home of my own. A family ...' His voice trailed, then he said, 'It's time I started thinking about something different.'

'Why don't you ask Uncle Nobby? He seems to have settled in to shore life. And now he's in charge of the seamen's hostel, he might be able to put in a word for you.'

After a pause, Uncle Len said, 'We'll see.' Another pause, then he asked, 'Have you seen Laura Marshall lately?'

'Not since my birthday. Her brother is having another series of operations so she spends quite a bit of time with him.'

'Do they ...?' He cleared this throat. 'Does Nobby still take her to concerts and things?'

'He visits her brother in hospital. But she's pretty busy with her canteen, feeding the rescue workers.'

'She's quite a woman, is Laura.'

As he emptied the teapot, Jane realised, from the expression on his face, that her favourite uncle was not just infatuated with Laura. He truly loved her. If only she could bring them together, Jane thought.

Her mother came into the room. 'I've moved Grace's things in with the girls, so you can have Betty's bed,' she said to her brother. As she noticed the sink, her smile changed to a frown and her voice sharpened. 'Janey! How many more times do I have to tell you not to empty the pot in there?'

Quickly, Uncle Len said, 'That was me, Nell. Sorry.'

'Oh. But Janey should have stopped you. She knows Fred wants the tea leaves for his roses. The girl's got a head like a sieve.'

Uncle Len looked troubled as his sister left the room. Then he asked Jane, 'Is she often like that?'

'Yes. But only with me.' Jane threw down the tea towel and fled to her bedroom.

When her tears ceased, she sat on the bed, thinking deeply. Her mother would criticise, whatever she decided. So she might as well stop worrying about trying to please everyone else, and think about herself for a change.

Even at the end of a day in the machine room, Rose managed to look glamorous, her fluffy pageboy bob bouncing on her shoulders, face-framing sweeps held in place with small combs, glistening lipstick matching her nail varnish. After the hug, Uncle Len held her at arm's length, smiling.

'Always said you'd grow up to be a real beauty, Rose. You ought to be a model, like Laura Marshall. Why don't you ask her how to go about it?'

Rose laughed. 'I have, Uncle Len. But she knew the right person at the right time. It's not so easy now. Anyway, I'm going to be a film star. All I need is a lucky break.' She kicked off her shoes. 'At least Old Mother Cohen will soon be too busy to keep nagging us.'

'How's that, love?'

'The girl in the office is leaving next month.' Rose turned to her sister. 'Fancy putting in for it, Janey?

It would be nice to work with Rose. But Mrs Cohen sounded dreadful. And there'd be fares to pay out of a meagre wage packet. 'I'll have to think about it.'

'Don't blame you for not jumping up and down. It's a crummy place to work. But if you're interested, just say the word.' Rose jumped up. 'I'm going over to the Palais with Edna after supper. Want to come, Uncle Len?'

'Not with my two left – Good God!' As Aunt Grace appeared in the doorway, brother and sister stared at each other. She was paler than usual, and her forehead and leg were bandaged.

'It was in the Aldwych,' Aunt Grace explained. 'I'd had lunch with Nobby at the Strand Palace and was on my way to the Law Courts when the wretched thing cut out.'

'We heard it come down,' Rose said.

Aunt Grace shook her head. 'Most of the people who ran into the Air Ministry were killed.'

Mrs Harrison filled her sister's teacup. 'Why didn't you come straight home, Grace?'

'These cuts are only superficial, Nell. And Mr Grierson needed a brief typed, ready for court tomorrow. That's if there's a court still standing.' Her voice was tearful as she said, 'Sometimes I wonder why I bother.'

Grandad said, 'You're just shaken up, girl. What you need is a drop of brandy.'

'It's not only today, Dad. It's everything.' Aunt Grace groped in her pocket for a handkerchief. 'A few years ago we enjoyed life, singing around the piano, daft games at Christmas, a week in Margate every summer. Now look at us.'

Nobody said anything.

'Len has seen things that will give him nightmares for the rest of his life,' Aunt Grace went on. 'So has Fred. Mum and Dad have lost their home, and Nell ...' She stared hard at her sister. 'You were the one with the looks. Now you just look worn out. You should be playing with your grandchildren, not looking after a houseful like this, and worrying about your son in some distant jungle.'

Gran muttered, 'And if he's still alive.'

The spoon clattered from Mrs Harrison's hand. 'Don't, Gran,' she whispered. 'I can't bear it.'

Aunt Grace drew a deep breath. 'That's what I mean,' she said. 'How much longer are we expected to "grin and bear it"? I can't even advise Janey about a career, because I don't know what to do about my own. When Edgar was killed, I settled for being a spinster and thought if I got to be supervisor of the typing pool I would be satisfied.' Slowly she shook her head. 'This might shock you, but I wish I could do something exciting with my life while I still have the chance. Nell, I will have a glass of brandy, please. And make it a large one.'

Slowly, Rose began to clap. 'Well said, Aunt Grace. My sentiments exactly.'

Tight-lipped, Mrs Harrison took the brandy bottle and a glass from the sideboard. 'I get fed up as well, Grace. Sometimes I wish I could run away and never come back. But, unlike you, I've got no choice.'

Taking the glass, Aunt Grace quietly said, 'I know. And it doesn't make me feel any better.'

The words stuck in Jane's mind for days. She had always felt that she would follow in her aunt's footsteps. But perhaps she should think again.

Marriage wasn't really on the cards. Even if she met someone she liked enough, once they had seen Rose they wouldn't look twice at her twin. And once she had seen them lusting after Rose, she would go off them, anyway.

But was it really worth years of study to end up taking dictation all morning and typing all afternoon? There had to be something better.

She watched Rose twirl in front of the mirror, wearing a new powder-blue dress, and thought how things had changed since she'd left school. No more little confidential chats at bedtime, sharing thoughts and dreams.

Rose wasn't the only one living in a world Jane couldn't yet understand. Once upon a time, she had felt quite comfortable with Bill and Sandy, despite the gap in ages. But now Bill was in uniform, and Sandy at King's College Hospital. When they talked about their new experiences, Rose understood the jokes and jargon, whereas Jane felt like a child listening in to the grown-ups. They tried to include her, but she didn't feel part of the foursome any more, and usually it was Rose who went out with Bill or Sandy.

When Rose had gaily tripped off to her third dance that week, Jane scowled at her own reflection and pulled at her plait. No wonder she was treated like a child. But the local hairdresser was hopeless with a pair of scissors, and Jane couldn't afford to go to Ilford and pay Maison Andre's prices. She wasn't earning anything from Madame Delia at the moment.

Suddenly she became angry. Very angry. She'd done everything her parents had expected, worked hard in school and out, but it was always Rose who was given the extra clothing coupons for pretty clothes, five shillings towards a dress, time off from chores to enjoy herself. It wasn't fair. For the first time, Jane was fed up with being the plain one.

Perhaps the answer was to find a job that paid well, even if it was in a factory. At least then she could buy some decent clothes, save for a holiday after the war. Not Margate, not even Torquay – somewhere exotic. Paris? Why not? If Mrs Marshall could go to Paris, and Madame Delia could go to Paris, then Jane Harrison could go to Paris.

The local paper was strewn across Rose's bed, left when she had finished checking the films on general release.

Jane turned the page and began to read the Situations Vacant column.

The V-1s were particularly active on Sunday morning, and tempers frayed. Nell Harrison's apple pie burned while she

170

was in the shelter. Rose smudged her nail varnish. Jane was secretly trying to write a letter of application for a job. Aunt Grace was called out for extra Red Cross duty. And their visitors were not only late, but Uncle Arthur insisted on going for a quick one with the menfolk, dinner ready or not.

If Uncle Len hadn't brought back a couple of bottles of Guinness, Jane felt sure her mother wouldn't have talked to any of them for the rest of the day. As it was, the atmosphere was decidedly frigid until Kathleen O'Connor arrived, wearing an obviously home-made 'Sunday best' frock. Her anxious little face scanned the living room.

'Glory be! You've got company. And here's me thinking it was this Sunday I was to come to tea.'

Jane laughingly assured Kathleen that it was indeed the right day, and introduced her to Uncle Len, who flirted outrageously with the girl, confessing that he'd seen some pretty colleens in his time, but none could match those glorious violet eyes. 'If only I was thirty years younger,' he sighed. 'Bet you're the apple of your daddy's eye.'

'Oh, no. That's Bridget, the darling child. She's the baby of the family. At least until next month.'

'Do you have many brothers and sisters?'

Kathleen counted her fingers. 'There's eight including me. Soon it'll be nine, God willing.'

Uncle Len whistled. 'That's a lot of mouths to feed.'

'Me mam's the happiest woman in the world. And Granny O'Connor says each new babe is a blessing from the Lord.' Kathleen grinned. 'Thanks be there's something they agree about, especially now Da's not around to keep the peace.'

'Is your father in the forces?'

'No, he's a steel fixer. He's been working down south on the new floating harbours.'

'The Mulberry?'

'That's right. So there's extra money coming in from the overtime and all. He's promised Mam a new dress as soon as the baby's born. Said she's not to go to the markets, but a good shop in the West End, like C & A's, Selfridges even. She's that pleased.'

'Sounds like he's very fond of your mother.'

'Do you know what he did yesterday? Told the foreman he

was taking the weekend off, jumped on a train and turned up, large as life, with a great bunch of roses. He'd only knocked on someone's door and asked if he could buy some of the flowers from their garden!'

'Weren't you expecting him?'

'Not at all. But he was worried about us with the buzz-bombs and all. Last night he took her to see *Frenchman's Creek*. Me mam reads Daphne Du Maurier over and over.' Kathleen smiled. 'And this morning we all went to Mass together. They wouldn't let me mam take the sacrament, of course, her being a Protestant, but it was lovely that the priest allowed her to sit with us.'

Gently, Uncle Len touched her cheek. 'If the others are anything like you, your dad's a very lucky man.'

Jane and Kathleen were playing rummy with Uncle Len and Grandad when the siren went again. And again. And again. Mrs Harrison suggested that Kathleen stay overnight. 'Your mother agreed it was safer than walking home if the raids were bad. Good job Vi went home straight after tea.'

Rose turned from the mirror. 'If I come in with you, Mum, Kathleen can have my bed. I shouldn't be too late.'

'You're not going out tonight, Rose. Not with those doodle-bugs coming over all the time.'

'Oh, Mum! You know I've been longing to see *Coney Island*.'

'I'm sorry, Rose. Your father made me promise before he went to work.'

'But it's got Caesar Romero in it. He's so dreamy. Go on, Mum. Don't be mean. Dad needn't know.'

Quietly, Uncle Len said, 'Take your Mum's advice, Rose. Hitler's really blasting us with them today. Talk of the devil, here's another ...'

There was no time to reach the shelter, so they dived under the nearest piece of furniture. The explosion was close enough to rattle the china in the sideboard, but there was no damage.

Jane peered at her mother, still on her knees under the gate-legged table. 'You all right, Mum?'

'No, I'm not all right.' Mrs Harrison was peeved. 'Just look at my knitting.'

The half-knitted sleeve of a child's jersey unravelled as Mrs Harrison tried to untangle the ball of wool.

'How on earth did you manage to get it around all those legs?' Jane laughed.

Her mother was not amused. 'If you think it's so funny, try sorting it out. Just don't lose any more stitches.' She pointed a finger at Rose. 'And you needn't finish doing your hair. You're staying in for once, and that's that.'

There was little sleep to be had that night. Rose was only persuaded to go to work by the knowledge that her father would soon be home.

Kathleen was anxious about her best dress. 'I don't want to get ink on it,' she told Jane as they hurried through the school gate. 'If I run all the way, do you think there'll be time to go home dinnertime and change?'

Jane's attention was caught by two prefects standing at the door. They were looking for someone.

'Kathleen O'Connor? Miss Bellinger would like to see you straight away, please.'

'Mother of God, now what have I done?' The Irish girl looked anxiously at Jane.

'Perhaps your mother needs you. She's near her time.'

The relief showed on Kathleen's face. 'It could be at that. Granny O'Connor can't manage all the little ones on her own.'

Halfway through the second verse of 'For those in peril on the sea', the prefect came back into the hall, looked along the rows of fifth-form pupils, and beckoned Jane. Miss Bellinger wanted to see her. She didn't know why.

When the prefect quietly knocked, then opened the door at a soft command, Jane drew in a sharp breath. Eyes closed, her skin pallid, Kathleen lay on the floor, supported by Miss Bellinger. There were tears in the eyes of the headmistress.

Suddenly, Jane knew it was not the baby. The news that had caused Kathleen to faint must be bad. Very bad indeed.

'All of them?' Aunt Grace whispered. 'It can't be true.'

Rose made a little gasping sound and sat down.

Mrs Harrison gulped. 'A direct hit on the shelter.'

'Where is Kathleen now?'

'Upstairs. I had to call Dr Norman in. He's given her a sedative.'

'She didn't have to identify the bodies, did she?'

173

'There weren't any to identify.' Mrs Harrison's voice was choked.

'Oh, God!' Rose began to weep. 'I couldn't bear it if it was my family,' she cried. 'Not to have them go like that. As if they'd never existed. It's too cruel.'

Jane turned away from the hatch. She had to keep busy. Try not to think about the enormous hole she had seen in the back garden. All that remained of a gloriously scatterbrained, generous, loving Irish family.

Even Gran only picked at her supper. Halfway through the meal, Kathleen came downstairs. She looked as though she was sleepwalking. 'I'd like to see the priest.' Her voice was flat and lifeless. 'Light a candle. Arrange things.'

With no bodies to bury, just two sacks, they hadn't given a thought to a funeral. Uncle Len broke the silence. 'I'll go with you first thing in the morning,' he said. The girl nodded. 'Kathleen,' he went on, 'you were so shocked, I took it upon myself to ask the police to try and trace your relatives.'

'Both families disowned us. For marrying into another faith. They won't ...' Abruptly, Kathleen stopped, staring at a library book on the mantelpiece, her expression anguished.

Following her gaze, Aunt Grace took the book and opened it. '*The Loving Spirit*,' she murmured. 'Daphne Du Maurier's first book. Jane brought it back with her.'

'Me mam said it was the most beautiful book she'd ever read.' A tear slowly rolled down Kathleen's cheek. 'She said the ending was sad, but happy at the same time. I didn't understand what she meant. I still don't.'

Aunt Grace drew the girl down onto her lap. 'The woman in the book was like your mother. She loved her family dearly and held them together, despite all the conflict. And her son carved her likeness as a figurehead on a boat, so that when she died, her loving spirit would always be there.'

Kathleen bowed her head. Then she looked up at Aunt Grace, the tiniest of smiles breaking through the tears. 'Now I understand,' she said.

On Friday, after the Requiem Mass, Uncle Len returned to his ship, and Aunt Grace moved back to the small bedroom, sharing it with Kathleen.

Several letters dropped onto the mat on Saturday morning. One, from the Irish Garda, confirmed that they were doing their best to trace relatives of the orphan child. Laura Marshall offered sympathy and help. A long, newsy letter from Aunt Peggy suggested bringing the dear little Irish maid to stay. And she'd made an appointment for Betty to take the poor little toad to the hospital, in the hope they would help him to walk better.

Betty's letter had been posted later. She'd heard at last from Jack's commanding officer, confirming that Staff Sergeant Taylor had not been instructed to fly behind enemy lines. An investigation was in progress, but so far had thrown no light on the matter. It was known that some Allied crews had been taken prisoner. Unfortunately, the Japanese were not cooperating with the International Red Cross and names were not released. He would communicate again with Mrs Taylor if further news was to hand.

Among the post, there was also a small brown envelope that Jane managed to slip quickly into her dressing-gown pocket. It was from the plant manager of a factory that made aircraft instruments. On Monday week she was to begin work on the assembly line.

Chapter Eighteen

Was this how Rose had felt? Like a criminal? Jane stared at the letter, remembering how she'd gone straight from school to the interview instead of a music lesson.

The manager had been polite enough, and she'd passed the aptitude test. It was the way the women had stared at her, not merely curious, but hostile. And their language, above the amplified *Music While You Work*, was foul. Could she really work in that atmosphere?

Perhaps she should have confided in Rose. But it would have been difficult, after the way she'd criticised her for being secretive. No, she would have to face her parents.

It was worse than she had anticipated. Mrs Harrison was shocked beyond belief. She could not bring herself to look at such a disloyal daughter, she declared. After all their sacrifices to give her a decent education, to go behind their backs like that! What on earth would the neighbours say? At first, Jane had almost decided to turn down the job, but the more her mother ranted and raved, the more appealing the offer became.

Eventually, Mrs Harrison announced that she was too disgusted to listen to any more, and left the room, instructing her husband to talk sense into the girl.

After reading the letter again, Fred Harrison said, 'We need to talk about it.'

Jane was never sure whether it was nerves or bravado that made her say, 'Oh, so I'm going to be allowed to talk, am I?'

'That's enough, Jane.' Her father's voice was angry. 'Sit down.'

'Sorry, Dad. But Mum didn't let me get a word in edgeways.'

'Your mother was very upset. So am I. Why didn't you tell us you'd gone after a job? At least we could have discussed it.'

Jane shrugged. 'I knew you'd try and talk me out of it. And I didn't know whether I'd get it or not.'

'But why this job?'

'I told you the other day. I can earn a decent wage straight away.'

Frowning, he studied her face. 'I never dreamed you were serious. I thought you were just fed up with exams.'

'I'm fed up with everything. Studies. The war.' Her voice rose. 'And most of all, I'm fed up with Rose getting away with murder and me being the one who gets nagged all the time.'

Elbows on the table, Mr Harrison rested his chin on his hands. Then he raised his head. 'I do understand,' he said with a sigh. 'But throwing everything away to work in a factory won't solve things.'

'Maybe not. But at least I'll have more money of my own. And time to go out if I want to.'

'Look, why don't you get a job in an office and have a rest from your studies for a while? It won't be so much money to start with, but you'd have your evenings free.'

'Wouldn't work, Dad. They'd insist I get more qualifications if I was going to be anything other than a filing clerk for the rest of my life.'

'Then complete the course and see how you feel after that.'

'You're asking too much of me.' Jane felt desperate. 'I can't face another two years' slog.'

Mr Harrison pushed his chair back. 'Do you know the real reason Mum and I are so upset? Not just because neither of our daughters is putting their education to good use. But because both of them were deceitful about it.' The pain on his face was almost more than Jane could bear. 'Rose was bad enough,' he went on. 'But I would have bet my life that you would never do anything underhand.'

Mrs Harrison stood in the doorway. 'Not any more we won't, though,' she said. 'You're a wicked, selfish –'

Her husband raised his hand. 'All right, old girl. I think Jane knows exactly how we feel.'

'No. She won't ever understand how I feel. Not till she

has children of her own and finds out what it's like to give them everything and have it all thrown back into your face.'

'You never talked like that to Rose,' Jane said. 'In fact, you were on her side.'

'Rose was different. She tried to get a decent job, but Mrs Cohen moved her. She couldn't help it.'

'I'm sick of hearing you make excuses for her. And I'll tell you something else for nothing. As soon as I'm old enough I'm joining up. Then you'll have Rose all to yourself.' Jane knew she was out of control, but she couldn't stop herself from shouting, 'That's all you've ever wanted, isn't it?'

Her mother was white with rage. 'Go to your room at once,' she demanded. 'And stay there till you've come to your senses.' She shouted up the stairs after Jane, 'I expect you to go down on your knees and apologise before I'll ever speak to you again, you ungrateful girl.'

Jane was beyond tears. She listened to her mother crying and her father talking downstairs, and knew she was alone. Dad would have to take Mum's side, no matter what. Aunt Grace would sit on the fence, but she'd be disappointed. So would Laura Marshall. And Peter.

The only one who would really understand was Rose, the sister she had come so close to hating. And after the things Jane had said downstairs, Rose was the last person she could approach for sympathy.

She heard Aunt Grace and Rose come home, and voices. Well, at least everyone knew the sorry story. Nothing to hide any more.

Suddenly the door burst open. Rose looked quite distraught. 'You're not really going to do it, are you?' she cried.

Surprised, Jane nodded.

The next moment, Rose grabbed her by the shoulders and was shaking her. 'I could have got you that job at Cohen's. You bloody fool!'

Jane pushed her sister away. 'You're the last one to talk,' she accused.

'No! I'm the best one. I know what it's like to work with people like that. They don't want anything better, and resent people who do. They're no-hopers.'

'Come on, Rose,' Jane scoffed. 'One minute you're telling

me I should have taken the job at Cohen's, the next you're complaining what a rotten lot they are.'

'But you'd be in the office there. Expected to behave differently. You don't understand what it would be like for someone like you to be working in a factory.'

'They can't all be common as muck, just because they didn't pass the scholarship.'

'Of course not. But there's always a hard core of troublemakers who won't leave it alone. You're not as tough as me.'

'If you can deal with it, I can. I might be tougher than you think. You've not changed that much.'

Rose's voice was low as she said, 'Oh, but I have, Janey. I've lost my dreams.' Speechless, Jane stared at her sister. 'It's true,' Rose went on. 'They were really rotten to me because I'd been in the salon. At first I didn't mind when they laughed at me. Thought I'd be able to show them. But they sneered every time I went round to the stage schools. Edna was the only one who ever wished me luck. In the end, I gave up telling them about it.'

'We never gave up believing in you, Rose.'

'I know. I gave up believing in myself.'

'But you're always saying –'

'Talk, Janey. Just talk. And I don't want that rotten world out there to destroy you like it's destroyed me. You're worth better.'

Jane turned Rose's head towards the dressing-table mirror. 'You're not finished yet, Rose,' she said. 'Just look at yourself. I'd swop places with you any day.'

The reflections in the mirror were opposite sides of the same coin, one golden-haired, peach-skinned, long-lashed, the other brown-eyed, sallow, with dark hair drawn back into an unattractive pigtail.

The blue eyes filled with tears. 'Don't envy me,' Rose whispered. 'Don't ever envy me.' She turned away from the mirror as though she found her reflection distasteful. 'Oh, Janey,' she sobbed. 'I've made such a mess of my life. If you only knew ...'

The office was little more than a cupboard in a corner of the storeroom, the window too high to allow a view. There was just enough room for the elderly desk, complete with splinters, a wooden chair that wobbled on the uneven floor, and a metal floor-safe that served as a table for two huge ledgers. They recorded every transaction since Mr Cohen had set up the business in 1919. As for the typewriter, Jane had never seen such an ancient one in working use. The keys had a tendency to bunch together as if in protest at their forced labour, covering Jane's fingers with ink whenever she attempted to free them, and two had snapped from their stalks. It would have been more efficient to write letters by hand, particularly since Mrs Cohen would not authorise a new ribbon until the typing was almost illegible.

Everything was covered in dust, the small amount of light too dim to illuminate Jane's desk, but showing only too clearly her spidery companions and the webs into which they scurried.

Jane began her daily battle with the broken drawer that housed the petty-cash book, and pondered her future. If she were to take Grade VII, Miss Palmer would need to know by the end of the week. But Madame Delia was planning to reopen her dancing school, and this was enrolment week for the autumn term.

Although Jane did not want to work for the Cohens for ever, she expected to work until retirement. Not for her the luxury of a husband to provide her worldly needs. Anyway, she didn't really think she was prepared to pay the price of marriage. It was all very well for Gran to say it was a wife's duty and didn't matter whether she liked it or not. Jane didn't think she could just 'put up with it'. So she would concentrate on a career.

Mentally juggling the things she needed to do with the things she wanted to do, Jane concluded that something had to go. Not shorthand or typing, they were essential. And certainly not Madame Delia. That left the choice between music lessons and book-keeping. She'd always wanted to achieve Grade VIII, but what difference would it make? In fact, if she went that far, her mother would become even more persuasive about teaching music from home.

That evening, she enrolled for two extra subjects, book-keeping and calculating machines, on Sunday mornings. The hardest part was explaining to Miss Palmer. She begged Jane to reconsider. It was dreadfully sad, and Jane was moved almost to tears when her friend and mentor leaned forward to kiss her cheek.

'You've been my special pupil,' she murmured. 'I shall miss you.'

'I'll visit you,' Jane promised.

Miss Palmer smiled, but shook her head. 'People mean to, but they never do,' she said. 'The important thing is to stay in touch with your music.'

The first 'mystery explosions' were just rumours. Nothing official. The Harrisons wondered if this was what Aunt Grace meant when she hinted at a second secret weapon.

Rose was telling Jane about a film when it happened. They were standing on the platform one September morning, watching for the train, and Rose was checking her handbag for matches. 'Let's move up a bit,' she suggested. 'I can have a fag in the front carriage.'

Jane could never say whether the ringing in her ears was caused by the explosion or the shattering sound as the heavy gas lamp fell only inches behind her feet, on the exact spot where she had been standing seconds before.

A porter shook his head as he gazed down at the wrecked lamp. 'Must be your lucky day, love,' he said.

A voice in the crowd asked, 'What caused it to fall down like that?'

Scratching his head, the porter said, 'Reckon it's one of them flying gas mains I've heard about. Here comes the train. Stand away from the edge, please.'

White-faced, Rose stared back at Jane. There had been no sound or sight to warn them. Nothing. It was just as Aunt Grace had predicted.

In the weeks that followed, only once was Jane actually able to 'see' a V-2 rocket. She was on her way to rehearsal, straight from work. As the train pulled out of the tunnel, Jane glanced out of the small diamond-shaped area of glass unprotected by mesh. Her attention was riveted to two small puffs of vapour, high in the sky, seconds before the carriage rocked to the double crack and blinding flash.

Jane found the daily attacks by V-2s less terrifying than the

V-1s. Not so her mother, whose nerves, once of steel, had now worn thin. Even the slightest noise triggered a reaction of trembling hands and fluttering eyelid. 'Don't slam the door,' she warned. 'It makes me jump.'

'I know, Mum.' Jane was very patient.

'I'm not sure how much more of this I can take, really I'm not.' Mrs Harrison's eyes filled with tears.

Grandad tried to comfort. 'It'll all be over soon, Nell. Our boys are pushing hard towards Holland.'

'That's all boys ever think about, fighting,' his daughter retorted. 'And if you can't be out there you stick pins in maps, pretend you're generals in Whitehall. It's all a big game to you.'

'Hold on, girl, that's not fair.'

'Fair! When has life ever been fair to women? We're the ones left mourning our husbands and sons.'

Jane wished there was some way she could ease some of the bitterness from her mother. There might be some flowers in Berwick Street market. Finding the stall and choosing the russet and gold chrysanthemums took most of her lunch period next day, so she tried a short cut back through an unsavoury area she usually avoided. One or two prostitutes glanced at her without interest. In a doorway, another was counting money into the hand of a furtive-looking little man with greasy hair. Probably one of the pimps Rose had told her about. He waggled his tongue at Jane, then went back to his business.

A group of Free French servicemen blocked the alley ahead of her and Jane side-stepped into the doorway of a nightclub, hoping they would pass, but they stopped to leer at a display of photographs of nude showgirls. As Jane eased her way through the soldiers, one turned to point out a photograph to his companion, laughing and pouting his lips in a kiss. Although they spoke rapidly, Jane understood enough to make her wonder what sort of girls would allow themselves to be the subject of such lewd comments. They were all attractive girls, with gorgeous figures, especially the one the Frenchman was pointing at, wearing little else but a sequinned headdress and a G-string. In fact, she looked rather like –

Jane's head spun and for a moment she thought she was going to faint. Oh, God! Not here. Not with these men.

She reached out for the support of a wall, but found herself grasped by one of the Frenchmen. 'Do you have a *malade, chérie*?' He looked concerned. 'Is your *maman* near?'

'No. I'm quite all right, thank you.'

'You dropped your flowers.'

'Thank you.' Panic-stricken, she grabbed the flowers and ran through the alley.

Mrs Cohen was waiting. 'You are five minutes late,' she remonstrated.

'I know,' Jane whispered. 'I'll make it up.'

'That is not the point. I expect you back at twelve thirty sharp. What's the matter with you? You look terrible.'

Jane collapsed onto her chair. 'I felt faint in the street.'

Mrs Cohen frowned. 'You're not pregnant, are you? I won't stand for any of that nonsense.'

'Of course not.' She thought rapidly. 'It's my period.'

'Gadding about too much at night, more likely. I hope you don't think you're going home.'

'No. But I must speak to Rose for a moment. Please.'

Rose knelt by Jane's chair. 'I'm going to take you home, no matter what Ma Cohen says.'

'How could you?'

'Did you knock your head? You might have concussion.'

'I saw the photograph.'

'What photograph?'

'The one of you with no clothes on. In that awful place.'

Slowly, Rose stood up. Eventually, she said, 'I hoped you wouldn't find out.'

'It was on the wall, for the whole world to see.'

'They promised me it would only be displayed inside.'

'Men were saying what they'd like to do to you. I was so ashamed.'

'I'm sorry.' Rose's voice was a whisper.

'Supposing Mrs Cohen found out? Or Mum and Dad?'

Rose swung round. 'You wouldn't tell them, Janey? Promise you won't.'

'Of course not. It would break their hearts. But why do it in the first place? Was it the money?'

Rose looked at the ceiling. 'I thought it was a foot in the door. At least, that's what Mick said.'

'And you believed him?'

'It sounds stupid now. But at the time it seemed so plausible. One of the showgirls broke her wrist and they needed a temporary replacement. Mick said it was a golden opportunity to get into the chorus line, and perfectly respectable. The girls at the Windmill are highly thought of, and talent scouts, et cetera, et cetera ...'

'How long have you been doing it?'

'A few weeks. I soon realised it wasn't the Windmill. We have to walk around, and that's not allowed in the legitimate theatre.'

'It's not even a theatre, just a sleazy club. I can't understand why you're still doing it.'

'I tried to get out of it.' Rose looked desperately unhappy. 'But I'd signed on the dotted line. They've got me just where they want me.'

Jane tapped a pen on the desk. Then she said, 'Not necessarily. What did Mr McGlusky say about talent scouts?'

'Just that they're always there.'

'Well, if they're not, he's misled you. And they're breaking the law by asking showgirls to move around. All you have to do is tell him your contract isn't worth the paper it's written on.'

Rose bit her lip. 'I don't know, Janey. The other girl will be out of plaster in a couple of weeks.'

Jane looked at her sister in amazement. Was this Rose talking? Once upon a time she would have taken on the world. Now it was as though all the spirit had been knocked out of her. Just like Mum.

'How many nights are involved?' she asked.

'Every night, except Friday.'

'Sundays?'

Rose nodded.

'When you're supposed to go to the pictures with Edna, and stay the night with her afterwards? Does she know about it?'

'No. She thinks I'm with an American. I sleep in the dressing room on Sundays.'

'And the other nights we thought you were out dancing till all hours.'

'I was, in a way.' Rose shrugged wryly.

Jane sighed. 'Oh, Rose! So many lies.'

'I've been a fool. That's what I was trying to tell you the other day.'

'If only you'd told me the whole truth. I might have been able to help.' Jane looked closely at her sister. 'I can't believe you're prepared to go back there. It must be ghastly.'

'Servicemen are a bit noisy when they're drunk, but generally they're harmless enough. Only want to ogle.' Rose pulled a face. 'It's the dirty-raincoat brigade I can't stand. You know what they're doing under the table.'

Jane felt sick. 'I won't let you go back there,' she said. 'If I have to go and tell them myself.'

'I've got to go tonight. It's pay night,' Rose appealed. 'But I'll tell them that's the end of it.'

'Let me come with you.'

'No. I don't want you involved. Anyway, you've got evening classes.'

'Blow that. You're more important.'

Rose hugged her sister. 'You're a brick, but I've got to pluck up the courage to get out of my own mess.'

'And tell Mick McGlusky to take your name off his books. He'll never make you or anyone else a star. All he's good for is spouting blarney. Try the others again.'

Rose smiled wistfully. 'If only I could believe ...'

'You can. But get rid of that wretched Irishman.'

Before Rose could answer, Mrs Cohen flung open the door. 'I shall deduct this time from both your pay packets. Rose, I want all those sleeves before you leave tonight.

'But you said you didn't need them till tomorrow.'

'I've changed my mind. And where's the urgent invoices I asked for, Jane?'

'On your desk, Mrs Cohen. I finished them before lunch.'

Rose pulled a face and mouthed, 'Cow' at Mrs Cohen's back as she followed her to the door.

Nell Harrison had a headache that evening. And a letter with an Eire stamp. As Jane went upstairs to fetch the Aspro, she heard sounds of weeping from Kathleen's room. It must have something to do with the letter.

After she'd taken the pills, Mrs Harrison handed the letter

to Jane. 'Saves me explaining everything,' she said. 'I'm so wild, words fail me.'

A strongly worded letter from a Miss Bernadette Delaney expressed regrets that the family were dead, but concluded that it was God's punishment to her nephew.

As far as the child is concerned, rather than have her continue to live among heathens, she can complete her education at the convent school I attended. Out of the goodness of my heart, I will pay for this, on condition that Kathleen goes on to take holy orders. In this way, she can attempt to atone for the sins of her father.

Silently, Jane raised her eyes. Aunt Grace took the letter. 'We all feel the same,' she said. 'Too angry for words.'

'No wonder Kathleen's breaking her heart,' Jane said. A dreadful thought occurred to her. 'Can this aunt force Kathleen to do what she wants? Is she her legal guardian?'

'It's possible,' Aunt Grace said. 'I don't know what the situation is according to Irish law.' She offered her sister a cigarette. 'I'll ask Mr Grierson in the morning.'

Mrs Harrison's hand shook as she lit the cigarette. She was smoking more, but it didn't seem to help her nerves. Jane thought again about the letter.

'We can't let Kathleen go to that dreadful woman,' she said. 'She's doing well at school, and her father promised she would go to university, even put money aside for it.'

'But he didn't believe in banks.' Kathleen stood in the doorway. 'Always said the safest bank was his pocket. So I'll have to go to Great-Aunt Bernadette.'

Fred Harrison smiled at Kathleen. 'There's a home for you here, if you want it.'

'If I want it?' Kathleen clasped her hands. 'There's nowhere in the world I'd rather live.'

'Couldn't run to university, of course, but Mrs Harrison and I are agreed that you're very welcome, if Miss Delaney will allow it.'

Jane asked, 'Did you ever meet the old lady?'

'No. Me da said she had a face like a prune crossed with a sour apple. And the main reason Granny O'Connor left Ireland was to get away from her.'

Jane lay awake worrying about her friend, her mother, her

sister. Where was Rose? She should have been home by now.

It was almost two o'clock when Rose finally came home. 'Switch the light on,' Jane whispered.

Rose looked weary as she unbuttoned her coat and threw it on the chair.

'Did you speak to Mick McGlusky?'

'Yes.' Rose unpinned her hair. 'He wasn't very pleased, but I thought I'd got away with it till he came round after the show. With Tony the Greek.'

'Tony the Greek! Nobody really has a name like that.'

'He does. And he's mean, with it.'

'But you stuck to your guns?'

Rose peeled off her stockings. 'At first I did, but Tony turned nasty, and I got scared. Sybil told me his henchman beat up a girl once.'

'We'll go to the police.'

'No!' Rose glanced at the wall, listened for a moment, then lowered her voice. 'No, Janey. If I do that, Mum and Dad will have to know.'

'But –'

'It's only a couple of weeks.'

'They're blackmailing you, Rose, and if you give in, they won't stop.'

'Once Gwen is back they won't need me. And I told Mick that's the end.'

Chapter Nineteen

For once, Rose kept to her word, ended her stint with the Soho club and told Jane she had no intention of contacting Mick McGlusky ever again. Gradually the spring came back to her step, the smile to her face. She had a new boyfriend, a Canadian she'd met at a Glenn Miller concert.

Chuck was repatriated to his wife and family in Oregon, but Jane suspected that his liaison with Madame Delia had not ended at the airport, judging by the number of air-mail letters. Jane wondered how the dancing teacher felt now that her husband might be coming home.

Nell Harrison wept as she stirred the Christmas-pudding mixture. 'It won't be the same,' she sniffed.

'Don't worry, Mum.' Jane greased the basin with a margarine paper. 'Mrs Marshall said it's the best wartime recipe she's found.'

'I meant Christmas, silly. Without little Johnny. And not knowing whether Jack's ...' Mrs Harrison pushed the mixing bowl towards Jane. 'It can go in the basin now.'

Carefully, Jane lowered the basin into the boiling water. 'I remember when Gran used to light the fire under that old copper to boil her puddings. The house was full of steam for hours, just like washdays.'

'And she always kept the biggest one back to mature for the next Christmas.' Mrs Harrison stuffed the hankie back into her pinafore pocket. 'That was when we had proper Christmas puddings, with lovely juicy raisins and rum to help it mature. Not like this pathetic little thing.' She untied her apron. 'I'm going to Romford with Rose now. She's set her heart on having a crushed-velveteen dress for Christmas, to wear to the Canadian Club dance. I'll have to let her have some of my coupons. Keep an eye on the pudding, make sure it doesn't boil dry.'

Jane lowered the gas. 'Take a torch, Mum. The fog's coming down again.'

The November peasoupers made an effective blackout. Even in daytime the streets of London were grey and misty, filled with shadowy figures, scarves and handkerchiefs held to their mouths. On those days Jane stayed in her little cubbyhole. Mrs Cohen insisted that she and Rose take their lunch break at separate times, so Jane usually revised homework while she ate her sandwiches.

One evening, Jane reached Tottenham Court Road Station before realising she'd left her shorthand book in her desk. The fog had thickened early that day and she hugged the walls as she hurried back to the office. With luck, Rose would be the one to open the door. She was waiting for Larry to pick her up straight from work.

Across the narrow street, Jane could just make out a small group of men outside Cohen's. They seemed to be arguing, quite heatedly, and she hesitated. One thing she didn't want was to be caught up in a fight. Then Jane realised they were surrounding a woman. She wore a scarf over her hair and was crying as one of the men pulled at her arm, and another raised a fist above her face. Jane wondered whether she should try to get help, but the street was deserted.

Suddenly, the woman cried out, 'Leave me alone,' and her headscarf slipped back. It was Rose.

Running across the road, Jane shouted, 'You big bullies! Don't you dare lay a finger on her!'

The two men threatening Rose turned to stare at Jane. No wonder Rose was scared. They were swarthy and beefy, wearing wide-brimmed trilbies. Even the short one looked villainous. She was shaking inside, but tried hard not to show her fear. The third man shuffled from foot to foot, looking up and down the roadway. It was Mick McGlusky.

So the two nasties were probably Tony the Greek and his sidekick. 'Who the hell are you?' one of them asked.

'I'm her sister, and we're going home now. So you'd better

189

leave us alone.' Jane hoped the quaver in her voice wasn't noticeable.

The short man looked at Mick McGlusky. 'Tell her,' he ordered, pointing at Jane.

'We've got another job for Rose.'

'I thought Rose made it quite clear that she's not doing any more nude showgirl work.'

'It's a solo dancing act. Rose always wanted to be in the spotlight.' McGlusky laughed nervously.

For the first time since Jane arrived on the scene, Rose spoke. 'But not as a striptease dancer.'

The short man moved in front of Rose. 'You've got no choice, lady,' he muttered.

'I told you, Tony. I don't want to do it.' Rose began to cry again.

'It's what *I* want that counts. Isn't that right, Giorgio?' He looked up at the huge man towering over the group.

'That's right, boss. And I think the lady knows what will happen to her if she doesn't do what you want.'

This was like something out of a very bad B-film. Jane put her arm around Rose. 'Then I'm afraid you're going to be disappointed. I have already asked someone to send for the police, and if you're not gone when they arrive, we will have no alternative but to press charges.'

Tony was shorter than Jane. He reached up to prod her in the chest. 'You won't do that, girlie,' he sneered. 'Because we have the trump card.'

'And what's that?'

'The last thing in the world Rose wants is her momma and poppa to find out what she was doing in my club. And if you have sent for the cops, which I don't think, I will make sure they know what their good little girl has been up to. I have photographs.'

Thinking quickly, Jane knew she had to sound confident. 'I don't know much about playing cards,' she said. 'But I seem to remember the expression, "ace up my sleeve".' Tony glanced at Giorgio. 'I've already told my parents,' she went on.

'Oh, no, Janey!' Rose cried. 'You promised ...'

Warningly, Jane squeezed her sister's arm. 'Sorry, Rose. I had a nasty feeling the blackmail wouldn't stop. So I decided it would be better coming from me than these thugs.'

Tony's laugh wasn't quite so sure. 'You're bluffing,' he accused.

'And that's not all.' Jane ploughed on. 'If you attempt to contact Rose, or her family, in any way, we will tell the police that you are not only breaking the law by having your show-girls move about, but employing girls under age. I believe Sybil is only fourteen.'

'I was told she was sixteen. And the English law it is diffi-cult to understand for a foreigner.' The little man blustered. 'No one can touch Tony the Greek. I am too big in Soho.'

Jane turned towards the doorway. 'But you're not big, are you, Mr McGlusky? You'll lose your licence if the police find out you've been sending under-age girls to his sort of estab-lishment.'

McGlusky was definitely nervous. She could hear it in his voice. 'Perhaps we ought to find someone else, Tony. I've other girls on my books.'

'I've seen your other girls. They're tarts. No talent. Rose is different. The customers like her.'

Two men turned the corner of the road. 'That's the police,' Jane said. 'Come on, Rose.' As she turned towards the strangers, Tony grabbed Jane's arm and muttered, 'Don't forget, cops can be bought.'

Jane shrugged off his hand and hustled Rose along the road, past the two strangers, towards the main road. She dare not look back.

The train puffed out of Paddington Station, heading for the red earth and pure air of Devonshire. In a few hours, Rose would be eating scones and jam by a roaring fire, pressed by Aunt Peggy to 'have some more clotted cream, my pretty'.

Jane breathed a sigh of relief as she handed over her plat-form ticket. At least Rose was safely out of the way, for the time being.

Persuading her sister had been hard work. She hardly stopped crying long enough to listen, although that made it easier for Jane to convince the doctor that Rose wasn't at all well. She'd never really shaken off that bad throat. And what with this attempt to steal her handbag last night, coming just as

191

she'd been told that her boyfriend had been recalled for active service...

Dr Norman had agreed that Rose needed a few days away. The bruises on her arm would soon fade, but she was obviously distressed.

The worst part had been lying to their parents. At first Mrs Harrison had wanted to go with Rose to the doctor, until reminded that the next-door neighbours were moving today, and she'd offered to help. It would be much more practical if Jane were to take her sister to Paddington, straight from the doctor's, before going to work. Mr Harrison had looked curiously at Jane, and she couldn't quite meet his eyes as she asked for change to telephone Aunt Peggy.

Now she had to face her employer, but even Mrs Cohen couldn't argue with a doctor's certificate to the effect that his patient was suffering from 'nervous debility'.

After the expected displeasure, Mrs Cohen insisted that her clerk work late for the rest of the week. Each night Jane ran to the Underground, and each morning she dashed downstairs to check the post, in case the Greek carried out his threat. Rose wrote that she was feeling much better, Johnny had grown tremendously and Aunt Peggy spoiled him rotten.

Uncle Joe is quite cheerful really, which is more than can be said for Betty, or Aunt Jessie. We took Johnny out to the farm yesterday, and it would have been dead miserable without the Italians. Benito makes me laugh, the way he keeps crossing himself every time he hears the news, and Mario is always blowing kisses at me. Actually, he's not bad looking, a bit like Anthony Quinn only shorter. You should have seen his face when Aunt Jessie gave him a plate of macaroni with a bit of grated cheese on top. Told her he's going to stay on after the war, become a chef and show us how to cook properly. Talk about cocky!

Rose went on to ask her father for ten shillings, her mother to pick up a skirt from the cleaners, and Jane to try and persuade the doctor to give her a certificate for another week. She'd met a Scottish mechanic in the RAF who'd asked her out, but he wasn't so much fun as Larry. Were there any letters from him?

Fred Harrison sent a postal order and his wife paid the cleaning bill, but Jane wrote back that Mrs Cohen threatened to keep Rose's wages if she wasn't back next Monday. And no, there wasn't any mail from Larry – or anyone else.

Two days later, Jane found herself strap-hanging next to Aunt Grace. As the train collected homeward-bound passengers at each station, she told Jane that Rose had telephoned her at the office. Said it was marvellous not to have to worry about V-2s or the fog, but she really needed that certificate. And if Mrs Cohen didn't pay up, Rose would soon tell her what she could do with the job.

'Actually, dear, Rose used stronger language than that, but I won't repeat it.' Aunt Grace fended off an umbrella. 'And as soon as she gave me a chance, I told her about our visitor last evening.'

Jane smiled. 'What did you say?'

'That he was a handsome young soldier, wearing the white cap disc of an officer cadet, and with a Military Medal ribbon on his chest. I explained that I was on my way out at the time, so I didn't know any more.'

'I bet Rose was curious.'

'Very.' Aunt Grace winced as a bowler-hatted gent trod on her foot. 'But I couldn't remember his name, just that he was tanned, as though he'd served overseas, and had a strong country accent. Here's Mile End. Excuse me ...'

When they were safely on the platform, waiting for the District Line train, Jane asked, 'Did Rose guess who it was?'

'I'm not sure.'

'Poor Jim was still answering Grandad's questions about his medal when I got home from the tech. I think he was embarrassed by all the fuss.'

'Who was he, dear? One of your schoolfriends?'

'No. His parents took us in when we were evacuated to Norfolk.'

'Of course. Now I remember. Was he the one who had earache?'

'No, that was George. He's still at school. Doris has been working at her great-grandmother's shop since Kitty left. Believe it or not, Mrs Oliver is ninety-four.'

193

'Incredible.' As a rumbling noise was heard in the tunnel, Aunt Grace peered along the platform. 'Why did Kitty leave?' she asked.

'She was pregnant by an American airman and moved over near the base. At least he married her.'

After they had squeezed into the carriage, Aunt Grace said, 'Where did the young man get his medal?'

'Syracuse. Something to do with destroying an Italian gun.'

'Quite an achievement to be recommended for OCTU.'

'Apparently, he went out as a corporal, and was made up to Sergeant in Sicily.' Jane glared after a woman who had elbowed her out of the way. 'Anyway, does Rose still want me to see Dr Norman again?'

'When I told her your mother had invited him to tea on Sunday, she said perhaps she ought to come home, rather than put your job in jeopardy.' Aunt Grace laughed. 'I don't know who she was trying to fool.'

'Jim had a bit of a crush on Rose when we were in Norfolk. But he was only fifteen.'

'Well, he's no country yokel. But he'll remember Rose as a schoolgirl. She's changed, too.'

'I know. Should be quite an interesting Sunday, don't you think?'

Sergeant James Edwards arrived early. 'Hope it's not inconvenient,' he apologised.

'Of course not.' Mrs Harrison took the small package. 'What lovely chocolates! You really shouldn't have.' She handed her pinafore to Jane. 'Put the kettle on, and keep an eye on the rock cakes in the oven.'

By the time Jane took the tray of tea into the living room, the men were deep in conversation. Jim had an air of quiet confidence that hadn't been evident five years ago. No wonder he'd been selected as a potential leader. As Jane studied his profile, he turned and smiled. She tried to fight back the blush, but knew her skin had turned quite pink.

'Do you still see the boys who were billeted next door?' he asked.

'The last we heard of Arnold, he was in the south of France with the Marines. And Sandy's doing well at medical school. Wants to become a surgeon.'

Jim raised his eyebrows. 'Never thought of Sandy as being ambitious.'

'Oh, yes. He's very determined. Rose says he won't get married or anything until he's got the right letters after his name.'

'Rose? I thought she was more friendly with Bill?'

'She is. They still meet up when he's on leave from the Air Force. But sometimes Sandy takes Rose out for a meal straight from work – if she's not got a date with her Canadian boyfriend.'

'Sounds like Rose likes to play the field.' Jim grinned at Jane. 'What about you? Do you have a boyfriend?'

Again Jane felt the colour rising. 'Good heavens, no! I don't have time.'

'Ah, yes. Your father told me about your classes. Do you still study music?'

'No, but I play for a local dancing troupe. Rose is their soloist. She's very good.'

'She always wanted to be a star.'

'Yes.' Jane stood up. 'I'd better make a start on the sandwiches.'

Jim carried the tray back into the kitchenette and insisted on wiping up. After some general chat about his training at Sandhurst, and her job, she said, 'I expect you think I was mean, not keeping in touch with your parents.'

'It's war, Jane. You've had things to put up with that never touched us. It wasn't till I went to your old address that I realised how sad it must be to have your home reduced to a blackened shell.'

'I was so ashamed that we'd let your mum and dad down, after all they'd done for us, I just couldn't think of the right words.'

'Dad knows it wasn't your fault,' he said. 'Sandy told him what had happened.'

'Really? He never said.' Jane smiled as she reflected what a good friend Sandy was.

'I don't think Dad ever forgave Kitty for lying to him,' Jim went on. 'Mum wanted to write to you, but she couldn't find the right words, either.'

'Well, I'm glad they don't still think badly –'

Their conversation was interrupted by a violent explosion that rattled the crockery. Jim's hand rested lightly on her shoulder. 'The rockets don't seem to stop people going out at night,' he commented. 'Theatres and cinemas are still busy.'

'We can just as easily be hit during the daytime.' Jane creamed butter and margarine together.

'Actually, I've been wondering whether you would like to see a film after tea. That's if you haven't any other plans?'

For a moment, Jane could not speak. The only plans she had were to discuss trial balance with Peter. How should one answer the first invitation? Rose always said not to appear too eager, to play 'hard to get'. But Jane could only stammer, 'That would be nice, if you're sure?'

'Why shouldn't I be?' She noticed how his brown eyes crinkled when he smiled. 'Is there anything particular you'd like to see?'

'Really, I don't mind.' Silly fool, she told herself, Jim won't know what's on locally. 'They say *Double Indemnity* is good.'

'I read the reviews. That'll be fine.'

'Good.' She hesitated. 'Rose won't be home till later this evening.'

'I'm in London till Christmas.'

He seemed relaxed, talked to Uncle Arthur about the problems of running a shop, Gran about his first impressions of London, and Kathleen about her future.

Jane was cutting the seedcake when Rose arrived – with Uncle Nobby.

'I thought I was supposed to be meeting you at nine o'clock,' Mr Harrison said.

'Changed my mind, Dad,' Rose said brightly. 'Phoned Uncle Nobby and asked him to meet me from the early train.'

'If your train had been late we'd have missed each other.'

Nell Harrison took her daughter's coat. 'The train wasn't late, Fred, so it doesn't matter. I'm glad that Rose was home in time to see Jim.'

Rose pushed a chair into the gap between Jim and Jane. 'I'm starving,' she said. 'Any more sandwiches, Janey?'

From that moment on, Rose dominated the conversation. She was her old self, telling outrageous versions of what she would say if Mrs Cohen didn't part up with her wages, and plying Jim with questions, mostly about his medal.

Uncle Nobby helped Jane and Aunt Grace with the washing-up. 'Smart young man, that, as well as brave,' he observed. 'Give me a fellow who gets his promotion in the field any day, rather than those who come in with a commission just because they've been to the right school.'

Carefully rinsing the bread-and-butter plate, Aunt Grace said, 'You seemed to be getting on very well with him, Jane. Are you going to see him again while he's in London?'

'I don't know. But he has asked me to go to the pictures tonight.'

'Well, you'd better go and get ready, dear. Off with your pinny. We'll finish these.'

Quietly, Uncle Nobby said, 'And watch out for your sister.'

'What do you mean?'

'You know what I mean. I love Rose dearly, but I'm just as aware of her antics as you are. Why do you think she came back early?'

'I expect she wanted to see Jim again, but Rose has a steady Canadian boyfriend now.'

'That's never stopped her before.'

Jane put on her new wine-coloured jumper and brushed her hair into a smooth roll around her head. For once it stayed in place, with the help of some small curved combs. The gilt scroll brooch, a present from Laura Marshall, showed up well against the colour of the jumper.

Rose raised her eyebrows. 'And where are you going, done up like a dog's dinner?' she teased. 'Got yourself a beau while I've been away?'

Jim stood up. 'We're going to the pictures.' He turned to Jane and smiled. 'That colour suits you.'

'Thank you.'

'What film are you seeing?' Rose asked.

'*Double Indemnity.*'

'Really? I was furious that it wasn't on in Torquay.'

Surprised, Jane said, 'But you don't like thrillers.'

'Whatever gave you that idea?' Rose picked up the local paper. 'Damn! It finishes today.' She looked appealingly at Jim. 'I don't suppose I could come with you? I'll pay for myself.'

197

'Do you mind?' he asked Jane. She had no choice.

Aunt Grace suggested that Peter go with them, to make a foursome.

'Good idea.' Peter beamed. 'They say it's a very clever plot. What about you, Kathleen?'

'Thanks just the same, but I'm just off next door to help Margaret with her homework. She's in my class at school.'

'Ah, the new neighbours,' Rose said. 'What are they like?'

'They're lovely people,' Kathleen said enthusiastically. 'And they're Catholics. And Mrs Ackroyd is expecting another little one in the spring. And –'

'That's nice.' Rose laughed as she picked up her handbag. 'I'll just pop upstairs and tidy up. Won't be a minute.'

Half an hour later, she was ready, looking stunning in a tight-fitting black skirt and V-necked blouse the colour of the sea in Babbacombe Bay on a summer's day. Jane noted the admiration in Peter's eyes. And in Jim's.

'Are my seams straight?' Rose asked her mother, hitching the skirt to reveal her shapely legs.

'Never mind your seams,' Mrs Harrison said. 'Where did you get those clothes? You were out of coupons.'

'Aunt Peggy let me have some. And she treated me to the blouse.'

'That was kind of her. Now, mind you wear a scarf. It's raw out, and you don't want another of your throats.'

'Do stop fussing, Mum. Anyone would think I was a child.' Rose took Jim's arm. 'Ready?'

Several times during the evening Jane remembered Uncle Nobby's warning.

On the way to the cinema, Rose managed to form the group into two pairs, with Peter and Jane at the rear. 'Do you think I've changed?' she asked Jim.

'Yes, but five years is a long time.'

'Janey doesn't change, though, does she?'

'No. And I'm glad.'

The queues were lengthy, and Jim rubbed his hands together. 'Hope we go in soon. It's cold enough for a fur-lined stick.'

Rose squealed with laughter. 'Oh, Jim! I'd forgotten your Norfolk sayings. We had some good laughs, didn't we?'

Jane was relieved when Peter summed up the situation, paid

for Rose's ticket and bought her a bar of chocolate. As the lights dimmed before the main feature, Rose whispered in Jane's ear, 'Can we swop seats? I can't see for this woman's hat, and you're taller than me. Annoyed, but unable to think of a way to refuse, Jane stood up.

'Why are you changing seats?' Jim asked.

'Rose can't see.'

'Then she can change with me.'

Rose quickly sat in Jane's seat. 'No, Jim. You stay on the aisle. You've got longer legs.'

A loud 'shush' from the row behind prevented further argument, and Jane sat down, aware of her cousin's sympathy on one side, and her sister's scent on the other.

Mrs Harrison made cocoa before Jim left and handed Rose a letter. 'Forgot to give it to you yesterday,' she said.

Rose gasped, 'It's from Bill. He's booked two seats in the stalls for the new revue at the Prince of Wales next Saturday. Everyone is raving about it.'

Jim said. 'It's good. I saw it on the first night.' He turned to Jane. 'Would you help me out with some Christmas shopping next Saturday? Perhaps we could see another film?' Stunned, Jane could only nod. 'Shall we meet in Selfridges' Restaurant, say one o'clock?'

'Oh, yes. Thank you.'

'Good. Thank you for the tea, Mrs Harrison.' He shook hands all round, holding Rose's hand just a fraction longer as he said, 'Give Bill my regards. Perhaps we can have a drink together while he's on leave.'

'Sure.' Rose's smile was stunning. 'And Sandy will be off-duty again next week. I'll fix it up.'

The following Saturday Jane watched Jim as he ordered lunch. Who would have thought the quiet country boy could become so self-possessed? Perhaps it could happen to anyone if they studied their peers and really wanted to break out of the rut. So why hadn't it happened to her? All week she had been excited about her date, yet here she was, worrying about her hair slipping from its roll.

Jim talked about a new book, but she could only mutter 'I see' in response. By the time the chops were served, she was so nervous, she dropped her knife on the floor. Jim reassured her it didn't matter as he asked for a clean knife, but she was sure he must think her an absolute idiot.

Helping choose a scarf for his mother and a toy for Kitty's child was easier. She knew how to shop. But she didn't know what to do when sitting next to an attractive young man at the cinema, feeling the rough sleeve of his tunic brush against her arm, sensing his warmth. Would he expect to hold her hand? She couldn't help remembering Rose's words, 'Jim thinks of you as a sweet little girl, Janey, so don't get any romantic ideas. I'm more experienced than you and I don't want you to get hurt.'

Jim placed a box of chocolates on her lap, but made no attempt to take her hand. Rose was right. Jane wasn't ready yet for boyfriends. Or they weren't ready for her. She edged away and tried to concentrate on *Gaslight*.

It was no surprise when Jim shook hands at her front door and declined her invitation for a cup of tea. But she was amazed when he invited her to a Christmas ball.

'Evening dress and all that. Do you like dancing?'

'Sorry. I'm no good at it. And I've nothing suitable to wear.' Miserably, she turned away. 'Why don't you ask Rose?'

At first she thought he hadn't heard. Then he quietly said, 'Perhaps I will,' and turned on his heel.

Chapter Twenty

'You're wasted there, Jane.' Laura Marshall picked up a flat pebble and skittered it across the shallow waves. It bounced once, twice, three times, before it was claimed by the incoming tide. Brushing sand lightly from her gloves, she looked searchingly into Jane's face. 'You know that, don't you?' she said.

It would be a good moment to explain why she had chosen to work in that dreary office: because Rose needed her. Mrs Marshall would understand, offer advice, but never break a confidence. That was the trouble. It was a confidence.

Uncertain how to answer, Jane looked along the beach. In little groups, her family and friends were taking an after-lunch walk on Boxing Day. Nell Harrison with Betty, who had asked Uncle Nobby to bring her home on Christmas Eve. Johnny perched high in a 'flying angel' as his grandfather chatted to Peter. Kathleen deep in conversation with Uncle Len, who had offered to become her guardian and put her through university. Uncle Nobby with his shipmate Robert, both bearing the scars of their experience. Aunt Grace playing 'I spy' with Bea Marshall and her grandsons. And Rose.

Her sister walked slightly apart from the others, head down and shoulders hunched against the chill wind that blew in from the Thames estuary. If it weren't for Rose ...

Choosing her words carefully, Jane said, 'I'd like to help Rose find something better first.'

'It won't be easy. She has no qualifications.'

'I know, but I want her to get away from that place. It's awful. And she's not well.'

Taking Jane's arm, Mrs Marshall walked slowly. 'Your

concern for your sister is admirable,' she said, 'but you must look to your own interests as well. Evelyn's firm will expand when the marketplace becomes competitive again, and you could carve quite a career for yourself.'

Jane faltered. She knew that wonderful opportunities like this wouldn't be plentiful once London was flooded with demobbed secretaries. 'Please don't think I'm ungrateful,' she pleaded. 'There's nothing I'd like better than to work in advertising.'

'So what's holding you back? Evelyn is desperate. She's running the agency almost single-handed, apart from a useless office boy and an old dear who came out of retirement.'

It was tempting. Good wages were offered for someone with shorthand-typing, the ability to prepare simple accounts and answer the telephone properly, and not liable to be called up before war ended. Jane knew Rose wouldn't think twice about such an offer. So far there had been no signs that Mick McGlusky or his unsavoury companions would pounce again. But suppose they did? Without Jane's support at hand, Rose might well give in to their demands.

No. She had to persuade her sister to look for another job. Anything, as long as it was away from Soho.

'I'd like to think about it,' Jane hedged. 'Do you mind?'

'Not at all. I expect you'll want to talk to your parents first, anyway.'

'No!' Jane tried not to show the panic she felt. 'Please don't say anything to either of them. Not till I've had a chance to make up my mind.'

'As you wish.' Jane sensed a slight withdrawal. 'But don't leave it too long. Evelyn needs to advertise the post straight away if you're not interested.'

'Of course. And it was kind of you to think of me.'

'Well, you seemed the ideal person to recommend. However ...'

They had almost reached the others before Mrs Marshall spoke again. 'From what I hear, your new neighbours are very good Samaritans.'

'Oh, yes.' Jane was relieved to change the subject. 'When Betty turned up, Mrs Ackroyd insisted the uncles sleep in their spare bed.'

'That's a thought.' Mrs Marshall laughed lightly. 'After

years of barely speaking to each other, Len and Nobby have to share a bed.'

'I know. Aunt Grace said perhaps they'll stop being so daft now.' Jane glanced sideways at her companion, but there was no reaction in her expression, just a thoughtful smile. 'And the Ackroyds offered to look after Gran and Grandad today.'

'That was kind. I wonder how they're getting on.'

Jane explained that when the Ackroyds had walked home from Mass with Kathleen, Mrs Harrison had invited them in to have a drink. 'It was quite interesting really. Mrs Ackroyd's mother used to own the little shop in Upton Park where Gran bought her hats. And Grandad found out that Mr Ackroyd's family up north are great pigeon fanciers, so he was well away.' Jane chuckled. 'Till Uncle Arthur arrived and nearly finished Christmas Day before it started.'

'What happened?'

'He offered to let them have a tin of ham and turn a blind eye to the points, if they were prepared to pay a litle extra. I nearly died.'

'Didn't he know that Mr Ackroyd was a policeman?'

'Mum hadn't had a chance to warn him. But Aunt Grace whisked him out into the kitchenette to help her open a bottle of brown ale. He kept out of the way after that.'

'Your uncle will find himself in prison again if he's not careful.'

'Mum keeps telling him that. But he's greedy. He even tried to charge us for the dried egg they brought, till Auntie Vi mentioned it was their contribution towards Christmas.' Jane sighed. 'Let's hope that next Christmas we won't have rationing. I don't know how Mum managed to give us such a spread. And that curry you gave us today was delicious. Where did you learn to cook like that?'

'We often cooked curry on the boat, and I brought back spices from the East.' Mrs Marshall paused and gazed across the Thames. 'Please God the war will be over by next Christmas. But I fear rationing is here for some time.'

Jane was shocked. 'I'd imagined that we'd tear up the ration books as soon as peace was declared.'

'If only it was that simple.' Mrs Marshall frowned. 'This country will never be quite the same again, I'm afraid.'

Thoughtfully, Jane frowned. 'Do you think the men will expect it all to be the same when they're demobbed?'

'If they do, they're in for a surprise. Especially the married ones.'

Jane nodded. 'It must have been nice for some of the wives to have money of their own. They won't want to give it up.'

'It's not just the money. The women have had to make all the decisions. That's bound to cause a few problems.'

Jane remembered the conversation she had once had with Peter ... 'If ever I get married, which is highly unlikely, I shan't want to spend all my time cooking and shopping. Otherwise, there's not much point in having an education, is there?'

'That's why ...' Mrs Marshall bit her lip, as though she had been about to refer again to the advertising job, then thought better of it. She smiled at her young friend. 'But don't put yourself on the shelf yet. You've years ahead of you to meet the right man.'

Jane shook her head. 'They've not been exactly queueing at the door to take me out so far. The only date I had was disastrous.'

'Jim?' Jane nodded. 'Don't worry, my dear. Most first dates, like wedding nights, are disastrous. But they do improve with practice, I can assure you.'

Jane felt herself blush. She would have liked to discuss wedding nights with Mrs Marshall. Her mother always evaded any attempt to discuss sex, Aunt Grace was too inexperienced, and Jane wasn't sure that she wanted to learn from her sister. Somehow she felt that Mrs Marshall had a very healthy, straightforward approach to the subject. But she couldn't bring herself to pursue it. Instead, she mumbled, 'I suppose so. But boys are bound to compare me to Rose.'

'Ah, yes. Rose.' Laura Marshall gazed at the solitary figure scuffing through the shingle. 'You really must learn to fend her off, you know.'

'I don't think she deliberately sets out to upset me.'

'Of course not. There's no malice in the girl. But she can't help poaching every male in sight, whether she wants them or not.'

'I know,' Jane sighed. 'And I can't compete with her. So it's better not to try, surely? Then I won't be hurt.'

Mrs Marshall stopped and grasped both Jane's arms. 'Hurting is part of being alive. I'm surprised at you, Jane.'

'But –'

'You've got to learn to stand up for yourself. And not only against Rose.'

'I don't understand.'

'Yes, you do.'

Mrs Marshall was right. Jane knew only too well what she meant.

Suddenly, the older woman laughed, breaking the tense atmosphere. 'Come on, let's help out those two lads of mine. They're no match against their grandmother.'

After a few frantic rounds of verbal word games, Bea Marshall left the boys and walked beside Jane. 'Rose seems a little on the quiet side,' she observed. 'Boyfriend problems?'

'Sort of. She hasn't heard from Larry since he went overseas. I think she was quite keen on him.'

A middle-aged couple walking towards them stared quite rudely as they passed Robert, the woman commenting in an audible voice, 'They should be in a home, where the public can't see them.'

Angrily, Auntie Bea glared after the couple. 'Don't they realise ...?' She checked her anger and turned to Jane. 'It's the first time you've met Robert, isn't it?'

Jane nodded. 'Every time I've visited Mrs Marshall, her brother has been in hospital. He seems to be coping with it remarkably well.'

'Robert copes with the pain. It's the stupidity of people that really hurts him. But, like young Kathleen, he has his Christian faith to keep him going.'

They walked quietly for a while, deep in their own thoughts. Although she knew Robert had been badly burned, Jane had been shocked when she first saw the shiny skin, puckered mouth, distorted eyelid. But within a few moments, she was only aware of the quiet charm of the man.

In front of them, Johnny giggled as his grandfather trotted and neighed, pretending to be a horse. Bea Marshall smiled.

'I'm glad Betty was able to join us. What exactly was she told? I wasn't there when she arrived.'

'Just that an American glider pilot who knew Jack is convinced he saw him being led away by a small Japanese patrol.'

'But I thought you said only Americans were dropping supplies to the Chindits.'

'They were, officially. But the pilot said Jack had tried to bribe him to swop places.'

'Why didn't he come forward before?'

'At the time he was injured, and local natives took care of him. He's only just been rescued by the American forces.'

'So your brother could be a prisoner of war?'

'It's a strong possibility. The British Red Cross are making further enquiries with the American Red Cross, and Mum is taking Betty to Whitehall tomorrow.'

Bea Marshall squeezed Jane's arm. 'We will pray for him,' she said.

'Thank you.' Jane frowned. 'Mum has been through so much. I don't think she could bear it if her hopes were raised for nothing.'

'Never give up hope, my dear. Don't forget, the American must have been posted missing, but he's alive. There's always hope.'

As Johnny's fourth birthday approached, Jane began her campaign to help Rose find another job.

Classified advertisements were avidly read, phone calls made in her brief lunch period. One or two jobs were quite promising. General office girl, no qualifications necessary. Rose pursed her lips. The City was dull. Telephonist? Not Kensington, the season ticket would cost too much. Waitress at the Corner House? Too hard on the feet. Cashier at the Odeon, free cinema tickets? Rose brightened at this, then shook her head. Unsocial hours. Jane despaired of being able to apply for an interview with Laura Marshall's friend. Sometimes she was so annoyed by her sister's lack of interest that she was tempted just to look after her own future. But Rose looked so unwell.

Madame Delia commented on it after the concert on Friday night. 'I know she misses the Canadian boy, and I'm sure she's anxious about your brother, but she should make an effort on stage.'

Jane agreed that Rose hadn't been at her best during her solo. 'I think she's got gastroenteritis,' she said. 'She's not been well since she went to that banquet with Jim. Said she thought the chicken tasted funny, but she hates going to the doctor.'

'Can't your mother persuade her?'

'Mum's a bit preoccupied with the news about Jack at the moment. But I'll try to get Rose along on Monday morning if she's no better.'

Madame Delia handed Jane an extra half-crown with her pay for the show. 'Give that to your nephew tomorrow, and wish him a happy birthday from me.'

Johnny's birthday would have been a great success, if it had not been for Herr Hitler and his rockets. Finally, Betty announced she couldn't take any more and would return to Babbacombe. Aunt Grace suggested she accompany Betty, and return late Monday. Now the courts were closed there wasn't so much urgency in the typing pool. She would telephone Mr Grierson from Torquay first thing Monday morning. Uncle Nobby frowned over his diary, discovered he still had a couple of days' leave owing to him, shook hands warmly with his oldest friend, and caught the night train to Torquay, with Aunt Grace and Betty.

It was just as well that Betty had taken Johnny to a safe area. The V-2s were relentless all day Sunday. Mrs Harrison restored the house to order, polishing with a ferocity that told Jane of her nervousness more than the startled jump which followed each explosion.

Jane wanted to talk to Rose, but her sister stayed in bed all morning, then straight after lunch put on her hat and coat, saying she was going roung to Edna's and they might go to a New Year's Eve party. She overslept on Monday morning, so it was all rush to get to the station.

The train was crowded and the sisters were separated. Jane watched in the hope that there might be a seat nearer to Rose. There was a vacancy for a seamstress in the paper she'd just bought. Suddenly, at Bow Road, Rose pushed her way out through the doors just before they closed. As the train moved

207

away, Jane saw her sister running along the crowded platform. Had she seen someone she knew? There was nothing Jane could do but go on to work.

Edna Browning was combing her hair in the dump of a cloakroom. 'Where's Rose?' she snapped. 'She borrowed two bob from me on Friday and didn't come round like she promised. My mum had to lend me the bus fare to get to Winnie's party.'

'But I thought –' Jane stopped abruptly. Not only did she not like Edna Browning, anything said would be all round Cohen's within two minutes. Jane untied her headscarf. 'She'll be in later,' she said.

'What am I supposed to tell Old Mother Cohen?'

'Nothing. I'll talk to her.'

When Jane made the excuse that her sister-in-law couldn't get to Paddington by herself with a small child, Mrs Cohen's face became even uglier, and she demanded that Rose come to her office as soon as she arrived. Jane positioned her chair so she could watch the staff entrance. It was vital that she intercept her sister before their employer's eagle eye spotted the errant girl.

She wanted to shake Rose, unwell or not. How dare she keep putting Jane in this impossible position? How dare she lie to her parents again? Where had she been yesterday afternoon and evening, if not with Edna? It must be a liaison with a boy. But she wasn't usually reticent about her dates. In fact, she rather liked to boast about her conquests. So what was different about this one? Oh, Lord! Perhaps he was married. Maybe Rose had seen him on the platform at Bow Road? Well, she needn't think that dear little Jane was going to sit around for ever covering up for her escapades. This time, Rose had gone too far. She was obviously going to get the sack, so she'd have to take any job offered. And Jane would telephone Laura Marshall.

It was another half-hour before her sister tiptoed along the passage. Jane pulled her into the cubbyhole and closed the door. Startled, Rose half fell into the only chair and stared at Jane. Her make-up had been renewed, with a vast amount of rouge and eyeshadow.

Jane tried to keep her voice low. 'Where the hell have you been?'

'Nowhere.'

'Why did you get off the train?'

'Oh, that ...' Rose looked away. 'I had to go to the lavatory. Is the old girl wild?'

'She's not the only one. Rose, I've had enough of your lies and your scheming.'

'All this fuss because I was taken short.'

'You weren't taken short all yesterday afternoon and evening, were you? And you weren't at Edna Browning's, either.' Rose's head jerked back. 'Where were you?' Jane persisted.

'Don't ask me.' Rose's eyes were filled with tears. 'I can't tell you.'

'That's what you said last time. And who got you out of the mess?'

'You can't get me out of this mess, Janey.' Rose's voice wavered as she jumped up, pushed Jane away from the door and fled along the passage. Jane followed her sister into the lavatory. Rose was being audibly sick.

Rose staggered out of the cubicle and leaned against the doorway, eyes closed. With her blotchy, smeared make-up, she looked terrible. But Rose wasn't the only one feeling nausea.

Miserably, Jane asked, 'How long since you had a period?'

Rose's eyes opened wide. Then she bent over the sink to splash water onto her face. 'I don't know.' Her voice was a mumble. 'I've been irregular for some time now."

'You're as regular as clockwork. And you got off the train this morning because you felt sick, didn't you? Come on, Rose. You've got to tell the truth.'

Slowly, her sister raised her head and studied the reflection in the mirror. The pitted glass did little to imporve the girl's mottled features. Ignoring the filthy towel, she dabbed at her face with her handkerchief.

Finally, she said, 'I never could keep anything from you, could I, Janey?' Tears mingled with the water still on her face as she choked, 'It's true. I'm pregnant. And I wish I was dead.'

Chapter Twenty-One

While the family waited for her father to speak, Jane glanced at her sister, staring into the fire, her thoughts far away. His cigarette finally rolled, Mr Harrison said, 'It will take careful planning, Grace. Neither of you has any actual experience.'

'Not of owning our own business,' Uncle Nobby said. 'But I've been in charge of the hostel for a while now, so I've got some idea of victualling, costings and so on.'

Every line on Gran's face registered disapproval. 'You must be mad,' she said. 'Both of you.'

Flushed with excitement, Aunt Grace laughed. 'I think it's the first really sane thing I've done in years.'

Mrs Harrison looked worried. 'But to contemplate such a thing, at your age!'

'I'm not fifty yet, Nell. What have I got ahead of me?' Aunt Grace answered her own question. 'Ten more years supervising a typing pool, then what?'

Angrily, Gran gathered her balls of wool together. 'You're comfortable enough here, with your family. What more do you want?'

Warming her hands at the fire, Aunt Grace said, 'A home of my own.'

'Oh, Grace.' Nell Harrison touched her sister's shoulder. 'This is as much your home as mine.'

'You've been good to me, Nell, and I'll always be grateful. But I really want to do this. We both do.'

The *Daily Mirror* slid off Grandad's lap as he stretched his legs. 'What made you think of it now?' he asked. 'Did Peg suggest it, or Joe?'

Uncle Nobby answered. 'Not sure, really, Pop. Joe mentioned that the landlord wanted to sell.'

'And Peg said she thought the house was too big for the two of them,' Aunt Grace carried on.

'Then Joe talked about the problems of finding a suitable place to rent. And I miss being near the sea. So we came up with our idea.' Uncle Nobby beamed.

Mr Harrison sat back in his chair. 'Wouldn't you be better off just running the place as a boarding house?' he said. 'At least to start with. It's going to make things harder if you're only taking in ...'

Gran found the word her son-in-law had not liked to voice. 'Cripples,' she said shortly. 'Don't beat about the bush, that's what they are. Cripples.'

Quietly, Aunt Grace said, 'We prefer to think of them as people who've been disabled through no fault of their own. Some through the war. Some may have been born with a handicap, like Johnny.' Gran lowered her eyes from Aunt Grace, sitting on the fender box. 'Watching Joe in his wheelchair made us realise there must be lots of people who can't go on holiday without help.' She smiled up at Uncle Nobby. 'And we thought it would be a good idea to convert the house into a comfortable and welcoming holiday home for them.'

'Why does the landlord want to sell after all these years?' Mr Harrison asked Aunt Grace.

'The old boy died suddenly just before Christmas. Left everything to his son. But he wants a quick sale. That's why it's so cheap.'

'A real snip.' Uncle Nobby limped closer to the fire. 'He's only asking just over a thousand for the freehold.'

Gran snorted. 'Where are you going to get that sort of money?'

'We've both managed to save a bit over the years,' Aunt Grace said. 'And my endowment matures on my birthday.'

'That won't go far. And what are you going to live on while the work's being done? Air?'

'I've been paying into a pension fund for years,' Uncle Nobby grinned. 'Don't worry, Ma. I'll look out for Grace.'

'But who's going to look out for me and Dad? Bet you haven't thought about that.'

Aunt Grace looked puzzled. 'I don't understand, Mum. You've often said that you wouldn't go back to the old house, even if it's rebuilt.'

''Course we won't. With my legs I couldn't manage. But suppose something happens to Nell?'

'Now, Gran,' Mr Harrison reproved. 'Nell and Grace aren't your only family. You'd be taken care of.'

'If you think I'd go and live with Herbert and Dolly, you can think again. And Arthur's too bloody mean to give anyone houseroom.'

Uncharacteristically, Grandad rounded on his wife. 'I don't think we should expect Grace to give up her plans just because of us, Rosie. We've had our life.'

'And had to make sacrifices for our kids.' Gran's mouth quivered. 'It was bad enough when Herbert went to the other end of the country, but I never thought I'd live to see the day when Grace would abandon us as well.'

'I'm not abandoning you,' Aunt Grace protested. 'I'll come up as often as I can, and you can stay with us whenever you want. Have a nice little holiday. We're going to keep a couple of rooms aside, just for the family. Aren't we, Nobby?'

'That's right, Ma. And I might be able to drive Joe's car. It was specially adapted for his wooden leg. Then I can come up and get you.'

'And pigs might fly.' Gran put her glasses away. 'When did the likes of us ever ride in cars to go on holiday by the seaside?'

Jane retrieved the ball of wool her grandmother had dropped. 'We used to go to that nice boarding house in Margate before the war, Gran,' she said. 'And you came with us when we went to Canvey Island.'

'That was different. We had a caravan. And we went by charabanc.'

'Then it will make a nice change for you to go to Torquay.' Jane smiled at her aunt. 'I think it's a smashing idea, and I'd love to see your conversion plans when they're worked out.'

Looking grim, Mrs Harrison said, 'Nobody asked your opinion, Janey. You'd better make up your Uncle Nobby's camp bed in the other room, while I help Gran upstairs.'

Aunt Grace said, 'But I really am interested in Jane's opinion, Nell, and Rose's and Kathleen's.'

212

Uncle Nobby agreed. 'They might come up with some good ideas. Rose?'

Only half attentive, Rose shrugged. 'If you want to do it, I think you should go ahead. Working in that stuffy solicitor's would drive me round the twist, anyway.'

As Jane handed round cups of cocoa, she noticed with concern the deepening lines etched around her mother's mouth. How on earth was she going to react to Rose's news? It could well prove to be the last straw. And would it affect Aunt Grace's plans? Jane hoped not. Her favourite aunt was so happy with her dreams. She deserved to have them come true.

Much as she loved her sister and sympathised with her predicament, Jane was furious that Rose's impulsive behaviour was about to place such an unnecessary burden on a family already stretched to the limit. How could Rose be so careless? She wasn't even sure who the father was. After much probing from Jane, she'd finally admitted it might be Larry, although she'd had a slight period after he went overseas. Not Bill. He was always too careful. Yes, of course mistakes could happen. The whole business was a mistake. Jim? Unlikely. There'd only been the one occasion, after the banquet. Pressed further, she hinted at the possibility of a fourth man, one she refused to name. Jane asked whether he would be prepared to do the honourable thing, but her sister had vehemently shaken her head. His plans for the future certainly wouldn't include a wife and child. Oh, Rose, Rose, Rose!

Jane sighed and followed her sister upstairs. Like it or not, they had to talk.

'Not now, Janey. I'm beat.'

'Yes, now. When are you going to tell Mum and Dad?'

'What am I supposed to say? You might be losing Aunt Grace, but you're gaining another grandchild. Oh, by the way, I've got the sack.' Rose laughed bitterly. 'How can I tell them?'

'They'll want to know why you're not going to work in the morning.'

'Not if I go up with you as usual, they won't.'

Jane made no attempt to contain her anger. 'So you're going to try lying your way through, just like last time?'

'I didn't lie. I just didn't tell them.'

213

'Same difference. And you can't keep it up for ever. What are you now – two months gone? It won't take long for Mum or Gran to notice something.'

'There may not be anything to notice.'

'You're not doing anything silly, are you?'

'Well, it's early days yet. One of the women at work was pregnant by an Aussie.' Rose picked up her hairbrush. 'She miscarried quite easily, just with hot baths and gin.'

'You mustn't! It's dangerous. Anyway, Mum would see.'

'That's why I haven't tried it yet. I'd need help.'

'Don't look at me.'

'Thought you'd say that.' Rose sighed. 'Still, there's more than one way to get rid of a baby.'

Dumbfounded, Jane stared at her sister. Finally, she said, 'Girls die through back-street abortions.'

'Not if they're careful. Trouble is, the woman wants twenty-five quid, and I haven't got it.'

'You haven't already approached someone? Oh, Rose! How could you?'

'I can't think of any other way out.'

'How did you know where to go?'

'Edna's cousin went to her last year.'

'Does Edna know about you?'

'Of course not. Nobody knows, except you. But I remembered her talking about a nurse who lived near the Ilford Hippodrome. Went to see her on Sunday.'

'You were out for hours. What happened?'

'Couldn't find the house. Then, like I said, the price was too much.' Rose paused. 'By that time, it was getting late, so I went into the nearest pub and watched everyone celebrating the New Year. The Year of Hope, they called it. Ha ...' The pathetic laugh broke into a sob. 'I've never felt so terribly alone.'

Swiftly, Jane gathered her sister into her arms and stroked the golden head. 'Shush,' she whispered. 'You're not alone. You've got all of us, and lots of friends.'

Rose raised her tear-stained face and groped for a handkerchief. 'Not friends,' she sniffed.

'Don't be silly, Rose. You're always the centre of a crowd.'

'Only because they want to see what I'm going to get up to

next. When I take the mickey out of someone, it makes them laugh. But there isn't one that I could really trust as a friend, tell my innermost thoughts to. Only you. You don't know how I envy you sometimes, Janey.'

'Me! For goodness' sake, why?'

'You've had real friends, like Theresa and Kathleen, Sandy, Peter. People admire and respect you. I'm just a good laugh, but not to be trusted with anyone's boyfriend.' Rose gazed at her reflection in the dressing-table mirror. 'I wish I'd been born with a nice nature instead of a pretty face.' She looked wistfully at Jane in the mirror. 'I don't know how to love.'

'Nonsense! You've had lots of boyfriends.'

'Oh, I know how to fall in love. And out. But not how to love someone so that they matter more than anyone in the world.' Eyes as brilliant as sapphires studied Jane's face. 'You're capable of real love, Janey, because you know how to give. I don't think it will ever happen to me.' Rose waved aside her sister's protest. 'I've never done it with a man I didn't like, but I haven't loved any of them. I don't even care who the father is. Does that sound terrible?'

This was no time for dishonesty. 'Yes,' Jane answered. 'But abortion isn't the only answer. And if you think it is, I'll have to tell Mum.'

'You'd better have a good alternative, then, because I've run out of ideas.'

'Go through with it.' Jane gripped her sister's hands. 'Of course they'll be shocked. But they won't turn you out. Mum will want to help take care of your baby.'

'Johnny will be back soon. I can't lumber her with another one.'

'He'll be starting at the special school next year, and it's about time Betty took more responsibility for him. Anyway, I'll be around, and Kathleen. And one day you'll meet someone who really cares for you and the child.'

'And they all lived happily ever after.' Rose grimaced. 'I wish I had your faith in happy endings.' For a long time they were silent. Then Rose said, 'Give me a day or two to work out how I'm going to tell them. Promise me you won't say anything. Please.'

Jane wasn't sure she trusted Rose, but she couldn't deny her plea. 'All right,' she agreed. 'But only on condition that you keep away from that woman.' Rose hesitated, then nodded. 'And,' Jane chose her next words carefully, 'I want you to contact the man you think is the father.'

With a sharp intake of breath, Rose shook her head. 'I can't,' she whispered.

'You must.' Jane was adamant. 'Even if, for whatever reason, you can't marry. He may be able to help. You'll need money. And he has a right to know.'

'Please don't ask this of me,' Rose begged.

'I'm not asking. I'm telling you. If you don't at least try to do things the right way, I'll go straight in to Mum and Dad now, and you can sort it out between the three of you.'

'You wouldn't.'

'Try me.'

The sisters stared at each other, each being defiantly tested. Finally, Rose's shoulders slumped. 'I can't promise that I'll be able to, but I'll try,' she said.

'That's all I ask. Now let's get to bed. We've both got a lot of thinking to do.'

Chapter Twenty-Two

January 1945 was a switchback month of freezing cold and thaw. When they weren't picking their way through ice and snow, Londoners trudged through slush, worrying about the safety of their loved ones, either at home or battling through Europe in conditions even more miserable. The end of the war was in sight, but the swift, soundless rockets continued their deadly journey. People disappeared without warning. Only a gaping hole showed where they had once stood; only an empty coffin to bury.

The Harrisons, together with thousands of British families, struggled to hold on to their sanity. Grandad read that the Burma Road had been declared open, and Nell Harrison telephoned the War Office again, but they had nothing to add to the 'unconfirmed sighting by an Allied pilot'. Aunt Grace met Uncle Nobby at every opportunity, poring over official documents. Kathleen applied herself to her studies, writing frequent letters to Uncle Len. And Rose went through the mockery of a daily journey on the District Line, leaving Jane to wonder how her twin spent each day. Rose was adept at evading confrontation.

Finally a letter from Laura Marshall forced Jane to shake the mound lying silently in the other bed.

'I know you're not asleep, Rose. We've got to talk.'

'It's too late.'

'It's only ten o'clock.'

'Well, I'm tired, even if you're not. I've been walking all day.'

'Where?'

'Mind your own bloody business.'

Jane pulled back the sheet covering her sister's face. 'I've got to know if you've contacted that man,' she demanded.

Rose tried to grab the sheet, but Jane was determined. 'Have you?' she repeated.

'I don't know where he is.'

'You're lying.'

'Prove it.' Rose's voice was surly.

'What about Mum and Dad? You promised.'

'Dad's on nights. I can't tell Mum on her own. Leave me alone, for Christ's sake.'

For a moment Jane was speechless. Then she flung back the eiderdown. 'If you don't turn over and listen to me, I'll throw a jug of cold water over you,' she threatened.

Slowly, Rose sat up. 'All right, I'm listening,' she grumbled, retrieving the eiderdown from the floor. 'What's so important that it can't wait another day?'

Jane took a letter from her handbag. 'This,' she said. 'A chance of a better job. But it will be offered to someone else if I don't contact them tomorrow.'

Rose glanced through the letter. 'Looks OK. But what's it got to do with me?'

'I want everything out in the open before I start. If Mum finds out I've been covering for you, she'll be livid. It'll be much easier if you tell them first.'

'For you, maybe, but not for me. I'm the one who's pregnant, remember.'

'And who's fault is that?'

'I'm paying for it now, aren't I? You don't know what it's like.'

'No. But I'd make sure I never got into that situation in the first place.'

'Hark at Miss Goody-goody. Bet nobody ever wanted to try it on with you.'

'I'd rather be a virgin than a tart.' As soon as the words were spoken, Jane regretted them. But the hurt was done, to both girls.

Scarlet-faced, Rose shouted, 'I'll do what I want when I want, and not just because some holier-than-thou little prig tells me to. Is that clear?'

Jane shouted back, 'You don't give a damn about anybody but yourself, that's what's clear.'

The row was interrupted by Gran banging on the wall. 'Shut your noise in there. I'm trying to get some sleep.'

Jane lowered her voice. 'Tomorrow I'm going after this job, and I don't want everything spoiled with rows over you.'

'Go after your bloody job. I don't care what you do.'

'Then you'd better try a bit harder to find the father. Because I'm going to tell Mum and Dad the truth at the weekend.'

The expression on Rose's face changed to anguish. 'You can't welch on me, Janey. You promised!'

'So did you. And I don't want some nosy neighbour asking Mum when the baby's due. It would kill her. You've got till Saturday, no longer.'

'You really mean it, don't you?'

Jane nodded.

Hunched on the bed, Rose lowered her head onto her kness. In a muffled voice, she said, 'I'll tell them when Dad comes home Saturday morning.'

'And the father?'

'I don't know. I'll try.'

'That's what you said last time. I want your word that you'll do something tomorrow.'

Rose raised a tearful face. 'Tomorrow! That's impossible.'

'You've got all day.'

Rose glared at her sister, then nodded reluctantly. 'You're a hard cow, Janey!' she cried.

'And you're a selfish bitch. Now shut up and go to sleep before Gran starts banging on the wall again.'

After Jane had switched out the light, she lay trembling, reliving the scene. As the anger waned, she wished she'd spoken with reason, not spite. But as she was about to whisper 'Good night', the memory of Rose's words taunted her, and she buried her face in the pillow.

The following morning, neither twin spoke to the other. Jane's thoughts concentrated on secretly arranging an appointment with Mrs Marshall's friend. It would be impossible to get to Piccadilly Circus, have the interview and be back at work in half an hour, but if she was lucky enough to be offered the job, it wouldn't matter.

Evelyn Reynolds was tall and angular, her wiry reddish-brown hair streaked with premature greyness and struggling to escape from the pins holding it in place. But it was her eyes that Jane found the most striking feature. Brilliantly green, they glowed as she held out her hand.

'You look younger than I expected,' she commented. 'But Laura tells me you have been nominated as one of the best students on the commercial course. Sit down and tell me about your practical experience.'

Producing her RSA and Pitman Certificates, most with distinction, Jane briefly outlined her work at Cohen's, then waited patiently while the older woman lit a cigarette and stared pensively out of the window.

Eventually, Evelyn Reynolds said, 'I'll be honest with you. The girl I saw earlier had advertising experience. But she talked nonstop, and I wasn't too happy about her reasons for leaving the other firm.' She smiled at Jane. 'I think we could work well together. Three pounds ten a week, two weeks' paid holiday a year, hours nine till five thirty, lunch one till two. And you would have to work every other Saturday morning. When can you start?'

At first Jane could only gape. It was too good to be true. Then she stammered her thanks, and asked if she could give Mrs Cohen two weeks' notice as she would like to clear up the end-of-year accounts before leaving, if possible.

The green eyes closed in concentration. 'That would take us up to the end of the month,' Evelyn Reynolds mused. 'And the new campaign for the Central Office of Information starts in February.' Her eyes opened. 'Have you registered for war work?'

'Yes, I had to once I was sixteen. Mr Cohen supplies a small quantity of shirts to the WVS, so I was cleared to work there.'

'Well, you can tell the officials you're covered here by the government work we do.' Miss Reynolds scribbled in a note-book. 'I would have preferred an earlier date, but your consideration to your present employer is admirable. Two weeks it is, then.'

Jane stood up. 'Thank you,' she said. 'If I can complete the accounts earlier, shall I contact you?'

'Please do, Miss Harrison. Actually, I'd like to call you Jane, if I may.' Jane nodded. 'Good. I'll introduce you to Miss Dawson and Victor when you start.'

Wanting to shout with joy, Jane raced down the stairs. She was free. No more Mrs Cohen. No more scrimping and scraping to make her wages stretch the week. More housekeeping money for Mum. And goodbye to that horrid little cubbyhole.

Not even the heavy grey clouds could mar her happiness. This was a lovely place. With an hour for lunch she would have time to window-shop in Regent Street or feed the ducks in St James's Park. She couldn't wait to tell Rose. Her mood saddened as she thought of their quarrel. They had argued before, but never like this. She hated being bad friends with her sister. Perhaps there was something she could take home, a little peace offering.

Across from the boarded-up area that had once displayed the Greek god of love, a department store advertised its January sale. She was going to be late back from lunch anyway. Might as well be hung for a sheep as a lamb.

The scarves were reasonable, but not quite to Rose's taste. Upstairs, a small queue was beginning to form at a counter where a delivery of silk stockings had arrived.

Clutching the small paper bag, Jane made her way through a gap in the restaurant queue. Then she stopped, took two steps backwards, and looked again. Yes, it was Rose. Seated at a table near the door, with a man. He was partially hidden by a service station, but Rose was leaning towards him in earnest conversation, his hand holding hers. This must be the one – the father of Rose's baby. So she had managed to find him!

Curious, but not wanting her sister to think she had followed her, Jane ducked behind a pillar. She heard Rose plead, 'You've got to!'

The man's low voice was drowned by the clatter. Suddenly, Rose shook her hand free and jumped to her feet. For a moment, it seemed as though she were going to strike him with her handbag. Instead, she cried, 'I knew it wouldn't do any good! You don't care about me at all, do you? All you care about is your bloody career!' With that, she ran sobbing from the restaurant.

Jane was about to run after her sister when the man stood up and turned towards the doorway. Heart thumping, she watched him pay the bill and leave the restaurant, a worried expression on his face. She could have touched his arm, he passed so close to the pillar where she stood, as though rooted to the spot, fearing that if he noticed her she would attack him publicly.

When the lift doors had closed behind him, Jane leaned against the pillar for support, trying to accept the fact that someone she had trusted, loved as a friend, could be so callous.

How could anyone put their career before honour? Sandy, of all people!

Chapter Twenty-Three

'And I expect you to work an additional hour tonight.' Myra Cohen spat the words at Jane.

'Sorry, Mrs Cohen, I have a dancing class to play for.'

Banging her fist on the table, Mrs Cohen raised her voice. 'Tonight or tomorrow, you will work an additional hour. And if that is not satisfactory, you can have the same treatment as your sister. Instant dismissal. Now get back to your desk.'

Jane was tempted to tell her employer just what she could do with her job, but bit back the words. Although the meagre wage packet was already in her handbag, the Cohens kept a week's salary in hand, and also owed her fifteen shillings overtime, which was usually paid at the end of each month, after a great deal of haggling. She would need another perm, and that would cost seventeen and sixpence at least. Better to write a formal letter of resignation and give it to her employer in the morning.

Then Mum and Dad had to be faced. Rose must keep her promise. The last thing Jane wanted was to have to tell them about the baby. But she was committed. Whichever way, there would be a big upset, and the news of her own change to a better-paid job would be of little consolation.

First, though, she must tell Rose she knew about Sandy. Advise her to go to his parents. They might be able to persuade him that the right thing was to put his responsibility before his career and marry the girl. If not, at least they were bound to help out financially. After all, it might be their grandchild he was denying.

Madame Delia was in a talkative mood and asked Jane to

stay on after the tap class was over. Jane was worried she might question Rose's continued absence, but the dancing teacher said she wanted to plan victory-celebration shows.

'The war has to end this year, and I want us to be ready for it. Do go and sit in the other room while I make a pot of tea. Then we can toss a few ideas at each other.'

Jane was glad of the opportunity to warm her hands at the coal fire, but watchful of the time ticking away. After they had roughed out a programme, Madame Delia lit another cigarette and reached for an air-mail letter tucked behind the ornate marble clock.

'I know I can trust you, Jane,' she began, 'and I feel it's only fair to put you in the picture.' The letter looked as though it had been read several times. 'Chuck is getting a divorce,' she said. 'He wants me to do the same and go out there.'

Not completely surprised, Jane asked, 'Does your husband know?'

'No. And I won't do anything until Bernard is repatriated. It has to be face to face, not a "Dear John" letter.' Madame Delia stared into the fire. 'It's five years since I saw my husband. He's been through experiences I can't begin to imagine. And I've not had an easy time, either. We'll be strangers. I don't know how to tell him.'

'Have you decided to go to America?'

The older woman looked up. 'I love Chuck,' she said, simply. 'It may take a while for everything to be sorted out, but I will join him, eventually. That's why I wanted you to know.' She smiled. 'Actually, I had to tell someone, and there are few I can trust not to gossip.' Her expression became a little anxious as she said, 'Please don't think too badly of me.'

'Of course not. It's hard for all of you. But it's nobody's fault. A lot of rotten things are happening because of the war.'

Madame Delia held Jane's gaze for a moment, then nodded 'You have a wise head on your young shoulders,' she said. 'Thanks for listening. It helped.'

On the homeward-bound bus, Jane thought about the conversation. It was true that rotten things happened because of the war. Madame Delia would never have considered leaving her husband if an attractive American sergeant hadn't offered love and companionship when she was vulnerable. And Rose ...

why couldn't she have been as generous to Rose as to Madame Delia? Perhaps because the war had nothing to do with Rose's predicament. Perhaps because she was frustrated that Rose had wasted her talent, succumbed to the easy way out. But Rose was her sister. Her twin. She had always been the strong one, the leader. Now she was the one who needed help. The reason didn't matter.

Nobody else could help Rose. Mum was too emotional, and Dad wouldn't understand. Aunt Grace would be supportive, but she was moving to Torquay. So it was up to Jane to offer sympathy and practical help. Reserve the anger for the man who wouldn't face up to his responsibility – Sandy.

Jane's blood boiled every time she thought about him. Was that the way he behaved at the hospital? Casual dalliances with nurses? Plying them with wine and a meal? Thank you and goodbye? But it was her sister who was left holding the baby – literally!

Although Jane wasn't sure of the best way to help, she would talk to Rose, try to work out a plan. Find out whether she wished to have the baby adopted. If she decided to keep it, Johnny's pram and cot could be used, but there would be other expenses. Jane's new job would ease some of the financial burden and she hoped Mr and Mrs Randall might contribute something.

Jane smiled as she wondered whether it would be a boy or girl. She could just imagine Rose with a golden-haired, blue-eyed little girl. Girls were more fun to dress, and Rose's clever fingers could stitch such pretty things. They must look forward to the baby, and she must help lift Rose's spirits, after her dreadful rejection at lunchtime.

It was almost nine thirty when Jane opened the back door. Her mother was rolling pastry on one end of the table, Aunt Grace ironing at the other. Straight away, Jane sensed an atmosphere.

'Where have you been?' Mrs Harrison snapped.

'The tap class. It's Friday.'

'I know it's Friday, but you're late, and your dinner's ruined.'

'Sorry, Mum. Madame Delia wanted to discuss the programme with me.'

225

'That's all very well, but I wanted you to polish the brass. And Gran is yelling for her cocoa.'

Jane unbuttoned her coat. 'I'll make the cocoa first, have my dinner, then do the brass –'

'Don't forget to put your slippers on. Don't want your muddy footprints all over the floor.'

'No, Mum.' Jane was already pulling on the sensible brown slippers her mother had bought her for Christmas.

As Aunt Grace stood on a chair to unplug the iron, she flashed a look at Jane which confirmed that things were not at all well in the household, before asking, 'What sort of day have you had, dear?'

Jane hesitated. She wanted to tell them about the new job. It might lighten the atmosphere. At first she had thought her mother knew about Rose, but she would have mentioned it by now. Something else must have happened to put her in such bad humour. Her own news could wait until morning. She must speak to Rose first. 'Oh, so-so,' she answered her aunt.

'Mrs Cohen on the warpath again?' Aunt Grace folded the ironing blanket. 'Rose came home in a foul mood.'

'Is she upstairs?'

Mrs Harrison banged the rolling pin onto the pastry as she answered, 'No. She came storming into the house, changed her clothes, had a dreadful row with your father, then stormed out again. I don't know what's wrong with you girls. You don't listen to anybody.'

'What did they row about?'

'She wanted to borrow some money, and Fred blew his top.'

'Did she say what she wanted it for?'

'Something about tickets for the pantomime. You know, the one with Renée Houston. Said she was treating Edna for her birthday tomorrow. I couldn't help her out, I'd already given her a pound on Tuesday and it left me a bit short. I've never seen your father so wild.'

'What did he say?'

'That he was fed up with her using the house like a hotel, only in for meals and out every night. I told him you were just as bad, but he made excuses for you. Then –' floury hands poised over the table, Mrs Harrison hesitated, as though the memory was painful – 'he ordered her to go upstairs and scrub all that muck off her face. That did it.'

'Oh, dear.'

'I won't tell you what she said, but if I'd talked back to my father like that, he'd have shown me the door, and no mistake.'

'And you've no idea where she's gone?'

'Didn't get a chance to ask, with all the shouting and yelling. Fred was so upset, he went off to work without his sandwiches. Then your grandmother started.'

'Because of the noise?'

'Among other things. Kathleen had the girl next door in after tea. For some reason, Gran's taken against the child. Thinks she's been nosing around their room.'

'Margaret! That's silly. She even asks permission to use our toilet.'

'I know, but Gran said her things had been moved, and Margaret went home in tears.'

Aunt Grace took the tray from Jane. 'I'll have a word with Mrs Ackroyd tomorrow, Nell. I'm sure she understands that Gran is old and gets confused.'

'Thanks, Grace. The last thing I want is bad feelings with the neighbours.' Mrs Harrison opened the oven door. 'Look at this liver and bacon. It's all baked up.'

'Never mind. It'll be all right with a drop more gravy. Go and drink your cocoa. I'll see to the apple pie.'

'Make sure you don't let it burn.'

Aunt Grace sighed heavily as she came back into the room. 'Nell doesn't appreciate you,' she said. 'Even after that dreadful row, she was still sticking up for Rose, telling Fred that he'd been too hard on her. Mind you, he really lost his temper. I thought he was going to hit her at one point.'

'That's not at all like Dad.'

'Then, when he said she was only interested in a good time, and dressed like a streetwalker, Rose became quite hysterical.' Aunt Grace swirled her cocoa around in the cup. 'Fred's under a lot of strain with his job, and this sort of thing doesn't help.'

'Mum's the one who really worries me. She looks so ill.'

'If only she could have confirmation about Jack. It would make all the difference.' Aunt Grace drained her cup, then looked at Jane. 'What's the real problem with Rose? You must know.'

227

Taken aback, Jane couldn't think of an evasive answer. Eventually, she said, 'Yes, I do know. But I gave my word I wouldn't tell anyone yet. And she promised to talk to Mum and Dad in the morning.'

'That's not very likely now, is it?'

'I'll have a word with her when she comes home. Hope she's not late. I'm dead tired.'

Aunt Grace took Jane's empty plate. 'Come on. I'll give you a hand with the brass.'

Before she went to bed, Jane picked up Rose's skirt and jumper from the floor, and tidied the dressing table. Then she put the paper bag with the stockings on Rose's pillow, and wrote a little note, 'Sorry I lost my temper. If I'm asleep, please wake me. I want to help. Jane.' For a while she read, trying to stay awake, but tiredness won the battle.

She awoke to her mother banging on the bedroom door.

'Janey! Rose!' Mrs Harrison called. 'I'm off to the butcher's now. If I'm in the queue early enough, I might get a sheep's head to make some brawn. Make some porridge for Gran, Janey. The milkman's coming along the road. Don't be late now, you two. You know what Mrs Cohen's like.'

Rubbing the sleep from her eyes, Jane rolled over, then sat upright. Her sister's bed was just as it had been last night. Bedspread pulled up, paper bag on the pillow, holding the stockings Jane had bought. And no clothes on the floor or thrown across the chair.

Rose hadn't come home.

Chapter Twenty-Four

Hurrying downstairs, Jane filled the kettle, willing Rose to come home before Mum found out. She tried to think calmly and rationally where Rose might be. Edna Browning – that must be it. After the row last night, Rose had gone there.

A tap on the back door interrupted her thoughts. It was Mr Ackroyd. He looked ready to drop.

'Sorry to be a bother, lass, but I wonder if you've a drop of milk to spare for a cup of tea. The Co-op comes later than your man.'

'Sit down for a moment.' Pulling her dressing gown closer, Jane ventured out of the front door and peered into the darkness. Old Ned was at the next gate, haybag around his neck, blanket protecting his back from the raw cold while the milkman made his deliveries. Long experience told him when to clip-clop the few paces to the Harrisons' gate.

In the kitchenette, her neighbour sat with his eyes closed. Jane put the bottles on the table. 'You look all in, Mr Ackroyd. Bad night?' As she searched for a jug, his words filtered through her troubled thoughts about Rose.

'Ilford again ... water everywhere ... Donald Stewart trapped under a beam ... chorus girls shivering ... thank God it wasn't a direct hit on the theatre ...'

Jane's mind was jolted into awareness. 'What theatre?' Her voice was urgent. 'Not the Hippodrome?'

'That's right. *Robinson Crusoe* was on.'

'Were there many casualties?'

'Mostly shock and bruises. The tank bursting made it tricky. Bit like the *Titanic* going down, water pouring over the footlights and the band still playing. But can you imagine the carnage if the rocket had hit the theatre, instead of that row of cottages?'

Jane had assumed that Rose would go to the Hippodrome on Edna's birthday. But they might have gone last night.

'Mr Ackroyd, did you see Rose?'

'No, lass, but they'd a full house. Was she supposed to be there?'

'She'd bought tickets for a friend's birthday, but I don't know if they were for Friday or Saturday.' Jane had to explain. 'She didn't come home, and I thought she'd stayed with her friend. But now I'm worried in case she might be in hospital.'

'There weren't many hospital cases from the theatre, Jane. Most of the serious casualties were from the cottages and the pubs. I'll go back to base and enquire if you like?'

'No.' Jane thought rapidly. 'Thanks just the same, but you need sleep. I'll go round to her friend's house first. If they're not there, I'll go to Ilford, see what I can find out. Mr Ackroyd ...'

'Yes, lass.'

'Don't say anything to Mum. You know how she worries.'

'Won't she wonder where you are?'

'She'll think I've gone to work. No point in worrying her for nothing.'

'You're right, pet. I'm sure you'll find Rose safe and sound. Probably having a fine old time with her friend.'

Jane raced upstairs and hurriedly dressed. As she pulled on her trousers, she heard her grandmother begin to shout. 'My money's gone! My emergency money.'

From the bathroom, Aunt Grace called back, 'For goodness' sake, Mum! You're always losing things. Where did you keep it?'

'Where I always keep it. In that pottery vase Janey brought me back from Torquay. I told you that girl had been going through my things. Now perhaps you'll believe me.'

'Do stop shouting, Mum. They'll hear you next door.'

'Good! She ought to be ashamed of herself. A copper's daughter, too. You go round and get my money back, Grace.'

'I'll do no such thing. You've probably moved it and forgotten.'

'No, I haven't. I counted eleven pounds seven and six in the vase yesterday morning. I might be old, but I'm not bloody senile.'

'Well, you'd better stop accusing people without any proof. And I don't want you worrying Nell. When I get back from work I'll help you look for it.'

Jane reached for her shoulder bag, then paused. If she had to go to the Hippodrome or a hospital to look for Rose, she would need something better than the description of a pretty blonde with blue eyes. Rose kept a file of photographs in her drawer. The one on top was a good likeness, although it made her look older. Hands cupping her chin, a seductive smile parting her lips.

When she tried to close the drawer, it jammed. A Post Office savings book was caught down the side. As she tried to straighten the crumpled book, Jane noticed the last entry, dated the day before, when five pounds sixteen shillings had been withdrawn, leaving a nil balance.

In the kitchenette, Aung Grace filled the teapot. 'You're ready early,' she observed. 'Is Rose up?'

Jane had to confide in someone, and Aunt Grace was unlikely to panic. Briefly and calmly, she told her aunt that Rose hadn't come home, and she was concerned she might have been injured by the V-2 near the Hippodrome.

'I'll come with you,' Aunt Grace said.

'Thanks just the same, but I'm sure I'll find her round at Edna's. Anyway, Gran will be yelling for her breakfast.'

Reluctantly, Aunt Grace agreed. 'But I won't go to work till I know Rose is safe,' she said. 'You'd better hurry. Fred will be home any minute.'

It took a while for Mrs Browning to open the door. Blinking sleep from her puffy eyes, she clutched a grubby dressing gown around her vast girth.

'Sorry to disturb you so early, Mrs Browning, but –' Jane began.

'So I should think, my girl.' Edna's mother glared from under a tangle of metal curlers. 'Fancy waking us up at this bloody hour of the morning. On a Saturday, too.' As she spoke, one yellow tooth protruded from an ugly cavern of a mouth. Rose referred to it as a 'pickle stabber'.

Again Jane apologised. 'I'm sorry. But I would like to speak to Rose, please.' She prayed that the woman would turn and bellow Rose's name. But she just stared.

'Rose? Why the hell should Rose be here?'

'I thought she was coming round first thing. To give Edna her birthday card.' It was pretty lame, but the best she could do.

'Haven't seen sight nor sound of the girl since before Christmas. Don't want to, neither, with her highfaluting talk of being a film star. She only fills Edna up with big ideas.'

'Do you happen to know whether they're planning to go out tonight?'

'Considering they had a flaming row last week, when your sister got the sack, I'd say it was bloody unlikely. Anyway, Edna's got a date up West tonight, with one of them Yanks. She didn't say nothing about a foursome.' Mrs Browning began to close the door, then paused, eyes narrowed. 'What do you want her for, anyway?'

'Oh … just to give her a message.'

'What message? She might come round later, seeing as it's Edna's birthday.'

'It doesn't matter, thanks just the same. Sorry to have bothered you.' Turning, Jane tripped over the broken front gate. She knew the woman was still watching, but she didn't look back, just hurried to the bus stop.

The area around the Hippodrome was chaotic. Under arc lights, firemen pumped away water as rescue workers dug steadily around broken masonry and splintered wood, in the vain hope that someone might still be alive. Small groups of people watched, grim-faced. A voice called for silence, but no answering sound came from under the debris, so the weary team resumed their gruesome task. Two Red Cross helpers carried a stretcher to a waiting ambulance, stumbling among the rubble. The body was completely covered, but an arm hung stiffly down from beneath the blanket. It belonged to a woman, an old woman with a work-worn hand. An elderly man standing near Jane brushed a tear from his eye as the ambulance drove away. Now Jane knew why Aunt Grace was always so quiet when she came home from a duty shift.

Carefully picking her way through the maze of hoses, an

elegant woman wearing a beaver coat offered cups of tea to two wardens. Jane approached them.

'Excuse me.' She took the photograph from her handbag. 'Can you tell me if you have seen this girl? I think she may have come to the Hippodrome last night.'

'Let's have a look.' The January morning was still reluctant to give light, so one of the men took a torch from his pocket. 'Pretty girl,' he commented. 'But I didn't get here till midnight. What about you, Bill?' His companion studied the photograph, then shook his head. 'Sorry, duck. I'd have remembered her if I'd seen her. But I'll make a note of her name and ask around.'

'Rose Harrison.'

The man added the name to his list, then asked, 'How old? Nineteen? Twenty?'

'Sixteen.'

'Who is she, love, a friend?'

'My sister.' The familiar look passed between the two men as Jane went on, 'Rose didn't come home last night, and I'm very worried.'

The woman with the tray hesitated. 'May I look?' she asked. 'Yes, I saw the young lady last night, but not in the theatre. I was taking my little Toby for his walkie when we bumped into each other. Literally. Her foot was tangled in his lead.'

Breathlessly, Jane asked, 'Did you see where she went?'

'Why, yes, my dear. She turned into number 22.' The woman pointed. 'At the far end, on the left.'

'You're sure it was Rose?'

'Oh, yes.' The woman returned the photograph to Jane. 'I thought what lovely hair she had, and what a pity –' She stopped.

'What do you mean, a pity?' Jane saw the look of embarrassment that passed between the two men.

The woman bit her lip. 'Number 22 is the nurse's house.' With her tray of refreshment, she moved on.

Suddenly, the last pieces of jigsaw puzzle fell into place. Rose hadn't intended to go to the theatre. She wanted to borrow money to pay the nurse. Gran's money! Rose had taken it.

The man called Bill said, 'Your sister might still be there. Do you want me to come with you?'

233

'No, thank you.'

Number 22 was shabbier than its neighbours, and the curtains were drawn.

The woman who opened the door a fraction was in her fifties, thin, with wary eyes. She didn't look at the photograph. 'Never seen her,' she said abruptly and tried to close the door, but Jane's foot was too fast.

'She was here last night. I have witnesses.' The nurse's eyes became even more hostile, but Jane held her ground. 'If she's here, I want to see her. If not, I want to know where she is.'

'How the heck should I know?' The door banged hard against Jane's foot.

'I could bring the police, if you prefer.' The pressure eased. 'Is she here now?' Jane asked.

'No.'

'Don't you usually keep your patients overnight?'

'Only if they have enough money. She didn't.'

'So you threw her out into the street afterwards?'

'I told her to go down to the pub and have a drink. That's the last I saw of her. God's truth.'

Jane wondered what the woman knew of either God or truth. 'Was that before or after the rocket fell?'

'Before. About an hour before.' The woman turned sharply towards a sound coming from a room off the narrow passage. The door was half open, and Jane's blood chilled as she noticed the trappings of the nurse's grim trade, stirrups hanging from the ceiling above a blood-stained bed, an assortment of instruments on a table, a bucket beneath it. Again, that low moan, like an animal in pain.

The woman quickly closed the door and turned back to Jane. 'It's not her,' she said, 'or I'd let you in just to shut your face. Now clear off.' This time the door slammed hard enough to push Jane's foot from the step.

Running back towards the arc lights, choking on her tears, she was consumed with a terrible anger. This was Sandy's fault. If he had any decency in him at all, Rose wouldn't have resorted to a back-street abortionist. And Jane wouldn't be searching for her sister in a public house, or what was left of it.

The rescue team stopped to examine Rose's photograph,

shaking their heads. But one called out to a pleasant-faced woman wearing the green uniform of the WVS.

'Mrs Wallace, didn't you bring blankets for the chorus girls last night?'

'That's right, Mr Brown. Poor things! It's a wonder they didn't freeze to death in those flimsy costumes.' Mrs Wallace turned to Jane. 'Are you looking for one of them?'

'No. It's my sister. I was told she might have been in the pub last night.'

Mrs Wallace took a pair of spectacles from her pocket. 'Oh, yes. I saw her in the toilet, crying her eyes out.' She smiled sheepishly at the man. 'It was such a perishing night, I decided to pop in for a glass of rum to warm me up before I went on duty.'

'Did you speak to her?' Jane cried.

'Why, yes, dear. The poor girl was so upset, I asked if I could help. She told me she was looking for somewhere to stay the night, but didn't have any money.' Mrs Wallace hesitated. 'She said she couldn't go home.' Jane closed her eyes as she thought of her sister's anguish. 'I suggested that she try the Salvation Army,' the woman went on. 'They're usually very helpful.'

'What did she say?'

'She was very grateful. Asked for the address. I'd have taken her there myself, but I was already late. So I gave her a couple of bob, and told her how to find it.'

'How long was it before the rocket landed?'

'Not long. But if your sister left straight away, she would have been safe. I expect she's tucked up in bed at the Sally Ann's right now.' Mrs Wallace looked at her watch. 'I should have gone off duty hours ago. Just let me get my bike, dear, and I'll walk round with you.'

For the first time, Jane felt hope as she waited by the remains of a brick wall. Nearby, a warden leaned heavily against the same wall, removed his tin hat and took a stub of cigarette from behind his ear. After it was alight, he glanced at Jane, noting her tear-stained face.

'Anyone looking after you, girlie?' he asked.

'Yes, thank you. The WVS lady is helping me find my sister.'

235

'Is that her?' He nodded towards the photograph, now a little crumpled. 'Let's have a look.' He smiled. 'Right little cracker, isn't she? Haven't seen her, I'm afraid.' When he looked closer. 'Wait a jiff. There's something familiar ...' He frowned, then stared for a moment at Jane's hand. 'Stay here while I check.' Still clutching the photograph, he strode towards a small concrete shelter at the corner of the road.

After a few minutes, Jane followed him, crunching across broken glass. Mrs Wallace talked to a colleague outside the WVS van, and Jane waved and pointed, to let her know where she was going. At the foot of a short flight of steps, she ducked and peered into the shelter. It appeared that they were using it to store things collected from the debris. Lit only by a hurricane lamp, scarves, hats, jewellery, cigarette case, lighters, a man's shoe, all were neatly laid out on a table.

The warden wrestled with something in a cardboard box. As Jane drew in a breath, he cried, 'Don't look!'

But he was too late. Jane had already seen the crimson-tipped finger adorned with a ring. A gold signet ring with a garnet. Identical to hers, apart from the engraved initials.

For the ring the warden struggled to remove was Rose's ring. And it was on Rose's finger.

Chapter Twenty-Five

An east wind drove sleet across the cemetery until it attacked Jane's face. In a strange way it was a relief to feel physical pain, but soon the icy needles numbed her skin so that again there was only coldness. Inside and out. Not even when the coffin was lowered into the grave could she feel anything. For the coffin was empty, apart from a finger. A ringless finger. Her mother wore the ring on a gold chain around her neck. 'Rose will always be next to my heart,' she'd whispered.

Jane barely listened to the recited words, '... hath but a short time to live, and is full of misery ...' True, Rose was full of misery on the day she was 'cut down, like a flower'. Fred and Nell Harrison scattered earth upon the lid of the coffin. 'Dust to dust ...' There wasn't enough left of Rose to become dust. One moment a stunning beauty, turning heads. Then nothing. Only a finger to show she'd ever existed at all. The one thing she'd feared. Where was she? Scattered in the hemisphere? Part of the dust-filled bowl scooped from the pavement? What had she been thinking, at the moment she had been 'delivered from the burden of the flesh'? Had she wished she was dead? Did she feel blessed as her last breath was stripped from her?

Fred Harrison supported his wife as her knees buckled. Before Jane could step forward, Aunt Grace had taken her sister's other arm. At her side, Gran sobbed and Grandad held a handkerchief to his face. Jane was sure that none of them gave 'hearty thanks ... deliver this our sister out of the miseries of this sinful world'.

It was over. The vicar closed his prayer book. Mourners walked away. More people than she'd expected. Even Uncle

Herbert had come down from Warwickshire, accompanied by his daughter. In her crisp Leading Wren uniform, hat at exactly the correct angle, cousin Evie was well on the road to achieving her mother's ambition. Aunt Dolly had sent her apologies, along with a huge wreath.

The school was represented by no less a personage than the headmistress. After speaking briefly to the Harrisons, Miss Bellinger came back to Jane. 'Your sister will be remembered by all who met her. Such a tragic loss.' She sighed. 'Her name will be added to the Roll of Honour.'

Jane thought of earlier honoured victims. Sweet little Theresa, evacuated to safety, but dead. Leslie Saunders, his bravery terminated at Dieppe. Marine Arnold Godwin had given his life at Anzio. Now Rose. Not killed on duty. She just happened to be in the wrong place at the wrong time. Walking out of a pub, after having an abortion.

'It's as though a light has been snuffed out.'

Jane turned towards the voice. Madame Delia watched the grave diggers stabbing at the frozen earth. She took a white chrysanthemum from her wreath and let it fall into the grave. 'It should be a rose.' Her voice cracked, and she turned towards Jane. It was the first time they had ever hugged. Then she stood back. 'I would like to hold a memorial concert. Do you think your parents would object?'

'Why, no. It's a lovely thought.'

Turning, Jane was surprised to see her music teacher. She had been right. Jane hadn't kept in touch. But there were no recriminations, just sympathy and sadness.

As Miss Palmer walked back along the path, she passed a man in Merchant Navy uniform. Uncle Len kissed Jane.

'Ruddy ship docked late, or I'd have made it,' he said. 'I just can't believe it. Not our little doll.' Head bowed, he stood at the graveside, then looked towards the group around the Harrisons. 'There's Herbert!' he exclaimed. 'Haven't seen him since before the war. Blimey, he's aged.' Uncle Len ran a hand through his grey hair. 'But haven't we all? Who's the little Jenny Wren holding his arm?'

'Evie.'

'Never! Last time I saw her she was playing with dolls.' Uncle Len's gaze wandered on to his parents, plodding slowly along the path. 'Christ! They shouldn't be out on a day like this,' he said, then apologised. 'Sorry, Janey, but at their age ...'

'They insisted on coming.'

'I'll give Nobby and Grace a hand. And you'd better not hang about too long, love, or you'll catch your death.'

'I just want to look at the wreaths.'

Uncle Len ran towards a small group of people offering condolences to her parents. Mrs Green; Daphne Jarvis and her mother; Mr and Mrs Ackroyd; Mrs Randall, nurse's cape billowing in the wind.

For the first time that day, Jane felt emotion, as she stared at the young man standing beside his mother, neatly dressed in dark suit and overcoat, black tie, grey trilby in his hand. How dare Sandy come here? How dare he pretend to be so solicitous, when it was his fault? Suddenly, he looked straight at Jane, then walked towards the grave.

She wanted to scream, 'I know!' She wanted to grab one of the spades and hit him with it, until he, too, was no more. She wanted to spit in his face. She wanted to shout, 'Murderer!' But she couldn't do any of those things. Not without telling everyone the sordid truth about Rose. Nor could she exchange courteous pleasantries with him.

Her predicament was solved by Laura Marshall arriving at her side before Sandy. She held Jane close, then said, 'My car's outside. Do you want to speak to Sandy first?'

Jane took the older woman's arm. 'I want to go home, please.' She shivered.

Mrs Marshall nodded and smiled towards Sandy, but Jane ignored him. 'Are the boys with you?' she asked.

'No. They want to remember only beautiful things about Rose. But they asked their housemaster if they could pray for her in the school chapel at the time of the funeral.'

Bea Marshall was waiting in the car with Kathleen. 'Laura insisted that I get out of the cold,' she apologised. 'I think she's afraid I'll get pneumonia again.'

'It's bitter,' Jane agreed. 'Gran and Grandad shouldn't have come.' She glanced at Kathleen and handed her a clean handkerchief.

'Won't you want it yourself?' Kathleen sniffed.

'Not any more.'

Jane had shed all her tears last Saturday, when she'd seen the finger and the ring. For an hour, she'd been unable to control the grief which threatened to tear her apart. Aunt Grace and Mr Ackroyd had followed the dreadful sound when they'd come looking for her. Now the well was empty.

Gazing silently out of the window as they followed the funeral cars along the dismal, grey streets, Jane recalled the events since Saturday morning.

When Mr Ackroyd returned the milk, he and Aunt Grace had become anxious. Jane hadn't come home, and neither had Rose. Leaving Fred Harrison asleep upstairs, his wife still queueing at the butcher's, they'd taken the bus to Ilford. Eventually, they'd brought Jane home in a taxi, still clutching the cardboard box with its macabre contents.

Nell Harrison had been in the kitchenette, cleaning a sheep's head. Jane knew that she would never again be able to look at a lifeless animal head without remembering her mother's screams. Her father hadn't made a sound, just turned a dreadful colour. It had taken an injection from Dr Norman to quieten Mrs Harrison's hysteria, brandy and hot-water bottles to restore life into the shaking form of Grandad. Gran rocked backwards and forwards in her chair, weeping bitterly, which Dr Norman considered better than bottling everything up inside. Kathleen had rushed straight up to her room and fallen to her knees. At first, Jane had feared that the reminder of death might prove too much for the child, but later the healing tears were heard.

Her father's reaction was the most frightening. He was too silent, his colour too deathly, eyes too haunted. It had been bad enough when his friends were killed at the Arsenal. But this time the grief was almost submerged by something else. Something Jane understood only too well. She, too, had not been given the chance to say 'Sorry' for the harsh accusations. Fred Harrison would not expect his wife to forgive him. But it wouldn't matter whether she did or not. Unless he could forgive himself, the guilt would gnaw at him like a cancer, until he was destroyed.

It wasn't until Jane went to bed, quite late, that she had been able to feel the full extent of her own loss. Opening the wardrobe door to hang up her skirt, she was confronted with pink satin, black velveteen, turquoise crepe, jaunty little pillbox hats thrown on the shelf, high-heeled courts tossed onto the floor. In the dressing-table drawer, the fragrance of Uncle Len's gift of perfume still clung to silk cami-knickers, and on the polished surface a scattered array of nail-varnish bottles, lipsticks and rouge pots told the story of Rose's life. Vibrant, sensuous, untidy, full of colour. But no accompanying reflection in the mirror, laughingly recounting a scandalous tale, turning this way and that to decide which earrings to wear. No frown of concentration as she brushed Jane's hair, drawing it back from the face, suggesting hairstyles, remedies for spots, brighter colours.

The stockings were still on Rose's pillow. And the note. Slowly, she tore it into tiny pieces. Too late for apologies. Turning back the cover, Jane had known the nightdress would be eau-de-nil satin, trimmed with lace. No sensible winceyette for Rose, whatever the season. Slowly, she sank down on her own bed, remembering the anger that had filled the room two nights ago. If only she hadn't kept on at Rose. If only ...

A light tap at the door and Aunt Grace came quietly into the room. They'd sat together, staring at the empty bed. Then Jane murmured, 'I've not only lost a sister, Aunt Grace. I've lost a friend.'

Her aunt stood up and untied the girdle of her dressing gown. 'Kathleen's cried herself to sleep,' she said, 'and I really need your company.' They'd cuddled up together in Jane's bed, not crying, not talking. Just before she drifted into sleep, Jane had thought, Dear Aunt Grace.

On Sunday the door knocker had tapped constantly from early morning. First Auntie Vi, who burst into tears as soon as she was through the door, then went up to her parents' room. Uncle Arthur had shuffled around for a while, then stood with his back to the room, peering through a crack in the drawn curtains. Peter was equally ill at ease. He squeezed Jane's arm before wandering over to the window to stand with his father. Kathleen had been taken under the wing of Mrs Ackroyd after Mass.

Various neighbours had called, but Nell Harrison stayed in bed, too distraught to talk to anyone, and Fred Harrison seemed oblivious to everything. Jane was examining the larder to see what food was available when Laura Marshall arrived, carrying a large casserole dish.

'I don't suppose anyone's had much chance to think about lunch,' she said. Then she, too, fell silent as she noticed the pretty blue umbrella she'd given Rose at Christmas, hanging on the hallstand. As she hung up her coat, she murmured, 'It just doesn't seem possible.'

It was a peculiar day, that first day of mourning. Frequent offers to make cups of tea, as if something should be done to help, but what? Voices in hushed whispers. Tears. Men clearing their throats before commenting on the weather. Jane wondering whether to pack away Rose's things, but deciding to wait until her mother was in a fitter state to make decisions. So she washed up and emptied ashtrays, which soon overflowed again. And all the time, her father remained wordless, staring inwardly at his tormented memories.

Monday had been easier, because there were practical things to do. A death to be registered. Funeral parlour to be visited. Phone calls to employers had to be made.

Myra Cohen interrupted Jane's attempt to tell her about Rose. 'I should have dismissed you along with your sister,' she shouted. 'You didn't have the nerve to confront me face to face –'

'Mrs Cohen –'

'Instead you left a letter on your desk, with false claims for overtime.'

'Please listen –'

'You stated quite clearly that you would work out your notice.' The woman was in full flow.

'I intended to –'

'And if you think I'm going to send your back pay, you can think again. Let me tell you, I am glad to get rid of the pair of you, especially that troublemaking sister –'

Jane yelled down the telephone, 'Rose is dead!'

Silence. Then Mrs Cohen said, 'When?'

'Friday evening. She was killed by a V-2.'

Silence again. Then, 'And you didn't have the courtesy to telephone me on Saturday morning.'

'We didn't know Rose was dead until Saturday.'

'That's no excuse for not being at your desk this morning. You haven't finished the balance sheet.'

'I'm sorry, but I can't possibly come in before lunch. There's so much to do before the funeral.'

'That's your parents' responsibility.'

'They are both in a state of severe shock. And, as you know, we have elderly grandparents to care for.'

'And I have a business to run, not a charitable organisation. If you are not here within the hour, you will forfeit every penny of your back pay.'

Shocked, Jane protested, 'You can't do that. I'm entitled to last week's wages, and my overtime for last month.'

'You're entitled to nothing, not even a reference, and I expect to see the completed balance sheet on my desk by lunchtime.' Jane had been prepared to make the effort until Mrs Cohen said, 'Your sister was a sore trial to me when she was alive, and she's still a problem now she's dead.'

Suddenly, the anger erupted. 'Well, here's another problem for you to be getting on with. I'm not coming in today, tomorrow, or ever. And you can stuff your back pay with your reference and your job.' With a glorious vision of Rose cheering her on, Jane had added, 'Right up your tight bloody arse!'

Chapter Twenty-Six

Slipping a carbon between letterhead and flimsy, Jane checked her calendar. Thursday 22 March 1945. Was it really only two months? She felt as though she had worked at the agency for years. That was mainly due to the matter-of-fact kindness of Evelyn Reynolds. When Jane had apologised for not having the promised references, she'd nodded, expressed her sympathy about Rose, and asked if Jane needed an advance on her salary. Laura Marshall had probably told her friend about the problems with Mrs Cohen.

There were only two other members of staff: Augustine Dawson and Victor Mole.

Miss Dawson was another of the Great War's spinsters, although, unlike Aunt Grace, she hadn't been a bereaved fiancée. There simply hadn't been enough men left to go around.

Her hair was coiled in the plaited earphone style fashionable some twenty years earlier, and her skirt barely cleared her ankles. Each morning, she would carefully take off her cloche felt hat, put on rimless spectacles, remove the cover from her typewriter and stare at the machine for a few moments. The duplicating machine was obviously a monster, waiting to cover her hands with ink, just like the typewriter ribbon when it needed replacing.

Perhaps because Jane was willing to help with these tasks, and answer the hated telephone, perhaps because she also dressed rather plainly, Miss Dawson took a liking to the new member of staff.

After the coarseness of the machinists at Cohen's, Jane

found her colleague a pleasant companion, and was quite happy to accept an invitation to take tea one Sunday in the tiny flat that was now home to the gentle spinster.

'Knightsbridge is quite convenient for the office,' Miss Dawson told her visitor.

'And for Harrods,' Jane observed.

'Indeed, yes. Not that I can afford to shop there so frequently now. But sometimes I indulge in a light luncheon or afternoon tea in their excellent restaurant, remembering the days when Papa took us for a birthday treat.'

Jane looked around at the curious mixture of good antique and clumsy Victorian furniture. 'Was the flat partly furnished?' she asked.

Her companion nodded. 'Fortunately, I managed to rescue some of the pieces from Wimbledon.' A land mine drifting along a tree-lined avenue had partially demolished the family home, killing her elderly parents in the process.

'That painting is beautiful.' Jane nodded towards the fireplace.

'It's a Turner. One of Papa's better investments. And my insurance against penury,' Miss Dawson explained, as she poured tea into delicate cups with gilt edging and offered a plate of wafer-thin cucumber sandwiches. 'Thank goodness the explosion did not damage Mother's Crown Derby.'

Jane's gaze wandered to the iced fancies on the two-tiered cake stand. Her hostess smiled. 'Baking was never a speciality of mine, although Cook did attempt to teach me. However –' she moved the cake dish a little closer to her guest – 'Fortnum and Mason's have a rather mouth-watering array, even in wartime, don't you think?'

'They look delicious.' Jane selected a pink creation. 'What happened to your cook? Was she ...?'

'Thankfully, Mrs Bennett was not harmed.' Miss Dawson dabbed at her mouth with an embroidered napkin. 'She now lives in Worthing. Quite close to Nannie.'

Sitting around a cosy fire on that chill February day, Jane had heard about a life vastly different to her own, a world of Edwardian elegance, garden parties and carefully preserved dance cards, signed by dashing young officers before they were called to the muddy fields of France, leaving genteel young maidens unprepared for a world outside marriage.

245

They discussed the lunchtime concerts at the National Gallery, and Madame Delia's dancing school. It was surprisingly easy to talk about Rose. Perhaps because Miss Dawson had never met her sister. But she was perceptive.

'It must be so dreadfully painful to lose a twin. I would imagine there is a special closeness. A sharing of life's experiences.'

Jane nodded. Not a day passed without her feeling as though part of her own being had been lost. She spoke of Rose's brightness, the star-struck dreams. She did not tell of the latter months. The bitter truth would remain a secret, even to the family. Especially to the family.

Aunt Grace had wondered why Rose should be outside the theatre, but Jane reminded her that Rose was unwell, probably needed some air. When asked what had been troubling Rose, Jane merely said they'd both had problems with Mrs Cohen and decided to leave.

Before her grandmother could remember the lost money, Jane had taken her savings book to the post office, then slipped eleven pounds seven shillings and sixpence into the pink handkerchief sachet in the next room. Gran was sure she hadn't moved her little nest egg, but the family were convinced, Margaret vindicated, and no one suspected Rose's involvement.

A few days after the funeral, Jane had received a letter in Sandy's handwriting. She took it straight into the living room and poked it deep into the fire. Whatever he had to say, it was too late.

But life would never be the same again. Her father had retreated into his private hell, and Mrs Harrison nursed her mother. As Uncle Len had feared, Gran caught a chill at the funeral, which turned to pneumonia. Grandad still read the newspapers, but with lack of enthusiasm, despite the war approaching its finale. He didn't even move the pins on his maps any more.

Aunt Grace tried to engross herself in correspondence from Torquay, but would often sit silently staring at Rose's photograph on the sideboard. And Kathleen retired to their room most evenings with her homework. Even Peter did not visit so often. It was as though the heart had been torn from the family.

Jane's salvation had been the new job. She had so much to learn, it left her little time to dwell on her thoughts. Madame Delia was planning her victory concert, and looking for something suitable to donate as a permanent memorial to Rose. The piano lid had to be opened again, although Jane still couldn't find the inspiration to play anything other than rehearsal pieces. It was easier to plunge herself into work.

Breaking free from her reverie, she typed the date and began to transcribe her shorthand. Just before lunchtime, Victor put his head around the door.

'Boss wants you, Jane – Miss Harrison,' he said, glancing at Miss Dawson. 'Said you're to take in the Fernley budget if you've done it. Better chop-chop. She's in a bit of a mood.' The door shut noisily.

Miss Dawson raised her eyebrows. 'A spot of military discipline would not do that young man any harm.'

Jane agreed. Victor Mole lived up to his name. Small and furtive, with beady eyes and acne. Always late, often careless, and sometimes cheeky just short of rudeness, he was a bone of contention to all who worked with him. He knew better than to chance his luck with Miss Reynolds, but had a regular running battle with Miss Dawson on points of order and the correct way to address people.

Evelyn Reynolds took the sheaf of papers from Jane. 'You've soon finished this,' she said, glancing through the columns of figures. 'And it's well presented. Let's hope the total is within their suggested budget. They're a tight-fisted lot, expect miracles on a shoestring.'

Jane nodded. 'I noticed that from their last letter, so I checked your figures against theirs. You've still got fifty pounds to play with, in case they change anything.'

'Well done!' Miss Reynolds smiled. 'That's exactly the attitude I like to see.' She slipped the top copy into an envelope. 'This has to be taken directly to the client, but I can't trust that wretched boy. Last time he missed the deadline with an important letter. Said it was because of a V-2, but I suspect he pocketed the taxi money and went by bus.' She unlocked a drawer and gave Jane two one-pound notes from a metal cash box. 'I hate asking you to do run-around jobs, but it is important, and I've just been called to a meeting with a new client.'

247

She pulled on her grey peaked hat. 'Would you type a covering letter and sign it p.p.? You know the sort of thing.' At the door, she turned back. 'I forgot to ask. How is your grandmother?'

'I think the new M & B tablets are helping.'

'Let's hope they are as successful as they were for Winston.'

'Thank you. Oh, Miss Reynolds,' Jane called after her employer. 'The petty-cash box ...'

'Botheration! I must be more careful.' She locked the desk drawer. 'Good job one of us has her wits about her.'

As Jane buttoned her coat, she glanced out of the window behind her desk. It looked out onto an interior well, with office windows on three sides. Immediately opposite, a middle-aged man tapped his pencil rapidly on his desk as he spoke into a telephone. He seemed rather cross. But the man in uniform on the floor below did not seem at all cross. He smiled up at Jane, and she raised her hand. Miss Dawson, using the pencil sharpener attached to Jane's desk, noticed the blush of her young companion.

'They truly are a handsome race,' she commented. 'Due to their Viking ancestry, no doubt.' Jane had noted the white-blond hair and blue eyes. Miss Dawson nodded as the sailor bowed in her direction 'Good manners, too.' Her smile was a little roguish. 'Has the young man been introduced to you?'

'Oh, no.' Flustered, Jane turned away and pulled on her beret.

'Well, he does seem to find this window interesting.'

'I hadn't noticed,' Jane lied. 'How long has he been at the Naval Headquarters?'

'He is a fairly new recruit, probably just eighteen. Four years ago, that floor was thronged with Norwegians who had escaped after the raid on the Lofoten Islands.'

'Have you talked to any of them?'

'I once had a most interesting conversation about Edvard Grieg with Mrs Petersen.'

'The grey-haired officer, with the kind face? She seems to take care of the younger girls.'

'Don't be deceived by her appearance, my dear,' Miss Dawson said. 'According to her colleagues, Mrs Petersen was a key figure in the resistance movement. In fact, she was captured by the Germans and sentenced to death.'

Jane was stunned. 'Did she tell you much about it?' she asked.

'Oh, no. Like most heroines, she is reluctant to discuss her deeds.' Miss Dawson studied the paper knife thoughtfully. 'To me, this is merely something with which to open a letter. To Mrs Petersen, it is a means of ending the life of a German guard, quietly.'

In the taxi Jane thought how war changed so many lives, to a greater or less degree. Some, including her parents, would never recover. Others would look for a new life elsewhere, as Madame Delia and Aunt Grace were doing. Those like Miss Dawson would find the changes a continuous struggle, whereas Mrs Petersen, whose experiences were too dreadful to contemplate, would probably exchange her uniform for an apron, go back to her homeland and try to pick up the pieces of her life again.

Jane's postwar plans had always centred on Rose. She had never been able to imagine a time without her sister to care for, worry about, quarrel with. To be the spinster twin wasn't a problem. But to be a lonely spinster was different.

Marriage had never been part of her plan. The idea of sex was not exactly repugnant, just something she rarely thought about. Something that seemed to give other people a lot of problems. But something that was obligatory in marriage. Would marriage now have to be a considered possibility for the future?

Probably not. Her limited experience with Jim hadn't provided much faith in her ability to attract a man. He'd not even made a pass serious enough for Jane to slap his face. So here she was, nearly seventeen, and only one date to sustain her through her old age.

Gazing out of the taxi window, Jane found that an image of blue eyes and a boyish smile blurred the London street. But the good-looked Norwegian hadn't ventured further than a wave. Even when they had once met in the entrance hall, he had only said 'Good morning' and hurried past.

It was lunchtime when she returned. Reluctant to go straight back, Jane was tempted to walk in the park. The morning sunshine had encouraged daffodils to burst into spring song, and a horde of hungry ducks waddled furiously in her direction as she paused by the lake, till they realised she had no titbits, quacked peevishly, and turned their attentions to a man in a bowler hat, umbrella hooked over his arm, who threw them a few crusts.

At the far end of the park, Buckingham Palace posed regally against the backdrop of blue sky and bare trees. Jane decided that, in future, she would bring her sandwiches here whenever possible, share them with the ducks, and watch people passing by. Most were in uniform, the flashes of Canada, France and Poland on their shoulders, many from the United States, and nearly all had a girl on their arm. Suddenly, Jane felt lonely. And hungry.

Someone was watching her from the other side of the little bridge. A young man with blue eyes and blond hair, the word *Norge* on the shoulder of his uniform.

'Hullo.' He smiled shyly. 'I thought it was you.'

How long had he been watching her? What should she say? Oh, dear! It was just as bad as being with Jim.

'I'm sorry,' he apologised. 'You were far away in your thoughts. Did I surprise you?'

'Yes. No. I mean ... I was thinking I should go back to the office.' What a stupid thing to say! Now he would probably think she didn't want to talk to him.

'It is time I also returned. Shall we walk together?'

'Why, yes. Of course.'

'My name, it is Olaf. Olaf Amundsen.'

'Are you a descendant of the polar explorer?'

'No. Sometimes I wish. I might be famous.' They both laughed, a little nervously. 'And your name? It is ...?' Olaf asked.

'Jane. Jane Harrison.'

'Jane. That is a good name.'

'I was named after my father's mother.'

'Is she a nice person, too, your grandmother?'

Jane felt herself blush. 'She died before I was born.'

'That is sad. But I am sure she was a nice person.'

They walked in silence for a few minutes. Then Jane said, 'Were you named after a relative?'

'My mother named me after the crown prince.'

'Is she in England with you?'

250

Olaf shook his head. 'When Norway was invaded, my mother was afraid my older brother and I would go into German labour camps. She sent us to her brother in Namsos. British Marines had landed there and she was hopeful they would take us to England.'

'And did they?'

'No. All was confusion. The Germans bombed Namsos until there was nothing left to destroy.'

Jane shivered as she remembered the Blitz of 1940. 'How did you manage to escape?' she asked.

'My uncle put me on a fishing boat that was going further north. I sheltered in the Lofoten Islands for a year. In 1941 your Commandoes brought me to England.'

'With your brother?'

'He stayed to help my uncle establish a resistance group. They blew up roads and bridges as the Germans advanced from Trondheim.'

'Is he still in Norway?'

Olaf's eyes clouded as he said, 'He was killed, together with my uncle, in the operation to rescue Lieutenant Petersen. You know, the lady who works in the room next to mine.'

'Yes, I heard she was captured.'

'She was a very important person. So the orders were that she was to be rescued, or killed, before she could give away any names or plans. But even though she was horribly tortured before Uncle Kris found her, she told them nothing. A very brave lady.'

'Your brother must have been very brave, too.'

'Yes. I am proud of Sven. And I miss him. He was not yet seventeen when he died.'

The same age as Rose, thought Jane. They crossed the Mall in silence and had begun to climb the long flight of steps below the memorial to the Duke of York when they heard the familiar explosion and watched the distant plume of dark smoke rising into the blue sky.

'Will they ever stop?' she muttered.

'Soon. It will be over soon.'

'I hope so.'

'The Milorg is very busy in Norway. They tell us it will not be long.'

'Milorg?'

'Our resistance fighters.' They were almost at the entrance to their building. Olaf looked up at the Norwegian flag fluttering in the breeze, then his gaze turned to the board listing the various companies. 'You work for the advertising agency. It is interesting?' he asked.

'Very. Of course, I still have much to learn, but I am glad I came to work here.'

'So am I.' He held out his hand. 'Goodbye, Jane Harrison,' he said. 'And thank you for allowing me to walk with you.'

'Goodbye.' Sadly Jane turned to press the button for the lift. She had hoped that Olaf might linger a little, but he was obviously anxious to get back to work. Suddenly, he ran back down the first flight of stairs.

'Excuse me.' His voice was breathless. 'I hope you do not think I am too ...' He looked at the ceiling as he searched for the right word. 'Fast? It is wrong word? But I am to see the film *The Way to the Stars*. And I should be so happy for you to accompany me.'

Chapter Twenty-Seven

'To Jane, with love from Aunt Peggy and Uncle Joe.' Jane looked at the small pile of cards, uncertain. When she'd picked them up from the mat, her mother had uttered a little cry. perhaps seeing only one set of greetings on the sideboard would not be a good idea.

As she arranged them on the dressing table, her aunt tapped on the door. 'Happy birthday, Jane!' She looked at the cards. 'Aren't you taking them downstairs?'

'Mum was rather upset just now, so I thought ... It's very hard for her.'

'It's hard for you as well. And it is your birthday.' Aunt Grace handed Jane an envelope. 'Nobby's on duty this weekend, so he asked me to give you this.' The card contained two pound notes.

'How very kind. I'll put it into my savings book.'

'I think he'd rather you bought something with it. And this is from me. Hope you like it.'

'Like it? It's lovely,' Jane gasped as she held up the navy handbag. 'Just what I needed. But it must have been very expensive.'

'It's about time you had a few smart things. Have you been given any other money?'

'A pound from Aunt Peggy, two pounds from Uncle Len.'

'Treat yourself to a pair of shoes to go with the handbag. And a new hat. That beret isn't fashionable enough for a secretary.'

'I'm not really a secretary. Only a typist.'

'Nonsense. You're keeping Miss Reynolds's diary, answering

her phone, writing letters off your own bat and working out schedules. Much more than a typist.'

'I enjoy the work, Aunt Grace. Honestly. And Miss Reynolds is very appreciative.'

'Good. But I still think you need some new clothes. You're seventeen now.' Aunt Grace paused. 'Is there anything suitable among Rose's things?'

Slowly, Jane shook her head. 'Rose was shorter than me, and not so skinny. Anyway, we had different tastes.'

'What about scarves and belts? Accessories can make all the difference, you know, especially when you're still wearing your old uniform.'

'I've outgrown most of my other things,' she said, 'and Mum said there's still plenty of wear in these.'

'You can see the ridge where you've let the hem down. It's a different colour. Now you're earning more you should be able to afford a new skirt. I saw some nice plaid ones in the Civil Service Stores.'

It wasn't possible to explain that she'd been trying to replace the withdrawal from her savings account. 'It's not just the money,' Jane said. 'Mum was short of coupons.'

'Because she was always giving some to Rose.'

'I know. But her funeral outfit was bought years ago, and had turned a funny green colour. I had to help her out.'

'Have you enough coupons for a blouse as well as shoes?'

'I think so.'

'Get a nice bright colour. Red would suit you.'

'Mum wouldn't like that. She said I ought to wear quiet colours for at least a year, as a mark of respect.'

Aunt Grace made an exasperated sound. 'All this fuss about wearing mourning. As though it has anything to do with respect, or grief. It's what we feel inside that counts.' Jane was inclined to agree, but didn't speak. 'Rose loved bright colours,' Aunt Grace went on. 'And she wouldn't want you to wear things that don't suit you, just to please the neighbours.'

'Fetch out no shroud for Johnny-in-the-Cloud,' Jane murmured.

'And keep your tears for him in after years,' Aunt Grace continued the verse, then frowned. 'Wish I could remember the rest.'

'Better by far for Johnny-the-bright-star,' Jane quoted, 'To keep your head and see his children fed.'

'How did you remember all that?'

'I copied it out from a magazine. *The Way to the Stars* was the first picture Olaf and I saw together, and the poem reminded him of his brother.'

'It reminds us all of someone we've loved and lost,' Aunt Grace said. 'Sadly, they were too young to leave children to be fed. But Rose would have approved of the sentiment. She hated humbug.'

Jane smiled. 'Thanks, Aunt Grace. I'll remember that, when I'm trying to convince Mum.'

'Well, you know what they say. There's no time like the present. You've got your birthday money, and the morning off before you meet your young man.'

The blush deepened as Jane spoke. 'He's not my young man. Just ... just ...'

'Just good friends, as the film stars say?'

'Yes. But I promised Mum I'd give her a hand with the spring cleaning this morning.'

'Not on your birthday, you don't. I'll help Nell this afternoon, and we can all pitch in tomorrow. Is Olaf coming to tea?'

Jane shook her head. 'Mum can't face meeting strangers just yet.'

'Pity. It might do her good. So what are you –'

They were interrupted by Kathleen. 'Happy birthday,' she said, handing Jane a package.

'Thanks a lot.' Jane kissed her young friend. 'How did you know I wanted an address book?'

'I guessed.' Kathleen smiled. 'Your mother wants to talk to the three of us. She's reading a letter from Torquay.'

Betty and Johnny were coming home. She was fed up. When Aunt Peggy was over at the farm, Betty had to look after the boy herself. He was a real handful. She just hoped Hitler hadn't got any more secret weapons.

'There's not been any rockets for a fortnight.' Mrs Harrison looked hopefully at Aunt Grace, who nodded.

'Should be safe enough now. We'll have to change the bedrooms around. Johnny's too big for the cot.'

'I know. I hate the thought of someone else sleeping in Rose's bed. But Betty and Johnny will have to go in there. Janey can sleep on the bed-chair downstairs.'

'You can't turn her out of her own room,' Aunt Grace protested.

'If I had my way, no one would use that room. I'd keep it as a shrine to Rose. But I've no choice.' Mrs Harrison ran a hand through her hair. 'What else can we do? It was bad enough when I had the cot in my room, let alone a bed.'

Jane's heart sank, but she couldn't think of a better solution. Kathleen worked it out. 'I'm thinking there's room for the bed-chair in Jane's room,' she said, 'and I'd be very snug on that, being small and all. With Aunt Grace in Rose's bed, Betty could have our room for herself and the little lad. What do you think?'

Jane thought it far better than sleeping in the dining room, Aunt Grace agreed, and Mrs Harrison only demurred a little. It was settled. Kathleen would move her things out immediately after breakfast. Where should she put them?

It couldn't be delayed any longer. Glancing at her aunt, Jane ventured, 'Mum, we really must decide what we're going to do with Rose's clothes.'

'Not today, Janey! How can you be so heartless? Don't you realise it would have been Rose's birthday?'

'Of course I realise, Mum. It's my birthday, too. Or have you forgotten?'

'Don't be silly.' Mrs Harrison eye twitched rapidly. 'I hope you didn't expect me to go out and buy just one card and present. Perhaps next year I'll be able to face up to it. But it's too soon. Too painful.'

Gently, Aunt Grace said, 'It's painful for Jane as well. We mustn't forget that, Nell.'

'I suppose so.' Mrs Harrison softened a little. 'Sorry, Janey. You do understand, don't you?'

Jane nodded. It was difficult to understand how hurting one daughter eased the loss of another, but she tried. 'When is Betty arriving?'

'This afternoon. I want you to meet her at Paddington. She can't manage on her own.'

'Mum, I can't! Olaf's taking me out for a meal, then we're going to see the new Ivor Novello musical. Remember?'

'Surely you can go another day? I can't leave Gran, and your father's working overtime.'

'Olaf has already booked tickets, and I've arranged to meet him at the Scandinavian Restaurant. There's no way I can let him know, even if I wanted to cancel it.'

'It's not a question of what you want. It's what I want that goes in this house, my girl.'

Aunt Grace said, 'I'll meet Betty. What time is her train due in?'

'Ten past five. But I thought you had Red Cross duty.'

'So I'll be late for once. There's not must activity at the moment, anyway, thank God.' She smiled at Jane. 'You go out and enjoy yourself, dear.'

Tight-lipped, Mrs Harrison said, 'I don't know how she can even think about enjoying herself, with Rose dead.'

'Listen, Nell. If being miserable would bring back Rose, I'd be the first with the sackcloth and ashes.' Aunt Grace tried to reason with her sister. 'And don't look at me like that. Just because Jane wants to go to the theatre doesn't mean she's forgotten about Rose.'

'If Jane thought anything at all of Rose, she wouldn't dream of gallivanting about with some foreigner on Rose's birthday. It's not decent.'

'That's not fair, Mum,' Jane cried. 'I loved Rose more than you know. She was my twin, for goodness' sake.'

'Nobody loved Rose the way I did,' her mother retorted. 'None of you. I was the only one who really understood her. And she'd do anything for me.'

'You never asked her to do anything. Only me.' Her frustration almost out of control, Jane faced her mother. 'In fact, you don't ask, you just tell me what you want done. Rose wouldn't have put up with it.'

'How dare you talk about Rose like that!' Mrs Harrison's face was white with anger. 'You were always jealous of her. It's wicked.'

'Stop it! Both of you.' Aunt Grace held up her hand. 'This isn't getting us anywhere. And you're upsetting Kathleen.'

Tearful, Kathleen had edged backwards towards the door. Taking a deep breath, Jane was about to apologise when her mother looked her full in the face, eyes full of contempt.

Stunned, Jane could only turn and run up the stairs. She'd always known her mother favoured Rose, but the thought that she herself was disliked had never entered her head. Yet there was no mistaking the expression in her mother's eyes. Totally devoid of affection. It was as though ... No. She wouldn't admit it into her thoughts.

One of the birthday cards fell from her dressing table as she flopped heavily onto the bed. 'Happy birthday, Jane,' she mocked.

Aunt Grace popped her head around the door. 'I'm off to work now, Jane,' she said. 'What are you going to do?'

'I'm going to take your advice and go shopping.'

Her aunt nodded. 'Probably the best thing,' she said.

'Well, I'm not wanted here, that's for sure. Did you see the look on Mum's face?'

'Don't take too much notice, dear. Nell's bound to be upset this morning. She'll have forgotten all about it by the time you come home.'

'Wish I could say the same. But thanks for offering to meet Betty. Don't know what I'd have done without you.'

Two hours later she had still not found a suitable pair of navy shoes, so she settled for black with a low wedge heel. At least they were better than school lace-ups. The blouse was just as difficult, but she eventually found a grey crepe-de-chine with a white scalloped collar and kept it on, putting the white shirt into the bag. Hats were always a problem. She tried most of the milliners in Ilford before deciding to go to Oxford Street.

A neat little navy felt with a bit of veiling didn't look too bad, although it was costly. The stores were quite festive, with their imaginative displays of flags, portraits of King George and WELCOME HOME banners.

Olaf was waiting outside the little café. 'You have a new hat,' he commented, as he ushered her inside. 'It is nice.' The restaurant was adorned with flags of Norway, Sweden and Denmark, and the waitresses wore attractive national costumes. After ordering meatballs in tomato sauce, Olaf pushed a package across the table. 'Happy birthday,' he said. It was the largest box of chocolates Jane had ever seen.

'How ever did you ...?' Words failed her.

'Ah.' Olaf grinned and touched his nose. 'An American sailor gave me ...' He looked for inspiration at the ceiling. 'A favour? Their clubs sell very good things, yes?'

'Very good indeed. Thank you. They look gorgeous. I can't wait to show them to –' Jane had been about to say 'Rose', then remembered. Olaf covered her hand with his own.

'It is sad as well as happy, this birthday of yours, yes? I understand. But next year will be a little more easy.'

Silently, Jane nodded. His hand was warm and comfortable. But her pleasure was short-lived. The waitress needed to put the tray on the table.

It wasn't until they were in the dark theatre that Olaf again reached for her hand. In the weeks since they had talked in the park, he had never once attempted to kiss or touch her. Not until this afternoon, in the restaurant. But this time it wasn't to comfort her. This time he caressed her fingers with his thumb, and she was aware that he'd moved closer. It was a surprisingly pleasant sensation.

Jane sneaked a sideways glance. He had a good profile, straight nose and slightly wavy hair brushed back from his forehead. Suddenly, he turned and smiled at her, a glimpse of white teeth in the darkness. Then he squeezed her hand gently before they both turned their attention back to *Perchance to Dream*.

As they walked along the Strand afterwards, Olaf tucked her hand into his arm. Jane softly hummed the beautiful melody of 'We'll Gather Lilacs'. She was desperately afraid of saying the wrong thing, as she had with Jim. This time it was much more important. After a while, she had to comment on the delight of seeing neon lights flashing again. The Civil Service Stores window blazed with light.

Olaf hugged her arm closer. 'You have waited many years for this moment, Jane,' he said. She smiled back, feeling a strange sense of breathless excitment. It wasn't only the lights of London she had waited for.

At the Underground station he bought a platform ticket. 'I wish I could take you home,' he commented, 'but I have to be back at my lodgings.'

'I know. It was a lovely evening. Thank you.'

He looked along the platform towards the sound of rumbling

from the tunnel. 'Is it possible that I may see you tomorrow?' he asked hesitantly. 'I could meet you at your home, if your parents would permit?'

Oh, dear. Now he would think that she didn't want to go out with him again, because he had held her hand.

'Olaf, I would like to, but ...'

'But?'

She searched for the right words. Words that wouldn't hurt or be misunderstood.

'My mother is not well. She can't get over losing Rose. And with Betty coming home ...'

'Of course. I had forgotten your sister-in-law. You must stay with your family. Will you be able to come to the cinema on Wednesday, as usual?'

'Yes, that would be – oh, no!' She covered her mouth as she remembered. 'Madame Delia has asked for an extra rehearsal. It's a special concert as a memorial to Rose. And Wednesday is my only free evening.'

Olaf's words were obliterated by the train thundering into the station. She stepped up into the carriage and turned to face him. 'I'm so sorry,' she said.

He leaned forward, as though to kiss her, but the guard shouted 'Mind the doors' and she had to jump backwards. As the train gathered momentum, she was aware of his solitary figure on the platform, hand raised, a disappointed expression on his face.

Melodies from the play waltzed inside her head. She tried to think of a way to meet Olaf outside work, but it was difficult, with exams coming up for her commercial course, and extra rehearsals. Jane fervently hoped that Olaf believed she really wanted to see him again. He was too nice to lose. There was only one night she might be able to wangle. Thursday was set aside to help with chores.

Jane's chin went up. She was not a child any longer, but a young woman. Entitled to some fun.

She'd expected everyone to be in bed. But Betty sat by the fire, a glass of sherry in her hand. Smiling. Actually smiling. And Aunt Grace positively beamed over the top of her glass. When she spoke, it was in her 'I'm ever so slightly tipsy' voice. 'Hullo, dear. Like your hat. Was the show good?'

'Lovely, thanks. Hullo, Betty. You're looking well.'

'Happy birthday, Janey. Sorry I didn't send you a card. I forgot the date.'

'That's all right.' Jane hadn't really expected anything. 'Where's Mum?' she asked. 'In bed?'

Betty shook her head. 'Johnny wanted a drink of water.'

'Oh? Is he speaking better?'

'No such luck. He just yells till he gets what he wants.'

Only because you never make any attempt to communicate with him, Jane thought. Expecting a frosty confrontation, she listened to the footsteps on the stairs.

Mrs Harrison had obviously been crying earlier, but she didn't look sad or angry. In fact, a wavery smile tried to force its way onto her face.

'Hullo, Janey,' she said. 'I've got such a birthday present for you.'

Chapter Twenty-Eight

'At least, I think that's what she said.' Betty concluded her disjointed account. 'You'll be able to find out better when you go to the War Office.'

'Let's try and get the story straight first.' Jane unbuttoned her coat. 'The Red Cross told you that a lady in America picked up a propaganda broadcast from Japan last December. A concert from a prisoner-of-war camp. Right?'

'Well, I don't know if you'd call it propaganda. They were just saying how well they were being treated.'

'And she didn't hear Jack speak.'

'No. They were all Americans and Aussies. And they were singing "A Partridge in a Pear Tree". You know, the one you play at Christmas.'

Jane didn't want to dampen the bright atmosphere, but she had to be sure. Gently, she said, 'It's sung all over the world, Betty. Tell me what happened next.'

'Well. One of the Yanks said a Limey he'd met in another camp had taught him the words.'

'There had to be more for them to think it was Jack.'

'Twin sisters were mentioned, one playing the piano. She thinks he was trying to let people know Jack was safe.'

'Did they give any names?'

'To tell the truth, I couldn't take it all in. But there was something about him being a glider pilot. Oh, Janey, it is Jack, isn't it? It's got to be.'

'Well.' Jane drew a deep breath. 'It certainly sounds promising. And it was rather clever of them to connect such a flimsy description to Jack.'

Aunt Grace raised her glass. 'Good old Red Cross,' she toasted. 'They look for different details. More of the human touch. The War Office is so tied up with red tape it can't see beyond rank, name and number.'

'Have you been in touch with the War Office?' Jane asked her sister-in-law.

'No. They frighten the wits out of me.' Jane reflected that her sister-in-law had few wits to lose. 'I hate talking to officials,' Betty went on, 'and Mum can't leave Gran, so I thought you or Aunt Grace ...'

Aunt Grace offered around her packet of Craven A. 'It's out of the question for me on Monday, I'm afraid. In any case –' she flicked on her lighter – 'they won't tell me anything, or Jane. You're the next of kin.'

'I can't go on my own. Janey ...?'

'We're very busy just now, but I'll see what I can do. Make the appointment first, then phone me at the office.'

'You do it, Janey. I hate using the telephone.'

'I can't get in touch with you, so you'll have to do it yourself. But if you give me the telephone number of the lady who phoned you, I'll contact her.'

'Oh, dear.' Betty pulled a face. 'I was so flummoxed I just said, "thanks very much", and put the phone down. Does it matter?'

'It would have helped, but never mind.' Jane yawned. 'I've got classes in the morning, so I'll go on up.' She smiled at her mother. 'That really was a smashing birthday present.'

'It wasn't the only nice thing that happened today, Janey. Mrs Ackroyd had a baby girl this afternoon.'

'Oh, how lovely! What are they calling her?'

'Rose.' Tears welled in Mrs Harrison's eyes as she murmured, 'Born on my Rose's birthday, too.'

'That's wonderful, Mum. Such a kind thought. You must be thrilled to bits.'

'She had thought of calling her Rosemary Jane, but I said Rose was a pretty enough name on its own, and Rose Jane didn't sound right. I knew you wouldn't mind.'

As she quietly undressed in the dark room, Jane wondered if she was being childish to feel so hurt. It would have been lovely to have been part of the newborn child next door, even if only the second name.

The time spent in the bleak Whitehall office was, as she had feared, lengthy and fruitless. As usual, 'further investigations would be made'.

But Mrs Harrison now had hope in her eyes and, to Jane's surprise, asked if she would like to invite Olaf to tea the following Sunday.

'Grace suggested it. You can ask the lady from your office as well. After all, you went to her home, and it's only fair to return the invitation.'

What would Miss Dawson think of their council house, Gran and Grandad, Johnny? Then common sense told Jane Miss Dawson was no snob, and it might help Olaf to feel more comfortable.

'Thanks, Mum. I'll ask them tomorrow.'

'You'll have to give me extra help with the polishing.'

Polishing came after washing-down of woodwork. 'Don't forget the tops of the doors, Janey. And the picture rails.' A new block of hearthstone whitened the doorstep, the front porch gleamed red with Cardinal polish, and the grate was black-leaded to a fine ebony.

'Blimey, Nell, anyone would think the King and Queen were coming,' Uncle Nobby commented, as Mrs Harrison cleaned his ashtray for the umpteenth time.

'I wouldn't be ashamed if their majesties did knock on my door.'

'Bet you'd tell them to wipe their feet before you curtsied, though.' Uncle Nobby laughed.

Watching her mother place a vase of daffodils in the centre of the crocheted table runner, Jane reflected that it was almost like old times. For the first time in months there was a spark of life, a pride in the home.

The door knocker rapped quietly. 'Oh, dear!' Mrs Harrison swiftly removed her pinafore and patted her hair.

'You look fine.' Aunt Grace grabbed the pinafore. 'Just go and sit in the living room with the others. It'll be better if Jane answers the door and introduces her friends to you.'

'But the kettle's not on.'

'They won't need a cup of tea for at least five minutes. I'll see to it.'

Her hand on the front door, Jane silently prayed, Please God, let Mum like him. Please.

Olaf ushered Miss Dawson into the hall, then shook hands with Jane. He carried several small posies of violets, charmingly presenting one each to Mrs Harrison, Gran, Aunt Grace, Auntie Vi, Kathleen and Jane. Miss Dawson handed Mrs Harrison a box of luxury biscuits.

'You really shouldn't have used your precious rations,' Mrs Harrison gasped.

'It is my pleasure. I rarely need all my points, and it was so kind of you to invite me.'

After a hesitant beginning, and the inevitable tray of tea, the conversation settled into a comfortable hum. Olaf talked of the parents and younger sister he hadn't seen for five years, their farm near Ulvik, and agreed with Uncle Nobby that the fjords were breathtaking in the spring, when apple blossom delicately replaced drifting snow. Then they chatted about the importance of navies, Merchant and Royal. It wasn't long before Grandad showed a keen interest in the discussion.

Auntie Vi, plainly as bored as her husband, tried to turn the subject around to the hardships endured by a small shopkeeper. 'It's not that we want more for ourselves, you understand. Everything will go to our Peter. His wife will be a lucky girl, indeed. He's so clever, you know.'

As she began to extol his virtues, Peter left the group and leaned over Jane, whispering 'Help' into her ear. They both escaped to the kitchenette.

'Poor Peter!' Jane giggled. 'How can you bear to be so rich, so clever, so ...'

'Handsome?' Peter cleaned his spectacles. 'Probably because it's true.' Laughing, he changed the subject. 'Where's Betty?'

'Aunt Grace persuaded her she ought to take the boy round to see his other grandfather. Thank God.'

'I'd heard he was a little horror.'

'Looks like an angel, behaves like a devil.' Jane tried to keep her voice casual as she asked, 'What do you think of Olaf?'

'He's OK.'

'Only OK?'

Peter studied the cup he was drying. 'He's intelligent, well-mannered, speaks good English, not bad-looking. Like I said, he's OK.'

'Oh.'

265

Peter looked at Jane. 'Do you think he's more than OK?'

'I like him, yes.'

'You'd better not like him too much. He'll be going back to his own country soon.'

'I know.' The thought made Jane miserable.

'Anyway, you've already promised to marry me.'

'When?'

'The day you started school. Don't you remember?'

'Oh, yes.' Jane leaned against the sink, recalling that she'd come home in tears because the teacher hadn't allowed her to sit next to Rose. To cheer her up, Peter had said he'd play mothers and fathers with her, and this time she could be the bride and Rose the bridesmaid.

Peter smiled. 'You said I was your favourite cousin and you wouldn't marry anyone else but me.'

'You're still my favourite cousin. So I'll let you sit next to me at tea.' Suddenly Jane remembered. 'How did you get on with your army medical?'

'Failed.' Peter grimaced. 'I've got to have stronger glasses. With luck, I may be able to finish my accountancy course before they shove me into the Catering Corps, or some other round hole waiting for a square peg.'

'I'm sorry, Peter.' Jane kissed his cheek with affection. 'Come on. Better get back to the others.'

'Or they'll start talking.'

They were still laughing when they returned to the living room. Jane was pleased to see the two maiden ladies getting on so well. They had much in common, apart from working at a desk and liking cats. Both were fond of the writings of Charlotte Brontë, the poetry of Wordsworth and the music of Schubert. Both also felt that in the aftermath of war, the role of women would be vastly changed.

'People have expanded their abilities beyond belief,' Aunt Grace commented. 'Now they will want to expand their opportunities.'

'As long as we do not lose too many of our values.'

Tibs purred and settled more comfortably on Miss Dawson's lap. Gran said nothing, concentrating on her crochet, but Jane knew she didn't miss a word.

The conversation moved on to comparisons between

working for a man or a woman boss.

'In many ways, Mr Grierson is an excellent employer,' Aunt Grace said, 'but I feel he regards the young ladies in the same way as their dictating machines. It would be nice to be appreciated, just occasionally.'

Miss Dawson smiled. 'We are fortunate to have such a considerate employer. Miss Reynolds always asks how one is, and I feel she really cares whether we are happy. Do you not agree, Jane?'

'Oh, yes. And it doesn't stop her from doing her job well, either.' Jane chuckled. 'Apart from a tendency to leave her desk unlocked when she goes out. I'm always concerned someone might read the confidential files.'

'And the petty cash. It was on top of her desk again yesterday. Fortunately, it was almost empty.'

Jane stared at her colleague. 'It wasn't your turn to work yesterday. Don't you mean Friday?'

'No, my dear. I'd left my umbrella drying in the ladies' cloakroom, and thought I might need it over the weekend, April being such an unpredictable month.'

'What time did you come into the office?'

'Let me see, about one o'clock, I believe. You and Victor had already left.'

'That's odd,' Jane mused. 'After I'd paid the milkman, I distinctly remember seeing several banknotes.'

'There was merely a small amount of silver when I found it. The lid was open.'

'Then the rest of the money must have been stolen.'

Miss Dawson looked troubled. 'I suppose suspicion will fall upon anyone who was in the building –' She ended the sentence rather abruptly.

Following her glance, Jane realised that Olaf was listening. Quickly, she said, 'Most work Saturday mornings. I saw quite a few from the oil company, and the accountant on the third floor was still at his desk when I left.'

Aunt Grace said, 'Anyone could walk in from the street.'

Miss Dawson shook her head. 'Strangers would be noticed.'

'Not if they were regular visitors, or in uniform.'

'The only uniforms we would not question are those of the Norwegian Navy, Miss Davies.'

'Not necessarily. We had a handbag stolen once,' Aunt Grace explained. 'The thief turned out to be the one person we had never thought of.'

'Who was that?'

'The telegraph boy. When charged, he confessed to other similar thefts.'

Miss Dawson sighed. 'Was he eventually caught in the act?'

'No. Bravado was his downfall. He couldn't resist showing off to his friends, one of whom was ... I believe the expression is "a copper's nark".'

Miss Dawson looked dumbfounded, as though such things were quite beyond her comprehension.

Jane said, 'But there were no telegrams yesterday, and the postman called long before I left.'

'What should we do?' Miss Dawson was obviously anxious.

'There's nothing you can do until tomorrow,' Aunt Grace said. 'Miss Reynolds can then decide whether she wants to inform the police.'

'The police?' Miss Dawson became even mor agitated. 'Oh, surely not.'

More calmly than she felt, Jane said, 'It will probably depend on how much money is actually missing.'

'That's not really the point, dear,' Aunt Grace said. 'The fact is, as Miss Dawson pointed out, you will all be under suspicion until the matter is resolved. And that is a very unpleasant situation, as I know only too well.'

Jane's apprehensions were interrupted by her mother calling everyone in to tea. Olaf asked if he might use the bathroom first. As usual, Gran took her time packing away her crochet, and shuffled slowly along the hall on Jane's arm. 'You won't have to look far for your thief,' she told Jane. 'Mark my words, it will be one of them foreigners.'

'Shush, Gran! Olaf might hear you.'

'Foreigners don't understand what we're talking about, any more than we understand their funny accents. Look at that girl next door. Can't make head nor tail of her.'

Jane laughed. 'They're as English as you and me.'

'No, they're not. They come from foreign parts up north. And I still say she only put my money back because I was making a song and dance about it.'

268

'Don't be silly, Gran. You mislaid it. Anyway, I thought you liked the Ackroyds.'

'Mrs Ackroyd is a Londoner, same as me. But he's a copper, and that girl has shifty eyes. I never did and never will trust foreigners.'

When Olaf sat next to Jane. he seemed pensive. Surely he couldn't have heard Gran? Perhaps he didn't like ham salad. No, he was eating without hesitation, but only politely answering when spoken to. Then she noticed that he frequently glanced at the framed photograph in the centre of the sideboard. Mrs Harrison followed his gaze.

'That's Rose. Isn't she lovely?'

'A most beautiful young lady.'

'You'd never think they were twins, would you? She was very clever, you know. Should have been a film star.'

'Jane told me her sister was a singer and dancer of great talent.'

Miss Dawson took a piece of Victoria sponge from the plate offered by Aunt Grace. 'I understand Jane is an accomplished pianist. Perhaps we could hear her play something after tea?'

Peter nodded enthusiastically. 'Play "Die Fledermaus", Janey,' he said. 'I'll turn the pages for you.'

Jane also played a scherzo by Schubert, and pieces from *Peer Gynt*. Finally, she held up her newest piece of music. 'I bought the selection from *Perchance to Dream* yesterday, but I haven't had a chance to practise it yet. Shall we try it?'

Miss Dawson was a surprisingly good mezzo-soprano, well suited to the lyrical Ivor Novello melodies. When complimented by Aunt Grace, she shyly said, 'My interest in music is inherited from my mother, who would sing to us each evening, accompanied by my sister on the pianoforte. Unfortunately, Adeline was not gifted like Jane, and poor Papa decided enough was enough, so he declined my request for singing lessons.' She handed Jane the sheets of music to replace in the stool. 'But you, my dear, are a fine musician, with a natural ability to sight-read. Do you not agree, Olaf?'

Gazing out of the window, Olaf appeared to be miles away. Recalled to the present, he quickly apologised, agreed that Jane was an excellent pianist, and suggested they should take their leave, before the rain became much heavier. Jane went upstairs to fetch their coats.

Suddenly, Auntie Vi's shrill voice rose above the general hubbub from the living room. 'Once people met Rose, they didn't have eyes for no one else, but Janey wasn't jealous. She may not be much to look at, but she's got a nice nature. I've always said Peter could do a lot worse.'

Mortified, Jane sank down on her mother's bed. She could not go down and face them, she just couldn't. It had been going so well, too. At least until teatime.

A key scratched in the front-door lock, and she heard the introductions of her father to Miss Dawson. Then her mother calling, 'Janey! Have you got the coats? They're waiting to go.'

Better get it over and done with. Her father was standing in front of the living-room fireplace, vaguely watching Miss Dawson make her farewells: 'I have enjoyed a simply spendid afternoon, and a delicious tea. Thank you so much.'

Shaking hands, Mrs Harrison said they must come again. 'But where's Olaf?' she asked. 'I want to introduce him to my husband before you go.'

He was in the dining room, holding the photograph in both hands. Startled, he looked up as Jane went into the room, and gently replaced the photograph on the sideboard. 'Such a beautiful face,' he murmured.

Sadly, Jane handed him his cap. Oh, Rose, she thought, you'll always compete for a lover, even in death.

First thing Monday morning, Miss Reynolds conferred with the managing director of the oil company, the accountant on the third floor, and Mrs Petersen. There had been no reports of anything missing from the oil company, but when the accountant checked the small roll of notes in his wall safe, he was five pounds short.

It was an uncomfortable day. Each person in the building was interviewed by Detective Sergeant Lomax, and those who had worked on Saturday questioned in detail. The sergeant was obviously experienced and noncommittal, but Jane couldn't shake off the feeling that she was regarded as the main suspect, having been alone in the office after Victor left. Miss Dawson confessed to the same feeling because she had returned to the office later. Victor shrugged his shoulders and said he didn't know what they were getting in a flap about. It was obviously one of the Norskies, wasn't it?

Later that day, Olaf signalled to Jane and met her on the stairs. He seemed ill at ease as he cancelled their date for Wednesday. 'We have many messages coming from the resistance groups, and I have to work late to decode them. It is possible that the war might end within a few days.'

'That's wonderful. Perhaps we can see the film at the weekend?'

'It is difficult just at the moment, I am sorry.' He did not look at her. 'Will you please to thank your mother again for an excellent tea. Now I must get back to my desk.'

Slowly, Jane climbed the stairs. He couldn't have made it clearer that he didn't want to see her again. Did he think she was a thief? Or was it because he'd seen Rose's photograph and suddenly realised how unattractive Jane was? Was this to be the story of her life? A few dates, then excuses?

Aunt Grace and Miss Dawson lunched together the following day. Miss Dawson told Jane that she thought the venture of Miss Davies and her friend was a splendid idea, and she was delighted with the invitation to visit them. Torquay had long been one of her favourite resorts.

Wednesday evening was dismal, especially having to explain why she was not out with Olaf. 'That's foreigners for you,' Gran said. 'Come here eating us out of house and home, then sling their hook.'

Betty was curious. 'Wish I'd been here Sunday. Mum said he was ever so good-looking. Now I don't suppose I'll ever see him,' she moaned. 'And Dad was rotten company. Kept talking about doing himself in.'

Jane fled to the kitchenette and spread a newspaper on half the table. Aunt Grace tackled the ironing on the other half and watched as her niece cleaned the brass. After a while, she said, 'It probably is only work, you know.'

'It's more than that, Aunt Grace. He's different towards me. And there's nothing I can do about it.' A tear dropped on the Buddha's head, followed by another, which slithered down towards his belly. 'Nobody told me it would be like this. Hurt so much ...' Her aunt's comforting arms around her, Jane wept for the first time since the day she had lost her sister. Now the tears were for her lost love.

The detective sergeant returned on Thursday, and Miss

Reynolds asked Jane to take her calls. A few minutes later, Victor was looking out of the window, when he cried, 'Something's up. The Norskie's gone all red.'

Olaf was replacing the telephone, and it was true. His face was scarlet. Suddenly he glanced up at Jane's window, quickly looked away, spoke briefly to his colleagues, and left the room. Miss Dawson raised her eyebrows, but Jane made no comment. After three restless nights, stifling tears into the pillow, she just couldn't talk about Olaf, although he was never far from her thoughts.

Reluctantly, Victor went off to the stationery room. He was soon back, without the flimsy paper Jane had requested. 'Guess what?' He was gleeful. 'The Norskie's gone into the boss's room. Told you he was the tea leaf.'

Miss Dawson recovered first. 'The sergeant is probably merely checking statements. Now will you please get back to work? We are waiting for that paper.'

When he returned, Victor had more news. 'That book-keeping bloke is in there now.' He smirked at Jane. 'Still fancy your boyfriend in handcuffs?' The grin was wiped from his face as the telephone rang. Miss Reynolds wanted to see Victor immediately.

Half an hour later it was all over. Olaf and the accountant were back at their desks, Victor had finished slamming drawers in the next room and was in the lift with the sergeant, and Miss Reynolds was in Jane's office.

'It is all very distasteful,' she said. 'If he'd kept quiet, he might have got away with it.'

'How did he give himself away?' Jane asked.

'He said if he was going to steal anything, it would be a large amount, not a measly twelve pounds ten from the petty-cash box. I'd not told anyone exactly how much was missing.'

'Was that enough for a conviction?'

'Probably not. But when Sergeant Lomax questioned him further, he couldn't bluff his way out of his own web of lies. He finally broke down and confessed. I almost felt sorry for the boy.'

'Are you going to press charges?' Miss Dawson asked.

'I don't think so. Instant dismissal without a reference will be quite a severe punishment for a first offence. But I'm not sure whether Mr Burdett feels the same.'

'The accountant?'

Jane was about to ask her employer why Olaf had been involved when Miss Reynolds said, 'Will you telephone the *Evening Standard* straight away, Jane, and place an advertisement for an office junior?'

Busy as Jane was the following Monday morning, she couldn't help noticing the buzz of activity in the Norwegian Naval Headquarters. One of the girls wore headphones as she tuned a small radio, surrounded by colleagues, all consulting small books and rapidly writing notes. On her way back from posting the contract, Jane saw Olaf hurrying along his corridor. At first she thought he was going to ignore her. Then he turned back towards the staircase.

'Have you any more information about your brother?' he asked.

'No.' Her voice was equally stilted, as she asked, 'Is there any news about the war ending?'

'There is much confusion, but Hitler is dead.'

'I'd heard rumours. Is it really true?'

'It is reported that he committed suicide, together with his mistress.' Olaf hesitated. 'Mr Churchill is making a statement later today, but we may have news before then. Now I must hurry. They are waiting for this code book.'

Jane called after him, 'Will you let us know?'

'Of course.'

It was difficult to concentrate on work. Every few minutes Jane swivelled around to look out of the window, and Miss Dawson stopped work until Jane shook her head. Curiosity also sent Miss Reynolds into their office more than was strictly necessary.

Just before lunch, Jane made a cup of tea, watching the window with one eye while she checked her typing. The eruption came so suddenly that she spilled her tea. The Norwegians were jumping up and down, hugging each other, crying. Olaf signalled to her.

As she ran down the stairs, Jane heard the shouts and screams of joy. She knew, before Olaf reached her.

'The Milorg have been given orders to lay down their arms,' he cried. 'Oh, Jane! Do you realise what this means?'

'It is over? Really over?'

'Yes. The war is over.' Unashamedly, he wept. 'Now I can go home.'

Chapter Twenty-Nine

Tagging on to the tail of a human snake singing and dancing the conga, Jane felt her senses reeling. She had only drunk one small glass of the near-lethal concoction, but it had been enough. Miss Reynolds, wisely realising that the Norwegian cocktail had rendered Jane, Miss Dawson and herself incapable of useful work, suggested they join the crowds in the streets outside.

Partly owing to the thought of losing Olaf for ever, and partly because there was still no official word, Jane felt in a strange state of limbo. The atmosphere was one of preparation rather than celebration. Ladders were hoisted to fasten bunting and pennants, windows filled with portraits of the three Allied leaders. A black scarf had been draped around the picture of President Roosevelt, whose frail health had also surrendered less than a month earlier. Onlookers admired the display, but there was not yet a feeling of triumph. Most wandered aimlessly, wondering when the announcement would come that would lift the lid off London. In Trafalgar Square, university students chanted, 'Why are we waiting?'

Finally, Miss Reynolds decided they might as well collect their handbags from the office and go home. Back in Piccadilly Circus, the anticipation of festivities had sparked off the giant conga and Jane was whisked into line by a jolly Jack Tar who'd obviously popped the cork for the victory that wasn't quite. At the second turn around the Eros pyramid, she spotted Miss Dawson, hat slightly askew, sandwiched between two Canadian soldiers. Eventually, Jane broke free and pushed her way towards Lower Regent Street, where a circle of women danced

'Knees up, Mother Brown' in the middle of the road. And there was her employer, kicking high.

Breathlessly, she rejoined Jane. 'I was press-ganged as well,' she gasped. 'But it was such fun. Did you see Miss Dawson?'

'Here she comes. Oh, my goodness!'

Waving as she tried to thread her way through a group of American soldiers, their colleague was suddenly lifted high by a giant of a sergeant, to be deposited on the pavement next to Jane and Miss Reynolds.

'Is this where you wanted to go, ma'am?' he asked.

'Why, yes.' Miss Dawson straightened her hat. 'Thank you so much.'

'My pleasure, ma'am. Now for my reward.' Before Miss Dawson could stop him, he'd planted a smacking kiss full on her lips. For a moment it seemed as though he was going to repeat the operation with Miss Reynolds. Then he looked over her head, said, 'Another time, ma'am. My troops are getting out of hand,' saluted smartly, and bulldozed his way back.

'Are you all right?' Jane tried to suppress a smile at the sight of her friend, mouth open, hands to scarlet cheeks.

'Oh, yes, thank you, my dear. Such a friendly young man.' Miss Dawson chuckled. 'But what would Papa have said?'

The streets at home were quieter. A few people were building bonfires and setting up trestle tables in readiness for street parties, but most were indoors. Grandad sat with his ear glued to the wireless, waiting for an announcement. Mrs Harrison barely listened to Jane's description of the London scene. Her back was playing up again. So was Johnny.

'He's got the devil in him today,' Kathleen said. 'I've read stories and tried to make a house of cards, but he won't be pacified.'

'Where's Betty?' Jane asked. 'Can't she look after him for once?'

Her mother spoke sharply. 'She's upset. And so would you be if you couldn't find out whether your husband was dead or alive.'

Gran grunted. 'She'd better buck her ideas up if Jack is alive. Fancy coming home to a miserable little bitch like that.'

'All I care about is that he comes home safe,' Mrs Harrison said.

'That broadcast was quite hopeful, Mum.'

'Anything could have happened to him since then, Janey. I've heard some terrible stories about the prison camps.'

'There's bound to be rumours.'

'Is that supposed to stop me worrying?'

Kathleen picked up Johnny and followed Jane into the kitchenette. 'Would all the excitement be in London?' she asked.

'More than round here, anyway. I suppose everything will liven up once there's an official announcement.'

Their patience was rewarded at twenty minutes to eight. 'An official announcement will be broadcast by the Prime Minister at three o'clock tomorrow, Tuesday afternoon, the eighth of May. In view of this fact, tomorrow will be treated as Victory-in-Europe Day and will be regarded as a holiday. The day following will also be a holiday.'

The strange feeling of anticlimax persisted through to Tuesday afternoon. It took the stirring voice of Mr Churchill to convince everyone that 'the German war is therefore at an end'.

Aunt Grace, Jane and Kathleen gave a rousing cheer. Gran wiped a tear. Grandad hoped the Commies wouldn't muck up the peace. And Mr Harrison patted his wife's shoulder. For a moment, Jane thought her mother had cheered a little, until the Prime Minister went on, 'Japan, with all her treachery and greed, remains unsubdued. The injustices she has inflicted ... her detestable cruelties ...' With a choked cry, Mrs Harrison ran from the room.

When Jane took up a cup of tea, her mother was weeping into the pillow. 'If only I knew for sure,' she whispered.

'I know, Mum.' Jane smoothed the hair back from her mother's forehead.

'You don't know, Janey. You don't know what it's like to lose everyone you love. First big Jack, then Lennie. And Rose, my lovely Rose! And young Jack still missing. If anything has happened to him, I've got no one.'

'You've still got me, Mum. And Dad. You've still got someone to love.'

Mrs Harrison opened her eyes wide and looked straight at Jane. It was a curious stare. Then she said, 'It's not the same', and closed her eyes again. Jane knew she would never forget that look or those words.

Aunt Grace stood in the doorway, holding a glass of sherry. 'Drink this, Nell,' she said. 'And try not to feel so bitter. Fred and Jane care a great deal about you.'

Nell Harrison stared hard at her sister. 'If Fred hadn't shouted at Rose, she'd still be alive. As for Janey –' Her glance was scornful. 'She hasn't even shed a tear for Rose. That's how much she cares.'

'You wouldn't say that if you'd heard her breaking her heart at Ilford. And Rose would have gone out that night, no matter what anyone said. Don't blame Fred. He feels guilty enough as it is.'

'So he should. I'll never forgive him, and he knows it.'

'That's a terrible thing to say, Nell.'

'It's how I feel.'

Aunt Grace sat on the bed. 'Attacking each other isn't going to make things any better. Don't forget Janey was cheated out of the best years of her life.'

'What about Rose? She was cheated out of everything. And I was cheated, too. I used to dream about her being a star. Marrying well. Now the only grandchild I'll ever have is poor little crippled Johnny.'

'That's nonsense. Jane won't be single for ever.'

'Her boyfriends don't last for two minutes.' Again that cruel glance. 'No, Jane's destined to be the old maid of the family. Just as you were.'

'I was engaged to be married, as well you know.' Flushed, Aunt Grace challenged her sister. 'And I know what it's like to lose someone I love. But I never used that as an excuse to hurt other people.'

'Edgar died thirty years ago. And how can you possibly know what it's like to lose a child?'

Tears glittered in Aunt Grace's eyes. 'I never thought I'd feel ashamed of you, Nell, but I am. And if they could hear you, Rose and Jack would be ashamed, too.'

Angrily, Mrs Harrison waved her arm, knocking the glass of sherry from Aunt Grace's hand. 'I don't care what you think of me. You'll be off to Torquay soon, and I'll be the one left behind to take care of everyone on my own, as usual.'

'Mum, please stop it,' Jane pleaded. 'You know I'll help as much as I can.'

277

There was no stopping Mrs Harrison. 'Fat lot of help you'll be,' she cried. 'You're always out playing the piano, or at the tech.'

'You should be proud of her.' Aunt Grace defended her niece. 'She's getting an award as best student.'

'And now the course has ended, I'll be able to spend more time at home,' Jane added.

'I don't want you to spend more time at home,' Mrs Harrison shouted.

'But you said –'

'You still don't understand, do you?' Mrs Harrison was beyond reason or logic. 'You were her twin. Two of you. Always together. Now there's only you.' The knife turned viciously in Jane's heart. 'I'll never to able to forget that Rose was taken from me. Because you'll always be there to remind me.'

The quarrel continued, long after Jane had fled. Her sobs drowned the words, but not the sound. It was the first time she had heard such acrimony between the sisters. Her own dull ache deepened as she remembered her mother's words. Words that made it clear she wished it had been Jane, not Rose, who had been killed.

Finally, Aunt Grace came into the bedroom, grabbed her coat and handbag and rushed out again. She would probably join her Red Cross friends for the rest of the day, Jane thought. And good luck to her. Somebody in this house had to find victory a cause for celebration. Troops coming home. Allies going home.

Her tears flowed freely as she thought of Olaf. He might be gone by Thursday. For a moment, she wondered which was worse, knowing she would never see him again, or seeing him but knowing the love was unrequited, as poor Uncle Len must feel whenever he saw Laura. Oh, God! Why did life have to be so bloody awful? Today of all days.

Downstairs, Johnny began screaming. Probably wanting his tea. Betty wouldn't budge, that was for sure. Jane heard Kathleen moving about in the kitchenette, trying to soothe the child. It wasn't fair on the girl. She was putting on a brave face, despite her own heartache.

Better go down and help. Keep out of her mother's way. Put

278

Johnny to bed. Help Gran upstairs after the King's speech. Just like any other day. But the tears wouldn't stop. Now they were for Rose, who should have been getting ready to go out and light up London Town. Rose, who hadn't come back to hear her sister say, 'Forgive me.' Suddenly, it was as though Rose were standing beside her, saying, 'I knew you didn't mean it, Janey, any more than I did.' Of course. They'd always been able to read each other's minds. Rose had known her sister had only spoken in anger. After all, hadn't Jane held her and loved her only days before? Jack's words when Theresa was killed came back to comfort Jane. 'Forget the guilt. Remember the friendship.'

Aunt Grace was back – with plans. 'Wash your face and put on some make-up,' she said. 'We're going up West.'

'I can't. There's tea to get, and –'

'It's all arranged. The Ackroyds are having a party. They've invited the Cliffords, old Mrs Trent and the Irish family from number 42.'

'Don't tell me Mum and Dad are going.'

'No. But the old folks eventually agreed. I think Gran's curious to see what the other neighbours are like.' Aunt Grace peered in the dressing-table mirror and dabbed powder on her nose. 'It's true what she says, they knew everybody at the old place. Now they have to be invited to a victory party to meet people who've lived in the same street for years.'

'Is Betty staying in bed?'

'No. She's going next door. Said she feels like getting drunk.'

'Why aren't you going, Aunt Grace?'

'Because I would like to be far away from your mother tonight.' The compact clicked shut. 'And I guessed you'd feel the same. So I phoned Nobby, and he's meeting us at seven.' Aunt Grace brushed powder from her skirt. 'Now blow your nose and splash cold water on your eyes. It'll take the redness down.'

Ten minutes later, Jane closed the front gate. As she glanced at the house, she murmured, 'I feel as though I never want to come back.'

They'd reached the corner before Aunt Grace answered. 'You could come to Torquay.'

It was tempting, but Jane knew she shouldn't make such a decision while she was feeling like this. 'Thanks for the offer,' she said. 'But I have to be practical. Mum might not miss me, but there's the others. And if Jack comes back, they'll need all the help they can get.'

'Well, don't martyr yourself for the family. If ever it gets too much for you, just remember what I said.' Changing the subject, Aunt Grace pointed to a cul-de-sac. 'Look, they've got a street party.'

Flags fluttered above tables placed end to end along the road. Children tucked into bowls of jelly and custard while their mothers, wearing Union Jack aprons and scarves, passed around plates of rock buns and cheered on the men who manoeuvred a piano out onto the pavement.

The journey was lively, strangers shaking hands and hugging. This time there was no mistaking the carnival atmosphere in London. Crocodiles of dancers sang out of time and tune with stout-hearted musicians. Hawkers vied with each other to sell buttonhole badges. 'Churchill for sixpence. Worth more,' yelled one.

They reached Whitehall just in time to hear the Prime Minister's speech from the balcony. 'This is your victory.' The distinctive voice, heard so often on the wireless, concluded, 'God bless you all.'

As she watched the familiar V-sign and listened to the deafening cheers, Jane put her mouth close to Aunt Grace's ear. 'Thank you for making me come,' she said. 'I'll remember this for the rest of my life.'

Aunt Grace nodded. 'Time to meet Nobby,' she mouthed. She had arranged to meet him on the steps of Jane's office.

'Not quite such a traffic jam here,' he said, after he'd kissed them. 'Wish Len could be with us, but he'll splice the mainbrace a few times, I reckon. Let's have some grub first.' He looked towards Piccadilly Circus. 'We'll never get through that lot.'

While they were debating, a voice behind them said, 'Excuse me.' Jane knew that accent. It was Olaf.

He shook hands and congratulated them on winning the war. Jane noticed his voice was strained, but it was Aunt Grace who questioned him.

'Are you working?' she asked. 'Today?'

'No.' He glanced at Jane. 'I should not be here. But I am trying to get a message to my parents. The radio operator is still on duty, but she cannot get an answer to her signal. Perhaps tomorrow.'

Uncle Nobby nodded. 'Not much more you can do today, old son. Why don't you join forces with us? We're looking for somewhere to eat.'

'Oh. That is kind. If you are sure?' Again he glanced at Jane. She didn't know what to say, so just smiled.

'Of course we're sure,' Aunt Grace said. 'But finding a place might be a problem. Any ideas?'

'The Scandinavian Restaurant is in hiding.'

At first Aunt Grace looked blank, then she understood. 'Hidden away?'

'That is so. And the food it is good. Follow me. I know a shorter way.'

There was one table free. After a small glass of powerful, colourless liqueur, compliments of the house, Jane's legs and arms filled with warmth, and it wasn't until she'd eaten the last morsel of chocolate cake that she trusted her numb lips to speak correct English.

'I'd like to go to Buckingham Palace,' she answered Uncle Nobby's question.

'Good idea,' agreed Aunt Grace.

'If we are fortunate, might we see the King and his Queen?' asked Olaf.

Not only did they see the King and his Queen, but also his daughters. By now it was almost dark, and London was well and truly celebrating. They sang the national anthem. They sang 'Land of Hope and Glory'. They sang 'There'll Always Be an England'. And still the people cheered for more and more appearances from their sovereign.

Suddenly, Jane realised that Aunt Grace and Uncle Nobby had been swallowed up in the vast crowd.

'Do not worry,' Olaf reassured as she searched. 'Your uncle said if we were to separate I was to stay with you.'

They shoved their way back into a quieter part of the Mall. 'You are not to be afraid with me,' Olaf said, as they walked against the flow of the crowd.

281

'I am not afraid. It's just ...'

'Yes?'

'Well, last week, you didn't want to be with me.'

He stopped. 'That is not true. I had too much work.'

'It was more than that. Be honest.'

'Honest? Was not that what you doubted? My honesty.'

'Never!' Jane was horrified. 'How could you think such a thing?'

'Your grandmother thought such a thing.'

'Oh, no.' Jane remembered only too well. 'Gran is old. She says stupid things.'

'She suspected me of being the thief.'

'Not really. She said the same things about the girl next door. But it wasn't true. I'm so sorry.'

They walked silently for a little while. Then Jane asked. 'Olaf, tell me. Why did you blush when the police sergeant asked to see you again?'

'Blush? What does it mean?'

'The face becomes red when embarrassed.'

'Ah. Yes, I was embarrassed. Because I did not wish you to think that I was ... what your aunt said ... a "copper's nark".'

Now it was Jane's turn to stop. 'Why should I think that?'

'I told them I had seen Victor. At the time, I did not realise the importance. But when they telephoned me again, to verify the times, I realised that he must have come back to the office. My evidence would make him a suspect.'

'But you did the right thing.' Jane walked slowly at Olaf's side. She had to know. 'Was that the only reason you did not want to ask me out again?'

At first she thought he hadn't heard, but when she glanced sideways and saw his troubled frown, she knew there was something else. Suddenly, he blurted out, 'Are you betrothed to your cousin?'

'Peter? Whatever gave you that idea?'

'His mother said several times what an excellent marriage it would be. And when we were walking to the bus stop, he told me ...'

They had reached the edge of a crowd singing, 'For She's a Jolly Good Fellow' to a girl climbing a lamppost, minus her skirt, closely followed by an American soldier, stripping off his jacket as he climbed. The crowd gasped as the American reached the girl, wrapped his jacket around her, and brought her down to safety on his back.

As the noise abated, Jane prompted Olaf, 'What did Peter tell you?'

'That you had promised to marry him.'

'And you believed him? Why did you think I went out with you, then?'

He shrugged. 'Perhaps to amuse yourself?'

Angry with Peter for saying it, and Olaf for believing it, she confronted her companion. 'I was five years old, and it's been a family joke for years. How could you possibly think I was that type of girl?'

He hung his head. 'I am sorry.'

'Just wait until I see Peter.'

'He is not entirely to blame. At first, all was well. Then I sensed something. I do not know. It was as though they did not like someone from another country. I felt like a stranger.'

'We welcomed you.' Her anger increased as she stared at him. 'All you did was look at Rose's picture. I knew you were comparing her with me.'

He looked shocked. 'It was not your sister I was looking at, but mine,' he protested. 'I was thinking that was how little Birgit must be looking now.'

She put a hand to her mouth. 'And I thought ...'

'What did you think?'

'That I was too unattractive.'

For a moment, Olaf gazed at her. Then he kissed her. It was the sort of kiss Jane had never been able to imagine. Gentle. Warm. Lingering.

Coming up for air, she couldn't hear his words for the singing of a group of Land Army girls. It sounded as though he was asking her to go away with him. But that was impossible. Eyes shining, she laughed and mouthed, 'I can't hear you.'

It still sounded like, 'Come to Norway with me.'

This was madness. The liqueur must have gone to her head. Stupidly, she stared at him.

Olaf threw back his head and laughed. 'I want to marry you.'

When she came up for air once more, Jane imagined she heard bells ringing and bands playing. She also imagined Olaf had just asked her to marry him.

'What did you say?'

As the land girls finished their song, Olaf shouted into the sudden quiet, '*Eg er glad i deg.*'

The cheering and clapping were not a figment of her imagination. Neither were his words. For, quite distinctly, against her cheek, Olaf said, in English, 'I love you, Jane.'

His arms tightened around her, but she had no intention of breaking away. Oh, Rose, she thought. Why didn't you tell me it would feel like this?